FOREVER UNDENIABLY YOURS

IMMORTAL HOLLYWOOD
BOOK TWO

STORMY O'HARA

For all the ~~girls~~ women who just want to be seen.
May you find at least one person in this world who truly sees you.

AUTHOR'S NOTE

Forever Undeniably Yours is a spicy vampire romance and contains on the page sexual encounters between humans and vampires, vampires drinking human blood, humans drinking vampire blood, some mild violence and a whole heap of cursing. There is also mention of foster care and adoption. It may not be suitable for some readers. Look after yourself and read with care.

ALSO BY STORMY O'HARA

Truly Eternally Mine

PROLOGUE

rix

*T*RIX *& Maverick's Rules of Engagement:*
No kissing on the lips (too intimate)
No oral (way too intimate!)
Bites only on wrist (no neck or inner thigh bites)
No glamouring
No cuddling
No holding hands
One time only
No calling or texting after
Never tell anyone, ever
Act like it never happened

I SLIDE off the back of Maverick Stone's Ducati motorcycle and stare up at his Malibu mansion. My heart's racing, and it's not just because the guy drives like a maniac.

Am I really going to do this?

When we came up with the rules of engagement, it felt like we were discussing a concept — the *idea* of us going back to his place together for a one-afternoon stand.

As I take off the helmet an ocean breeze catches my green hair, and a charge of excitement rushes through me. As I pass the helmet to him, his fingers brush mine. Cool, but strong. The guy has huge hands, and while part of me thrills at the idea of those hands all over my naked body, there's a very loud voice somewhere in my brain telling me that *this is a very fucking bad idea, Trix!*

Because Maverick Stone may be sexy as it gets with his blue-green eyes that you just want to drown in, messy, dirty blonde hair you can't wait to run your fingers through, perfectly angled jaw line and biceps for days, but he is also kind of an asshole. He's one of the biggest movie stars right now, and he knows it. We passed six billboards with his face on them just on the way here. He has a reputation of being hell to work with, and from the little time I've spent with him, I can now confirm that Maverick Stone's ego is even bigger than his mansion. He's never seen in the tabloids with the same woman twice, and the list of women he's had sex with has got to be longer than this coastline.

Oh, and he's also a vampire who wants to have sex with *me. Right now.*

It's been an insane 24 hours. First, I got glamoured by a vampire in a trucker hat at Vincent's, a vampire club in West Hollywood, then we had to go save my best friend Poppy from a pack of werewolves while her new boyfriend staked his evil ex-wife to Certain Death.

When it was all over and everyone else was going home to their own beds, or their lover's beds, I found myself being propositioned by Maverick Stone in a diner across the road from the Hollywood Forever Cemetery.

Life sure knows how to surprise you!

"You okay?" Maverick asks, his blue-green eyes sparkling in the midday sun. He shakes his hair out of his eyes like a dog, but this guy is no golden retriever. I catch his scent on the air. How does a vampire who's spent all night in a cemetery somehow still smell like saltwater and clean laundry? He puts the helmet in the compartment at the back of his motorcycle, and I take the moment to check out his rear. *Nice.*

"Trix?"

"It's bigger than I expected," I say, staring up at his house, which looks like something from *Selling Sunset.*

He lets out a laugh and then looks at me with... *concern?* I didn't know Maverick Stone could *do* concern.

"Look, Trix, if you've changed your mind about this, I can just take you home, or wherever you want to go. No problem."

But there is a problem, two actually. Because having sex with Maverick Stone is a really fucking bad idea. But there's nothing I want more.

CHAPTER ONE

rix

"A BLOOD BOND forms between vampire and human after the partaking of The Bite. This bond creates a psychic connection between the two that will stay active for approximately three to six months after The Bite is given. Glamouring the victim after The Bite ensures a clean breaking of this bond and freedom for both parties."

The Fraternity of the Everlasting Rose Handbook, page 82

I DRIVE the van up to the entrance of the Starlight Studios lot, stop at the gatehouse, open my window and yawn at the security guy.

"Shit, sorry," I tell him, covering my mouth.

It's three-thirty a.m. and I've been awake all night baking and making sandwiches.

"Can I help you?" he asks.

"Trix Delaney, and this is Ali Yoon." Ali leans over me and gives him a wave.

"And…?"

"Oh, we're Trix and Treats," I say.

"Catering?" he asks, eyeing up my old van with the bright orange and green Trix and Treats logo on the side.

"Craft services," I tell him.

There are two types of food services on a movie set. The caterers make full meals for the stars and important people, and then there's us, craft services. We feed all the people who don't get scheduled lunch and dinner breaks — the technicians, make-up artists, wardrobe, background artists. Anyone who doesn't get the luxury of a trailer or a lunch break will come to our table whenever they get a few spare minutes to grab a sandwich, coffee or sweet treat to help keep them going through what I've been told can be a very long day.

"What movie?" he asks, frowning down at a tablet.

"I don't know. Brandon Curtis is producing it."

"Brandon Curtis produces half the movies for Starlight," he says, clearly getting annoyed now.

"He just told me to be here at four a.m."

"This is highly unusual."

"I guess I can call him," I say, pulling my phone out from the console.

"You have Brandon Curtis' number?"

"Yeah, he's a friend of mine."

He looks at me like there's no way someone like Brandon Curtis, a rich, successful movie producer and director, would know someone like me.

"Hang on," he says, disappearing into his gatehouse.

"What do you think the movie is?" Ali asks. She claps her

hands together, and her huge baby-pink Jack-o'-lantern earrings jiggle around. It's still a few weeks away, but Ali's had her pastel witch Halloween decor up since the fifth of July. "I hope it's a romance!" She squeezes her hands together like she's saying a prayer.

I go to take a sip of my coffee, but it's empty. I shove the cup back in the holder.

"I hope it's a horror," I tell her. "The last thing I want is to spend the next two months on the set of a romance movie."

"Did something happen with you and Ben?" she asks.

"I broke up with him."

"What? When?"

"About a month ago, I guess."

"Why didn't you tell me?"

"We weren't that serious," I shrug.

"You were together for what? Six weeks? That's pretty serious for you. Why did you break up with him?"

I ended it for the same reason I always do. So I could end it before he did.

And also, he wasn't Maverick Stone.

"It just wasn't right," I say as the security guy finally comes back.

"Stage nine," he says, shoving passes and piles of papers at us.

"Thanks," I call back to him as I drive through the now open gate.

And suddenly I'm on the other side. I'm *in*.

I've spent so much of my life wishing for this, wanting to be *here*, working in movies. And now, it's finally happening. Only instead of driving through that threshold as an actor, I'm here with a van full of soup and sandwiches.

But even though my acting career never took off, I'm so grateful I found another passion in life.

I'm also so glad I found Ali. We bonded instantly over our love of good food and bad movies when I hired her just a few months back. Trix and Treats started getting booked for more events than I could handle on my own. It didn't hurt that I used to be movie star Max Montrose's private chef. When I started my company, he recommended me to everyone in Hollywood.

But this is my first time working on a movie, and I'm nervous as hell. A lot is riding on this. If it goes well, this could open up the possibility of more jobs like this, and hanging out on movie sets is still a dream come true, even if I'm just serving soup.

Ali finds the map in the pile of papers and starts giving me directions through the studio lot. We weave through huge soundstages, special effects studios and then we drive past a park and some restaurants and bars that I'm not even sure are real or part of a set. Eventually we find ourselves at stage nine where a woman carrying a clipboard waves us to a place to park.

I stop the van and take a deep breath.

"Trix," Ali says, grabbing my hand and giving it a squeeze. "You're going to kill this."

I turn off the engine and then turn to her. "*We're* going to kill this," I tell her, with a forced smile.

BY NINE A.M. I've already learned that time moves differently on a movie set. The last six hours have felt like both three days and also five minutes.

The huge soundstage that was almost empty when we arrived is now full of people, and there's a buzz of excitement in the air as everyone rushes around drinking way more coffee than I prepared for.

Right in the center of this gigantic building, a crew is

putting the finishing touches on two sets — an entire coffee shop on one side and a whole office floor on the other. I've heard the title *"Double Agency"* being mentioned. Some kind of spy movie, maybe? Sounds cliché, but at least it's not a romance. Apart from a few dates with Ben that didn't go further than a kiss goodnight, I've been in a dry spell romantically for eighteen months, and I don't need that being rubbed in my face every day at work.

Our table is set up away from the action, right near the exit. We have sandwiches, soup, key lime bars, pastries and fruit and definitely not enough coffee at the station we've set up with our portable coffee machine and milk steamer.

"Hey, is that Brandon Curtis?" Ali asks, pointing towards the sexy older blonde man looking dapper as ever in a full suit.

Brandon peers into a TV screen, deep in conversation with Ziva Mohanty. Ziva is a big deal in Hollywood. She's only in her early thirties, already a huge success *and* looks like a catwalk model with her glowing brown skin and long dark hair.

"He looks busy. I'll talk to him later," I tell her.

"Good morning," says a beautiful blonde woman who looks to be in her late forties. "I'm Radha, Brandon's assistant."

"Nice to meet you," I tell her. "I'm Trix and this is Ali."

"What can we get you?" Ali asks with a smile.

"Two coffees, black. Thanks."

I make her drinks, she gives me a wave of thanks and takes them over to Ziva and Brandon.

Brandon immediately puts his down on the desk without taking a sip. But why would he? Brandon Curtis, with his Carey Grant looks who dresses like he's a 1950s mobster, *is* a vampire after all.

I stare off into the distance at Ziva, wondering if she's a

vampire too. Vampires basically run the whole movie industry, so it wouldn't surprise me if she was.

She takes a sip of coffee, and has that look on her face, like *thank god for this caffeine!* She's probably human.

"Can I grab a black coffee?"

I look up at an attractive guy in a black t-shirt and black jeans. He swipes a hand through a thick head of messy dark curls and gives me a smile. I have a feeling I've seen him before but can't figure out what movie or TV show I've seen him in.

"Sure," I tell him.

"We're going to need more coffee," Ali says.

"And way less oat milk and decaf," I say. "Everyone is drinking it black."

"Oh, you have oat?" the guy asks. "Can you make a latte?"

"Sure." I say and get to work steaming his milk.

"Now that I know you have lattes, you'll be seeing me a lot. I should probably introduce myself. I'm Finn," he tells us.

"I'm Ali, that's Trix."

I give a little wave.

"So, what do you do on this movie, Finn?" Ali asks.

"Small supporting role," he says with a shrug.

"Ooooh, what's the role?" Ali asks.

"Bad guy," he says with a playful grin.

Ali makes a choking sound. She's always had a thing for bad boys.

"I haven't seen any big stars here yet," I say, handing him his drink. "Who else is in this thing?"

"Juliette Cortez," he says. "I'm so excited to work with her."

"Oh, she's amazing!" Ali gushes.

"Right? She was due on set an hour ago, but she's not here yet. Both the leads are already running late. Ziva is freaking out."

"Typical movie stars," Ali jokes with a giggle.

"If you want to know who's here and when, you should be able to see all the call sheets and everything on the app."

"App?" I ask.

"Yeah, here—" he shows me his phone and then helps me download it to mine.

"I need a login," I say.

"You can use mine." I hand him my phone, and he logs me in.

"Thanks, Finn. I'll ask Brandon for my own log in when I get a chance."

"It's no problem."

I start scrolling through the call sheets and can't see any days where there aren't at least a hundred people on set.

Finn's eyes narrow at me. "Wait a second, have we met before?" he asks, pointing his coffee cup at me.

Ali's eyebrows rise in my direction.

"I don't think so."

And then I suddenly remember. Finn was at Vincent's that night. Before I got glamoured, before Poppy got kidnapped and before I went back to Maverick's Malibu mansion for the six best orgasms of my life.

"Mr. Stone's on the lot!"

My stomach bursts into flames at the sound of his name. But no. There are plenty of Mr. Stones. It could be anyone. It's not him. It can't be him.

"Mr. Stone!" someone else shouts.

And then I see him. Well, his back covered in a red and black check shirt that strains to fit over his broad shoulders.

He's here. The man who's haunted my dreams for the last eighteen months. I know it's him. I would recognize those arms anywhere, even covered in a shirt.

I never thought I was going to see him again, but he's *here*. And that means that this is *his* movie.

Oh fuck!

"I gotta go!" I tell Ali.

"Are you okay?"

"Yeah, I just — I need to go get more croissants from the van!" I tell her, and I run out of the soundstage as fast as I can.

CHAPTER TWO

$\mathcal{M}$averick

JULIETTE: I can't access the fucking app!! Is it 7am tomorrow?
  Maverick: Yep. Bright and early, welcome to Hollywood, baby!
  Juliette: My first feature film OMGOMGOMGOMGOMG!!
  Maverick: Try to play it cool on set tomorrow.
  Juliette: I can't promise anything! See you tomorrow!

As I WALK onto the soundstage, the familiar hum of energy and excitement lifts my spirits. There is nowhere on earth I'd rather be than here with all these people who have a shared vision and will do anything it takes to bring it to life and make it a success.

Well, there is one place I'd rather be. But I can't think about that right now. I need to stay focused.

Brandon's hot blonde assistant Radha approaches me. "Please follow me, Mr. Stone." She gives me that look. The one I see on most women's and a lot of guy's faces. The look that says — *take me back to your trailer and bend me over your bench seat.*

But while it's a tempting offer, one I'd normally take her up on, I'm a little off my game lately.

"Where's your assistant?" she asks as she leads me out to the back of the soundstage to where the trailers are.

"I'm between assistants right now."

She raises an eyebrow as she unlocks the trailer with my name taped to the door. "Well, if you need anything, anything at all, please do just let me know. I know I'm Brandon's assistant, but I'm more than happy to—" She cracks the door open and then steps back, right in time for three other people to appear, rushing into the trailer ahead of me.

"Thanks, Radha," I say with a nod.

I step into the trailer where one woman holds up a bunch of skin-care products, another holds a comb and the third is hanging a black suit up by the window.

"Mr. Stone!" the woman from makeup beams at me. "Please take a seat. I'm Candy. I'll be your personal makeup artist. That's Cassie," she says, pointing to the woman who's combing out my hair. "And that's Crystal," she adds, nodding towards the woman behind us, who gives me a shy smile.

"You hardly even need this," Candy says as she slathers moisturiser all over my face. "Your skin is perfect!"

"It's my diet," I tell her. I don't tell her my diet is the blood of pretty women just like her.

Cassie starts putting some product in my hair. "When was your last haircut?" she asks.

"It's been a while." I don't tell her it was in 1939. Vampires don't age, so our hair can't grow. It can be cut, but within a few hours it will be back to the same length. "I only let my private hairdresser cut it," I tell her. "I'll get him to trim it every few days for consistency in the movie."

"Maverick!" Ziva Mohanty, hot director and very hot woman, appears behind me in the mirror.

Another woman that I would have happily worked my charms on in the past, but lately I've only been horny for one thing, and it's not Ziva or any of the other gorgeous women currently in my trailer.

Even my Donnas don't do it for me like they used to. Donnas, a slang term for blood donors, are like vampire groupies, human girls who enjoy The Bite. It's a very pleasurable sensation for humans to be bitten by us, and once they get a taste of how good it can be with a vampire, they sometimes get a little addicted.

"We're going to start with filming the meet-cute," Ziva says. "Have you got your lines down?"

"Of course I have my lines down," I tell her.

Vampires don't have problems remembering lines. I can read a script once and it's memorized forever. Unfortunately.

"Have you run the lines with Juliette?" she asks.

"Not since the read-through."

"When I see her, I'll send her to your trailer to run it through."

But Juliette never comes to my trailer.

Half an hour later I'm standing on the set of a coffee shop, dressed as a CIA agent in a black suit, white shirt and black tie, which I loosen a little.

"Do we like the tie loosened?" Ziva asks no one and everyone. "Or does John Stannic have a sharper look?"

There's a chorus of nods and noise, and it seems they like my tie loose.

"Let's start with the blocking and run through the lines a few times before we roll," Ziva says, staring down at her script.

I take a quick look around the set. "Where's Juliette?" I ask.

"Juliette?" Ziva's head practically spins in circles looking around.

"Where *is* Juliette?" asks Brandon.

Radha types violently on her phone and then looks up. "According to security, she hasn't arrived on the lot yet."

"Somebody call her!" Ziva shouts, and suddenly everyone starts shouting and running around trying to find Juliette.

But Juliette never arrives on set.

CHAPTER THREE

I SIT IN THE VAN, take some shaky deep breaths and wipe my sweaty palms on my apron in an attempt to calm myself.

A very vivid memory of Maverick Stone bending me over his kitchen counter slams into my mind and sends my pulse soaring.

I didn't know this was going to be a fucking Maverick Stone movie!

I would never have taken this gig if I'd known!

An absolute fucking lie.

Ever since our one-night stand, I've been secretly hoping we would bump into each other again. At every Hollywood party I've catered, I've been like a hawk, checking the crowds for those broad shoulders, that messy, dirty blonde hair, that grin that would have my panties down in the back of the kitchen for him in a heartbeat.

I keep trying to tell myself it's just the blood bond, but

according to Beth, a friend I used to work with at Vincent's, a blood bond is not supposed to last this long. I'm not supposed to still be having sex dreams about him eighteen months later.

It's like he's everywhere. It's Maverick's face that flashes through my mind whenever I'm on a date with some other guy, when I'm sitting in traffic, when I'm in the shower. Memories of how freaking good it was with him hit me at the worst possible moments. Dinner with the family? Suddenly I'm remembering him lifting me up onto his kitchen counter like I weigh nothing. In line to pay for gas? I'm re-living the way he kissed my neck and told me I tasted like sugar and lime, his *favorite*.

I try to remind myself that to him I was just the girl that was *there* when he wanted to "drink blood and fuck," as he so delicately put it *when he propositioned me*.

But he didn't fuck me like I was just convenient.

I bite my lip and throw my hands over my face.

How the fuck am I going to go back in there?

A knock at the window startles me. "Shit! Ali!"

She pulls open the door and frowns at me. "What's going on? Where are the croissants?"

I wish I could just tell her the truth. That I slept with Maverick Stone, and I can't go back in there and see him, especially not looking how I do from not sleeping all night!

But we had rules. *Never tell anyone, ever.*

I look at Ali's concerned face. Maybe it's been long enough. Maybe it's okay to share it with someone and lighten this load I've been carrying. I open my mouth to tell her, but something stops me. My integrity? My loyalty to Maverick? The blood bond? The words are stuck. I can't say them.

"It's just a lot, isn't it?" I say. "All the people. The pressure."

"Trix, you're one of the hottest caterers in town."

"*We're* the hottest caterers in town," I tell her.

"And it's just craft services," she adds. "I doubt anyone that important will even eat at our table. They'll all be getting catered meals from Cate's Catering."

"God, I hate Cate's Catering," I groan.

"Me too."

I take a deep breath. She's probably right. The set is busy. There are hundreds of people here. Maverick is a vampire. He doesn't even eat or drink. Even if he wanted to pretend, he'd just get his assistant to get his coffee for him. I may never even see him or have to talk to him.

"Come on, let's get those croissants," Ali says with a reassuring grin.

But it's not reassuring enough.

"WE NEED A STAND-IN!" Ziva yells.

"Hey," Ali says, giving me a nudge in the ribs. "You used to do acting, why don't you be a stand-in?"

"Me? What? No! I need to be here."

Ali frowns. "Everything is under control here, Trix."

"Get me someone!" Ziva barks to one of the assistants.

I try to hold her back, but Ali runs towards the set and disappears into a swarm of people.

I shake my head and notice my hands are still shaking as I take a bite of one of my famous key lime bars. Damn, it's good, even if I say so myself. Coconut, sugar, lime, it's a rectangle of pure key lime pie goodness.

"Trix! Trix Delaney!" someone calls out.

Oh shit.

"We need a Trix Delaney on set!"

Ali, what have you done?

"Someone get me Trix Delaney!"

Radha appears in front of me.

"Key lime bar?" I ask her, holding up the bar I've been eating.

"You're wanted on set."

"Me? Why?"

"We need a stand-in."

"Anyone can be a stand-in. Why does it have to be me?"

"Everyone else is busy," she says.

"I'm busy."

She looks around. "No one is here."

"Yeah, but they *could* be."

"I've got it!" Ali says, reappearing beside me with a grin. "Go be a stand-in!"

Radha gives me a look that says no is not an option, and so I follow her through the crowd and onto the set even though my brain is saying *no! Don't do this! Go back and hide under the table with your croissants and sandwiches where it's safe!*

Someone shoves a script in my hand, and I realize I'm still holding the bar in my other hand. I look around to find someone to hand it off to, but there is no one, so I shove the rest of it in my mouth and start chewing.

My cheeks are still full of cookie, coconut and lime when he turns around. I put a hand over my mouth to prevent the crumbs from hitting the ground.

Goddamn, if he isn't even sexier than I remembered. How is that even possible? In my mind, Maverick Stone is already *the* hottest man on the planet, but now here he is, looking even better than he has in my dreams and my fantasies.

Fuck me!

He's staring down at his script dressed like the most fuckable CIA agent anyone has ever seen. His black jacket somehow both fits him perfectly and also strains tightly over the broadness of those shoulders I remember so vividly grabbing onto while he was making me come. His tie is a little loose, making him look like he's had a hard day at the office, and I have a sudden urge to throw myself at him, straddle him, shove his jacket off and release some of that pressure for him.

I stand gawking at him like some obsessed fan, but he doesn't even look up at me. I can only imagine what he would see if he did. Glitter eyeshadow that looked okay at two-thirty this morning sliding off my eyelids, faded green hair in a tangled top knot, white tee under an orange and green Trix and Treats apron, comfy baggy mom jeans I love but that do nothing for my figure.

That he fucked me at all is a goddamn miracle.

Don't do that, Trix. You're hot. You're totally fuckable. He could've had anyone, but he wanted you and you rocked his fucking world.

"Okay," Ziva says. "This is the meet-cute at the beginning of the movie. Except it's not, because these two already know each other."

My stomach flips because, oh my god, this is literally us.

Ziva points at me. "Lucy, you're the barista at John's favorite coffee shop. There's one closer to his office, but he comes in here because he likes you, and you always give him extra cream on his iced lattes."

"Uh, okay," I say.

"Let's run the lines and get a feel for things," she says.

"Can I get a coffee?" Maverick reads from his script, still not looking up at me.

Why won't he look at me? Does he even know it's me standing here? Does he even *remember me*? Or was I just a notch on a very tall bedpost?

It's for the best. If he looks up at me, if he finds me with those blue-green eyes, I will either melt into a pool of goo or I will have a panic attack and die.

"Cappuccino, latte, long black, short black...?" I read, my own eyes stuck safely to the script and not on the dirty blonde scruff on his jaw that felt like heaven as it rubbed against my nipples.

"What's *your* drink?" he asks.

"Oat latte with salted caramel syrup." That actually sounds pretty good. I make a mental note to get some caramel syrup for the coffee station tomorrow.

"That's a girl's drink."

"Well, I am a girl." I clear my throat and look up at Ziva. "Sorry, but—"

Everyone goes quiet, and I can feel hundreds of eyes on me, except for Maverick's. His eyes stay glued to his script.

"Is something wrong?" Ziva sighs.

"Well, how old is this character? She's played by Juliette Cortez, right? So mid, maybe even late twenties?"

"Yes," says Ziva. "And?"

I point to the script. "Well, the whole exchange is pretty sexist anyway, but that's standard for this kind of movie, I guess—"

"I wrote this script," Ziva frowns at me. "It's the most female-friendly action movie ever written."

"Okay, so you get what I'm saying then. I just think maybe this should at least be *woman* instead of *girl*?"

What am I doing telling Ziva Mohanty how to do her job? I'm just supposed to be a stand-in!

"That's a *woman's* drink," Maverick says, not even taking a beat.

"Well," I risk a look in his direction, but his blue-green eyes are still trained on his script. "I *am* a woman."

"Give me two," he says. "Large."

"She makes his drinks," Ziva reads. "She places them on the counter, but he only takes one. Can we have Lucy's line?"

"Hey, you forgot your drink," I read.

"That one's for you."

Ziva claps her hands. "And then that's where the terrorists come in, guns blazing, shooting up the coffee shop."

Of course they do. I wouldn't expect anything else from a Maverick Stone movie, even one written by a woman.

"I like the change to woman," Brandon says.

"Me too, it feels sexier," Maverick says, finally looking up and catching my eye.

And I fucking *melt.* Those sex dreams have nothing on Maverick's real-world gaze on me.

His eyebrow quirks a little, and my mouth opens, something about to come out that I know I am going to regret immediately after.

"Hi," I say.

Hi? After eighteen months of missing this guy's cock in me like I've lost a limb, all I can say is *fucking* hi?

But worse than that, instead of saying *hi* back like a normal person, he just turns and starts having some private conversation with Brandon. Who also hasn't even said hi to me, by the way!

"We need to start filming! We need to film something!" Ziva shouts to no one in particular. "Where the fuck is Juliette?"

CHAPTER FOUR

averick

I HURL myself onto the tiny bench seat couch in my trailer and throw a hand over my eyes.

Fucking Trix Delaney!

As soon as I saw her there in that cute as hell orange and green apron, it was like the last eighteen months never even happened.

I've had blood bonds before. I like women. I like biting them. I like fucking them. Sometimes I glamour them afterwards if it's in both our best interests to do so, but not always, so the blood bond is far from a foreign concept to me.

But this. Still wanting her eighteen months later. Thinking of *her* every time I'm about to bite another woman. Being totally unable to *fuck* another woman because she's not Trix.

This is hell on earth.

I hit call on my best friend Max's number.

"Maverick?" he answers quickly.

"Hey buddy," I say. "You busy?"

"Just doing some promotional work for the movie."

"It's great to see you working again."

"I think we've made something really special. Have you started on *Double Agency*?"

"Yeah. Actually, that's the reason I'm calling."

It's not the reason I'm calling.

"Juliette didn't show up for filming today."

"That is strange."

"Yeah, and no one can get hold of her."

"How can I help?"

"I'm not sure yet. I'll go over to her place after filming. Not that we can do much filming without her."

"I'll see what I can find out."

"Thanks." I take a breath. "That's not the only reason I'm calling, though."

"What's going on, Maverick?"

"Just out of interest, when you've had a blood bond with someone, what's the longest it's ever lasted for?"

"It's been a long time since I've had a blood bond with anyone but Poppy."

"Yeah, but think back."

"A few months, I suppose. But even then, it's always been strongest for me at the start, the first few weeks. After that it sort of fades."

"That's normal, isn't it?"

"Maverick, why are you asking me this? You have much more experience with blood bonds than I do. Is everything alright?"

"Yeah, yeah. Just this one girl, *woman,* can't seem to let me go," I say. "I still think about her."

"You glamoured her?"

"No."

"I rarely condone glamouring, but perhaps in this instance it's for her own good, and yours. If you're still thinking of her after all this time it must be absolute hell for the girl."

Why does the idea of Trix going through hell over me make me so fucking hot?

But that was one of our rules of engagement, no glamouring.

Trix said she wanted to remember it.

The way she looked at me when we were reading earlier makes it damn clear she remembers every single touch of my hands on her thighs, every kiss of my lips on her neck, every single thrust of my cock.

Jesus, I wish someone could glamour me!

"I need to go," I say. "Let me know if you find out anything about Juliette."

FILMING WRAPS EARLY without Juliette and Ziva makes a plan to skip some of her scenes for the next few days just in case she's unwell. She's not unwell, she's immortal, but you can't tell that to an entire cast and crew of humans. *Mostly* humans.

"I can drive, or follow you in my car," Brandon says as everyone starts packing up around us.

No one wants anything bad to happen to Juliette, but finishing at 4 p.m. is a short day in the movie industry and the crew buzz around like they're grateful for it.

"She lives out in Pomona," I tell him. "I can get there faster on my Ducati."

"Let me know as soon as you find out anything," he tells me with a gentle clap on my back.

I nod and make my way through the hustle and bustle of

the set and out into the sunlight, silently thanking the lizard gods for the blood of the lizards that can turn vampires into daywalkers and then I crash straight into Trix and a tray of cakes.

"Oh my god!" she says, dropping to her knees to pick them up.

"Shit, sorry." I crouch down to help.

"I don't need your help," she says, waving me away.

Crashing into someone is not very vampire. Our senses should stop us doing that kind of thing. So what the hell just happened? The sun in my eyes? Did I not take enough sun serum today? Was I going too fast? Was she just in my way and I didn't see her?

Maybe it's some kind of magnetic force pulling us back together—

I shake my head, emptying it of that thought. I don't believe in fate or destiny or any of that bullshit. But it is weird that she's here. I wonder if she orchestrated this, got this job because she knew I'd be here, because she wanted to see me again.

My heart does a little skip at the idea that she'd go to those lengths to see me again.

But it's far-fetched. Caterers don't get to choose what movies they work on.

"Don't just stand there!" she says, her warm brown eyes scowling up at me and I'm reminded of the way those eyes filled with such deep contentment after she'd screamed her way through her sixth orgasm of our time together.

"Do you want me to help or not?" I ask, smirking at the memory.

She scowls at me. "I just want you to go away."

I hold up my hands. "If we're going to be working on this movie together for the next few months, we should at least be civil, don't you think?"

"Civil? Like how you didn't even acknowledge me earlier?"

"What?"

"When we ran through lines together and you didn't even look at me!"

"Wait, that was you?"

"Fuck you!" she says, piling the last of the squashed cakes back onto the tray.

"Of course I knew it was you." I knew it was her from the moment I caught her summery scent of sugar and lime from across the lot.

She stands up, holding the try of squahsed cakes covered in bits of dirt between us. "You still could have acknowledged my existence."

But if I had looked up at her earlier, if I had glanced in her direction and she'd looked back at me, I wouldn't have been able to pretend that I didn't know her. I wouldn't have been able to just stand there and *run lines* when all I wanted to do was take her into my trailer and spread her out over my bench seat.

I take a quick look around. No one is paying any attention to us, but I still lower my voice. "That was part of the rules, right? That we'd never tell anyone."

"You don't need to act like you don't even know me."

"But how would I know you?"

Her pretty mouth twists as she considers what I'm saying. There is no way on earth that me and Trix should know each other. We met at a vampire bar when she was glamoured out of her mind.

"When people say — hey Maverick, how do you know Trix? What am I supposed to say?"

"That we met at a bar? Or that we have mutual friends? It's not a crime for us to *know* each other."

"If we say we met at a bar, people are going to get the wrong idea."

She rolls her eyes. "Oh, you suddenly care about your reputation?"

I ignore the dig. "Poppy and Max are keeping their relationship out of the media. If it gets out that we know each other because of mutual friends, it will only take five minutes for someone to find out about them."

"If we don't know each other, we should stop having this conversation," she says.

"Ah, but we know each other now," I say.

"What?"

"This can be our meet-cute, our origin story."

What the fuck am I saying? Why am I calling this a meet-cute like it's the start of something?

There's no version of reality in which me and Trix can start something.

"Oh sure. We met when you bumped into me and all my leftover bars and cakes, which took hours to bake and that I was going to drop off at the soup kitchen by the way, crashed to the ground, and then you didn't even help me pick them up!"

"I tried to help!"

"Whatever, just — stay away from me." She turns and walks towards her van, and I can't help thinking about what that ass swamped in those mom jeans looks like naked.

WHEN I GET to Juliette's place and let myself in, I'm not too surprised to find it's just a small, modest house in the suburbs. Juliette got her start on a TV show that was a colossal hit, but the pay on those things is not always great, especially when you start out as an unknown. Her social media following blew up, and she started getting brand deals, but judging from the amount of handbags and designer clothing scattered around the place, I'm guessing most of those were in exchange for goods, not cash.

Juliette was made vampire only a few years ago and was recruited by the Fraternity of the Everlasting Rose, a secret society of vampires shortly after she went viral. Lottie, the ex-president of the Fraternity, had her eyes on Juliette as someone with influence and power who would make a good addition to the elite community. When Lottie recruited someone, it was always for her own gain. She wanted to be able to influence the influencers.

Anyway, all this means that Juliette isn't as rich as those of us who've been around for decades or centuries.

"Juliette?" I call out, my voice echoing through the house.

A splotchy black and white cat comes running down the stairs and starts meowing at me like it's starving to death.

I find a bag of kibble in the kitchen and fill its empty bowl. The thing inhales its food like it hasn't eaten in days.

"Where's your mom?" I ask as it gobbles like crazy.

When I try calling her again, I hear ringing in the other room. I follow the sound and find it's coming from one of the designer handbags in the living room. I'm not usually the kind of guy to go through a woman's purse, but I make an exception this time. Her purse contains her phone, keys, a sealed white envelope and three different black eyeliners. Juliette wouldn't go anywhere without her phone or her eyeliner.

Something isn't right.

I try to unlock her phone, but it needs her fingerprint. Vampires have a lot of skills, but getting into someone else's iPhone isn't one of them.

I check every room in the house, but she's not here.

I rub a hand over my jaw.

This is definitely not right.

It's then that the envelope in my hand catches my eye.

It's addressed to the Fraternity.

31

CHAPTER FIVE

rix

"Was that—?" Ali asks, her eyes widening as she watches Maverick shove his helmet on and straddle his motorcycle. The same motorcycle I straddled that day. My arms wrapped around his waist, my legs wrapped around him, and my body pressed up against him as we drove through the city. It was thirty-five minutes of adrenaline-fueled foreplay.

"Huh?" I ask her, throwing the cakes in the trash and putting the tray in a crate for dirty dishes in the back of the van.

"You were just talking to—" she says, staring at the hot as fuck way he revs his motorcycle and then rides off the lot way too fast.

"Maverick Stone," I finish for her. The taste of his name in my mouth still tastes like the sweat on his strong shoulders.

"Oh my god, what was he like?" she squeals.

Hot, huge, hard, and a surprisingly generous lover.

"He's an ass," I tell her.

"Oh, what? No!"

"You've heard that about him, haven't you?" I say, loading the last of the trays into the van.

"Yeah, I guess," she says, helping me with the doors. "But I just thought it was tabloid gossip. I try not to believe anything I read online these days."

"Well, you can hear it from the horse's mouth. Maverick Stone is an ass." I slam the door closed and make my way into the van.

"Ass or not, you have to admit it's still pretty cool to be working on a *Maverick Stone* movie."

"I don't really care." I hit the gas, but I don't speed away like he did. I drive a little under the speed limit, there are people walking around *everywhere.*

"Trix, aren't you even just a bit excited about it?"

"Yeah, sure. I am excited. I know this is a really big deal for us. I'm just tired, I guess."

"It was a big day, even with the early finish."

"Yeah, can you believe a thirteen-hour day is *short* for these people?"

"We are these people now!"

I throw her a smile as we exit the lot. "I guess you're right." I open the window and yell, "We're movie people now!"

Ali laughs. "Hey, do you want me to help with the food prep tonight?"

"No, you get some rest. We have another early start tomorrow, but we don't need to be ready on set until five. I could probably pick you up at four thirty, and we'll still make it in time."

"Trix, you can't cook all night and be up that early."

I just shrug. I knew this was going to be intense, but I couldn't say no to the opportunity.

"It'll be okay for a few days. Once we're in our groove, the two of us won't need to be there all the time."

"What if you take tomorrow off?" she suggests. "I can drive over to your place, pick up the van."

"Let's do the first week together, and then we can figure out a way for us both to get some downtime." I suggest.

It's not that I don't trust Ali to set up a coffee station and put out a bunch of sandwiches, but Trix and Treats is still my baby, and I want to make sure my baby is okay before I hand her over to someone else.

The other reason I don't want her to do it is that I hate the idea of staying home when I know Maverick will be on set again tomorrow.

"Beatrix, honey, do you think it might be time to consider a professional kitchen?" My mom stands in the corner of our very large kitchen, a frown forming under her dark brunette bangs.

I have all the permits that allow me to cook from home, but it was only ever supposed to be a temporary situation. It turns out though that hiring a professional kitchen is expensive, and while my business is doing well, I'm still paying off all my set-up costs for the equipment, the van, the t-shirts, business cards, everything else I spent money on. It was not cheap to get this thing off the ground. Before I started my business, I hadn't been good with money. Everything I earned went on nights out, cosmetics and clothing. But I want to make Trix and Treats work, which means being as responsible as I can with my money.

"I don't have the money for it yet," I tell her.

"Honey, we can help you with the money. We can invest in your business."

"Letting me use the kitchen is all the investment I need right now," I say.

"Oooh, what's this? Crab?" My dad appears and takes half a sandwich off my tray.

"Dad!" I slap his hand away.

"This is some good crab!"

"It's banana blossom," I tell him.

"Banana what now?" he asks through a bite.

"Jerry," Mom admonishes before looking back to where I'm wrapping the sandwiches that haven't yet been eaten. "Can I help you, honey? I can help wrap something."

"It's just easier if I do it myself."

"What if I stir the soup?" she asks.

"Oh, shit! The soup!"

"Language," says my dad.

"Thanks, Mom. Sorry, Dad."

It might look like the perfect scene — a happy family, a big house on the edge of Beverly Hills, but the truth, as it is for most people who live around here, is less shiny than it appears. Jerry and Suzy adopted me when I was already ten years old. Before that, I'd been in and out of foster care homes after my biological mother gave me up when I was just a baby.

I am so grateful for everything they have given me, but it hasn't been the easiest path to walk.

When people find out where I live and what my parents do — my mom is a Beverly Hills realtor and my dad works in big tech, they assume I'm Beverly Hills all over, even with my green hair and occasional bad attitude.

I've accepted their money in the past. When I went to theatre school and then went back to culinary school, I let them pay my tuition, but only my tuition. I still worked part-time jobs to pay my rent and expenses.

I didn't want a free ride then, and I don't want a free ride with this. I want to make this business a success all on my own.

"I think the soup is under control. Is there anything else I can do, honey?" she asks.

My immediate reaction is to say no, but she looks so happy to be stirring the soup that I decide to give her another job.

"Could you cut those sandwiches over there in half? Triangles."

"You got it!"

I send her off to bed when all the sandwiches are cut. She grins at me and gives me a big warm hug. "I'm so proud of you, honey," she says. "Are you sure you don't need any more help?"

"No, I'm nearly done here, thanks, Mom."

I'm not nearly done, though. I stay up well past midnight finishing the bars and muffins, and when my head eventually hits the pillow, I only sleep for three hours before my 4 a.m. alarm goes off.

CHAPTER SIX

M averick

"I, Juliette Cortez, hereby resign from the Fraternity of the Everlasting Rose. I no longer believe that the organization operates in the best interests of vampire-kind, and so I submit my resignation. It would do all other vampires in the Fraternity well to consider their own involvement in this outdated secret order and to look to the future instead of the past when it comes to vampire legacy, influence and affluence."

I THROW the letter onto Brandon's marble dining table, between the crystal wine glasses filled with blood and the crystal carafe of blood in the center.

Vampires don't have a reputation of being particularly nice, loyal or honest, and so it's rare for us to make friends, but I have a couple. I met Max on the set of a western back in the late fifties. We had a shared love of film and trauma bonded over the vampiric experience. It wasn't long before he'd managed to get me an invitation into the Fraternity of the Everlasting Rose, the most exclusive secret society in the city, for vampires only.

Although our relationship has mostly been professional, I do consider Brandon a friend. He used to host wild parties at his Hollywood Hills mansion back in the day. He'd call in so many Donnas and Dons that we'd all end up high on blood. After a Donna ended up drained in a pool, the parties stopped. That wasn't the kind of reputation he wanted his parties to have, even though it made them even more attractive for some of our kind.

Brandon is an old vampire, and apart from his reputation to party, he's never been involved in a scandal and always remained on good terms with most of the vampires in LA.

When Max killed Lottie, our previous president, that made him next in line to run the Fraternity. But it wasn't something he wanted, so he stepped aside to let Brandon lead us into the future, and most of us were pleased to have him as our president, especially after decades of un-hinged Lottie running the show.

Meanwhile, I was chosen to be the vampire councilor for the Order of Concordia, another secret society that aims to protect the interests of all supernaturals in the city. No one fought me for that title. No one else wanted it. Weekly meetings with a werewolf, a fae and a witch are not every vampire's cup of tea. In fact, many vampires still think the other races of supernaturals should be extinguished.

"You found this at Juliette's house?" Brandon asks, taking the letter from the table and gesturing for me and Max to sit down. "But no sign of her?"

"No. Nothing was taken, no sign of any struggle. But her phone and purse were still there."

Brandon opens the letter and reads it. "This was typed on

a typewriter," he says, turning it around in his hands before passing it to Max who raises a dark eyebrow, his blue eyes examining it carefully. Max was turned in the twenties and still has that gloomy silent movie star look about him.

"There was no typewriter at her house," I say.

Max runs a hand over the back of his dark hair. "This is most unusual."

"It doesn't sound like her." I show them my phone with my most recent conversations with Juliette.

"Perhaps she was just trying to sound more formal in her letter," Max says.

"Maybe," I say. "But why would she quit the Fraternity and go AWOL from the movie?"

Brandon shakes his head. "I spoke to her just a few days ago, and she was beside herself over the film. She couldn't wait to start filming her first motion picture."

"Movie," I remind him. "No one says motion picture anymore."

"Slip of the tongue," he says, taking a sip of blood. "And she's given me absolutely no indication that she was unhappy in the Fraternity."

"None of this adds up," Max says. "I could ask Henrietta to read the tarot or—"

Brandon shakes his head. "Let's not alert anyone outside of this room to this situation just yet. There may be a reasonable explanation for it all. But in the meantime, we should be vigilant."

"We're vampires, we're always vigilant," I say. I take a drink of the blood, and while it's a decent drop, it doesn't satiate me at all.

Nothing satiates me anymore.

"You should get some security," Brandon tells me. "I don't need both of my leads going missing."

I just laugh. "I can handle myself."

"I'll hire you a team, have someone watch your house and someone shadow you. I believe you need a new assistant as well?"

"What happened to Joanie?" Max asks, referring to my most recent assistant. "You slept with her, didn't you?" he accuses.

I don't answer. I don't tell him I *tried* to sleep with her but couldn't go through with it. I don't tell him that for the first time in my life I glamoured a woman into thinking we *did* have sex. I have a reputation to protect after all.

It was a moment of weakness with Joanie right after I'd been with Trix. An attempt to rebound, to forget Trix and move on with my bachelor life. But as I was standing there, staring at Joanie's naked body on my bed, all I could think about was Trix lying there naked. I felt dirty, like I was cheating. Which was insane, because the rules were simple — it was only ever going to be one time with Trix. Well, three times. But those three times, *holy fuck—*

"For god's sake, Maverick!" Max sighs. "That's the third assistant in a row!"

I just shrug.

"Are you ever going to settle down?" he says, like settling down is a totally normal thing for vampires to do when it is the complete opposite.

I laugh, and so does Brandon. And so would any other vampire who was in this room.

"Just because you're all loved up and insufferable doesn't mean the rest of us want to be," I tell him.

"Vampires are not creatures of fidelity," Brandon agrees.

Max gives me a look. "I'm happier with Poppy than I ever was chasing chorus girls."

"That's you, that's not me," I tell him. "I'm personally still very interested in chasing chorus girls."

Something within me says *that's a lie,* but I push it away.

Sure, I have spent a lot of time over the last eighteen months thinking about Trix Delaney, but that doesn't mean I would want to be with her and *only* her for the rest of eternity!

"I appreciate the offer, but security is unnecessary," I tell Brandon, changing the subject.

"I can't make this movie without you," Brandon says. "I need to know where you are at all times. This is non-negotiable."

Max gives me a look. He knows I'm not good with people telling me what to do. But I get the feeling that Brandon is not going to let this go until I give in.

"Fine."

I LEAVE the letter with Brandon and make my way home, weaving my motorcycle through the heavy LA traffic until I hit the beach. The ocean always feels like coming home, whether I'm staying in my own house or on the other side of the world.

I kick off my boots and double-check the garage is locked before heading into the house. I don't usually worry about locks all that much. If an intruder entered my place while I was home, great. A free meal. But there's something about the whole Juliette thing that has me on edge.

I grab a glass and a bottle of blood from the wine rack and then slide open the doors to the back deck that looks onto the beach. I take a seat on the grey outdoor couch, and a memory of Trix invades my thoughts. It was a hell of a night. We had sex three times, each one even more perfect than the one before. When she needed a little rest (I never need a rest) I ordered her a pizza, and we sat out here. Her showered and naked under my robe, me in a pair of black boxer briefs, basking in the last of the daylight and the afterglow from such great sex.

Of course, I remember the sex, but right now what comes to mind is the way her hair felt on my chest as she laughed at something dumb I said. The way she leaned into me, pressing her head into me while her whole body shook with laughter. The sound of that laugh is forever etched in my memory.

I take a sip of blood and it's fine from the bottle, but never as good as from the source. I grab my phone from my pocket and find the number for Vincent's so I can get them to send me a Donna for the evening. It's one of their more exclusive services that I've taken a lot of advantage of in the past.

But like I have for the last eighteen months, one week and six days, I can't bring myself to tap the call button.

CHAPTER SEVEN

Trix

MY HEART THUMPS *wildly as Maverick throws his keys into a wooden bowl by the door. We walk into an open-plan space with high beamed ceilings. There's a living area, which is all cream couches and rugs, light wood and some dark accent pieces that look mid-century. It opens out onto the most gorgeous view of the beach. On the other side of the space is the kitchen, which is modern, clean and white. It's the complete opposite of what you'd expect from a vampire's mansion.*

Three movie posters sit on a wall above an enormous TV screen, each one from a different era with a different actor's name, but all of them are him. *An old western starring Mason Jones, an eighties cop movie starring Jason Rose and the first Road Rage movie that made Maverick Stone famous this time around. It's a reminder that he isn't just a random guy, he is a fucking immortal.*

"Take off your shirt," he says.

Heat flushes through my body at his demand, and I look down

43

at the image of an avocado with a moustache on my t-shirt. When I dressed for work yesterday morning, I was not expecting to end up here. Like this. With Maverick Stone demanding I take off my shirt. If I had, I would have worn something much sexier.

"Do you want to take showers first?" I ask, running my fingers over the hem of my shirt.

"Why?"

"I haven't changed my clothes in over a day."

"Then that's an even better reason to take them off."

"Take yours off."

He grins at me and pulls at the back of his own t-shirt, pulling it over his head and throwing it on the ground, and holy shit the guy is ripped beyond belief! He has a couple of tattoos on his chest, a cross and a rose, some other symbols I can't make out. They look old, ancient even. These are not the tattoos of a man who walked into a hipster tattoo studio and asked for something that would look cool. But knowing this only makes them look even cooler.

"Now it's your turn," he tells me, his chest muscles tensing as he walks towards me. "Take off that ridiculous shirt."

"You think Mr. Avocado is ridiculous?"

"If you don't take it off, I'm going to take it off you."

I hesitate as he closes the space between us.

I grab my hem and pull it off, revealing an old polka dot bra I did not expect anyone to see today.

"Shorts too," he says, pressing his hard as fuck chest into me.

I'm surprised to find his skin is actually a little warm.

"What's with your skin?"

"What?" he asks, pulling back and frowning at me.

"It's not icy cold."

He lets out a laugh. "I'm not that old."

"How old are you?"

"I was made during the war."

"Which war?"

"World War II."

"Shit, really?"

"That's not something I really want to talk about right now."

He steps closer to me again, and I put a hand on his stomach and, oh god, it is like a rock.

"So, wait, why aren't you cold?"

"The older the vampire, the colder the skin. You should know that from all the vamps you've been with."

I release my hand and step back. "I haven't been with any vamps!"

"Sure."

"Why would I lie?"

"You might want me to think you're more innocent than you are."

"I'm in your house half-naked. I'm clearly not that innocent."

"You're not half naked," he says, sliding one of my bra straps down over my shoulder. The promise of what he's going to do next heats in my belly, "yet."

MY ALARM GOES OFF, and I'm reeling from another Maverick Stone sex dream. I have them so often now that it's an unusual occurrence *not* to have one.

The dream is always of our day and night together. Sometimes I dream of him undressing me in his living room, sometimes it's when we did it in the kitchen, sometimes it's when he took me in his bedroom, sometimes it's the shower — but it's always like I'm not just *dreaming* it, I'm re-experiencing it all over again. Every time I wake up, it's like it *just happened* for the first time.

The blood bond is supposed to make you think about the vampire who bit you, so that you keep wanting more from them. It's supposed to make you available for their bite whenever they want to drink from you. It's supposed to be like a crush that eventually wears off and then disappears when the vampire loses interest in you.

It's not meant to be a year and a half of the same fucking sex dreams!

I quickly shower, but instead of just throwing on some old jeans and a t-shirt like I did yesterday, I make a bit more effort with a leopard print skirt and an Elvis t-shirt. I put my faded green hair up in a topknot, swipe some orange glitter eyeshadow over my eyelids and put on a pair of glittery gold lightning bolt earrings. With a bit of mascara and some lip-gloss later I'm ready for another day on set.

"You look nice today, Trix," Ali says as she finishes setting up the coffee station.

"Oh, what?"

"Not that you don't always look nice. I think it's the eyeshadow. It really brings out the gold in your brown eyes."

I warm at her sweet compliment. "Oh, thanks, Ali. You look nice today too."

She's wearing a black dress and her lucky clover earrings. She has clearly made an effort too.

Are we both this pathetic for our crushes?

"Oh, this old thing?" she giggles, and then she blushes as she sees Finn heading towards us.

I give her a look. "Here comes the bad guy."

Finn arrives at the table and lets out a swooning sound as he takes in the spread. He grabs two croissants and bites into one. "Thank god for craft services!" he says.

Ali giggles again.

"Can I get one of those magic lattes?"

"Sure!" Ali moves to the coffee machine, and I notice she takes extra care in making his drink.

"Did you hear? Juliette is still missing," he tells us.

"She's *missing*?" Ali asks.

He nods. "I overheard some assistants talking. Maverick went to her place last night, but she wasn't there. No one knows where she is."

"Oh, shit!" I pull out my phone and check her social media. I've been following her there for years. "She hasn't posted for five days," I tell them.

"That's not that long," Ali says.

"It is for her. She usually posts three or four times a day."

"Rehab," Finn says, taking another bite of a croissant.

"I doubt it," I scoff. Juliette is a *vampire*, she's not going to be in rehab.

"That sounds about right to me," Ali says. "All that pressure can mess with big stars."

The rumor blazes through the lot like wildfire. Everyone who comes to get breakfast or coffee is talking about Juliette in rehab.

"Do we know when she's getting out?" one technician says to another as they sip their espressos.

"Don't you have to be in there for at least a month? Is the movie getting postponed?"

"They're going to pause filming and I'm going to be out of a fucking job again," says a woman from wardrobe.

"I'm going to put together a care package for her, filled with her favorite beauty products, and take it to her," says a guy from makeup. "Anyone know which clinic she's at?"

But of course, no one knows which clinic she's at, because none of it is true.

But if she's not here, and she's not in rehab, where the hell is she?

CHAPTER EIGHT

*M*averick

"No one knows when she's coming back?" Ziva asks over coffee and pastries in my trailer. The space is small, but me, Ziva and Brandon have somehow managed to squeeze into the small booth table in my trailer.

I don't usually enjoy food, but these pastries aren't half bad. They do make a hell of a mess though.

"Nope," I tell her.

"Okay, let's not deny the rehab rumor," she says. "It may or may not be true, but we don't want anyone to know that she's missing."

"But how do we film without her?" Brandon asks, tapping his fingers on the table and sending crumbs flying all over me.

"Let's just film all the scenes without her," I suggest. "Until we know."

"She's in so many scenes. After the massacre at the coffee

48

shop, she's basically with you the whole time!" Ziva picks up a pastry and takes a huge bite.

"My scenes at the agency with Finn. We could start there." I suggest. "Get all of those done."

"Makes sense," Brandon says. "Let's do what we can today. Have all the other CIA agents and background artists ready."

"And what if we're done with those scenes and she still doesn't turn up?" Ziva asks.

I run a hand over my jaw. "We could use a stand-in. Film my scenes and lines at least. Then, when she eventually shows up, which she will, we can film her on a green screen and just add her into the shots in post-production."

"God, I *hate* filming like that! I want it all to feel as real as possible!" Ziva looks like she's about to cry.

I point to my script on the table. "We're already using green screens for more than half the shots in the movie. What difference does it make if Juliette is green-screened in?"

"This is just not what I want," Ziva says, sounding like a teenager who's not getting their way. "How are we going to get the *intimacy*, the *chemistry* with a stand-in?"

"Maverick had great chemistry with Trix," Brandon says.

My heart lurches into my throat. "What?"

"Who?" Ziva asks.

"Trix, the woman who stood in yesterday," Brandon says.

"The *caterer*?" Ziva looks shocked at the idea.

Brandon hands her the plate of croissants, and she takes another one. "Let's shoot everything we can without Juliette over the next few days, and then we can work out where to go from there. Don't panic yet. She'll probably walk in tomorrow not even realising she missed a few days." His influencing words put Ziva at ease.

"We have options," I assure her. "We'll film everything in the office, then we can film my shots in the coffee shop."

"We can easily film all coffee shop scenes without Juliette," Brandon adds.

"We'll use a stand-in," I say. "Apart from her lines, you could film the whole thing without even seeing Juliette's face, not until we're out on the street."

Brandon nods. "That scene is chaotic. No one will know it's not her as long as we get a good wig that looks like Juliette's hair for the stand-in."

"We can use the wig that was made for her stunt double," I say.

Ziva makes a sound like she hates everything about this.

"If there's not as much intimacy in those scenes, it's no big deal," I assure her. "That can build later in the movie. But at least that gets us filming. We can still get a lot done without her."

She looks at me and nods. "Well, it's not like we have any other options, is it?" She stands up and clutches my shoulder. "Maverick, thank you," she says. "This is not exactly a situation I had planned for, and your support and advice is appreciated."

"Just make sure I get my producer credit," I tell her.

"Absolutely," Ziva replies with a forced smile. "Assuming Juliette comes back and the whole thing doesn't end up on the cutting room floor."

"According to her contract we are already within our rights to re-cast." Brandon says. "Maybe we should consider it."

Ziva shakes her head. "I can't even think about that right now. She'll show up soon. She has to."

Me and Brandon exchange a look. We both know that's not going to happen.

"Re-cast," I mouth at him.

He nods.

CHAPTER NINE

averick

Dirty Cop, five stars

Jason Rose excels in this iconic cop movie from 1983. To those people who have reviewed this and called it "eighties trash" or "another pointless cop movie" you have completely missed the point and obviously understand nothing about cinema!! And to the person who reviewed this and called Jason Rose's acting "an abomination", YOU are the abomination!!! Jason Rose may have died tragically in a motorcycle accident in the late nineties, but he will forever live in his incredible movies of that era and the hearts of those who truly understand cinematic genius.

@Filmmmbufff3456

I smack my hand on the desk. "I don't care about procedures, I care about *results*."

There's a too long pause while I wait for my scene partner to respond.

"If you don't follow procedures, you'll be fired," he eventually says.

Two minutes of filming and I already can't stand this guy. Finn Huxley has been in exactly three other movies. One uncredited, one still in post-production and the other was a kid's movie from years ago about a dog that absolutely bombed. Even a dog couldn't redeem it. The rumours that his mom is dating our casting director seem very fucking likely because he clearly doesn't know shit about acting.

I give Ziva a look, and I can tell she's regretting this casting decision.

Some people are great in an audition, but when they're on set, they can't handle the pressure of the job, and they lose it. Finn is losing it. He's forgetting his lines, emphasizing the wrong parts of the lines and is just *so* *u*nconvincing as a double agent who's secretly working for the bad guys.

"Give us a minute," I say, holding a hand up to Ziva and the crew.

Ziva yells "Cut," and everyone starts talking and rushing around us again.

"Finn," I say, putting a hand on his back and guiding him to a quiet corner of the set. "What's going on, man?"

He sweeps a hand through his dark curls. "Nothing." But his heart rate is way too high. He's nervous as fuck.

"Take a breath and sort your shit out," I tell him.

"My shit is sorted," he snaps.

"No, it isn't.

"Maybe it's my scene partner that's the problem."

My eyebrows shoot up. The fucking nerve of this guy!

I stare into his eyes, and while I don't exactly glamour him, I definitely use my influence on him. I need him to be *good* in this movie, so *I* look good in this movie. "This *is* your first serious movie," I tell him. "So fucking act like it."

His gaze softens, and I know my influence is working.

"You're here, man. You've got a part in a Hollywood movie. You're going to be a movie star, so start fucking acting like one."

Something in his expression changes, like he's realizing that "movie star" is also a role that you have to play.

Good.

"Fuck that other movie you did. No one will care about it or even remember it if you show up and do a good job in this one."

"No one remembers it anyway," he says.

"Yeah, because it sucked. But let me tell you something. Every single person in this room has worked on a movie that sucked. Our job is to make sure this one doesn't suck. And so *you* need to stop sucking and start acting like a movie star who's acting like a CIA double agent and start doing it well."

"I'm going to be a movie star," he says wistfully, and I wonder if I used a little too much of my vamp juice on him.

"Yeah."

"I'm a movie star," he says, his eyes glazing over a little now.

Ah, fuck.

I've definitely over-done the influence thing. It may seem like I do this all the time. I mean, I *could*. But I very rarely have to. Most people just do what I want them to because I'm Maverick Stone. And when they don't, I usually just let it go. I've never been into taking someone's free will. Where's the fun in that? These days I mostly just use my glamour on the Donnas so that they don't tell anyone what I am.

And I definitely never used my influence on Trix. Although it's tempting to use it on her now to get her to at least talk to me. But it has to be her choice. Always.

He claps my back like we've been friends for decades, even though he can't be more than twenty-seven years old.

"Thanks, Rick."

"Never call me Rick again," I tell him.

He laughs and points a finger gun at me. "Sure thing, *Rick*."

Okay, so I might glamour him to stop calling me that later.

"I'm ready, let's go from the top of the scene," Finn says, walking back onto the set with a new confidence in his step and a much more normal heart rate.

Ziva shoots me a look, and I just shrug.

"Rolling!" she calls out, and a few moments later, "Action!"

I smack my hand on the desk. "I don't care about procedures, I care about *results*."

"If you don't follow procedures, you'll be fired," Finn says. "And none of us want to see that happen. You're one of our best agents."

"I am *the* best, and it's because I don't follow procedure," I say.

Finn makes a face like he's eaten something sour. "I think you should emphasize the word *don't* in that line."

"What?"

"I think it would be stronger that way."

"What the fuck?"

I look over at Ziva, and she just shrugs.

"Try it, Maverick," she says.

I gape at her for a second and then remember we're still rolling.

Fine!

"I am *the* best, and it's because I *don't* follow procedure," I repeat.

"Better," Finn says with an annoying smirk on his face.

"Can we just get on with the scene?" I practically growl at the guy.

"I think you'll get it this next time," Finn says.

I look over at Ziva, waiting for her to put him in his place. But all she says is, "Try it again from the top."

"WHAT THE FUCK WAS THAT ABOUT?" I ask Finn once we're finally done filming for the day. It's late and I'm tired. Not physically, but tired of his *shit.* My influential pep talk seemed to have such a powerful effect that the guy went from being a total mess to having the biggest ego on the lot, even bigger than mine! But my big ego comes from decades of work, of proving myself, of top-rated movies, of awards and accolades. I deserve my big fucking ego. All he's done is a shitty movie about a dog that no one liked!

"What was what about?" he asks.

"Your attitude."

He just laughs. "Just doing what you told me, *Rick.*"

"Rein it in a little, will you? You won't get another gig in this town if you get known for being an asshole to work with."

He laughs. "It hasn't stopped you from getting work."

I glare at him. Hard.

"I get work because I'm damn good at my job. I've earned every role I've ever had. You haven't earned shit, especially not the right to be an asshole."

"Is that how it works?" he asks, pulling off his tie. "You *earn* the right to be an asshole to everyone?"

"That's not what I said."

"Nice working with you today," he says, clapping a hand on my shoulder. "I see we're filming together again all day tomorrow. I'm really looking forward to it." He gives me a wink, *an actual fucking wink,* and then he's gone.

I walk towards Ziva to complain about the guy and then I decide not to. Maybe he'll be more chill tomorrow after my influence wears off a bit. And if he's not, I could always glamour him into being less of a pain in the ass.

But I have to admit, his acting was a hell of a lot better after he changed his entire personality.

I walk towards the craft services table without even realizing I'm doing it. The only thing I want after this tiring day is to see Trix's face, eat another one of her croissants and then take her back to my place and experience a repeat of last time.

"Mr. Stone!" Ali beams at me. "Amazing work today," she says.

"You watched some of the filming?"

"Uh huh, I snuck away for a little while and got to see you and Finn in action. He's very good, isn't he? Everyone is calling him the next Maverick Stone!"

What the actual fuck?!

"Oh!" She nervously plays with a shamrock earring. "I didn't mean — of course there can only be one of you — I just — shit, sorry." She looks like she's about to go crawl under the table.

"He's not bad," I say. "But no way in hell is he the next Maverick Stone."

"Do you want something to eat?" she asks, like a muffin will fix the situation.

I look at what's left on the table. There's not much — a couple sandwiches and a few bars. I pick one up and inhale the scent of Trix. Lime and sugar, with a little coconut. It even has a little green layer of icing on top.

"What is this?"

"Key lime bar," Ali says. "It's Trix's signature treat."

I take a bite, and it's heavenly. It tastes like Trix's sweet skin, and I'm suddenly back there, tracing kisses over her shoulder, down towards her perfect breasts—

"I guess you like the bar?"

My eyes fling open, and there she is. Looking cute as ever in an Elvis Presley t-shirt.

I finish my bite, and our eyes lock. "I love it," I tell her.

I hold her gaze for a little too long. Her pulse quickens, and her face heats, spreading those splotches of pink I'm so familiar with over her cheeks.

"Elvis fan?" I ask.

She looks down at her shirt and then back up again. "Yeah. I guess."

"I knew him," I say.

"Oh my god, what?" squeals Ali. And then her face squishes up for a second before she lets out a laugh. "Oh, that's a joke, right? You're not old enough to have known Elvis!"

I look at Trix. "We used to hang out in Vegas together."

"Sure," she says, but I can tell by the flicker in her eyes that she wants to know more.

"Come by my trailer sometime and I'll tell you about it." I don't really know what I'm asking. For sex? For a chance to talk? For an actual conversation about Elvis? I'd give her any of those options.

I grab the last key lime bar and give her a nod. "If you want."

And then I walk off, listening to Ali's squeals of excitement and the pounding of Trix's heartbeat. Our interaction has affected her. Good to know she's not completely immune to my charms.

When I get back to my trailer, I sit and savor every single bite of her key lime bar while I reminisce about Trix's soft skin under my lips and dream about what it would be like to kiss her on the mouth.

CHAPTER TEN

rix

I LET OUT *a little moan as his fingers trace circles over my shoulder.*

His face softens a little. "I'm your first?"

"Not first first. But first vampire. Yes."

"I was under no illusions that you were a virgin."

"What the hell is that supposed to mean?"

"Nothing."

I step back from him. "This was a stupid idea. I should just — go."

"Trix, I didn't mean anything by it. It's just that you're sexy as hell, and I'd find it very hard to believe that you haven't had men climbing all over each other to have a chance with you."

I just glare at him, folding my arms over my chest. "Oh, so you think I just fuck anyone who's interested?"

"That's not what I'm saying! Just that I'm sure you've had

offers!" He runs a hand through his hair in frustration and, holy shit, I love making this guy mad.

The way his muscles and jaw tighten when he's pissed just does *something to me.*

"Not as many as you," I say, like it's his fault he's completely irresistible.

He turns in a frustrated circle, giving me a 360 view of his incredible body.

"Let's add something to the rules of engagement," he says, stepping in close to me again, so close I catch his saltwater, clean laundry scent. "No talking about previous sexual experiences."

"No ex talk, got it." I mime zipping my lips.

"No talk of lovers, exes, one-night stands. I don't want to hear about any of it. And I'm not telling you about any of mine."

I nod in agreement.

He closes the space between us again and cups my cheek in his very large hand. "When it's just us, I want it to be just us. I don't want anyone else here. No ghosts of the past. Fuck the past."

I nod again, and his hand falls away.

"Are you with me?"

I just keep nodding.

"For fuck's sake!" He mimes unzipping my lips and leans in towards me.

"Nuhuh!" I tell him, pushing his lips away with my fingers. "No kissing, remember?"

"Fuck that rule," he says, leaning in again.

"If we start being loose with the rules, who knows where this will end?"

"Oh yeah? If I kiss you right now, where do you think this will end?"

"Dating, marriage, three kids and a mortgage?" I joke.

Shit, I hope that comes out like a joke!

He laughs, and instead of running away, he just leans in closer to play with a tendril of my hair.

"Well, I don't date. I'm never going to marry. I can't have kids, and I already own this place along with a decent property portfolio."

"You can't have kids?"

He shakes his head. "My sperm is nonviable."

Oh.

"So, protection?"

"Unnecessary. I can't catch anything and can't pass it on either."

Oh, god.

My stomach flutters at the thought of not just having sex with Maverick Stone, but doing it without protection, nothing between us, just full skin on skin with Maverick Fucking Stone.

"Okay, so if you won't let me kiss you on the mouth..." He kisses my cheek, and holy shit, he might as well be kissing my pussy because it sends shivers of pleasure through my whole body. "How about you use that sexy mouth to tell me how you want it?"

MY ALARM GOES OFF, and I throw my phone across the room. If I have to continue to endure these sex dreams, I would at least like to experience the actual *sex* part, not just all the talk leading up to it!

I close my eyes and think of the first time we had sex in the kitchen, but it's no good. My memories are just not the same as the *dreams.*

I feel like I've hardly slept. Again. But it's been over a week since they started filming, and true to my word, me and Ali are going to start splitting our shifts. This morning, Ali will drive over here, we'll pack the van, and she'll drive it to the lot while I follow in my car. As soon as we're set up, I'll drive back home and get straight back into bed. I'll finally get some decent sleep and hopefully the next instalment of my sex dream, the part with the actual sex in it!

A moment with Maverick from yesterday plays in my mind as I shower. I haven't seen much of him this last week. He's been busy on set or hiding out in his trailer, but yesterday he came by the table and grabbed a stack of key lime bars. The way he looked at me with those bright blue-green eyes that feel so at odds with his smoldering, brooding, bad boy personality had my heart skipping a beat, and I knew he could tell. When he caught my eye and bit into the bar, it was like he was biting into my neck, and my pulse went crazy.

I'm suddenly struck by a memory of his teeth sinking into my wrist, and a shadow of the ecstasy of The Bite hits me. My fingers move down to my clit all by themselves, and when I think about Maverick's bite it takes less than a minute for my body to tense and then explode.

I turn the shower water onto cold in an attempt to regain my senses, I just end up shivering, and not in a good way.

I dress in jean shorts, not the ones I was wearing the day I went to Maverick's, but a faded black pair. I wear them over tights since it's been chilly for LA the last few days. It's getting to that time of year where you never know if you should wear a sundress or a hoodie or both.

I throw on a bright orange Trix and Treats t-shirt with an oversized pink cardigan on top. I swipe on a little silver glitter eyeshadow, add some matching silver disco ball earrings and put my hair up in two space buns above my ears.

"WHY DON'T YOU GO HOME?" Ali asks me at around 7 a.m. "I promise you I've got this, and if anything weird happens, I'll call you."

I make a face at her. "What if I'm asleep? I won't know you've called."

"I'll call your mom. She'll send someone over to wake you."

"You've got all the bases covered," I say. "I guess the student has become the master!"

"Don't go that far. I can hand out sandwiches all day, but unless everyone here wants to eat PB and J, you'll still have to make them."

I make myself an oat latte from the espresso machine and pop the lid on. "Okay, I'm outie!" I tell her with a wave. "I'll miss you!"

"I'll miss you more!"

"Text me every five minutes!"

"Voice note me every thought in your head!"

"BFFs forever!" I call back to her with a string of blown kisses and then, as I turn towards the exit, I nearly smack into Maverick Stone. *Again.*

"Watch where you're going, you oaf!"

He laughs. "Why don't *you* watch where *you're* going?"

"I am!"

"You were looking in the opposite direction."

"You don't know anything about me!" I snap.

He smirks at me, that killer smile doing things to me I wish it wasn't. He lowers his voice. He's dressed in gym shorts and a tank top like he's just been to the gym, and his arms are practically bulging. "I know a *lot* about you."

It's true. Sure, I've had sexual experiences before Maverick, but *nothing* like it was with him. He knows where and how I like to be touched. He knows that sometimes I scream when I come. And he knows about my sexual fantasies. Sharing them seemed like a good idea at the time, but now—

"Whatever, I'm going home." I start to storm past him, but he grabs my arm, and the touch is electric. It's the first time he's had his hands on me in over eighteen months, and it's even realer than the realest dream.

"Get off me!" I jerk him off me, even though all I want is for him to grab me with both arms and shove me against a wall and have his way with me.

Fuck, I'm a mess.

"Ziva and Brandon want to talk to you."

"What? Why?"

"I'm just the messenger," he says, holding those large hands up in surrender.

"Why you?"

"Can't I just come and say hi?"

"No, you can't!"

I turn on the heel of my checkerboard Vans and storm back towards the set where Ziva and Brandon are staring into their little monitors.

"Trix!" Brandon says. "So lovely to see you."

"You wanted me?"

"Hi, Trix," says Ziva.

"Hi."

"We have a proposition for you," Ziva says. "Juliette is still unwell and not able to make it to filming. At this stage, we're not sure when she'll be back."

"We want you to stand in for her," Brandon says.

"Like I did before?"

"Exactly," Ziva says. "We're hoping Juliette is back to filming as soon as possible, but in the meantime, we can't pause filming. We need someone to stand in, someone for Maverick to work off."

A butterfly finds its way into the cage that is my belly as I consider the idea of Maverick *working off me.*

"We liked your chemistry together," says Brandon.

A second butterfly enters the cage.

"We can film Maverick's lines with you and then when Juliette is back, we'll film her lines. We can put everything together in post-production, and no one will ever know that

Juliette and Maverick weren't on set together," Brandon explains.

"Mostly we just need a body, someone who can act and support Maverick," Ziva says.

"What do you think?" Brandon asks. "I know you're busy with craft services, but you've got your assistant to help."

"And we will pay you, of course," says Ziva.

"How much?"

"It really depends on how long it is until Juliette comes back, but how about five grand a week?" Brandon suggests.

Five grand a week? Holy shit!

"Seven," I tell him.

"Done."

Shit, I should have asked for even more!

But even if Juliette is gone for just another week, seven grand would pay off all my business debts and then some.

"And I get paid for at least one week, even if she's back tomorrow."

"Of course," Brandon says.

I should have asked for two weeks.

"Excellent," Ziva says, beaming at me. "I think it would be good if you and Maverick could get together in his trailer and run some scenes we want to film today. Does that work for you?"

"What? *Now?*"

Ziva laughs. "Yes, now."

And so instead of going back to my car to go home and sleep, I walk towards Maverick's trailer.

CHAPTER ELEVEN

$\mathcal{M}$averick

"Silver should be avoided at all costs. Silver is not deadly to a vampire, but silver bullets can slow a vampire down, silver chains can keep a vampire bound, and drinking liquid silver can cause a vampire to fall into a deep sleep. If a vampire comes into contact with silver, the best thing to do is stay calm. Writhing or thrashing against silver will only cause more damage, even if it is just superficial."

The Fraternity of the Everlasting Rose Handbook, page 290

I'm just out of the shower after a session in the studio gym and my run-in with Trix when there's a knock on my trailer door. It's not like I need to work out. When vampires are made, their physique stays as it was at the moment they were turned. I'm lucky I was turned when I was at peak fitness, but running and lifting weights still feels good in my body, and I enjoy feeling fit and strong. When I'm in my home gym, I lift heavy, heavier than any weight in the gym. I could throw a fully stacked barbell easily a hundred meters, but in public I need to tone it down. I must admit, I enjoy pretending like it's no big deal to lift the heaviest weights in the place while the other actors and studio staff watch with open mouths.

I'm still shirtless and drying my hair with a small towel when I open the door. And there she is. Trix Delaney. Her mouth drops open a little as her eyes drop to my naked chest. Her pulse speeds up, and I'm fairly sure it's because of my body, not the coffee in her hand.

"See something you like?" I grin.

"Put a shirt on," she tells me, but all I hear is her telling me to take my shirt off moments before I fucked her in my kitchen.

I give her a smirk and turn around, flexing my back muscles for her enjoyment before returning with a shirt in my hands.

I lean on the door frame. "What can I do for you?" I ask, even though I know exactly why she's here.

"I'm your stand-in."

"Yeah, I heard something about that."

"Ziva asked me to come over so we could run some scenes."

"Come in." I open the door for her but make little effort to move out of the way, forcing her to brush past me on her way up the steps and into the trailer. Her scent of sugar and lime hits me and takes me back to our night together, the time in the kitchen, in the bed, watching the sunset, that damn *shower*.

This last week, I've been trying to avoid her. Every time I see her, all I want is *her*. It's been driving me crazy to see her walking around the lot in her colorful shiny outfits, but it's driving me even crazier trying to stay away from her.

I keep reminding myself that it was one time only for a reason. No good can come from trying to pick up where we left off. Our one-night stand was only special because it was *one night.* And an afternoon.

"Can you please put your shirt on?" she pleads, pulling her fluffy pink cardigan around her shoulders.

"I'm a little warm from my run," I tell her, ignoring her request.

"Whatever," she shakes her head. "Do you want to run scenes or not?"

"Or not."

"You're making this unnecessarily hard for me," she tells me.

"When I'm hard for you, it's always necessary."

A dark eyebrow raises into a tendril of green hair that won't stay in place.

I've gone too far. She's going to throw her coffee on me or storm out and have me done for harassment. Fuck, I'm an idiot.

"Sorry." I shake my head and pull the t-shirt over my head. "I'm being a dick."

"Yeah, you are. Look, I don't want to be your stand-in any more than you want me to be, but I need the money, so can you just stop with the innuendo and read some lines with me?"

"Why do you think I don't want you to be my stand-in?"

"Uh, because of the rules of engagement."

"Which one?"

"I don't know! I can't think of which one, but we said it was one time, and we'd never talk about it and act like it never happened, and now we're thrown together in this insane situation and—"

I step towards her, her fruity sweet scent driving me wild

and I wish that we'd never created any rules, because all I want is to bend her over the fold-out table and fuck her until she makes that whimpering sound that's like music to my dead ears.

"I'm more than happy to have you as my stand-in," I tell her.

"Oh?"

My smart mouth starts saying words before my brain can catch up and stop it. "And for the record, in case you're wondering, I'm still more than happy to fuck you anytime."

A blush spreads over her cheeks as her pulse speeds up. "What?"

"I know we said one time only, but if you ever wanted to revisit the rules, maybe we could make our time working together on this project a little more fun."

"This is highly inappropriate," she frowns.

"I'm just putting it out there. I'm just being honest. I don't want to be anything less than honest with you. Not ever. And so, I'm just trying to say that I think we had a good time together, and if you wanted to have a good time together for the next couple of months, or however long this film takes, I'm willing."

She pauses for a second, and once again I wonder if I've read her all wrong. The high pulse, the blush, the nervous excitement at being in my presence.

Maybe it is just the caffeine. Shit!

She takes a sip of her coffee and then looks up at me, those soft dark eyes giving her away. She wants this as much as I do.

"Right now?" she asks.

"What?"

"You want to fuck right now? When we're supposed to be running lines?"

I let out a laugh and then shrug. "Sure, if that's what you want."

She takes a pause and looks down at the lid of her coffee cup for what feels like forever.

"But if it's not what you want, just say so, and I promise I won't bring it up again. I'll be purely professional from now on."

Her lips twist, and she looks up at me. Fuck, she's gorgeous.

"All the other rules still stand. We're only changing the one that says it's one time only."

"Well, we already broke that rule by doing it three times."

She rolls her eyes playfully, and I know we're both remembering those three incredible times.

"Okay," she says.

Wait, what?

I didn't really expect her to say *yes*, and I certainly didn't expect her to want to do it *right now*.

"Are you serious?" I ask. "You want this?"

She shrugs. "Yeah, sure. Why not? You're right. It was kind of fun the last time."

"*Kinda* fun?" I move closer to her now, closing what's already a very small gap between us in this tiny space. I run my hands over those familiar shoulders and make my way down to her waist. That fucking waist! I'm reminded of how it felt to hold her there while I came inside her, and I'm instantly hard.

I bring a hand up to cup her beautiful face and look into those dark eyes, enlarged with her desire for me.

"No kissing," she reminds me.

"Yeah, yeah, I know." I can't believe this is going to happen. I've been wanting this for months. Eighteen fucking long months. And now she's here again.

I'm not much of a religious guy for obvious reasons, but I

mentally thank god or the universe or whoever is in charge, for bringing us together again.

All that bullshit about this not being a good idea was just that. Bullshit. Who fucking cares about rules? Who cares that she's human? Who cares that she'd be the first human for me to be with more than once in — fuck, I don't know how long.

Yes, I do. Lizzie. 1942.

I push Lizzie from my mind and run my fingers over Trix's glorious warm cheek. Goddamn, I want to kiss those lips. I move a stray piece of hair away from her eye and then—

"Oh, fuck!" I yell, clutching onto my thumb.

"What?!" she exclaims, jumping back. "What is it?"

I stare at my throbbing thumb and see tiny shards of silver have wedged themselves into my skin.

"Silver!"

"Huh?"

"Why are there silver bits in my thumb? Fuck!"

She lets out a howl of laughter.

"What is this? Jesus! Fuck!"

"I can fix this," she says, still laughing. "But you have to calm down."

"Ah, motherfucker!"

"I'll be back in two minutes!"

"Where the hell are you going?" I call to her as she disappears out of my trailer back towards the lot.

I thought I was going to get laid, not get stabbed to death by tiny silver shards! I stomp around the trailer like a child who's slammed their finger in a door until Trix returns with a pair of tweezers.

"Sit down and quit being such a baby."

I sit on the couch and pout while she plucks the shards out of my hand.

"What the hell?" I ask her when she's done. "What are these things?"

"It's my eyeshadow," she says.

"There's real silver in there?"

"It's eco glitter, but I had no idea the flakes were real silver."

She watches, dumbstruck, as my thumb heals over in seconds and then all the pain is gone.

"You're kind of a wimp for a vampire," she says. "Does silver really fuck you up that much?"

I grimace. "It wasn't that bad. It was the surprise of it more than anything."

She lets out a giggle, and it's the most beautiful sound I've ever heard.

"So, silver doesn't kill you? Just maims?"

I nod. "It just slows us down."

"So, I should keep hold of that eyeshadow."

"If you want to fend off vampire advances, sure."

"What else can maim you?" she asks.

"That's secret information."

"Sunlight?"

I give her a look. "Clearly not."

"How do you walk around in the sun all day?"

"Lizard juice."

She laughs again. "What?"

"There's a lizard that lives in the desert near here. If we drink its blood, we become daywalkers."

"Does it have any side-effects?"

"For some of us. Not much for me."

"Crucifixes? Holy water?"

"No."

"Garlic."

"No."

"Just silver."

"Pretty much."

I don't tell her about elm, ash and yew wood.

She takes another look at my hand. "Are you okay now?"

I shake my head. "There's only one thing that would make me feel better," I tell her.

"Let me guess. A hot cocoa and an early night?"

"That's a vampire's worst nightmare."

"Sure." She laughs, her eyes crinkling cutely at the corners before they fall on my mouth. She bites her lip, and I know she wants me just as much as I want her.

"You," I tell her. "You can fix me."

She bites her lip, and we both just stare at each other for a moment.

"My eyeshadow will get all over you," she says.

"So go take it off."

She gives me a shy smile. "How about tomorrow I don't wear any?"

I've never thought of naked eyelids as so damn sexy until now.

"How about I just put up with the pain?"

A knock at the door stops me from taking a step towards her again.

"Maverick, Trix! You're wanted on set!"

CHAPTER TWELVE

rix

Winning the West, *five stars*

Oh man, I miss the days when movies were made like this!! No green screens, no special effects, just damn good acting in real world settings! Real horses, actors doing their own stunts, filmed in real locations, these were the good old days of cinema!! Mason Jones gives an unbelievable performance in this one. It's absolutely his best movie. If you're new to Mason Jones movies, this is the place to start. That's not to say that Best of the West *or* West Goes East *are not incredible movies, but this one is a standout. And to the person who gave this one star and said it was "boring as fuck" but gave that piece of shit Max Montrose movie* Love Delayed *five stars you should grow a brain!!*

@Filmmmbufff3456

. . .

AS SOON AS I'm back out in the daylight and fresh air between Maverick's trailer and the lot, it hits me just how stupid I almost was.

I am not over Maverick Stone. I know it was just one day that turned into night, but I'm still not over it. I'm not over him. I haven't moved on. The last eighteen months have been hell, and to do it again, to put myself through that, would be absolute self-annihilation.

No, I will stick to the rules. I will not have sex with Maverick Stone again.

"Hey, wait up!" he calls to me, but I keep walking — fast.

"I need the bathroom!" I call to him.

I splash my face with water and then stare at myself in the grimy mirror. "Don't do it," I tell myself. "Be strong."

I fluff up my space buns, and after a few deep breaths I head back inside. An assistant immediately shoves a script at me, and then Ali appears by my side.

"This is so exciting!" she beams.

"Are you going to be okay without me?" I ask her. "This is all kind of — sudden."

"I'll be fine! You go live your dreams!"

"I'm just a stand-in," I tell her.

"You're still acting on a real-life movie set!"

And then the realization hits. She's right. I may not get to be *in* the movie, but I'll be helping to make it happen, and not just because I served some coffee and cakes.

"I gotta go," I tell her. "Good luck!"

"I got this, *you* got this!"

We high-five and then I walk towards the coffee shop set where everyone is assembled. I find a spot to stand with a bunch of other people — technicians, makeup, background artists dressed in casual clothes and a group of actors dressed in black balaclavas.

One of them pulls his balaclava off. Finn! He gives me a wink and walks over to me.

"You're standing in for Juliette, that's cool."

"Yeah, I guess," I shrug. "Have you heard anything about where she is?"

"I heard Serenity House," he says. Serenity House is well known for being a rehab clinic for celebrities. In fact, I don't think you can get in there unless you're at least a B-list celebrity.

"She was always talking about being sober on her socials," I say, knowing full well she's not in rehab, anyway.

"Doesn't mean she wasn't on hard drugs."

"I guess being a celebrity is tough," I say. "Sorry, I guess you're a celebrity?"

"Kinda," he laughs. "My last movie didn't exactly get rave reviews."

"Oh, you did a movie? What was it?"

He gives me a look like either he's upset I don't know what the movie is, or he doesn't want to tell me. I'm not sure which. "*Hound of the Bakervilles*," he says.

"Sorry, I haven't heard of it."

"It was a movie about a family and their dog."

"Oh, how cute!"

He shakes his head. "It sounds better than it was. I have a rom-com coming to streaming next month, but maybe after this movie comes out, I'll be a real celebrity," he shrugs.

There's something about Finn that I'm really drawn to. He's got to be in his late twenties, but he's got a boyish charm about him. There's something about him that just feels *easy.*

If only I could have a crush on someone like Finn, just a normal, cute guy who won't bite me or live forever.

But where's the fun in that?

"Quiet on set!" Brandon calls out over a megaphone, and everyone suddenly stops talking.

"We're about to film the coffee shop scene," Ziva calls out to the group. "We really have to get this right, because we only have one chance to destroy this set. We'll be filming from many angles to make sure we get everything we need, but I really need everyone on their game for this."

She looks around at the group. "Where the fuck is Maverick?" Ziva asks.

"Right here," he says, appearing behind her and making her jump.

He's dressed in that black suit again, tie slightly loosened, his hair hanging just a little over his forehead. And damn if he isn't fucking *fine*!

No, Trix, no!

"Okay, let's start with the coffee order scene, then we'll move onto the massacre," Ziva says.

"Should we get the stand-in into a green suit?" asks one of the technicians.

Ziva frowns over at me. "Why isn't she in a green suit already? Yes, get her into a green suit! Now! Jesus, why can't people just do their jobs?"

A pretty brunette I think is called Crystal who especially loves my blueberry muffins grabs my arm and pulls me through the studio and out into the wardrobe trailer. It's full to bursting with costumes, a sewing machine on a fold-out table and threads and scissors everywhere.

"What size are you?" Crystal asks.

"Four," I tell her.

"You're very petite. I think you're a two. How do you buy clothes without knowing your size?" She tuts as she grabs a tape measure out of her pocket and then I stand there getting prodded and poked while she measures me.

She disappears and then comes back moments later with a green spandex jumpsuit.

"I have to wear *that*?"

"It'll make it easier for post-production to add Juliette into the scenes."

"But I'll look ridiculous!"

"People wear them all the time on set, it's no big deal. I'll leave you to get changed."

I get out of my t-shirt and shorts, piling them up on a chair in a corner, and pull the suit on over my tights. I take a look in the full-length mirror and sigh. This is the ugliest, most unflattering thing I've ever had on my body.

Crystal comes back in and harrumphs at me. "Put the hood on," she says, grabbing a bit at the back and yanking it over my head. "Better."

"I look like a slug."

"A cute slug though," she says with a tired smile. "Now, come on."

I walk back towards the set, dreading the moment that Maverick sees me in this thing. Just a few hours ago he was trying to seduce me, but after seeing me in this outfit, he'll never think of having sex with me again!

But that will be the best thing that could happen right now!

I walk a little taller, proud of the fact that I look so un-fuckable right now. This is exactly what I need to look like!

When I get back to the set, the background artists are in place, the guys with balaclavas are nowhere to be seen, and Maverick is standing behind the coffee counter talking to Ziva.

His eyes fall on me, and his mouth drops open.

It's working! He no longer finds me physically attractive!

"Great, Trix, can you get behind the counter? All I need from you is to read the lines, just like we did last week."

"It's easier to fix later if she doesn't hold a script!" someone shouts.

"She's not a real actor!" Ziva shouts back.

Well, that stings.

"I know the scene," I tell her.

"You do?"

I nod and pass the script to a hand that appears nearby.

"Okay, let's roll."

A bunch of things happen next. A heap of people call out "striking!" and everyone starts to run around in circles.

Someone with a clapper stands in front of us and when Ziva shouts "action," they read the scene number and clap it together and even though I'm standing here dressed like a slug, I can't help but feel so freaking excited that I'm making a movie!

"Can I get a coffee?" Maverick asks, so smoldering in his suit on the other side of the counter that I want so much to jump over so I can climb him like a tree.

Oh, fuck, what's my line?

"Cappuccino, latte, long black, short black…?" I ask him.

"What's *your* drink?" He has that twinkle in his eye, just a hint of a flirt. He's clearly acting. If this was real life he'd just ask the server back to his place for blood and sex.

"Oat latte with salted caramel syrup," I reply.

Oh, I totally forgot to pick some of that up!

"That's a woman's drink."

"Well, I *am* a woman."

He pauses for a beat, and his eyes narrow at me.

"Give me two!" someone shouts, giving him his line. "Large!"

"I'm sorry, but what the fuck is this?" he says instead.

"What the fuck is what?" Ziva sighs.

"I can't work with this," he says, looking at me like I'm a slug that got in his mug of blood.

"With what?" asks Ziva.

"With this green suit!"

"What's wrong with my suit?" I ask, putting my hands on my hips.

"You wanted a stand-in so that I could vibe off someone, but how can I vibe off this shit?"

I gasp. "You're calling my suit *shit*?"

"I'm calling this whole thing shit," he says, shaking his head. "I can't work like this!"

Now it's my turn for my jaw to drop. I can't believe how much of an asshole he's being! He could have just said, "Hey, Ziva, I'm not sure I can work with the green suit", but he's making this into such a *thing*.

"Cut!" yells Ziva. She lets out a sigh. "Maverick, if you can't work with the suit, we'll lose the suit. Easy."

Crystal from wardrobe yanks me by the arm and takes me back to the trailer.

"Well, this is going well so far," I say to her, pulling the stretchy hood back down, revealing very squashed green space buns.

"You haven't seen anything yet," she tells me.

CHAPTER THIRTEEN

Maverick

TRIX, *dressed in nothing but one of my way too big for her sweatshirts, tucks her feet up under her on the outdoor couch and grabs another slice of post-sex pizza.*

The clouds are turning the color of peach and mango sorbet over the beach, and it's a most perfect evening. One of the best I've had in a long time.

"You really don't want a slice?" she asks.

"Honestly, I'm just enjoying watching you devour that thing."

She's ravenous. The two orgasms I've already given her have clearly burned some calories because she eats like she has sex, like she's starving for it. I wonder if she'll be up for one more round.

"More for me," she shrugs, taking another bite.

I pull her legs over me so that they're in my lap.

"Too intimate," she tells me, but she doesn't immediately move away.

"What? Why? It's just your legs." I run a hand over her naked calves, making goose pimples appear all over her legs.

"Exactly," she says. "It's too relationship-y." She pulls her legs back and hides them under herself again.

"Sexual fantasy," I say, trying to bring us back out of the "relationship-y" energy.

"Excuse me?"

"What's your sexual fantasy?"

"I can only have one?"

I grin. "You can have as many as you want. I'm just asking for one."

"I think we've ticked a few of them off the list already," she tells me.

"Yeah? Tell me which ones we did."

"Well, when you bit me," she says, a light flush hitting her cheeks.

"That was a fantasy of yours?"

"I nearly did it with another guy, another vampire," she tells me. "But I was too scared."

"You weren't scared of me?"

The idea that she felt safe with me, safe enough to let me bite her, warms in my chest.

"I was, a little, but I was more excited. So, I guess I felt the fear and did it anyway."

"Was it worth it?"

"You couldn't tell from all the moaning and screaming?" A soft smile appears on her face just before she takes another bite of the pizza she's over halfway through eating.

"What else?" I nudge. I want to hear more about how much of a sex-god I am.

"Well, when you did me in the kitchen—"

"That was—"

Well, we both know what that was.

"I've always liked the idea of—" she stops for a second, taking *the moment to eat a bit more pizza. "Is this too intimate? Talking about this stuff?"*

"No, this is just sex talk. Tell me, what do you like the idea of?"

"People watching me." Her face flames. "Like watching me having sex."

I lean forward. "I'll fuck you on the beach right now," I offer.

She gives me a playful kick. "The thing is, I don't really want to do it. Not in reality. I just like the idea of it. Playing pretend."

"Did you like it when I fucked you by the window in the kitchen earlier? The idea that someone could have seen us through the windows?"

"Yeah, but the windows are tinted, right? Right?" She suddenly looks horrified.

I let out a chuckle. "They are, but I get it. It's fun to pretend they aren't." I raise an eyebrow at her. "I love walking around the house naked pretending everyone on the beach is looking up like who is that sexy beast?"

She lets out a howl of laughter. "I bet you do!"

She takes another slice of pizza and asks, "What about you? What's your fantasy? I guess you've done them all already?"

"There's one I haven't done," I start. But holy shit, I would love to do it with her.

She nearly drops her pizza.

"This is top secret. Stick it on the list of things you can't tell anyone about."

"Your secret is safe with me."

"STILL NO WORD FROM JULIETTE?" Ziva asks as she takes a seat in the tiny booth in my trailer opposite me and Brandon.

I shake my head, trying to focus on the matter at hand. Juliette. This movie. Not dreams of conversations about sexual fantasies with Trix.

I don't sleep much, and I very rarely dream, but when I

do, it's always of our afternoon, evening and night together. Last night I drifted off in bed, listening to the sound of the crashing waves and letting them take me back to Trix. I dreamed of her, and it felt so real that in the morning I reached over to touch her, so sure that she was with me.

But she wasn't.

"I've hired a private investigator who's looking for her, but we're fairly certain she's in rehab somewhere," Brandon says. "None of the clinics would give us any information due to confidentiality, so it's difficult to know which one she's in," Brandon says.

We're still going with the rehab story for now.

"It just doesn't seem like Juliette," Ziva muses. "She's been such a big promoter of the sober lifestyle."

"Yeah, well, most of what you see online is bullshit," I say.

"I'm assuming you've got in contact with her family and relatives?" Ziva asks. "They don't know anything? She's not staying with any of them?"

That's a hard no. Vampires absolutely *do not* stay with family or relatives. For most of us, as soon as we're made, we fake our deaths, change our names and never contact our families again.

I shake my head. "None that we can track down."

"We might need to make a statement," Brandon says. "Hashtag Find Juliette is trending."

Seeing Brandon sitting there in his suit and old school hairstyle talking about hashtags has me stifling a grin.

"What do you mean?" Ziva asks.

I slide my phone over.

Ziva frowns down at the comment section on Juliette's last post from over two weeks ago now, a promo for a perfume brand. It's full of people calling bullshit on the rehab rumor.

. . .

@JULIETTELOVER666 NO-ONE BELIEVES this bullshit about you being in rehab.

@moviestarmaddnessss889 She's not in rehab! She's gone missing! Heard it from those working on set of her new movie! No one knows where she is!!

@wellnessgirly777 Maybe she's got depression?

@supersoccormom1988 We will find you, Juliette!

@juliettelover666 #FindJuliette is trending!!!!

"IT APPEARS that the hashtag Find Juliette is indeed trending," I tell her, tapping on it and seeing that it's been used over ten thousand times already.

Ziva presses her lips together.

"The real question we should be considering," asks Brandon, "is whether we should re-cast her."

"Waiting for her is holding up production," I say simply.

"Re-casting will hold up production too. God only knows how long it will take to find the right Lucy for our John." Ziva throws her head back and wails.

"I don't want to be the one to say it out loud," says Brandon. "But since we don't exactly know where she is, she could be — well, she could be anywhere." What he means is that she could have suffered the Certain Death. There would be no finding a body if she had. She would just turn to black ooze. "The reality of the situation," he continues, "is that Juliette may not be available for filming this movie. Ever."

We all sit in silence as we realize what this could mean for us, for this movie, our careers, and of course, for Juliette.

"You're right." Ziva takes a deep breath. "Juliette's out. We need to re-cast."

The tension in the room is palpable.

"But Juliette is hot right now," she says. "Without her, does this movie still stand a chance?"

I clear my throat. "It's still a Maverick Stone movie," I remind her.

"But there are loads of Maverick Stone movies," she says. "We need an edge with this one. We need a way to promote it that's not just the usual bullshit interviews or cast drama rumors. Maverick Stone threw a TV or whatever. I was really excited about Juliette using her social media, sharing the movie process with her fans, getting them excited about it now so that when it comes out next year, they're already emotionally invested."

"I may have a solution," Brandon says. "But let's just see how filming today goes first. I have an idea for how to get a little more heat and chemistry between Maverick and the stand-in, Trix."

Like we need any more heat and chemistry!

Ziva nods. "See you both on set in half an hour."

She leaves, and we're finally able to speak freely.

"Let's call in Henrietta," Brandon says. "See what she can pick up on Juliette."

Henrietta is Max's personal assistant. She's excellent at her job, partly because she's a very powerful and talented witch. She's also the counsellor for the witches in the Order of Concordia.

"I'll drop by Max's tonight and discuss it with her."

"Thank you, Maverick."

Brandon looks worried. It's an unusual expression on his face. He's usually the epitome of cool.

"You're worried," I say.

"Vampires don't just go missing. I suspect some kind of foul play. I just don't know what kind."

"I feel it too. None of this feels right."

"Hopefully, Henrietta can shed some light."

"She usually does."

WE'RE FILMING a car chase scene today. It's just after the coffee shop massacre, which we did eventually manage to film yesterday, with Trix still in the fucking green suit. I spent over an hour arguing about it with Ziva and Brandon, and in the end, I had to endure it. Most people look ridiculous in those suits, but the way it showed off every single curve of Trix's gorgeous body was so damn distracting! Eventually, after throwing my hissy fit, Finn glaring at me like I was being a diva, I reigned it in and suffered through it.

In today's scene, John has just pulled Lucy out of the coffee shop. They get in a stolen car, and they drive through the city, crashing into everything as they're chased by Finn and the other bad guys.

There are two sets. One set is a street-front where the car is waiting for us, this is where we'll run to, I'll grab her, throw her into the car, all while shooting some bad guys. On the other set is a duplicate car sitting on a raised platform in front of a green screen. This is where we'll shoot the rest of the chase.

Fucking green screens. I miss the days when movies were *real*, when action happened in real time, in real places. With real cars, real horses, real actors doing real stunts. I always used to do my own stunts. I still do when we're not using a fucking green screen. I miss the days when there was none of this inserting actors who've gone missing into scenes in post-production.

But here we are, and I guess there's no going back to the good old days.

I walk onto the set of the street, just getting a feel for it, trying to imagine myself as John Stannic, secret agent, good guy, perfect shot, great with women, none of it is too far-fetched, and the irony is that in real life I'm more John Stannic than John Stannic himself.

"Trix," says Ziva.

The sound of her name alerts me to her presence even before I pick up her sugar-lime scent through the crowds of other perfumes and scent profiles.

I turn, but I don't see Trix. I see Lucy Montague, raven-haired beauty, coffee shop barista and secret spy for the Russian government. The woman John falls for, not knowing that she's secretly married to the guy played by Finn. But Finn, the bad guy, doesn't know that Lucy is a double agent, and she's *actually* working for the CIA, so John gets the girl in the end after all! Ha!

This movie is so ridiculous.

I can't keep my eyes off her. Trix is dressed in tight dark blue jeans, high boots, and a black tank-top revealing a *lot* of cleavage. She's wearing a wig of long dark curls, and her makeup is movie-thick, covering her freckles unfortunately. They've given her dark eye makeup and a deep red lip.

And while she looks damn hot, she doesn't look as hot as she did that night I had her stripping off her Mr. Avocado t-shirt in my kitchen.

Someone hands her an apron with the coffee shop logo on it. She puts it on and then I watch as Ziva goes through the blocking with her, showing her where to stand, where to run to. "Just let yourself get grabbed and thrown around by Maverick."

A flush hits her cleavage, and she better be thinking about me throwing her around. She nods. "Sure."

"Remember, no one knows yet that you're working for the Russians or that you're secretly secret service. So you need to seem like an innocent barista in all this, even though you're not."

"Got it," she says with a nod.

"Let's run through the blocking!" Ziva calls out. "Maverick, Trix, everyone, places."

"You look—" I try to find some words that won't make her pissed.

"What?"

Great, I didn't say a word, and she's still pissed.

"I don't know," I say.

"Gee, thanks," she replies dryly.

"Grab her wrist and run her to the car," Ziva says.

I grip Trix's wrist firmly in my hand and suddenly remember the way it felt to bite her there. The way she so quickly went into ecstasy at the feeling of it, and the way her warm blood tasted better than anyone's I've ever had.

"Run, Maverick!" Ziva shouts out.

I run towards the car, pulling her with me. She trips and stumbles after me until I swing open the car door. I throw her into the driver's seat and then push her over into the passenger seat, all while she scowls at me.

"Damnit, we should have been filming! That was perfect! Let's roll, from the top!" Ziva shouts.

This time it's even better because Trix is even more pissed with me for having to do it again.

When I shove her into the car and close the door, she shoves me back. I bring my hands up in surrender. "I'm trying to save your life here!" I ad-lib.

"Well, you don't have to be an ass about it!" she snaps back.

Ziva yells cut, and I'm sure we're about to get into shit for going off script. Some directors love when actors do this, but Ziva is also the writer. Usually messing with lines doesn't fly with writer/directors, even though she was fine with Trix's change to the first scene.

She gives a thumbs up and starts watching replays on the monitors as I make my way over to her, Trix trailing behind.

"One take and it was perfect," she says, grinning and clapping her hands together.

"What do you think, Brandon?"

"These two are electric," he says.

Brandon and Ziva exchange a look.

"What?" I ask.

"I think we've just found a solution to all our problems," Brandon says.

M averick

"I, Linda McKinley, hereby resign from the Fraternity of the Everlasting Rose. I no longer believe that the organization operates in the best interests of vampire-kind, and so I submit my resignation. It would do all other vampires in the Fraternity well to consider their own involvement in this outdated secret order and to look to the future instead of the past when it comes to vampire legacy, influence and affluence."

"ANOTHER ONE?" Max frowns down at the letter, and I take a seat at the dark wood table in the war room of his Hollywood Hills mansion.

Henrietta gives me a stern look over her glasses, her red curls dancing around her head like snakes.

I don't have one at my place, but rooms like this are common in vampire homes. We have incredibly good hearing, and the only way to stop a vampire from hearing you talking about them is to go into a soundproof room like this one. Tomes of ancient and some more recent books on all things mystical, magical and supernatural fill shelves around us. Max had this room put in shortly before marrying Lottie. Lottie was old, and her vampire hearing was better than anyone's.

Max pours us short glasses of whiskey. Yes, we're vampires. Yes, we prefer blood. But while whiskey no longer gets us drunk, it still feels nice in the hand.

"I don't understand," he says, running a hand over the back of his neck. "*Two* resignations from the Fraternity?"

"Linda would never resign," I say. I've known Linda for decades, she was my leading lady in some of my best movies.

"I'm sure you're right," he says, frowning at the typed words on the paper.

"When was the last time anyone resigned?" I ask.

He looks dumbfounded. "According to vampire law, a vampire may leave if they wish, but why would any vampire wish to leave? Why turn your back on the most powerful vampires in the city?" He takes a sip of whiskey. "No one resigns from the Fraternity. It is unheard of. The only vampires who have ever left the Fraternity did not leave by choice."

He's referring to the Fraternity uprising in the fifties when many of our kind were given the Certain Death after speaking out against our then president, Lottie's father, Renauld. It was a war between vampire and fae, vampire and vampire.

I quickly shake those memories out of my mind.

"Where did you find this letter?" Max asks.

"Brandon found it in his trailer this afternoon."

"Is Linda filming anything at Starlight Studios?"

"No, that's the other thing. According to security, she was

never on the lot today. Brandon had his P.I. look into it, and apparently, she was scheduled to board a flight to Barcelona at midday, but she wasn't on the flight. We've been unable to locate her. Just like with Juliette."

"This is all most perplexing."

"And that's exactly why I'm here. I wanted to borrow Henrietta."

She shoots me a look. "I am not an item of clothing that you can just *borrow*."

Great, now I've pissed off a witch.

"That's not what I meant," I say. "I just wanted your special — *perspective* on the situation."

She scowls at me and then harrumphs as she pulls a deck of tarot cards out of her bag and starts shuffling.

"Okay, so what's the question?" she asks.

"Where is Juliette?" I ask.

"The cards don't really work like that. I could try a map and pendulum, but it helps to have someone with me who has a strong connection to her. I certainly don't, and from what I'm sensing—" She narrows her eyes. "Despite what the tabloids say, you're not that close to her either?"

I shake my head. I barely know her. We'd met in passing a few times, at the audition, at a script reading. That was it. The tabloids ran an entire story based on us being romantically linked just from a picture of us standing near each other.

"I'll see what I can get from the cards. I'll ask for something general about what's going on with this situation of vampires resigning from the Fraternity, and we can go from there."

She shuffles for a long time, and I feel myself falling into a kind of trance as I stare at her purple nail-polished hands shuffling over and over. It reminds me of my time in Las Vegas, where I did indeed party with *The King*. After the war had ended, when I was still a younger vamp, all I wanted to do was drink blood, have sex and use my influence to win at gambling, and there was no better place to be than Las Vegas for that.

Eventually, Henrietta starts placing the tarot cards out.

"What do you see, Etta?" Max asks.

"Give me a minute," she says, shushing him.

I take a sip of whiskey as I watch her face squish up in concentration.

"I don't think either of them are in any kind of immediate danger," she says eventually.

"That's all you get? From all those cards?" I ask.

"It's a good start," Max says. "Etta, please continue in your own time."

She waves her hands over the spread, umming and aahing over the cards as she wiggles her fingers.

"Seven of Swords. I see deception."

"I think you're going to need to be a bit more specific," I tell her.

"A threat." She purses her lips and looks at the reversed cards around her. "It's very dark."

"What do you mean, dark?" Max asks. "Dangerous?"

She shakes her head. "It's like something is veiling my ability to see."

"What would cause something like that?" asks Max.

"It may just be that my connection to these women is so weak, and no one here has a strong connection with either of them." She looks up at me. "Well, I see you and Linda romantically linked but it was a long time ago."

"It was one time," I tell her.

"Can you pick up anything else? Why did Linda miss her flight?" Max asks.

Henrietta shuffles the cards and places some more down. "I see only darkness."

Henrietta is usually a lot better than this, but she's not on form tonight.

"Never mind," Max says. "Perhaps you can try again later."

Some kind of revelation crosses her face. "I think I'm seeing darkness because Juliette and Linda are in darkness." She shakes her head again, sending her curls flying. "And I'm not *allowed* to see more than that. Magic may be involved."

"Another witch or fae magic?" Max asks.

"Witch."

"What would a witch have to do with vampires resigning from the Fraternity?" I wonder out loud.

"I'm not sure yet," she says. "But I can keep trying."

"Thank you, Henrietta." Max places a hand on one of hers, and the light catches the shiny ring she's wearing on her left hand.

"You're engaged?" I ask.

"Yes, I am." She looks down at the ring numbly. If I was the kind of guy to ever want to put a ring on a woman's finger, I hope she'd be a bit more enthusiastic about it.

"Congratulations," I tell her.

"Thank you." She packs the cards up into a neat pile. "Any other questions?"

"I want to know about the movie. With Juliette missing, we're looking at making the difficult decision to re-cast her. Is it the right thing to do? And will it still be a success without her? I just want some—"

"Reassurance?" asks Henrietta, looking at me with a little more kindness than she's shown previously. "That's what most people go to the cards for."

"Maverick, perhaps we should let Henrietta rest," Max suggests.

"It's okay," Henrietta says as she starts shuffling. "I don't mind."

She shuffles fast and lays out cards quickly. She's a lot

more confident about this reading than the last one. Smiling, she sighs over the cards, and her eyebrows shoot up more than once.

"What do you see?" I ask.

"Juliette was never supposed to be in this movie," Henrietta says, her voice going all soft and whimsical.

"What?"

She looks up at me. "Juliette won't be in this movie."

"If Juliette isn't going to be in the movie, who the fuck is?"

Henrietta gives me a smile. "Somebody else. Somebody even more talented and deserving of the role."

"Will the movie be a success with this *new person,* whoever they are?"

"Six of Wands but also the Knight of Cups... It depends on what your definition of success is, but there will be success, in some form... eventually."

"So not a box office hit, but it may become a cult classic?"

"I see you experiencing success, but in an unexpected way."

Great, whatever the fuck that means.

"You can't just focus on the outcome," Max says stoically. "You have to enjoy the process. The art of creating good cinema."

"You can enjoy something and still want it to be a success," I tell him.

"I never thought I'd do another movie. I was done. It had been over a decade since I'd been in the public eye. I was worried people would wonder why I wasn't aging, but I was also *bored* with the whole thing. Sure, it's Hollywood, it's the movies, but it's the same thing over and over again and it can get stale. Working on *Angels All Around Us* made me remember what I was in it for. The *craft,* the *meaning,* the *acting.* Telling a story, connecting with humans and my own humanity in the process."

"Jesus, Max, do you have to be so fucking deep? I just want to make another blockbuster."

"To what end?"

"What?"

"Well, what for?"

"Because it's what I do. It's what I'm good at."

It's not the only thing I'm good at. There are two other things I've received critical acclaim for — the way I fuck and the way I obliterated the enemy during the war. But I don't want to make money off either of those.

"Haven't you got enough money?" Max asks.

I let out a laugh. "You've always been the most phil-anthropic of us vampires, Max," I say. "But you have to understand that some of us like nice things."

"My house is full of nice things," Max says. "But life is empty without more meaning, purpose. Something *more*."

"Okay, I think that's enough pep talk with a vampire for tonight," I say, scraping my seat back and standing up. "Thank you, Henrietta. We'll go ahead and re-cast the movie."

I've known Henrietta for long enough to trust her advice, even if I don't always understand what the hell she's talking about.

CHAPTER FIFTEEN

Trix

Poppy: I miss you! How is everything in Trix world?

Trix: Life is so crazy lately. All I do is bake all night and stand in for Juliette all day!

Poppy: When do you sleep?

Trix: Sleep?! What's that? LOL!

I'M SUMMONED into Ziva's trailer at seven a.m. the next morning. We finished filming at eight last night, and then I went home and baked until two. It's been weeks since I've had a good night's sleep. Exhausted doesn't even begin to explain how I feel.

Ali has been great with looking after everything on set, but I really need to find a way to bake and sleep at the same time.

I yawn and take a sip of the three-shot latte I made for myself while I caught up with Ali.

I've already been in makeup, but I don't have my wig or costume on yet. I love my green hair, but I have to admit it's fun playing someone else, looking like someone else. It's so easy to get into character when you don't look or feel like yourself.

It's also easy playing Lucy Montague because she's trying to hate John Stannic almost as much as I'm trying to hate Maverick Stone.

I look at him sitting there at the table in his trailer, biceps about to burst out of his CIA suit.

I squeeze into the booth in the tiny free space next to him. I try to avoid touching him, which leaves one of my ass cheeks half off the seat.

"Can you just sit on the seat?" he asks, squishing himself further over.

"I'm fine," I say. "I like sitting like this."

We haven't been alone again since the eyeshadow incident in his trailer and while part of me desperately wants to finish what we re-started that day, the other part of me knows that was just a moment of weakness. No good can come from having sex with Maverick again. No good at all. It's been hard to avoid him on set while standing in for his love interest all day, but I've found ways to do it. Standing as far away from him as possible until Ziva calls action, walking off set the instant she calls cut. Just never showing up when I'm supposed to run lines with him in his trailer and then blaming it on some catering emergency.

Ziva ignores our interaction while Brandon looks from me to Maverick and back again.

"We want to talk to you both about an idea we have."

Maverick already looks pissed. "What idea?"

"Juliette won't be returning to make the movie," Brandon tells me.

"So, we need to make some decisions about re-casting," Ziva says.

"That's where you come in," says Brandon.

Ziva gives me an excited grin. "Trix, we want *you* to play Lucy Montague."

Maverick's eyes practically bulge out of his face at the same time I let out a very loud laugh.

"What?!" we both say at the same time.

"Juliette is out of contract," Brandon says.

"And the two of you have incredible chemistry." Ziva turns to Maverick. "It's better than anything we saw in the screen-test with you and Juliette."

"But *she's* not a name," Maverick says.

"She's not a name, but we believe this can bring an edge to the film," Ziva says.

"What's the edge?" Maverick attempts to fold his arms over his chest in the tiny space.

"Trix is the edge," says Ziva.

"How does a nobody from craft services bring an *edge* to a Maverick Stone movie?" Maverick asks.

My mouth drops open.

A nobody? I wasn't a nobody when he was fucking me in his kitchen!

"You know what? Fuck you," I say, jumping up from my seat. "I'm not a nobody. I run a very successful catering company that keeps your whole cast and crew fed, watered and caffeinated while you prance around waving a fake gun in the air. I'm also a trained actor in case anyone gives a shit. I went to fucking Juilliard!"

"*Wait, you* went to Juilliard?" Maverick asks, shocked by this revelation.

"Is that so hard to believe?" I glare at him.

"Let's all just take a beat," Ziva suggests.

But I don't want to take a beat. I want *air*.

I storm out of the trailer and head towards the soundstage.

"Trix, wait!" Ziva calls.

I stop and turn, but only because I still need the stand-in money and the craft services job.

"What?"

"Look," she says, approaching me cautiously. "Maverick can be — difficult."

"*Really?*"

"But he's also incredibly talented and very famous. And so we have to treat him — kind of like a bomb."

"A bomb?"

"You see, if he goes off, he will destroy this whole lot. Everything here will fall apart without him. All the staff, the cast, the crew, even the caterers. Without *him*, there's no need for the rest of us. We all like to think that a movie can't be made without each and every person here, and that is true, but everyone here is replaceable. Except for Maverick Stone."

I let out a sigh.

"Please don't tell anyone this, but Juliette is missing. We're telling people she's in rehab, but we have no idea where she is, when or even *if* she'll show up for filming. We could pause the project until we know, but that will cost us a *lot* of money. What we'd really like to do is keep filming. But we need you."

"You said everyone can be replaced. So, replace me."

"We could find someone else, go through the re-casting process, but that will take time, and you're already here."

Story of my life.

"You and Maverick, you are sensational on screen together."

"But I'm not a name."

"No, but your story is fantastic. We think we can really spin it in the movie's promotion."

For a second I think she means everything that happened between me and Maverick, but no one knows about that but the two of us. "What story?"

"Juliette doesn't show up on set. A nobody from craft services stands in for her, but her chemistry with Maverick Stone is off the charts. So, when we still can't find Juliette a few weeks later, she gets replaced by the stand-in."

Little tingles go up my arms at the idea of this, especially the bit about us having chemistry. But I didn't need her to tell me that. I experienced it firsthand. Three times. Then those tingles turn into absolute shivers as I realize what she's offering me—a chance to *be* in this movie. "It is a pretty good story," I admit.

"We want you on social media documenting the whole thing."

"What?"

"You're a regular, relatable person. You're not a Maverick or Juliette. It's a dream come true for someone like you."

"Someone like me?"

"For a regular person to suddenly be a lead opposite Maverick Stone! That's the definition of the Hollywood dream!"

"Right."

"One word of advice though?" she says. "Try to find a way not to let him get to you so much. The chemistry is great on screen, but we don't want you two at each other's throats off set."

"You're assuming I'm going to do it."

"Yeah, I am."

This is all you've ever wanted, Trix. This is still your biggest dream.

I pause for a moment. Of course I'm going to do it. How could anyone in their right mind say no to this opportunity?

"What's the pay?" I ask her.

She lets out a laugh. "How about we discuss that in your trailer?"

"*My* trailer?"

"Yes, Ms. Delaney, you get your own trailer now." She walks off towards someone with a clipboard. "We're going to need another trailer!"

CHAPTER SIXTEEN

Trix

MAVERICK STONE IS KNOWN for being "discovered" while working as a bartender at an exclusive bar in downtown Hollywood. Brandon Curtis, one of Hollywood's most influential producers and directors, ordered a whiskey and immediately knew that Maverick had star quality. Curtis invited him in for a screen-test and a few weeks later, Maverick was filming the first movie in the block-buster Road Rage *franchise.*

Maverick Stone Wikipedia page

AFTER A LONG DAY OF FILMING, packing up the crafts table and dropping off the leftovers to the soup kitchen, I park the van outside my house and immediately recognize the black town car parked across the road. I grab the bags of produce from the back, hurry inside and see my best friend, Poppy, standing in the kitchen chatting to my mom.

"Poppy!" I drop the bags and wrap my arms around her.

Me and Poppy met while working at the Montrose estate. Poppy was Max's domestic help, and I worked in his kitchen for about six months. Poppy quickly went from dusting his shelves to being his live-in lover, but we ended up becoming best friends as we bonded over oat milk lattes, boy talk and me practicing all my recipes on her.

We don't get to see each other so much anymore and seeing her here after such a huge day gives me the warm fuzzies.

"I'll leave you girls to it," says my mom, wondering out of the room.

"Thanks mom," I call to her as I pull back and take a good look at Poppy. Her brunette hair is tied back in a messy bun with a few stray tendrils turning red as they catch the light. She's dressed in cute boots, designer jeans, a crisp white V-neck t-shirt and around her neck is a gold locket which probably has some of Max's hair in it or something equally as weird. Also, are those earrings real diamonds?! She looks... expensive. Not a surprise considering Max, who's a legit billionaire probably pays for all her clothes now.

"You look great," I tell her.

"Yeah? I'm still trying to get used to the whole brand-new clothes thing," she shrugs.

"It's so great to see you, Poppy," I say. "And I really want to catch up, but I also have a heap of food prep to do for tomorrow."

"I'll help you!" she says with a grin.

I raise an eyebrow. "Don't take this the wrong way, but maybe you can just watch?"

She pouts. "Just give me something easy to do."

I grab some cookies from the bags. I'd usually bake them from scratch myself for the base of the bars, but these ones

I've bought are still good and I don't think anyone will be able to tell once all the other flavors are in them.

I throw the packs at Poppy. "Crush those."

She gets crushing and I get to boiling some cashews on the stove to soften them up faster.

"So, I heard about your big break," Poppy says. "Congratulations!"

"How do you know about that already?" I ask.

"Maverick told me."

Just hearing his name makes the butterflies in my cage do little flaps in my belly.

"What? When did you speak to Maverick?" Saying his name out loud sends the butterflies spinning in circles.

"He was at our place when I left. We just shared a pizza. He's been over a lot lately. So has Brandon. They're always hanging out in the war room talking about secret vampire business."

The butterfly does a little dance as I remember how Maverick ordered me a pizza that night, even though he didn't want to eat any of it.

Then I wonder if the three of them hanging out in the war room has anything to do with Juliette's disappearance. Juliette is a vampire, and after the whole werewolves trying to eradicate vampires from the earth thing from last year, a sudden gush of fear rushes over me. But no, Maverick is strong and he's ex-military. He's the last person I need to worry about.

"Wait, Maverick ate pizza?" I ask.

"Yeah, he did. Vampires are so weird with their eating habits. Max won't eat anything for a week and then suddenly gets a craving and eats an entire cake. Sorry, I'm babbling! How are you? You must be ecstatic!"

I start grabbing ingredients out of the bags at my feet. "I should be, shouldn't I?"

"This is your big break! What you always wanted!"

I pause. "I wish I was more excited, but I'm just kind of… not, I guess."

"Why not? What's going on?"

I throw a bag of limes on the counter. "Well, first of all, I still have to feed everyone on set—"

"Okay, Trix, you need to tell them to hire another caterer."

"Nope. No way. I worked my ass off for this job."

"But now you have *another* job, as the *lead role* in a Hollywood movie." She smacks the cookies a little too hard and bursts a bag, sending cookie crumbs flying out all over the kitchen floor. "Oh, shit. I'll get it." She grabs a broom from the corner and starts sweeping up.

Okay, this is exactly why I shouldn't have accepted her help. I love Poppy, but she's more of a hindrance than a help in the kitchen.

"Yeah, but what if it doesn't work out?" I ask her, throwing some limes on a chopping board. "What if Juliette comes back tomorrow and they don't need me? Or what if I do the movie and it's a huge flop? What if I never work on another movie again and I've ruined my fallback?"

"Well, isn't it better to have been in one Hollywood movie than none? Even if it sucks? And catering will always be there for you."

I throw a bag of shredded coconut next to the limes. "Yeah, I guess."

"There's something else on your mind."

I take a pause. "Isn't this enough?"

"It's a lot. But you're resourceful and courageous and you're going to be a big, big star!"

I grab a knife and start cutting the limes into segments. "Yeah, but first I've got to squeeze these limes."

"If you're not going to quit, you at least need help in the kitchen."

"I have Ali."

"Trix, you can't do everything yourself."

"Yes, I can," I almost snap at her. I put the knife down and look at her, holding the broom, trying her best to help me even though she's kind of a disaster in the kitchen. "Sorry, Poppy. It's just that Trix and Treats is really important to me."

"I know and if I could, I'd come over and help every night, but I have finals coming up soon."

"How is college going?" I ask, grateful for the change of topic and a chance to get back to chopping.

"It's definitely harder than I expected," she says, scooping up the cookies with a dust pan and brush and putting them in the bin. "But I'm loving it. And working at the shelter is the best. I just brought home another cat yesterday."

I let out a laugh. "How many cats do you and Max have now?"

"Thirteen. But we're only fostering most of them."

"Sure, sure."

"Well, it's too heartbreaking to leave them there when we have this whole mansion."

"When I think about the size of Max's mansion, I think you should have at least a hundred cats there."

"That's exactly what I've been telling Max."

"How's Callie? Is she coping with all the new cats?" Callie is an adorable little black cat that showed up at Max's mansion one day and took his heart. Just like Poppy did.

"She's taken ownership of Max's suite. No other cats seem brave enough to go in there."

"Of course she has, little princess!" I start squeezing the limes into a big bowl.

"I just love her so much," Poppy says with a smile. "Now, what job can I do next?"

"Grab a bowl and mix the cookies with some coconut oil." I measure it out for her and then she gets mixing.

"This smells so good," she says, practically sticking her head in the bowl.

"I'll give you a pack to take home."

She gives me a grin. "It's okay, I can just have Claude pick some up for me."

"Who the hell is Claude?"

"Our new butler. James left, remember?"

Oh, yeah. James was the fae butler who was tethered to Max for seventy years and was finally freed when he helped Max stake Lottie to Certain Death.

"How are you holding up?" I ask her, pausing my chopping to look over at her. It's been eighteen months since Poppy found out her brother was a vampire, and a bad one at that.

"With the whole Aiden being a part of a plot to kill me and Max and all vampire kind?" she asks.

"Yeah."

She shrugs. "I guess I'm doing okay. Trying to just keep busy, you know? Focus on school and the shelter. It helps."

"You're allowed to grieve."

"I keep trying to remind myself of that, but then I remember how he tried to hurt me and Max and that he's still out there somewhere." She takes a breath. "This will sound awful, but it would have been easier to mourn him if he'd just died a normal death, not been turned into a vampire and gone to the dark side."

"I'm so sorry Poppy. I know I've been a kind of distant friend lately, but I'm always here for you. I hope you know that."

"I'm always here for you too, Trix. I know something is

going on with you, and when you're ready to talk about it, I'm here, okay?"

I nod and then get back to the cashews on the stove that are now ready to be blended into a thick cream for the key lime bars.

"And if you need money for your business, I'm sure Max would be happy to invest—"

"Look at us," I say, ignoring her offer. "You're back at school living your dream of becoming a vet, and I'm going to be in a movie!" I let out a forced laugh.

"All our dreams are coming true," she says. "We've come a long way since we were both living in the staff quarters working for Mr. Montrose!"

"We sure have."

Poppy grins and hands me the bowl of very badly mixed cookies.

"Thanks, Poppy."

She helps me for another hour as we catch up, but when I eventually realize that her helping me is making this take twice as long, I send her home to get some sleep.

"I know it's ages away, but are you still catering our Christmas party? With everything so busy for us both, it might be the next time I'll get to see you," she says, as I walk her to the door.

I don't miss how easily Poppy refers to the party at Max's mansion as *ours*.

"You know you should really be there as a guest, not catering the party."

"I can do both. I'll bring a dress. But I think I'll be at Brandon's Thanksgiving party before that. I'm assuming you'll be Max's plus one?"

"Oh, I forgot about that! Yes, I'll see you there in a few weeks."

"Already looking forward to it."

"Text me and let me know how filming is going."

"Sure. Good luck on your finals!"

We say our goodbyes, and I head back into the kitchen with a sigh.

"Honey?" Mom appears at the doorway dressed in her pajamas.

"You're already going to bed?"

"Well, honey, it is nearly eleven."

"What? How is that possible?" I check my watch, and she's right. I should be going to bed right now, not just about to start making sandwich fillings. "Oh god, I still have so much to do."

I grab the cutting board and look down to slice some gherkins and notice my hand is shaking slightly.

Mom gives me a look like she's noticed it too. "Beatrix, let me help you."

"Poppy just tried to help and now I'm further behind," I say.

She folds her arms and gives me that look. "Do I need to remind you who taught you to cook?"

I drop my shoulders and my defenses.

"Trix," she says, rubbing a hand over my upper arm. "I *want* to help you." She gives my arms a squeeze. "Remember when you first came to us? You hated it here—"

"I didn't hate it."

"Yes, you did. You wouldn't take anything from us. You threw all your pillows and blankets out of your bedroom and slept on the floor. You wouldn't wear any of the new clothes or shoes I bought for you, and you wouldn't eat any of the cakes in your lunchbox."

"I was just… going through it."

"I know honey," she says. "But things changed when we started cooking together. If you made the cakes with me, you'd happily eat them. The first time I saw you smile was when you took a bite of a lemon bar we'd made together."

The memory of that moment stings at the back of my eyes. My earliest memories were happy ones. When my birth mom gave me up my paternal grandmother took me in until she died, no one else in my family wanted me and I got placed in foster care. I'd help my grandmother cook these huge meals for the whole neighborhood. It's a distant, fuzzy memory that I don't even know for sure is real, but when I started cooking here with Suzy, it felt like that. It felt like family.

"I remember you looked up at me that day, big brown eyes, and you asked if we could make some cakes for the homeless." She places a hand on her heart and looks like she's holding back the tears as well. "We started baking like crazy, do you remember?"

I nod.

"We used to take everything we made to the soup kitchen in your old neighborhood."

"I still take stuff there," I tell her.

"What?"

"After events, I take all the leftovers there."

"Oh, honey." She wraps her arms around me and I blink back the tears. The last thing I have time for tonight is tears.

"How about I just help you get a few things prepped and in the oven? You can take care of the rest on your own," she says.

Everything within me wants to say *no*, to push her away, to tell her I don't need her help, to remind her I can do things on my own and I'll be just fine, just like I was for the first ten years of my life.

But I'm so tired. I don't even know what my problem is, why I find accepting help so hard. I don't know if it's some-thing I inherited from my birth mother, or something I picked up in foster care, or what. But it's like it's just not possible for me to say, "Thanks, Mom, I'd really appreciate your help."

So I say nothing while Mom grabs an apron, and as she ties the strings, I stop pretending that I don't know what it is.

I don't want to rely on another person, because other people let you down. Other people give you up. Other people get sick and die and leave you in the hands of absolute strangers. Foster moms forget to pick you up from school. Foster sisters promise to always be there and then get adopted out before you do.

My mom and dad have always been there for me, but there is a safety in not needing to rely on anyone else. I'm safe when I don't need anyone.

"Honey?"

"What, Mom?"

"Where are the recipes?"

I slide the tablet over to her and bring up the recipe for raspberry and white chocolate muffins.

"Oh, these do sound delicious," she says, as she goes about locating the ingredients.

I didn't ask for her help, but I don't throw her out of the kitchen, and so I consider it small progress towards my issues.

If I had a spare hour, I'd go see my old therapist about all this, but even with Mom's help, there's still too much to do.

Three hours later, everything is finally done, and I'm looking forward to a good four-and-a-bit hours of sleep.

CHAPTER SEVENTEEN

rix

I LOOK over towards Maverick's pristine white kitchen that overlooks Malibu beach. "The bedroom is too intimate," I tell him.

"You have intimacy issues."

"And you don't?"

He doesn't answer, and I realize in that moment that, of course, we're both as fucked up as each other when it comes to intimacy and relationships. Me — always throwing myself at the most inappropriate, closed-off, unavailable men I can find, running for the hills if any one of them turned out to be half decent. Him — hooking up with Donnas and asking me point blank in the diner if I wanted to fuck.

We're both hot messes, and that's exactly why we're here, doing it like this.

My heart speeds like his Ducati on Route 101 as I realize this is it. I'm about to have sex with Maverick Stone.

He tenderly moves a strand of hair away from my face. "If not the bedroom, where?"

"I want to do it in the kitchen."

I've barely finished the sentence when he lifts me up by my ass, my legs wrapping around him on pure instinct, and damn if it doesn't feel so right to be wrapped around him like this. And then suddenly he's lowering me down onto a kitchen counter.

"Shorts off," he mumbles as he flicks my button and yanks my jean shorts off with a little wiggling around from me to help. And then I'm sitting here on his kitchen counter in my ugliest pair of underwear, unable to wait another second to have this gorgeous Adonis inside me.

I grab his shoulders and pull him towards me. His fingers are in my panties in an instant, flicking my clit and feeling their way confidently over my wetness. I gasp, and he lets out a deep moan.

"Are you ready?" he asks. "You feel ready."

I give him a nod. "Yes."

ANOTHER EARLY WAKE-UP call and another Maverick Stone almost-sex dream. At least this time I feel like I've actually had a bit of sleep, and *nearly* got to the sex part.

I get ready, throwing on a green Trix and Treats t-shirt, a pair of mom jeans, and a swipe of aqua blue glitter eyeshadow, *not* the silver one, even though I have zero intention of ever being in a compromising situation with Maverick again. The dreams will have to suffice.

I pack up everything Mom helped me make last night and drive the van to Ali's place.

"I just can't believe it!" Ali gushes, her pineapple earrings dancing. "*You're* going to be in the movie!"

Everyone is more excited about this than I am.

Is this normal? Why am I not more excited? What's wrong with me?

But while Ali goes on and on about my future life as a movie star, I realize that it's just that I already mourned this dream. This path already didn't work out once, and when that happened, I *grieved*. For a *really* long time. And now I'm supposed to just be happy that it has somehow risen from the ashes and resurrected itself like some walking dead dream I'm meant to be thrilled about?

But it doesn't work like that. When a dream dies, and you go through the process of (eventually) letting go and moving on with your life, it's not like you can just flick a switch and go back to where you were before.

Trix and Treats is my baby now. My *new* dream. And I can't just hand her off to some babysitter while I go try to live an old broken dream that could easily break my heart a second time around.

I'm not ready for another heartbreak.

I have already made peace with this never being my life. I accepted I was never going to be a professional actor. I *moved on* with my life. I followed a different path.

There's a part of me, and it's a big part, that doesn't even want to act anymore. A part that wants to just focus on baking and prepping sandwiches and feeding people and making a name for myself in a different new way.

But this zombie dream won't stop banging on the door.

"Oh! Did you get the fruit?"

The word "fruit" brings me back to Ali's monologue.

"Shit, I forgot."

"We can swing by the market."

I look at the clock. "We'll need to be quick."

WE'RE NOT QUICK. I find a selection of coffee syrups and spend at least ten minutes deciding on the flavors I think the crew will like. And I have fun doing it. I actually *enjoy* looking at all the bottles and choosing the ones I think will make the crew happy and peppy for a few hours before they come get their next one.

This is what makes me happy. Making people full and happy.

When we finally get on set and get our table set up, I place the salted caramel, raspberry, coconut and apple pie syrup by the coffee machine where everyone will see them.

I'm in my own world, fantasizing that I'm the owner of the most successful coffee shop and bakery in Brooklyn, or somewhere equally exotic. I nearly jump out of my skin, dropping the bottle of raspberry syrup when I hear a gruff "Hey!" from behind me.

My heart hammers in my chest as I avoid his gaze and instead look down at the bottle that's thankfully still in one piece.

"You okay?"

I look up, and there he is. The guy who was just about to fuck me in my dream.

Maverick is dressed in low hanging jeans, a dark blue t-shirt that stretches over his shoulders like it's trying really hard to fit him. Those blue-green diamond eyes of his penetrate my soul while he tries to hide a laugh.

"Must you?" I ask him with a hard glare. "You're stealthy, we get it."

"What are you doing here?" he asks.

I hold up the bottle of syrup. "What does it look like?"

"I mean, why are you still doing catering?"

"First of all, I'm not *doing catering*. It's craft services."

"Right."

"And secondly, because it's my *job*."

"Your job is acting in this movie. You should be chilling out in your trailer and learning lines."

"I haven't even signed a contract yet or been told where my trailer is."

God, it sounds so weird, so Hollywood, to be talking about *my trailer.*

He frowns. "I'll get someone onto that ASAP."

Why am I so suddenly turned on by him taking charge of this situation? A flash of him taking charge in the kitchen hits me, and I turn around, averting his gaze to make myself a raspberry oat cappuccino. I feel his eyes on my back as I work the machine.

"You can't keep doing craft services and work on the movie," he tells my back.

"I'll figure it out."

He lets out a sigh, and I turn around, immediately wishing I hadn't. He crosses his arms over his chest, and his biceps bulge. Goddamn he's sexy as hell.

"You'd better figure it out. I need you rested and focused."

"Was there something else?" I ask, turning back to the coffee machine.

"What are you making?"

"Raspberry cappuccino."

"Sounds good. I'll take one."

"You don't drink coffee."

"Maybe I can change."

I blink at him. Is he talking about coffee or something else?

"You seriously want one?"

"Yes."

I sigh and go about prepping a second cup and frothing enough oat milk for both of us. There's something about pouring enough milk in the jug for both me and Maverick that makes the butterflies in the cage wake up again. It feels… domestic. *Relationship-y… intimate.*

I quickly get that idea out of my head and just focus on pouring the milk in a pretty heart-shaped pattern.

I hand him the drink. "It's not your usual, but it does have a red tint."

He looks down into the cup and laughs. He *laughs*!

My nether regions give a little shiver as I think about his actual drink of choice — blood, and how glorious it felt to have him drink mine.

I try to empty my brain of all sex-related thoughts, but it's honestly impossible when he's a walking advertisement for it. "Do you want something else?" I ask when he doesn't walk away.

"Yeah, I want you to quit this catering gig and focus on the movie."

"I can't. It's my livelihood. Imagine someone asking you to give up movies so you could focus on some pet project?"

His eyes turn Atlantic Ocean stormy. "This movie may be a pet project to you, but it is *my* livelihood, and I don't want anything to fuck it up, especially not you being half asleep every damn day because you're working what's essentially six full-time jobs."

"Yeah, well, I'm working on a solution. I just—"

"Let me help you."

"No."

Saying no to him is a lot easier than saying no to my mom. I don't feel bad about it at all.

"Let me help you, or—"

I frown at him. "Or what?"

"I'll get you fired from the movie."

Blood rises to my face. My mouth drops open, but no words come out.

"I *want* to help you. If you're sleeping at least six hours a night or whatever is the amount you people need, and not stressing over baking cakes for the sound guys or whatever, the movie will be better. I really care about this movie, and so I need you in a good place."

Ali reappears and stops short when she sees me talking to Maverick.

"Maverick Stone! Oh, shit!" she says. "Oh, sorry! Oh, god!" she gushes. "Can I get you something? Do you want something to eat? A drink? What can we do for you?"

"Nice to see you again, Ali," He gives her a grin, and a bit of an eye twinkle, and I'm taken back. Since when did Maverick Stone have any manners? He's certainly never shown me any.

Not that I wanted him to have manners when we were in his kitchen that afternoon...

"I'm just trying to get Trix to let someone help her."

"Yeah, good luck with that. If you can, you'd be the only one. I've been telling her for ages to let me do more, and now that she's *in* the movie, she can't be driving sandwiches onto the lot at four a.m. every morning."

"You leave your house at *four a.m.?*" Maverick looks like he's about to throw over our table and carry me out of here fireman style. I would 100% let him if he did. Even though I'd be pissed about the sandwiches.

"Ali, I forgot the key lime bars. Could you go get them?" I ask her.

"Yeah, of course!" she disappears in search of the key lime bars that are already out on the table. Maverick's eyes glance at the bars and a big label saying "key lime bars" including ingredients and allergens.

"That's my favorite, by the way," he says, his eyes flicking back up to mine.

Holy shit, he likes my cooking. Why is that making me want to throw my own table over and fling myself into his arms?

"I thought you didn't eat."

He grabs a bar, takes a bite and as he closes his eyes, something crosses his face, something *real*. Something like… happiness?

"You didn't want any of the pizza that night—"

His eyes meet mine for a second too long. "I prefer sweets."

"Max is the same," I muse. "Is that a—" I'm about to say vampire and then stop myself, just in case someone overhears this weird conversation. "Is that a thing for you guys?"

"Kinda," he says, finishing the bar and then licking his fingers suggestively.

I look down at my coffee and realize I haven't even tried it yet. I take a sip. It's good. Sweet.

"If you like sweet stuff, you might actually like the coffee."

He brings it to his lips. Those soft, sexy lips that have been all over my body. Well, apart from the two places I want them most.

"You're right. I do like it."

Why does it make my heart swell to know that he likes my coffee and my bars? That he enjoys something I made for him?

"Is there any silver in that eyeshadow?"

I shake my head.

"When I put it on this morning I kind of forgot that makeup would take it off anyway," I say, taking another sip of coffee.

He takes another sip of his and we just stare at each other, taking sips of coffee.

"Come by my trailer."

I shake my head.

God, why am I shaking my head? Why am I not just ripping my clothes off and letting him take me here and now?

"It's a bad idea."

"If you change your mind, meet me at my trailer after you're done filming."

"We're not filming together today?"

"Haven't you checked the app?"

"I can't get it to work."

He sighs. "You're filming some dream sequence this morning. Traumatic childhood memories or something."

"Great."

I haven't even had time to look at the script. Shit. Maybe he's right. Maybe I can't do it all.

"Yeah, like anyone wants to relive that," he says.

"Trix, the van was empty, I couldn't find the — oh, they're already here!" says Ali, looking confused.

"My offer still stands," Maverick tells me. "Anytime you want it."

He grabs three *more* key lime bars and walks off.

"What did he want?" Ali asks.

He wants to fuck me in his trailer, and if it wasn't for the emotional torture I'm still reliving from the last time, I would be following him over there right now.

I said no this time, but I know that at some point my willpower will disintegrate into tiny little cookie crumbs and I'll find myself bent over his bench seat having the time of my fucking life. Until it all falls apart and I'm left with more broken dreams, a broken heart and Maverick Stone sex dreams haunting every moment of sleep for the rest of my life.

"Nothing," I tell her.

CHAPTER EIGHTEEN

$\mathcal{M}$averick

"I'VE ALWAYS HAD this fantasy that I'm just a regular guy," I tell her.

"Wow, that's dirty!" She laughs, and I want to reach out and grab the tendrils of that sound and wrap them around me so that I feel like this forever.

I roll my eyes playfully at her. "That's not the whole thing."

"Okay, you're a regular guy and—"

I take a beat. Am I really going to tell her this? I've never told anybody this.

"I told you mine!" she pouts.

Those lips, fucking hell! I want to just rip up that invisible rule book we made and make-out with her on this couch all night.

"It's the 1950s," I start.

Her eyes light up like she can't wait to hear this now.

Okay, fine.

"I'm newly married and I have a house in the suburbs," I continue. "I come home from work and my wife, who's very fucking sexy by the way, is wearing a dress in that fifties style — big skirt, tight bodice. She's made me dinner and been waiting for me to come home."

"You don't even like food!"

"It's not about the food, it's about what happens next."

She squirms a little in her seat. "Okay, so what happens next?"

"I give her a little kiss hello, because in this fantasy, kissing is permitted."

She lets out a playful laugh. "And then what happens?"

"And then I turn her around, bend her over the dining table and lift her dress."

Trix is no longer laughing. I can tell she's back in the kitchen with me, getting bent over the counter. She swallows.

"And then what?"

"I think you know what," I say, my eyes holding hers. "I fuck her. Hard."

Trix's face heats and I can't help it. I've cast her in this fantasy. She's the one I'm imagining fucking over my dining table.

She grabs the last slice of pizza. "Okay, but what about the dinner? She worked hard on that, I hope you're going to eat it even if it's gone cold."

I let out a laugh. "Yeah, sure, after we've fucked, we sit at the table all prim and proper and eat the meatloaf or whatever."

"Is that something you want for real?" she asks. "A wife, a regular life?"

I shake my head. "I just like the idea of it. A woman who's just mine. Who doesn't want anyone else. I've never—" I take a breath. "I've never had the desire to be committed to just one woman."

She pauses and then asks, "Why do you think that's your fantasy?"

"Why is yours to be watched?"

"Because I have a desperate desire to be seen."

"That's very self-aware of you."

She shrugs. "Everyone wants to be seen," she says. "What about yours?"

"Why don't you tell me since you're so good at analyzing sex fantasies."

"You want someone," she tells me.

"What?"

"You have a secret desire to be monogamous."

I throw my head back and laugh. "Trust me, monogamy is the last thing I want or need," I tell her.

She shrugs. "Well, what do I know? I'm not actually a sex therapist. I'm just a caterer."

"You're a lot more than a caterer, Trix. A lot more."

I'VE BEEN SLEEPING MORE than usual lately, and I know it's because of the dreams. Whenever I sleep, I always dream of Trix. I dream of her legs wrapped around me, of her laughter carrying out over the deck towards the beach, of the way her dark eyes smoldered when she suggested we go for round three.

As a vampire, I could have gone all night long, but for a human she matched my desire in a way I've rarely experienced with other human women.

Of course, everyone wants a piece of Maverick Stone. The girls I hook up with, they're thrilled to be with me, but it always feels a little cold somehow, like they're only interested in this shell, this *idea* of me. They don't really care if it's good for me, or even if it's good for them. They just want the experience of fucking a movie star.

I'm not real. I'm just a fantasy to them.

When I have an itch that needs scratching, I don't care. It's mutually beneficial. I get my itch scratched, and they get their fantasy lived out. I often glamour women after I've given them The Bite, just to keep our vampire community safe, but I don't bother glamouring them after sex. Most of the time, no one would believe them anyway. But still, they get the memory of being with me. I'd always thought of it as my philanthropy.

But I didn't realize how empty my encounters even were until that night with Trix.

That night we spent together was anything but empty.

I wish I could put the dreams and the thoughts of her that are never far from my mind down to the blood bond, but it doesn't work that way. I'm not supposed to be obsessed with her. It's only supposed to make the *human* act like a teenager with a crush so hard it feels like life will end if their crush doesn't look their way.

But that's how I feel now, every fucking time I walk onto the lot.

Like right now, I'm walking out of my trailer and my eyes are *everywhere* just hoping for a glimpse of her.

That's how I bumped into her that first day on set. I wasn't looking where I was going because I was looking over at her van, hoping to see her there. It wasn't the universe pulling us together. It was me acting like a fucking fool.

I pull at the tie I'm wearing, already in my costume and ready for filming.

Today we're filming the helicopter scene. Everyone has seen it a billion times in these movies, but these scenes still get the audience excited and on the edge of their seats every time.

The thing *I'm* most excited about is that I'll get to be close to her all day.

I run a hand over the back of my neck as I look over towards the crafts table. I catch a glimpse of green hair, and my body reacts by walking right over to her with no idea of what I'm going to say to her when I get there, but I'm Maverick Stone, I can always improvise.

"Maverick!" Ali gushes.

"Morning, Ali," I say. "Trix."

She gives me a look like she's already pissed at something I've done.

"Shouldn't you be in wardrobe?" I ask her.

"Ziva said they're going to film you falling out of the helicopter first." She gestures over to a set where a helicopter sits on a raised platform in front of a green screen. "I won't be needed for a couple of hours."

"Right."

"Want a coffee?" Ali asks me.

"Thanks, Ali."

I wish it was Trix making my coffee, but I also wish she would just quit this whole catering thing and focus on the damn movie!

"Espresso? Latte? Cappuccino? Oh my god, I feel like I'm in the movie!" Ali laughs. "We have all these syrups too! Salted caramel, coconut, raspberry—"

"Raspberry," I say.

Trix gives me a look.

I shrug. "You got me hooked."

She blinks her dark eyes, her naked lids reminding me of my standing offer to take her in my trailer anytime she wanted. She's still yet to take me up on that offer, but the quickening of her pulse and the way she busies herself to do anything but look my way suggest she still wants it.

But I've put the offer out there enough now. If she wants it, she can come to me.

"Do you want anything else?" Ali asks while she warms the milk. "The breakfast bars are superb."

I take a bar from the table. "Grains," I say, doing a weird zombie voice.

Why am I being so awkward? I'm never awkward!

"Ancient grains," Trix says. "They're very good for your digestive system. If you have one."

I let out a laugh at that.

Ali hands me my coffee. "Enjoy!"

"Thanks." I take an inhale over the hole in the lid, and it smells just like the one Trix made for me.

I hold my cup up in a kind of cheers to them both and then walk through the crowds and onto the set.

We spend hours getting the shots we need of me hanging out of the helicopter. I hang onto its leg with one arm, then the other, I pull myself back into the helicopter a bunch of different ways and then *finally* Ziva calls someone to go get Trix from her trailer.

"I'll go," I offer. "I want to talk to her about some ideas I have for the scene on the walk over," I lie. I have no ideas. I just want to see her.

Jesus, Maverick, can you just stop acting like a teenager for two minutes?

But I never got to do this when I was a teenager. I never got to swoon over girls, feel awkward and excited around them, I never got to sneak glances and daydream about taking them to bed.

I barely had a childhood. Born to a farming family in South Dakota in the early 1900s, I was working before I was walking. Enlisted by my father into the army at thirteen, and that was it for my innocence. I was big for my age, but even if I wasn't, no one questioned your age in those days. If you could point a gun straight, it didn't matter.

And so all this fawning and yearning and sneaking glances is new for me, even after all this time.

I find my way to Trix's trailer, which is right at the end of the row of trailers and knock on the door.

"Trix?"

There's no answer and I wonder if she's even here, but I didn't see her by the crafts table, and I *looked*.

"Trix? We need you on set."

Still no answer.

I give her a minute and then knock a few more times before trying the handle. The door opens and I call to her again.

Not sure if I should be worried about her or if I'm just acting like a creep, I step inside.

And there she is, curled up into a ball, dressed in her costume and wig, fast asleep on the bench seat with that fuzzy pink cardigan covering her like a blanket.

My heart does a little flip as I realize that even though we spent all that time having sex, this is the first time I've seen her asleep.

And this feels just as intimate, maybe even more so, than everything else we did that night.

I place a hand on her shoulder and give a little squeeze. "Trix," I whisper, not wanting to startle her. "Trix, wake up."

She doesn't move and so I try again, a little louder this time. She startles, her eyes flick open and her whole body shudders awake.

She lets out a scream, and I step back.

"Are you Edward Cullen-ing me?!" She grabs the cardigan and tries to cover herself.

"What?"

"How did you get in here?"

"I just walked in. You left the door unlocked." I take another step back, giving her space. "You're wanted on set."

"Oh, shit!" She jumps up and touches the hair of her wig. "Is my makeup okay?"

"Hair and makeup will touch you up on set."

She pulls on her long boots and storms out of the trailer like it's somehow my fault that she fell asleep.

"You're doing too much," I tell her as I catch up with her fast strides. "You can't keep helping out with craft services and be in the movie."

She stops and turns to glare at me. That glare that feels like delicious fire in my bones. "I'm not just *helping out*, I am running a successful business!"

"You can't do both!"

"I can and I will! Watch me!" She turns and storms off into the soundstage.

"The helicopter will turn, and you'll slide out," Ziva tells Trix. "Your instinct will be to hang onto something, don't. Just reach your arms out."

Trix gives me a look from her seat in the helicopter. "And he's going to catch me?"

"Yes."

"What if he doesn't?"

"Then you'll fall to your death," I tell her.

She just glares at me even harder.

"You'll land on the crash mats below. It's not that far down," one of the crew assures her.

She looks out of the helicopter at the mats below. Her pulse is racing, and it's different this time. It's not the race of her heart I hear and feel whenever I'm close to her. It's not excitement or desire, it's *fear*. She's afraid of heights. The idea that I get to save her from something she is *actually* scared of, even if it's just a few feet down very much appeals to my superhero complex.

"Trix." She turns to look at me, a hint of that fear in her eyes. "I won't let you fall."

Her pulse races even faster and I see little sweat beads form above her lip.

"Let's try it first without the movement of the helicopter," Ziva says. "So you know the blocking. I'll talk you through everything."

I give her a thumbs up.

"Look at each other… and run the lines," says Ziva.

"Put on your seatbelt," I say.

"You sure you know how to fly this thing?" Trix asks.

"I can fly anything."

"Okay, John, you go to the controls… now Lucy, you're falling out, hold out your arms."

Trix leans over, but not that far. She's scared to even just practice like this without the helicopter moving on the gimbal. I grab her wrist, and she looks at me like this touch between us does something to her just like it does to me.

"Lucy!" I call out. "Hold on!"

"And then after a whole lot of flailing, you pull her back into the helicopter," Ziva says.

I pull her in towards me, so that her body is tight against mine, her head in my shoulder.

"I told you to wear a seatbelt," I say.

"Yeah, that's great, let's roll!" Ziva says.

There's sound and movement below us, lights blaze, a sound boom appears above us and Trix looks like she's about to vomit.

The helicopter jolts, and Trix grips my arm.

"Sorry!" yells a technician.

Trix realizes that she's still holding onto me, and she lets go, moving back into her seat. The helicopter jolts again, and she reaches out for me, grabbing my leg this time.

I let out a laugh. "You okay?"

She looks at her hand on my leg and then quickly removes it. "I'm fine."

"How about you tell me the truth? You're scared of heights."

"No, I'm not. I'm just nervous about filming."

"You know I can tell, right? I can hear your heart beating."

She folds her arms over her chest, pushing her breasts up and giving me a great view of her cleavage.

"Trix," I say.

She doesn't look at me.

"Trix."

She turns and gives me that glare. "What?"

"I promise. You won't fall. I've got you."

CHAPTER NINETEEN

rix

THE HELICOPTER STARTS MOVING, and I honestly think I'm going to die.

We're not in a real helicopter, we're not really in the sky, just a few feet in the air over a big stack of crash mats, but those few feet feel *very* far down right now.

We start filming, run the lines, and then thankfully, before I have to fall, Ziva calls "cut".

"You're going too far with the fear thing," she tells me from the safety of the ground. "You're a double agent, a spy, remember? You wouldn't be scared of heights!"

"Okay, but what if she is?" Maverick calls down to her.

Ziva just looks up at us, her frown lines definitely deeper than they were at the beginning of filming a few weeks ago.

"What if Lucy is scared of heights? It could bring some more depth to the character."

"Sure, but how's she going to run along the top of a train or parachute down from this helicopter in the next scene?"

"Maybe she feels the fear and does it anyway?"

I look over at Maverick and realize he's helping me. He's trying to make this easier for me.

I liked it better when, as much as I wanted to fuck him, I still knew he was an asshole. Right now, he's helping me. He's being... *sweet?*

Ziva taps a pen on the script in her hand and considers it for a minute.

"Okay, let's try it. Lucy, you're scared, but you're doing it anyway!"

I look at Maverick. "Thanks."

"For what?"

"You know what."

"No, I don't."

I shake my head at him, and Ziva yells "Action!"

We run the lines, and when it gets to the part where I'm supposed to fall out of the helicopter, I don't even have time to wonder how I'm going to do it, or where my arms are supposed to go, because the helicopter tips and I'm suddenly in free fall. It's like everything happens in slow motion. I'm sliding feet first out of the helicopter, trying to grab onto anything I can, but I can't reach anything. Fear takes over as I realize there is nothing to grab onto. Maverick is not going to catch me. I'm going to fall, and while there are crash mats beneath me, if I fall on my head, it will still do some serious damage—

I squeeze my eyes closed, bracing for the crash landing, but suddenly a firm hand grips my wrist and even though I'm dangling out of a helicopter, I have never felt safer than I do in his grip.

"Good!" yells Ziva. "Now flail around, Lucy!"

I don't have to try. My legs are already kicking around desperately.

"I won't let you fall," Maverick tells me, going off script.

"A bit more flailing!" Ziva calls out.

And just when I think my arm is going to rip from its socket, Maverick yells to me — "Give me your other hand!"

It's not in the script either and it's not how we practiced, but I reach up with my other arm and he grabs it, easily hauling me up into the helicopter and pulling me close to him. It's nothing like we rehearsed. He wraps his arm around me and pulls me in closer, moves some wig hair from my sweaty forehead and then places a kiss on it.

What the fuck? A forehead kiss?!

I melt into his embrace, turning to complete goo as he tightens his grip around me.

"I told you to wear a seatbelt," he says.

I let out a laugh, and Ziva yells," Cut".

But Maverick doesn't move his arm, and I don't make any effort to move either. It's too comfortable, even with the sound boom and the lights and the hundreds of people around us. I never want to leave his embrace.

"We got it! Another perfect take! You two are on fire!" Ziva says after a few more moments.

Everyone claps and then starts running around setting up the next scene, which is us parachuting out of this helicopter together.

Maverick keeps his arm around me as he pulls his phone out of his pocket.

"This will be a great photo for your social media." He grins, snaps the photo and then lets me go. "Give me your number, and I'll send it over to you."

I shake my head. "No."

"What? Why not?"

"We said no swapping numbers."

"That was before we were working together."

"Still stands. Just send it to my social account."

"Which is—?"

"trixandtreatscatering."

"You need socials for your acting. Has anyone got you an assistant yet?"

"An assistant? What? No."

"I'll get someone on it."

"I don't want an assistant!"

"Too bad. You're getting one."

I wriggle out of his embrace and look around. "Can someone let us down, please?"

Maverick gives me a grin and just slides right out of the helicopter, landing easily on the mats below.

"Jump and I'll catch you."

"What? No!"

"I got you!" he calls up to me.

"No, I'm not going to just jump out of—" The helicopter begins to turn and I'm sliding out again before I can even try to find something else to hold on to. I let out a scream as Maverick and the mats come hurtling towards me.

And then I'm in his arms, in a fireman hold.

"I'll never let you fall, Trix. I promise." His blue-green eyes twinkle at me, and it's too fucking much.

I thump his steely shoulder. "Put me down!" I demand.

He lets me go, I slide out of his firm embrace, and then I run. I actually *run* through the soundstage and back to my trailer.

CHAPTER TWENTY

rix

Happy Halloween Trixters! There's no rest for the wicked so we have a full day of filming today, but I have baked some extra special witchy treats for the cast and crew! We also have the biggest bowl of candy you've ever seen in your life at the craft services table today!

Images:

1. Me dressed in a skeleton hoodie holding a tray of my Halloween GF pumpkin muffins

2. My signature key lime bars with bright green icing and gummy worms

3. Sanderson sisters triple tofurkey sandwiches

4. The biggest bowl of candy everrrr!

5. Pumpkin pie lattes

#maverickstone #secretagency #trixdelaney

. . .

@FIELDOFPOPPIESSS HAPPY HALLOWEEN BESTIE!!

@wellnessgirl I don't usually do sugar these days, but I would for a bite of one of those muffins! Yummm!

@juliettelover666 WHAT THE FUCK??! WHY HAVE THEY RE-CAST JULIETTE??

@moviestarmaddnessss889 WHO IS THIS RANDO??? WHERE IS JULIETTE?

"WHAT ARE you going to wear to the party tonight?" Ali asks as we pack away for the day. I only filmed one scene and managed to take a nap for an hour in my trailer, but I'm still dog tired and totally forgot that everyone was going to a Halloween party at the bar on the lot tonight.

"I think I'm going to skip it."

She gasps. "What? No! You promised me you'd come! I can't go alone!"

"Ali, you've made friends with almost everyone in this gigantic room. You'll be fine on your own. And besides. I have too much to do. I have to get all this back, start on tomorrow's baking, *and* they want me to post more on social media even though everyone hates me."

"They don't hate you," she says. "They're just jealous."

"Sure."

"If you come for just *one* teeny tiny drink, I'll come back to your place after and help you bake all night long if we have to."

"Why is it so important to you?" I ask, passing her an empty tray with just a few crumbs left from the key lime bars. It's suddenly everyone's favorite.

And then I see Finn walking over, and Ali's eyes glaze over like she's joined a cult of Finn worshippers or something.

"Will I see you two over there soon?" he asks, shifting a backpack on his shoulder.

"Yeah, definitely!" Ali beams.

He gives us both a wave.

"You've got a thing for the bad guy."

Finn doesn't have a huge part in the movie, but it's a damn good part. His character starts off as this young guy who's practically running the department John Stannic works for because the four other guys above him have all been shot. But it turns out he's running the criminal gang who are using both the Americans and Russians to do their bidding, and it was him who shot the four other agents. It's perfect for Finn. He has the whole boy next door thing going on. He's unsuspecting, and yet always kind of looks like he's about to get you into some kind of trouble.

"Chances are high that he's just a rebound, but I need to do *something* to get over Rebecca, and if Finn Huxley can't get me over her, no one will."

"Why do you need me to come?" I moan, grabbing the last few trays and making my way out to the van.

"I need you as my wing-woman."

"What if it goes really well and you don't even need me to stay?"

"Then I'll help you bake tomorrow night?" She makes a pathetic pleading face at me that I can't say no to.

I sigh. "Fine. One drink."

WE LEAVE the van where it is and walk about fifteen minutes to the bar, which is bursting full to the seams with people wearing crazy Halloween costumes. I guess a movie lot is a great place to find a costume. I feel completely underdressed in my skeleton hoodie. Even Ali has changed into a red fairy costume.

We squeeze past rabbits and ghosts and drag queens and make it to the bar. I order a Coke, and Ali orders a tequila sunrise. She is so not here for one drink only.

Once we have our drinks, Ali spots Finn, who's gone all out with his costume — nothing but a black bandana around his forehead.

"What are you meant to be?" I ask him.

"Karate Kid."

"You know that's not what they wear in karate, right?" Ali laughs.

"Best I could do on short notice."

"You forgot about the party?" Ali asks him.

"I forgot about Halloween."

Ali gasps, and the two of them quickly get into some banter about Halloween, which leads into the Karate Kid movies, and it's not that I don't have a secret crush on Johnny Lawrence, but within minutes I'm bored out of my mind and so clearly the third wheel here.

I give Ali's wing a nudge. "I'm going to go."

"Oh, no! Not yet!"

I down my Coke. "I really need to get baking. You look like you're fine. But you have a great night, okay?"

"I can come with you," she says halfheartedly.

"No, stay. You work so hard, you deserve to let your hair down."

I wave a quick goodbye to everyone else and wander out of the bar to walk another fifteen minutes back to the van.

I just wasted half an hour walking around the lot. But I smile when I think of Ali and Finn deep in conversation. She does deserve this night, and if it helped her to have me there for five minutes, I'm glad I did it.

My smile quickly disappears as I get to the trailers and see my own personal Halloween horror movie playing out before me.

Maverick Stone has his tongue down a very attractive woman's throat. She's wearing a short, tight red dress with red stilettos. Her hair is blonde and huge. I have no idea who she's dressed as, but she's a fucking bombshell.

And the sight of her arms wrapped around him, her mouth on his — it stops me in my tracks. It's like my blood stops moving through my body, and I think I'm going to actually be sick.

Just hours ago he was telling me he'd never let me go. Just days ago he was telling me his offer to fuck me in his trailer still stands.

And now he's here with *her*? Whoever the fuck she is!

What the actual fuck?!

He holds her face in his hands, and all I can think is, *why her*? Why isn't it me standing there with his tongue in my mouth?

I mean, sure, it was in the "rules" not to kiss me, but it's so easy for him to kiss this woman who he hardly knows? Maybe he does know her. Oh, my god. It never even occurred to me that he could be dating someone.

But he told me quite clearly. He didn't do monogamy.

I turn and start walking the long way back to my van so I can avoid them both.

"Trix!" he calls out.

Why?

I turn and he's waving me over.

Why, why, why?

"What do you want?" I call out to him from across the street.

"Why are you leaving the party so early? Where are you going?" he asks as the woman links her arm into his. She's stunning. She has to be a model.

"Home."

I stomp away from them both and after about five

minutes I finally reach my van. But there, leaning against my door, is Maverick.

"Your vampire speed tricks don't impress me. But shouldn't you be careful running around that fast around here?"

"Babe, this is a movie set. Nothing looks weird here."

"I'm not interested in whatever you have to say. Just go back to making out with your girlfriend or whatever she is. And don't ever call me *babe* again."

"I told you. I don't do relationships."

"So, what is she then?"

"Just a Donna."

"Don't be so disrespectful," I tell him, opening my door. "She's not *just* a Donna. She's a person with feelings."

He looks like he's in pain. "She gets it. She gets who I am, what I am, what I want and need."

Right, and I don't?

I yank open my door. "If she's so perfect for you, go fuck her and suck her blood and stop hassling me."

"I didn't mean to hassle you. I just wanted to talk."

"About what?"

He runs a hand through the back of his hair. "I don't know. About my offer, I guess. Because you were into the idea, and then suddenly you weren't—"

"It was just a moment of idiocy," I tell him.

"Oh, because you'd have to be an idiot to have sex with me?"

"No. I wasn't an idiot to do it the first time," I say, feeling the heat moving up my body as I vividly remember his thick cock inside me.

"The first three times," he adds, leaning towards me.

"But it would be really stupid to do it again."

"Why?"

I swallow. I don't want to tell him I haven't thought about

anything but fucking him and baking cakes for the last eighteen months.

"Just go back to your Donna," I say, getting in the van and slamming the door.

He taps on the window, and I open it, sighing at him. "What?"

"What if I don't want to go back to my Donna?" he asks, his voice gravelly and rough and making me want to take back everything I just said. "What if I'd rather be with you?"

"If I meant anything to you, you wouldn't be making out with some other woman right now."

"You're the one who said no to us hooking up again. You didn't give me any indication that you would change your mind. What am I supposed to do? Just sit around and wait for you to change your mind about my offer?"

"Do whatever you want," I tell him.

"Trix," he says, his voice low and gravelly and sexy as hell. "Say the word and I'll—"

"You can't just treat people that way. You should—"

I look over at where the woman is, and she's flirting shamelessly with some other guy who's just appeared.

He looks over at her completely unfazed. "I told you, she gets it. She means nothing to me, and I mean nothing to her."

"And that's what you want from me? For us to mean nothing to each other?"

His jaw clenches. "No, I—"

"It's so easy for you to just *kiss* her? Some woman you don't even care about? After everything from that night, you wouldn't even kiss *me*?" The words roll off my tongue without a chance for my brain to think better of it. The last thing I want is for him to think I'm jealous. But I've never been more jealous in my life.

"You made the rules," he says, like all of this, everything I'm feeling right now, is my own fault.

And I guess it is. And this is *exactly* why I need to distance myself from him. This raging fire within me, this fear, this anger, this anguish, this kind of suffering just hurts too much.

I need to get over him, and fast.

"We *both* made the rules," I say, turning on the ignition.

"I'm happy to break any of them at any time. You want me to kiss you? Just say the word. I'll kiss you right fucking now."

I open my mouth, ready to tell him the word, to slide out of the van, to tell him to kiss me right here, right now, to tell him to push me up against the van and kiss me as hard as he fucks, when I hear a voice call out—

"Maverick? Honey bunny?"

He rolls his eyes. "I've claimed her," he says, like this explains any of his actions. "It makes it easier for her to find me."

"You *claimed* her?"

He nods. "It means no other vampire can drink from her but me."

"I know what it means," I snap. "I've heard you claimed half the Donnas in the city."

"Want me to claim you?" he asks with a smirk. "I'll do it right now."

"No, thanks."

The woman appears and gives him a smile. "Honeybuns, where did you go?" she pouts at him.

"I just needed to make sure Trix got home okay," he tells her.

"Bye, *honeybuns*," I tell him as I get in the van and start it up.

"Get home safe!" The woman calls out to me.

And then hot tears fall from my eyes as I think of him spending a night with her like the one we had together.

CHAPTER TWENTY-ONE

rix

I'M ALREADY LOOKING at a sleepless night ahead of baking, but I don't go home. Instead, I find myself parking the van just up the street from Vincent's.

Of course, most of the people standing in line don't know it's a vampire bar. They just think it's an eccentric place decorated in an art deco twenties style where a big band plays covers of new songs.

But this is where vampires hang out looking for someone to drink from and have sex with. Most of the vampires that hang out here follow the rules, but not all of them. Both me and Poppy have been glamoured by vampires here who didn't play by the rules.

And tonight, I don't want to play by the rules.

I just want to feel better.

"Trix!" Dave, the bouncer, greets me with a smile. "Where have you been, chicka?"

"Busy," I tell him. "I started my own catering company."

"Oh, go girl!" He gives me a high five.

"What about you? I thought you left Vincent's?"

"This place has a habit of sucking you back in."

"I know exactly what you mean."

"Coming in?"

"Yeah. Is Cass here tonight?"

He gives me a look that says *Trix, don't even go there.* "Why?"

"I just wanted to ask him about something."

"You want your job back?"

"It's — of a personal nature."

"Trix, I'm in no place to judge, but be careful with Cass and Vinnie."

"Dave, I used to work here, remember? I know the deal."

He gives me a warning look and then lets me through, telling the girl at the door not to charge me, and then I'm back, standing in the bar that holds so many memories for me.

I worked here for months when it first opened, before I even knew it was a vampire bar, before I even knew that vampires existed. It was here that I discovered the deepest, darkest side of Hollywood.

When I worked here, I had a huge crush on one of the owners — Cassius. He was so sexy, powerful, his energy was intoxicating. When I found out he was a vampire, it all made sense. I should have been scared working here, but I wasn't. I was intrigued and kind of excited. I knew vampires were dangerous, but they were also sexy as hell.

But still, I didn't get too close to them. I was an interested observer, watching them come and go, watching the Donnas take them into the back room for a quick drink and usually sex too, while I just served drinks and fantasized about maybe one day doing it with a vampire. That was all it ever was, though. A fantasy.

At least it was until I met Maverick.

Cass wanted to bite me one night. He called me into his office and told me he was going to bite me. Just like that. No asking if I wanted it, just — "Trix, I'm going to bite you now."

It was hot as fuck, and part of me wanted to walk over and just let him do it, but I was scared. I shook my head, and when I told him no, that I was too scared, that I wasn't ready, he fired me.

He could have glamoured me, wiped my mind and made me forget it all. He could've made me forget vampires existed, but he didn't.

I learned it's a kink some vampires have. By vampire law, they are supposed to make humans forget they exist, but sometimes they like knowing that you're out there, terrified of them, or horny for them. Usually a bit of both.

I was scared to let Cass bite me, but when Maverick asked, it was an easy yes.

I don't know why. I don't know what it was about Maverick that made it so easy for me to give him my wrist. I just felt so *safe* with him.

I knew he wasn't going to hurt me. He wasn't going to let me fall.

And then I think of him kissing that woman and I walk up the stairs towards Cass's office.

I knock, but there's no answer, then I try the door, and it opens. I step in and look around the room filled with plush twenties style furnishing and a heavy oak desk, but don't see Cass anywhere.

"You wanted to see me?" Cass asks, appearing out of the shadows like a — vampire.

I jump, and he laughs.

He looks gorgeous. Light brown waves of hair frame his

perfectly angled face. He's not as buff as Maverick, not as broad, but he's muscular, strong. Of course he's strong, he's a fucking vampire.

I get straight to the point. "I want you to bite me."

He laughs again. "Oh, Trix. That offer has long since expired." He grins at me, revealing his fangs and making me realize right away that this was a big mistake. "But I find it most interesting you've finally come back. It rarely takes so long, but still. They always come back eventually."

I fold my arms over my chest as he eyes me up and down.

"Want to be a Donna for our next client?"

"No, I don't. I choose who bites me, where and when."

"That's not how it works, sweetie," he tells me. "If you want The Bite, you take it from whoever is willing to give it to you."

I swallow and try to keep my cool even though everything within me is telling me to run the fuck out of here right now and stay away from vampires *forever*.

"But maybe, for you, I could make an exception."

Oh, fuck, what am I doing?

"Come here."

For a moment, my feet don't move. But if Maverick is drinking from someone else tonight, why can't someone else drink from *me*? I try to remember how good it felt to have his fangs in me, how the ecstasy of that moment took me and made me feel like nothing else ever had.

Will it feel the same with Cass?

Will he only take what he needs? Will he stop in time? Will I even care once the ecstasy of The Bite takes over?

Why didn't I worry about any of this when I was with Maverick? I just let him bite me — no fear, no worry, no hesitation.

Cass sits down in the large leather armchair in the corner of his office.

"Sit," he tells me, gesturing to his lap.

"I'm nervous," I tell him.

"You want me to be gentle?"

I nod.

He grins at me. "A vampire virgin," he says.

I shake my head. "I've had The Bite before."

"Oh, you have?" he asks. "Who from?"

"I'd rather not say," I tell him.

He raises an eyebrow. "Then you know what to expect."

I walk towards him. I *have* to get Maverick out of my system. And blood bonding with Cass would be a way to do that. I'd stop dreaming about Maverick and start dreaming about him instead. Right?

Suddenly I'm petrified. This isn't what I want. Not with Cass.

Oh, shit.

"Sorry, but I think I've changed my mind," I stammer.

"I'll be nice, I promise," he says with a fanged grin that unsettles me even more.

I'm about to step away, but he speeds towards me, grabs my wrist and pulls me onto his lap on the chair. He wraps an arm around me, looks into my eyes, and the guy I thought I remembered — the hot, sexy, powerful vampire Cass that I had crushed on so hard for so many months isn't here. This is someone else. He's changed.

Or maybe I have.

His mouth moves to my ear, giving me all the wrong kind of goosebumps.

"You'll like it, I promise," he says, taking my wrist and pulling up the sleeve of my skeleton hoodie that suddenly doesn't feel so cute now I'm worried about getting drained.

"I don't want to," I tell him. "I'm sorry. I just — I'm a bit confused right now. I thought I wanted it, but now I don't... Please let me go."

"How about you let me take that confusion away for you?" It's almost tender in a way, and for a second, I think maybe I should just let him do it. Just let him take the edge off. Just have a moment of something that isn't work, making sandwiches, learning lines or thinking about Maverick.

He grabs my wrist and brings it towards his mouth.

His teeth pierce my skin, but instead of ecstasy all I feel is fear. A scream escapes my lips as I jerk away from him. I don't know how I do it. He must be a thousand times stronger than I am, but I somehow manage to get out of his grip. I fall to the floor and then scramble on hands and knees towards the door.

He just sits in his chair and laughs. "You'll be back, Trix!" he calls to me. I finally get to my feet and run out of the office, down the stairs and through the club.

I run until I'm safe inside my van.

I've played a dangerous game tonight. My heart is beating like a wild thing, adrenaline coursing through my veins.

And then I just laugh hysterically, because I'm still alive, and at least for just a few moments, I wasn't thinking about Maverick Stone and his Donna.

CHAPTER TWENTY-TWO

rix

"ARE YOU READY?" he asks, his fingers running along my opening. "You feel ready."

I give him a nod. "Yes."

Less than a second later, he moves my panties aside and pushes his cock into me. It's the most glorious feeling in the world — his thick cock stretching me out to fit him perfectly.

"Too much?" he asks.

I shake my head. "Give me more."

He pushes in deeper, and I groan.

"Oh, fuck," he moans into my neck. "You're glorious."

"More," I beg him as he pumps into me like a man who's been living on an island with no female company for the last decade.

He pulls my bra down, and my breasts tumble free. He groans as he takes one in his hand, gripping the counter beneath me with the other.

He gives my nipple a squeeze, and I let out a little scream.

"You okay?"

"Just shut up and fuck me!" I tell him.

He grins at me, those fucking blue-green eyes sparkling like aquamarine diamonds or whatever the fuck shines that intensely.

He keeps going, and every thrust feels like a step on the stairway to some vampire sex-dream heaven.

His hand moves from my nipple down to my clit. He squeezes me between his thumb and forefinger, and it's so divine I can't hold on—

"Holy FUCK!" I call out, arching my back and letting the quiver and shake of the beginning of an orgasm hit me. "Maverick, fuck! Oh, my god!" I let out a scream as my climax hits its peak.

I ride the waves of my orgasm, and he grips my waist, thrusting steadily into me while I bask in the magic of a Maverick Stone induced come-fest.

"I want you from behind," he tells me.

He doesn't have to ask me twice. As soon as he pulls out, I jump down off the counter and turn to face the magnificent view of Malibu beach while Maverick pulls my panties down to my knees and grips my waist again...

So, it turns out that getting half bitten by another vampire has done nothing to ease the grip that Maverick Stone still has on my sex dreams.

Fuck.

And even worse than that, the puncture marks on my wrist that I had thought would be healed by the morning are most definitely *not* healed.

When Maverick bit me, he rubbed a little saliva into the bite marks afterwards, and they instantly healed. But Cassius Blake is nothing like Maverick Stone and going back to ask him to heal them is not an option.

The good thing about acting on set is that I don't have to

do my own hair and makeup. So, I just take a quick shower, throw on a Trix and Treats t-shirt and a pair of acid-wash jeans and then go stock the van with the pathetic amount of food I still managed to make last night.

But it's okay. I have a plan. I can make the sandwiches there. I grab the bars, cookies, and the sandwich ingredients and pack the van.

I'm about to leave when I notice the vampire bites on my wrist. It's going to be very obvious to anyone who knows anything about vampires what they are.

I grab the first-aid kit from the back of the van and wrap my wrist in a bandage.

"You still got all this done?" Ali asks as she helps me unpack the van and set up our table.

"Everything but the sandwiches. I'm just going to put the ingredients out and people can make their own."

"Genius," Ali says. "You could do this every day."

I shake my head. "It's a one off. It'll get us through today, but people shouldn't *have* to make their own sandwiches."

She gives me a look.

"What?"

"It's too much, Trix!"

"I can handle it," I tell her. "I've got to get into hair and make-up now though."

She hands me a coffee with coconut syrup and then shoos me off.

I get my hair and makeup done, and I almost look like a person who has slept for over two hours. *Almost.*

"You look like hell," Maverick says, as I step out of the hair and makeup trailer towards wardrobe to get a clean costume.

"Thanks," I say, not even bothering to look up at him.

"What happened to your wrist?"

"A burn. Hazard of the industry."

I can feel his scowl on me without even looking up at him.

I stop and face him, folding my arms in front of me. "What?"

"This is exactly why I told you to quit catering. The other caterer who does the main meals for us can—"

"Everything is under control."

"No, it isn't."

I just glare at him and then turn and walk into wardrobe, slamming the flimsy trailer door behind me.

Maverick has no say in how I live my life. He's not my boyfriend, he's not even my friend, he's not my anything!

We are nothing to each other.

Visions of last night's dream dance through my mind, and I try to blink them away while the guy from wardrobe hands me my costume for today. Same thing I wear every day — tight jeans, revealing tank top, high boots.

I roll my eyes. "Doesn't this woman ever get to wear a sweater?"

The wardrobe guy just looks at me. "No."

I take my costume, hoping not to run into Maverick again, but he's outside my trailer waiting for me.

"Why are you still picking up your own costume? They should deliver it to your trailer."

"Maybe because I'm just a stand-in."

"You have the role now. They should treat you the same way they'd treat Juliette."

I just laugh. "In what world would I get treated the same way as Juliette?"

"After this movie comes out, you will."

"Sure."

He grabs my good wrist and forces me to look at him. "Trix, when this movie comes out, you'll be a movie star."

"Whatever."

"Can you stop being such a pain in the ass and realize exactly what's at stake here?"

I glare at him. "Your career?"

"And yours."

"I don't have a career."

"But you will. You're living someone else's dream right now, and you're not taking it seriously. If this movie does well, you'll be hot property in the industry. You can get another movie, and then another, TV, whatever you want. This can be the start of an incredible career for you. But if you're too busy fucking around making sandwiches—"

"I'm not *fucking around making sandwiches*! I'm running a highly successful catering business!"

"If it's so successful, why can't you pay for a kitchen? For a team to help you?"

"I could pay if I wanted to!" A half-truth. I could take money from my parents, or get investment, but I don't want investment. I don't want anyone else getting to decide how I run my business.

"If you won't listen to me, I'll go to Brandon."

"Snitch," I tell him before turning on my heel and storming back to my trailer.

"Jesus, Trix!" I hear him groan from behind me.

I bang the door of my trailer open and then lock it behind me this time. I throw my costume onto a chair and try to breathe. My whole body is shaking from being so close to Maverick, from the heat of our argument.

I go to rub my hands over my face, but remember I'm already made up. I make myself a coffee at the tiny coffee maker, hands shaking as I throw in three sugars. I add some cold water and throw it back. It makes me feel even shakier, but at least I'm awake.

I put my costume on and look in the mirror. My bandage is in no way subtle.

Fucking fang bites.

I should have just let him drink from me. At least then he would have closed the wounds.

I could call Poppy. I could get Max to close the wounds, but Max is Maverick's best friend. There's no way he wouldn't tell him.

I can't ask Brandon. He's probably already regretting his decision to cast me in this movie.

There must be other vampires on set, but I'm not sure exactly who. And anyway, it's not like I can go to a stranger and have them heal my bite wounds. Can I?

It's still early, but I decide to give Beth a call anyway. She worked as a Donna at Vincent's when I worked there, and at least I know she's discreet.

I'm so relieved when she answers.

"Trix? It's like eight a.m., what's going on?"

"I need some advice."

"Yeah? Sure," she says, sleepily.

"How do you get rid of bite marks?"

"The vampire who bit you has to close them up with saliva."

"Yeah, I know, but say the vampire didn't close them up."

"Who the fuck didn't close your wounds?"

"Doesn't matter," I tell her. "Is there any kind of home remedy?"

"Trix, no. It's not a normal wound."

"Just tell me what to do."

She yawns. "You have to get a vampire to do it for you. It's the only way."

"You know anybody who could help me out and be discreet about it?"

"I'm not working as a Donna at the club at the moment," she tells me. "I got claimed."

"Good for you." For a Donna, getting claimed is a big deal. Getting bitten by just one vampire instead of all the freaks at the club is definitely a step up.

"I could get my vampire to help you. He works around there."

"Yeah? When could he come?"

"I don't know," she says. "I'll have to call him. Oh, you might already know him," she says. "You're in that movie too now, right?"

My stomach twists at the thought of what she's going to say next.

"It's Maverick Stone," she yawns.

"Maverick."

"He's the vampire who claimed me. I'm sure he'll be happy to help you. He's a great guy—"

"Thanks, but no thanks. I'll handle it." The butterflies in my ribcage catch on fire in a fit of rage.

"Okay, talk again soon?" she asks, and I know I've been a shitty friend. This is the first time I've reached out to her in ages, and it was only because I wanted something.

"Yeah, when this movie wraps, let's hang out and catch up."

"I'd love that!"

We say our goodbyes and I end the call.

Maverick really wasn't kidding when he said he'd claimed half the women in this city.

CHAPTER TWENTY-THREE

$\mathcal{M}$averick

"ALL WOUNDS MUST BE HEALED and sealed by the vampire who made them on the human donor. To leave a wound unsealed and unhealed is to leave a mark that not only causes a potential for our kind to be discovered, but it is also in terrible taste. It is more acceptable to kill your prey than let them walk around with bite wounds. This is the height of vulgarity and will not be accepted in high vampire society."

The Fraternity of the Order of the Everlasting Rose Handbook page 390

I GET BACK to my trailer with the coffee Ali made me. It's not as good as the one Trix made. Well, it's probably fine. I just wanted Trix to make it for me.

Maybe it's because of my fucked up fantasy I told her about. The one where I have a wife who cooks me dinner and lets me fuck her over the dining table. Maybe it's the idea that she's making the coffee for *me*, that she wants me to enjoy it, that she's doing it because she wants to make me happy.

Fucking hell, I can't believe I told her about that.

It's not like I'm some sexist guy who thinks women belong in the kitchen. It's just a monogamy fantasy. Something I can never have in the real world. Something that I can't let myself want except in fantasy form.

I get dressed and ready, looking forward to another day on set with her. Another day of being close to her, even if I can't have her.

A little while later I'm standing in front of a train carriage and a green screen waiting for Trix to appear so we can film some shots of us jumping off the top of the train. She's going to hate this, but I can't wait to do my macho bullshit and put her at ease.

She walks towards us, and she looks as hot as she always does in her costume. The way those jeans cling to every curve, the way that tank top shows *almost* too much makes me want to rip those straps off her shoulders — I suddenly realize this is what every man, and many women will be thinking when they watch this movie. Fuckers. But they can't have her. They won't get her the way I've had her. The way I so desperately want her again.

I can't believe how much I fucked up with my Donna last night. Of course, I never expected Trix to be there. If I'd known she would come back to her van so quickly, I would have taken my Donna somewhere else. I just needed something, someone to help me forget her. Trix has made it abundantly clear she doesn't want to be with me again, and I was sick of feeling like I was losing my mind over her. I thought if I did it with a Donna, maybe I could take my mind off it for a little while. But just like it has for the last eighteen fucking months, it was pointless. As soon as I kissed her, I knew I wouldn't go through with it. I knew I couldn't bite her or fuck her. I just *didn't want to.* Me, Maverick Stone, not wanting to bite and fuck a beautiful woman who was so damn up for it.

But that's not what Trix saw. She didn't see my thoughts of her, my decision to just drive my Donna home and go to bed on my own. All she saw was me kissing someone else.

I'm such a fucking idiot.

"What's wrong with your wrist?" Ziva asks Trix as she walks onto set.

"This?" she holds up her wrist. "It's just a burn."

I'm about to open my smart mouth, tell Brandon and Ziva she's still cooking all night, but I hold my tongue. She's already pissed enough. She looks way too tired to take any more arguments, and I need her in good form for this scene.

"Can we get makeup to cover it?" Ziva waves over someone from makeup.

Trix grabs her wrist. "I'd rather not."

Ziva's eyebrows shoot toward the ceiling. "It's not a choice, Trix. You can't keep the bandage on."

"Can't we fix it in post?" she asks. "Put a green bag over it or something?"

"We can edit a burn out, but a whole bandage is annoying," someone calls out. "Covering it with makeup is easier."

"Uh, okay. Can you give me two minutes in my trailer? I just need to—" She runs off before anyone can stop her.

"What the fuck, Trix?" I ask, catching up with her outside. "You can't just run off set like that."

She ignores me and just keeps stomping away with me following on her heels.

She storms into her trailer, and I stand outside, pacing. I have a line I won't cross, and it's here. I won't go in unless I'm invited. Not because it's a vampire thing — that's bullshit.

If a vampire wants to get into your house, they will get in. It's just that she doesn't want me in there right now. I should respect that. Really, I should.

I bang on the door after a few minutes. "Trix!"

When there's no answer another few minutes later, I forget my pretend manners completely and barge in to find her eyes red as she tries to pat make-up onto her wrist.

"Fuck!" she says when she sees me.

I grab her wrist, and when I see the bite marks, my insides feel like they have caught alight. "Who did this to you?" I growl. "Who fucking did this?!"

"It doesn't matter," she tells me. "Can you just — fuck!" She blinks and stares at me. "Can you just fucking fix it? Please?"

"First, you tell me who did this to you." I grab her by the shoulders and stare into her eyes. "I can glamour you into telling me, but I'd rather you just trusted me enough to tell me."

"Trust *you*?" she laughs. "Trust you with your ten thousand claimed women?"

"Jesus, is that what this is about? Are you *jealous*? Baby, I'll claim you anytime you say the word."

She lets out a laugh. "That's the last fucking thing I want!"

Well, that stings.

"Who's this guy? I can tell he didn't claim you."

She scowls at me. "Why? Because no other vampire would think I'm worthy of claiming?"

"No, because I can't smell another vampire on you. And usually, when someone claims you, it's because they—" He runs a hand over his jaw. "They get close to you, and the scent sticks around."

"I didn't fuck him, if that's what you're alluding to."

Slight relief moves through me, but it's not enough. "If you want The Bite, I'll give it to you anytime," I tell her.

"Even if that's all you ever want from me. And I would *never ever* leave your wounds open like whoever the hell did this to you. I will rip their fucking head off when I find out, and I *will* find out whether you tell me or not!"

"Can you please just heal it so we can get to filming?" she pleads.

"Tell me who. And I will."

She takes a breath. "Cass," she whispers. "From the club."

It takes me a second. "*Cassius?!*"

She nods.

"Cassius fucking Blake did this to you?!" I grab her forearm and look at the marks on her. "Cassius gave you The Bite and then didn't close your wounds? Even for that evil bastard, this is messed up." I glare at her now. "What the hell were you doing with Cassius Blake?"

"I know him," she says. "And I was in the mood for — you know."

"Of all the vampires, fucking hell, Trix. Anyone would have been better than that piece of shit. Even me!"

"What's wrong with him?"

"He's murdered more humans than any other vampire I know, that's what."

The blood leaves her face.

"He could've—" I don't even want to think about what he could have done to her.

I have to stop myself from asking — *how was it? Was The Bite good with him? Was it better than it was with me? Did he fuck you? Did you think about me when he was inside you?*

No, she told me she didn't fuck him, and I have to believe her, or I will lose my mind.

"Only the worst of the worst leave the wounds," I growl.

"Well, he didn't really get a chance to close them."

"What do you mean?"

"I ran away."

"What?"

She sighs and looks down at where I'm still gripping her forearm.

"I thought I wanted it," she says, her chin wobbling ever so slightly. "The Bite. But when I got there, when he was about to do it, I changed my mind."

Another wave of rage hits me, and now I'm really seeing red.

"He bit you when you didn't want it?"

"It's not like—"

"Don't you fucking dare suggest any of this is your fault."

"I went there to get bitten. I changed my mind at the last second."

"You told him no, and *then* he bit you?"

Holy fuck, my head is about to explode.

"How much did he drink from you? Did he drink too much?" I take her face in my hands and look into her eyes. "Are you feeling okay? Are you feeling weak?"

She shakes her head, as much as she can with my hands clamped on each of her cheeks. God, it feels good to hold her like this. I just wish it was under different circumstances.

"No, he didn't drink from me. He just bit my wrist, and then I ran."

"You got away?"

"Yeah."

"He just — let you go?"

"I guess so. I'm not stupid. I know he could've kept me there."

"You're playing with fire, Trix." I run my thumbs over her cheeks. "These guys, Cassius and Vincent, are the worst kinds of vampires. You're lucky to be alive right now."

She nods her face as I hold it in my hands. "Yeah. I know. It was so dumb, but I just—"

"You just what, sweetheart?"

Whatever she was about to say, she's decided not to.

I let go of her face, take her wrist gently in my hand and look down at the puncture wounds she's tried to hide unsuccessfully with makeup.

"I'll heal these over, but first you have to promise me something. Stay away from Cassius. And Vincent."

She nods. "Okay."

"I mean it, Trix. If you want to fuck around with vampires, that's on you, just anyone but Cassius, for fuck's sake."

"You think I want to fuck around with vampires?" She scowls at me.

I point to her wrist. "What do you call this if it's not fucking around with vampires?"

Fuck, if she wants to fuck around with vampires, why can't it just be me?

"If you want The Bite, you ask me, okay?"

She shakes her head. "I don't want it anymore."

"Once you've had The Bite, you always want more. I'm assuming that's what this was. Some attempt to get that feeling again. That feeling you had with me that night?"

A flush hits her cheeks, and I know I'm right.

"If you want that feeling, you come to *me*. Any time."

"Me and half the women in the city? Do I have to make an appointment?"

If only she knew that I hadn't had sex in over eighteen months, the longest I have ever gone in my whole life without it. But whenever it had been on the table, I didn't want it. I didn't want to put my cock in anyone but *her*. Had I bitten women since then? Yes. Had I enjoyed it? Partially. It was just food to me now. I hadn't felt true pleasure drinking blood since I'd been with Trix. Which is why right now all I want to do is heal these wounds and then make some new ones in her neck that I will absolutely heal up when we're done enjoying each other.

I don't tell her any of that.

"No appointment is necessary," I tell her.

I run some warm water and gently wash the wound with soap, getting all the makeup off. Not totally necessary, but it feels right to clean her skin first, like I'm washing off her attempt to hide something from me. Like I'm washing off Cassius' hold on her.

She winces.

Why fucking Cassius?

I hold her wrist gently with one hand, and I lick my index finger of the other. She watches with interest — no, this is more than interest. She watches me with *gratitude and awe.*

I slide my finger over her wrist, making tiny circles over the wounds.

She lets out a little moan.

"Feels good, doesn't it?" I ask with a smirk. It's nothing like The Bite, but when vampires heal their wounds, it gives a nice little tingle.

She looks up at me and bites her lip.

Fuck.

"Promise me, Trix. You want to fuck around with vampires, let that vampire be me. I would never hurt you like this. I'd never hurt you at all."

$\mathcal{M}$averick

I TRY my best to film the scene, but my mind is elsewhere. Trix is terrified of even *getting* on top of the train, and I'm in such a rage that I can't help her like I want to. I can't promise her that everything is going to be okay when all I can think about is Cass's fangs in her wrist.

All I can feel are flames of wrath that need to be quenched immediately. And definitely before I can focus on filming.

Ziva yells "Cut" again for the eighth time, and I run a hand over the stubble on my jaw that never grows beyond this length.

"Maverick, what's going on?" Ziva asks, stepping towards us.

"Can we pause filming for a few hours?" I ask after just five minutes of getting nowhere.

"What? Why?" Ziva's brow knits together, and I know she

won't like this, but she also won't like any of the shots she's going to get with me in this mood.

"I have to take care of something. I can't concentrate until I do."

She looks over at Brandon, and he just shrugs. The thing about Ziva is that no matter how pissed she is with me, she knows she needs to keep me happy. And so she does.

"Can you be back by six? We could still try to get a couple of hours in."

I give her a nod. "I promise when I'm back, I'll be in better form. We both will."

I flash a look in Trix's direction. She looks at me intensely, pressing her lips together in worry.

Those damn lips!

I don't even bother to change out of my costume, which I know wardrobe will complain about later when it comes back covered in black vampire goo because I will kill the fucking bastard, and then I run out of the lot towards my motorcycle.

I'm just about to start the engine when I sense Trix running up behind me. I turn, and the way she runs to me in that damn outfit, that too low-cut tank top that makes her breasts look fucking unbelievable.

"Maverick, what are you going to do?" she asks, stopping right beside me.

"I'm going to go give Cassius a piece of my mind."

"Don't do it," she begs. "He's not worth it."

"You told him no, and he bit you. That's against vampire law."

"So tell Brandon and take it to vampire court or whatever it is you do."

"Sweetheart, going over there to fuck him up *is* vampire court."

Part of me wants to do what she asks, but I won't be able

to calm the fuck down until I've beaten the shit out of him or at least tried my goddamn best.

I get on my motorcycle and ride, leaving her in my dust. But at least on the lot with Brandon, she's safe.

I ride fast, weaving in and out of traffic under bright LA skies, thanking the lizard gods that I'm not in some coffin somewhere unable to do anything about Cassius until nightfall.

I knew I had feelings for Trix. That was fucking clear, but this protective feeling, this wanting to keep her safe at all costs when I haven't even claimed her — that's something new. It feels wild. *I* feel wild, and I have no worries at all about taking on that little weed Cassius.

But Cassius is not so much of a weed as I remembered, especially when he's standing next to his brother Vincent.

"She said no, and you still bit her," I growl at him, walking towards where he's standing near the bar.

Cassius turns to me, looks me up and down and then lets out a laugh. "What are you to her? If you haven't claimed her?"

"A friend," I say.

Vincent laughs at that. "Vampires don't have friends."

"Maybe *you* don't," I say. "But *I* do. And Trix is one of mine."

"What are you here for, Maverick?" Cassius asks. "Some kind of retribution? You know I'll kick your ass, just like I used to during training exercises."

"It could be fun to watch him get his ass kicked again," says Vincent. The two of them are like different sides of the same coin. Their faces are all sharp jaws and straight noses, but Vincent's long wavy hair is black while Cassius has light brown, almost blonde hair.

The Blakes weren't made for the vampire army, they were recruited. Already a few hundred years old, they were stronger than the rest of us, and they were also psychopaths who gave no value at all to human life. Cassius and Vincent killed with no regard for which side their victims were even on. They even killed our own soldiers, just for their own fun when the mood struck. They were out of control assholes during the war, and I doubt much has changed.

I was lucky not to be in their unit, but they were never far away, and neither were the stories of what they were getting up to. Everyone was terrified of them, and rightly so.

But standing here now in their almost empty West Hollywood vampire bar, I'm not terrified. I'm just seething with fury.

Although honestly, I wasn't expecting to see both of them. Taking them both on may be a different challenge. One I may not be entirely prepared for.

"What is she to you?" I ask him, trying to stall while I figure out what to do here.

"Ah, I see!" Cassius says with a vicious smile. "You're here because you're *jealous.*"

Vincent puts a glass of blood on the bar. "See? This is exactly why we have the claiming system. It avoids all these kinds of *misunderstandings.*" Vincent seems bored with this already. "One of you just claim her already."

"The thing is," Cassius says, taking a step towards me, "if she wanted to be claimed by you, what was she doing here, begging me to bite her?"

The idea that Trix had come here and *begged* him for anything makes me sick to my stomach.

"She said no, and you bit her anyway."

"You want to know what really happened?" Cassius asks and then continues without waiting for an answer. "She told me she wanted it. She *wanted* me to bite her. I didn't seek her out. I didn't go after her. She walked into my club and into my office with that look on her face. You know the one they have?"

Vincent nods. "Lustful desperation. Like they'd do *anything*, even sell their soul to have you fuck and bite them."

"That's the one," Cassius says with a smirk.

I very much doubt that was the look on Trix's face last night, but I can't ignore the fact that he's partly right. She did come here. That was her choice. She might have changed her mind, but at first, she wanted it. She wanted to be with Cassius.

I'm suddenly reminded of our conversation last night. She was upset about my Donna. Holy shit, did she come here because she thought I was with a Donna?

"You see, Trix and I know each other, did you know that?" Cassius asks with a sly smile.

I didn't, but I don't admit it.

"She used to work for me. I was her boss. I used to bite her all the time."

What the fuck?

"I fucked her too. She's surprisingly good."

Fuck red, now my vision turns to black.

She told me she didn't fuck him last night, and I believed her. She also told me that night we were together, that first time, that I was her first vampire, that I was her first bite.

I take myself back to that moment, the first time I bit her. The nervous but excited look in her eyes. The way her head tilted back at the ecstasy of it.

"You know what these Donnas are like," Cassius continues. "They tell you all sorts of fucked up shit just for The Bite."

I let his words slide off me. I trust Trix. I believe Trix. She had nothing to gain by pretending she hadn't done this before.

Cassius is the one lying. Of course he is. He never fucked her. He barely bit her. I try my absolute best to believe that.

"Trix isn't a Donna," I bark.

"Maverick, if a girl comes into my office begging for The Bite, what else is she but a blood whore? I left those marks on her because that's what she is, and I wanted everyone to know how up for it she—"

He doesn't finish his sentence because my fist is in his mouth.

Laughing, he wipes a drop of blood from his lip. "You have to do better than that, Maverick."

I punch him again, harder, and again and again, and he just stands there like none of it is getting to him.

"You forget I'm two hundred years older than you and quite a bit stronger."

Okay, I still don't regret coming here, but maybe I should have brought Brandon and Max with me.

He punches me in the gut, and I take a few steps back. Fuck. He is strong.

But I don't care. I don't care if I get the absolute crap beaten out of me, I'll fight for Trix's honor.

I run at him and grab him around the neck, squeezing as hard as I can. "You fucking leave her alone," I tell him.

"She's the one who can't leave me alone," he rasps before grabbing my shoulders and shoving me back onto the empty dance floor.

The few customers in the club scream and run away. No one wants to be in the middle of a couple of vampires fighting over a girl — not girl, *woman.*

I run at him again, throwing my shoulder into him. This time the hit lands him on the ground. I straddle him and hold up my fist.

"Don't fucking touch her again!" I yell, punching him in his stupid face.

He just laughs.

"And when a woman says no, it means no, you fucking asshole." I punch him in the face three more times.

He keeps laughing, and so I keep punching until he eventually stops and glares his steely gaze up at me.

"You broke vampire law. If I had a stake, I'd do it," I tell him. "I'd give you the Certain Death, right here, right now."

"You wouldn't stand a chance, but even if you did, then what do you think would happen? My brother Vincent would do the same to you. Unlike some people, I *have* protection."

He's right. The security team that follows me everywhere go by car and are always half an hour behind me due to traffic. There's no one coming to back me up.

"Just leave the girl alone, Cass," says Vincent, like even he's sick of Cassius' bullshit. "No Donna is worth this."

Cassius' eyes narrow like being told off by his brother is worse than anything I've said or done since I arrived here.

"You can have any other girl in the city," Vincent adds, standing over us now like a school principal come to break up a schoolyard fight. "And he's right, Cass. You did break vampire law."

"I don't give a fuck about vampire law," Cassius says, pushing me off him and bringing himself back up to standing while I stay on my knees for a few moments trying to compose myself.

"Neither do I," says Vincent. "But we hardly need the Fraternity coming down here and causing shit for us. They still have some power."

"For now," Cassius says, dusting down his jeans and glaring at me.

"You could have joined us if you were willing to abide by the rules," I tell them.

"Fuck the rules," Cassius spits.

"Leave her the fuck alone," I demand, even though I'm the one on my knees.

"How about this," he starts. "I won't go after her, but if she comes in here again asking for The Bite, she's going to get it, even if she does change her mind at the last second."

I lunge towards him, landing another punch in his pretty angular face before Vincent pulls me away from him.

"We've got the message," Vincent says. "Now get the fuck out of our club and don't come back."

CHAPTER TWENTY-FIVE

rix

HOURS PASS, and the mood on set shifts from a vibe of —
okay, Maverick is the star, so let him do whatever he wants
— to everyone starting to hate on him.

I drift aimlessly between trying to get some rest in my
trailer, attempting to learn lines, obsessing over the nasty
comments I'm getting on socials now that I've taken Juliette's
job and hanging out with Ali at the crafts table. But mostly I
can't stop worrying about Maverick. I know he can hold his
own, but Cass and Vince can hold their own too.

I make myself another coffee, trying out the apple pie
syrup this time. When the sweet caffeine hits my throat, I
immediately catch another buzz, and I'm fairly sure I can
stay upright for at least another few hours.

The crafts table is busy. Everyone is hanging around and
eating more than usual because not much can happen now
until Maverick comes back.

"He's always doing this," complains a guy who works in wardrobe as he grabs another pumpkin muffin. "I'm so sick of his diva bullshit!"

"If it wasn't for us, there would *be* no movie!" complains one technician as she finishes off another key lime bar.

"How long are we supposed to *wait*?" asks a woman from makeup who's on her third coffee.

"As long as it takes," I snap at her.

She looks down her nose at me like now *I'm* the problem.

"Do you have any idea where he went?" Ali asks me.

I shake my head. I hate lying to her, but it's not like I can tell her that he's gone to beat the shit out of a vampire who tried to bite me last night.

And yes, sure, I told Cass no, but I also put myself in an incredibly dangerous situation. If I'd had any idea I'd end up with those bite marks and that Maverick would go down there and all this would happen, I never would have done it.

Maverick going to see Cass is also reckless, and so fucking unnecessary, but the idea of him beating the shit out of Cass for what he did makes my heart leap and my nether regions damp.

Trix! Stop it! Do not go there again with Maverick!

"Who knows?" I'm suddenly unable to stop thinking about Maverick's wet finger making healing circles of saliva over the wounds Cass left on my wrist.

The way his fingertips slid over my skin was so sensual, so—

"Trix?"

"Huh?"

"I said, did you want to eat something? Make your own sandwich, maybe?"

I grab some bread and slap on some condiments, lettuce, tomato slices and gherkins.

"Okay, tell me what's happening with you and Finn," I say,

taking a seat behind the table and changing the subject. I make a waving motion for her to spill.

"Oh, yeah, Finn..." she looks over to where Finn and some of the other actors are standing around drinking coffee and eating the cookies I'm not even sure I remember baking from last night.

"I think that kind of fizzled out," she says.

"Oh, how come?"

"He told me that while he was up for having some fun, he wasn't looking for anything deep because he had feelings for someone else."

"What a dick!"

"Well, at least he was honest, right? I could've slept with him and fallen for him and then found out. That would have been worse."

"Yeah, I guess."

"And then Rebecca called."

I roll my eyes. "Ali, no!" Rebecca was not exactly a dream girlfriend. She cheated on Ali twice, and when she wasn't cheating, Rebecca's eyes were always roaming.

"She's like a drug to me. I don't know how to stop being so addicted!" Ali says.

I take a breath to tell her to get a grip, but it's not like I have any of this figured out.

"Please, just be careful. Look after your own heart."

"Yeah, I know," she tells me. "I just never want to be one of those people who locks their heart away so much they miss out on something really special, you know?"

I blink at her.

"Oh, shit, I didn't mean *you*."

"I didn't think you meant me. But I do now." I chew on my sandwich while Ali figures out how to stop digging this hole.

She shakes her head. "Oh, no! I really don't! It's just that—"

"What?"

"Well, your longest relationship was what? Two months?"

"Six weeks." I say through a bite, and then when I finish, I add, "But I'm not going to settle for just anyone. And you shouldn't either."

"You think I'm settling for Rebecca?"

"She cheated on you. *Twice.* I get that you don't want to miss out on something special, you don't want to hide your heart away, but she's not good for you. She's not good *to* you. You deserve better."

Ali sighs. "You're right. I know. But I just don't know how to let her go."

"Yeah, well, I don't have the answer to that one."

A gherkin slides out of my bread as a rumble of noise moves through the soundstage.

"Mr. Stone is back on set!" Ziva's voice booms out. "Ten minutes!"

"Speaking of—" Ali says.

My eyes flick to her. "What's that supposed to mean?"

"It's pretty obvious."

"What is?"

"You have a crush on Maverick Stone." She wiggles her eyebrows.

"I do not!"

"Don't keep your heart too locked away." I can tell she's giving me a look, but I only have eyes for Maverick as he walks back onto the set looking all bloody and sexy and messed up. I want to run to him and hold him and wipe away the blood and dirt from his face. I want to tell him he's an idiot but thank him for defending me. The idea that he's all banged up because of *me* is way too hot and way too stupid.

"Gotta go," I tell Ali as I rush back onto set to find out what happened.

"What the hell happened to you?" Ziva asks him.

"I had to go and—" he shoots me a dark look. "Deal with something."

"Well, next time can you deal with it after filming and also not in your costume please?" she moans.

"Some things can't wait."

"I actually like it," Brandon says. "By this point in the movie they've already been on the run for over twenty-four hours. He should look like hell."

Maverick raises an eyebrow in Brandon's direction.

"At least lose the jacket," Ziva says.

He slips the jacket from his shoulders and hands it over to a hand that appears.

Damn he looks good for someone who looks like hell.

He rolls his sleeves up to just under his elbows, revealing the bulging muscles of his ripped forearms and I swear I can hear the entire cast and crew gasp.

"Can we get makeup to get some of the blood off his face at least?"

Someone comes over and starts working on him.

"We need you both on top of the train," Ziva says.

I take another look at how high it is. "Shouldn't we use body doubles or something for this?" I ask.

"We will for some shots, but we need close ups of you on top of the train and some of you both jumping off."

"It's very safe," says one of the stunt guys who sets up the crash mats. "Just don't land on your face."

Great.

"You went to see him?" I ask Maverick as we both step around to the back of the train where there's a ladder to help us get up.

"Doesn't matter."

"It does matter. You left all these people here wondering where the hell you were."

"Fine. Yes. I was beating the shit out of Cassius. *For you.* So don't fucking complain to me that I wasn't here."

He climbs the ladder and then looks down at me with a sigh before reaching out a hand to me. "Come on."

I ignore his hand and begin to climb, even though I'd rather do just about anything else than stand on the top of a train with Maverick right now.

"I didn't ask you to," I say. "That's all on you."

"Fine," he says, stepping up onto the train carriage like it's nothing. It probably is nothing to him.

My head pops out over the top of the carriage and then I'm stuck like a deer in headlights. Not just because of all the lights on the set, but because it's *too damn high.*

Maverick tuts at me and then holds out a hand. "Stop being such a baby," he tells me.

My ego loses out over my fear, and I let him pull me onto the top of the carriage.

I hear the clapper and realize they're already filming.

I wobble as I try to get my footing and he's immediately there, hands on my waist, holding me steady.

Those hands on my waist, fuck! Even here in front of all these people, standing on this fucking *train,* this feels so damn good.

"I know you're exhausted but can you please just *try* to stand on your own feet for five minutes?" he complains.

God, he always knows how to ruin a moment!

I give him a shove, and I nearly fall backwards, reaching out to him to stop myself from falling. I grab his shoulders as those big strong hands find my waist again.

"This is good stuff," I hear Brandon say to Ziva.

"Lines!" Ziva calls out.

"We're going to have to jump," he says.

"What? No way! We need what's on this train!" I step out of my faux annoyance at him and into character like a pro.

"We'll have to get it another way, unless you want your head ripped off in the next twenty seconds."

"Look towards where the train is going," Ziva calls out. "You realize how close the tunnel is and that you'll have to jump."

I don't need to realize it, I'm already petrified.

"Okay, now jump," she tells us.

I look down at the crash mats below which are once again *way* too far away.

But I don't have any time to pause, because Maverick hooks his arm around my shoulders and pulls me off the train, sending me plummeting towards the crash mats. I land wrapped safely in his arms.

"I thought you said you'd never let me fall," I say, trying to catch my breath and wiggle out of his embrace.

"I caught you, didn't I?"

He gives me a squeeze, and it feels so good here in his arms. So safe.

"I know I said I'd never let you fall," he whispers into my neck. "But sometimes in life it's unavoidable. But if you ever do have to fall, I'll fall with you, okay?"

CHAPTER TWENTY-SIX

$\mathcal{M}$averick

"FRATERNITY MEETINGS SHOULD BE HELD NO LESS than once per month but may be called at any other time if there are pressing matters to attend to. Fraternity meetings are an opportunity not only to speak on vampire matters but also for the vampire elite to work together in business, industry and the arts to collectively wield more power and influence over humanity. All members of the Fraternity must attend or have a justifiable explanation for their absence. Three missed meetings without explanation results in immediate expulsion from the organization."

The Fraternity of the Everlasting Rose Handbook, page 498

BRANDON HAD ALREADY PLANNED a Fraternity meeting for later this week, but when a third vampire resigns, we know that we can no longer keep this between just me, Brandon and Max and an emergency meeting is called.

So instead of sitting on my back deck at home watching the stars twinkle over the ocean, reminiscing over my night with Trix like I always do when I'm out there, I'm trapped in Max's war room with the remaining 29 members of the Fraternity. The most influential and powerful people — *vampires* in LA.

Christian Stadler places Vivian's resignation letter in the center of the table.

"Someone has Vivian," he says, his jaw tight beneath the dark moustache he sports, a style that was popular in the late eighteen-hundreds when he was made.

Christian and Vivian have been one of Hollywood's power couples since the dawn of Hollywood. He was a producer, and she was his leading lady who he turned after he decided he couldn't live for all eternity without her. They used their influence to amass a huge amount of wealth and started Starlight Studios, the movie studio we're currently filming *Double Agency* in. They aren't hands on these days, instead preferring their life of luxury — cruises, travel. They are famous for having tried the blood of every race and culture in the world.

It's obviously not wonderful that Juliette and Linda are missing, but the fact that Vivian is missing is *very bad.*

"Where is she? What is this?" Christian demands, hitting the table with a fist. "She would *never!*"

"This is a resignation letter, not a ransom note," says Rose Chan, a newer member of the Fraternity and CEO of the biggest streaming service of the moment.

"*That's* not her signature." Christian points aggressively to the bottom of the letter. "And now she's *gone.* And she would *never* leave the house without her purse and wig!"

Unfortunately for Vivian she had been struggling with

hair loss before she was made due to the harshness of 1930s peroxide.

"This isn't the first resignation letter we've received," Brandon says calmly. "Juliette and Linda have also both resigned."

The group gathered around the table erupts in noise.

"Please everyone, stay calm," Brandon says.

"Stay calm?" Screeches Sloan Paxton, an eternally eighteen-year-old brunette who thirty years ago was in Hollywood's Brat Pack. She was in every teen comedy made within a ten-year period. You wouldn't pick it from looking at her, but she's an absolute computer geek and now runs one of the most successful special effects studios in Hollywood.

"How do you expect us to *stay calm* when someone is out there *stealing* vampires?!" she shrieks.

"It's impossible to kidnap a vampire," says Rose.

"Quiet, please!" Brandon's voice booms over the group and quiet descends. "I would ordinarily agree with you, but while Juliette and Linda have both resigned via letter, we also don't know their whereabouts."

"Perhaps we ought to check the signatures on the other letters," Max suggests.

"*You* knew about this?" Sloane glares at Max across the table. "Why are you getting special treatment?"

"May I remind you," says Brandon, "that after Max staked Lottie, by vampire law he became the president of the Fraternity. It is only because he handed the responsibility over to me that I'm your president and not him. I consider him to be second in charge here, I hope the rest of you do as well."

A murmur of vague agreement passes around the table.

Brandon retrieves the other letters from the inside pocket of his suit jacket. "I will have my investigator look into

Vivian's whereabouts, and I will have someone check these signatures."

"So, what do we do now? Just wait to be fucking kidnapped?" Sloan glares at the letters on the table.

"No one is getting kidnapped," I say, finally sick of all this shit. "Maybe they just needed a break."

"Then why are all these letters *exactly* the same?" Sloane demands, shoving them in my direction.

I look at the letters and she's right. Same paper, same typewriter. Even the signatures look similar.

"We will find these women," Brandon assures everyone.

"Of course they're all fucking woman," Rose says with an eye roll. "Why are none of the *men* from the Fraternity going missing?"

"Why weren't we told about this as soon as you got the first letter?" Sloan scowls.

"We didn't want to cause worry in case it was nothing. A prank. Juliette just trying to get attention for her social media," Brandon says.

"Typical," Rose says. "A woman goes missing and your immediate response is to suspect it's attention seeking."

Sloan stares up at me. "So, what? Someone is kidnapping all Maverick's ex-girlfriends?"

A low growl escapes from Christian's throat.

I glare at her. "Linda and I were involved briefly decades ago and nothing at all happened between me and Juliette or Vivian."

"Sure." She rolls her eyes just like an eighteen-year-old even though she's at least sixty years old.

"What's the connection here?" I tap the letters on the table. "Maybe this will help us figure it out. Why Juliette, Linda and Vivian? Why them?"

"Were they in cahoots?" Max asks. "Did they plan this together?"

Christian shakes his head. "Vivian couldn't stand Juliette, and Linda was only an acquaintance."

There's more head shaking and murmuring around the table.

"Juliette was about to start a movie," I say.

Christian rubs a hand over his moustache. "Vivian and I were about to sign a contract to buy out another studio. She never showed up to the meeting. I couldn't sign without her. That deal will fall through if she's not back soon and I *need* this deal to go through!"

The guy seems to care more about his deal than he does about his missing wife.

"What about Linda?" Brandon asks. "Does anyone know what she was working on?"

"She was about to fly out to film a Telenova," says Rose.

Chuckles and scoffs burst out around the table.

Judgmental assholes.

"I considered a Telenova at one point," I say. "There's significant money in it and the way those fans idolize the actors in those shows is quite something."

"Linda does love being idolized," Max says.

"We all love being idolized, but Telenova?" Sloan giggles like she's making fun of someone in the cafeteria.

I choose to ignore her existence like I've tried to do for the last forty years.

"It may be a coincidence, but it looks that they're resigning and then going missing right when they have something big to lose," I say.

"They're not resigning. They are being kidnapped!" Sloan switches from bitchy to angsty in seconds.

I'm so glad I was made at 35 and not at 18.

"We will find out what's going on here," says Brandon. "But it may be best to avoid making big plans or signing any contracts."

"I'm not going to put my life on hold," Rose says. "And I'm certainly not going to give in to this deranged idea that someone out there has the ability to kidnap a vampire. We can look after ourselves."

"Vivian is a vampire, and *strong*," Christian tells her. "If she can get taken, anyone can."

"We don't know that anyone is being kidnaped," Max says.

"If they are being kidnaped, who would be taking them?" Christian asks. "Who would have my precious Vivian?"

"Lottie Luelle," says Sloan, staring at her nails.

Her name ricochets off the walls, and the room goes silent.

"Lottie is dead," says Brandon.

"Yeah? Who saw her body?" Sloan asks.

"I did," says Max. "I put the stake through her heart. I saw the blood turn black. She was dead when we left her in the crypt."

"Sure, sure."

"What? You think Lottie Luelle is some kind of zombie vampire walking around kidnapping members of the Fraternity?" I laugh.

Rose nods. "There is something about it that feels like her. The drama of it all."

Max's eyes shift like he's considering it. "It can't be her."

"An accomplice, perhaps?" Christian suggests. "Was there anyone she was close to before she was killed?"

Max, Brandon and I exchange quick glances.

Brandon clears his throat. "We will find out who's doing this, get our friends back and get retribution. If you have any leads or any concerns, contact me immediately."

The tension is palpable. Nothing like this has ever happened before. Like Rose said, vampires don't just *go missing.*

"Enough of this doom and gloom." I scrape back my chair to stand. "How about I order us some Donnas and some Dons and we eat?" I release my fangs and grin.

Good old Maverick, always ready to get the party started.

The energy in the room instantly changes from worry to excitement. No matter how old a vampire is, no matter how many centuries they've lived, they rarely give up the chance to drink and fuck.

"Please make your way down to the parlor," Max says, opening the door for everyone to exit.

"Get comfortable and we'll have some humans for you to feast on soon," I assure them.

When everyone has left but me, Max and Brandon, I shove the door closed behind me.

"Aiden," Max says as soon as we know no one else will be able to hear us.

"How would Aiden pull something like this off?" I ask. "He was only made a few years ago. He's weaker than all the vampires who've gone missing."

"At first I suspected the werewolves, but there's no way they would be capable of such a thing," says Max.

"Neither would a very young vampire working alone," I say. "Maybe he could get to Juliette somehow, but there's no way he'd be strong enough to take on Linda and Vivian."

"Maverick," Brandon says. "Set up a meeting with the Order. Bring up the fact that Vivian is missing. See if Claudia's heart rate rises, if she knows anything."

I nod. "Will do. But there's no way it's werewolves. They're too messy, too unorganized."

"What about James?" Brandon asks.

Max looks up at him. "James would never be a part of something like this."

Brandon gives him a tight-lipped smile. "I know you think he's your friend, but the fae have never really moved on after all that happened to them at our hands many decades ago, and what was done to James—"

"They just want to move on with their lives now," Max says.

"I'll see what I can find out. From both of them," I say.

We stand there in silence for a few moments, each of us thinking, trying to figure out what the hell is going on.

"Let's not leave our guests waiting," Max says. "I do wish you wouldn't call the Donnas here though, Maverick. Poppy will be furious with me."

"Oh Max," Brandon says with a laugh. "You know you can enjoy more than one human woman at a time. In fact, it's often better that way."

"I only want one," Max says, pulling open the door and gesturing for us to follow him down the landing.

"One of you will have to call Vincent's for the Donnas though. I'm banned from Vincents," I say.

They both stop and turn to look at me.

Brandon raises an eyebrow.

"What did you do?" Max's dark eyebrows knit together in my direction.

"Just the usual shit," I tell him.

"It must have been something extra to get you banned."

I run a hand over the back of my neck. "Cassius bit Trix," I tell them.

"Cassius who?" Max asks, like there are *so* many Cassius' running around.

"Blake?" asks Brandon.

I nod.

"Fucking hell!" Max explodes. "What's she doing messing around with a vampire like Cassius!?"

His response doesn't surprise me. Trix worked for him for nearly a year before she started her own company, and she's also his girlfriend's best friend. He still thinks of Trix as someone who needs his protection.

But she doesn't. She only needs *mine*.

"They didn't hook up," I tell him. "It wasn't like that."

"What was it like?" Brandon asks.

"She went to see him, told him she wanted The Bite."

"Dear god," Max says, wiping a hand over his forehead.

"Then she changed her mind, said no, and he bit her anyway."

Their expressions both darken.

"That's where you went the other day in the middle of filming. To Vincent's."

I say nothing. I don't have to.

"You should have told me. I would have come with you, ripped his fucking eyes out," Brandon says, with disturbing calm.

"That's against vampire law," says Max. "We could have him staked."

"You want me to stake Cassius Blake?" Brandon asks. "It's not that the idea doesn't appeal, but the Blake boys and their minions have been eyeing up the Fraternity for a long time."

"Do you think they have anything to do with the vampires who are going missing?" I ask, the idea suddenly dawning on me. "Like you said, they never got membership with us. Do you think that's what this is about?"

"It's definitely something to consider." Brandon turns to Max. "How is Henrietta doing? Has she found anything?"

"No," says Max. "She keeps saying she's struggling to see anything clearly. She can't get a location on anyone who's missing. But now that we have a few leads, perhaps she'll be able to find something. I'll get her to read on Vivian and the Blake brothers."

"See if she can pick up anything on Aiden too," I tell him.

"Alright," Max says. "But let's keep this between us for now. Poppy doesn't need to know."

"Poppy doesn't need to know what?" Poppy appears from a doorway and gives Max a look like he's not getting any tonight unless he explains himself.

"My love," Max says, jumping up and moving towards her. "It's nothing, just vampire business. I thought I told you to stay in the library?"

"You promised you'd never lie to me," she says, giving him that look that women give their partners when they're in trouble.

"Poppy, I just didn't want you to worry—" he looks over at us. "Excuse me, gentlemen."

Poppy folds her arms and glares at him. He slides a hand down to the small of her back, guides her into the library and then closes the door behind him.

Brandon and I walk down the stairs, but instead of heading towards the party, I pause.

"I think I'm going to sit this one out," I tell him.

"Maverick, it's been months since I've seen you enjoy yourself with a Donna. Are you quite alright?"

"I'm just not in the mood for people," I tell him. "And it's a big day of filming tomorrow."

"Drink from a couple of girls, and you won't need any rest tonight."

I shake my head. "I'm good."

He gives me a concerned look and then puts his hand on my shoulder. "Enjoy your solitude."

As I walk out of the mansion towards my motorcycle, the very clear sounds of Max grunting and Poppy moaning drift down from the library window above me.

"Jesus, they make up quickly," I say to myself.

And then I get on my motorcycle, wishing every time me and Trix got into it we could make up like that.

CHAPTER TWENTY-SEVEN

rix

"YOU'RE TOO SHORT," he says. "Don't move." He squeezes my hip and then disappears, leaving me there bent over his kitchen counter with my ass in the air in anticipation of what's coming.

I bite my lip as I listen to him moving around the kitchen.

"Stand on these," he says, shoving a pile of coffee table books under my feet. He grabs my waist again, and it feels so good, so right.

"Perfect," he says to himself, lining himself up to me.

I brace myself. His cock is huge, and this is going to be a lot, but holy fuck I've never wanted anything more!

He pushes fast and deep inside me, and I let out a scream.

"Fuck, sorry," he pulls back, and his thrusts become shallow.

Too fucking shallow!

"Don't be sorry, and don't you dare stop!" I beg. "I can take it. I want more. Give me all of it."

"God, you're so fucking perfect," he says, his thrusts a little deeper now.

"More," I groan. "Give me more."

"Who knew you were such a dirty girl?" he laughs softly.

"I'm not a girl, I'm a woman!" I shout back at him.

"You dirty woman," he says with a chuckle, finally thrusting deeper now, thank fuck! "But only ever dirty for me. Only mine."

I let out a soft giggle at the fun awkwardness of this dirty talk.

"Tell me I'm right!" he demands.

I'm enjoying his cock inside me and his hands on my hips too much to have a clue what he's talking about, but I go with it. "You're right!" I yell out as his cock slams into me again.

"Tell me, gorgeous," he says, his thrusts getting faster now. Damn, he moves fast! "Tell me I'm the only guy for you."

I raise an eyebrow out at the ocean. Maverick Stone has a monogamy kink? That's unexpected.

"Tell me," he begs, his thrusts becoming even harder and faster, threatening to push me over the edge of this countertop, out this window and down into a sea of pleasure within me.

"I only want you," I say, realizing with sudden deep certainty that it's true. "You're the only guy I ever want to fuck!"

He thrusts into me hard, his hands gripping me tighter. His orgasm is so intense, I can feel it pulsing through my body, like I'm having another orgasm too.

Oh, fuck, I am having another orgasm!

I gasp, gripping the wood of the countertop and pushing back into him while he groans and pushes back into me hard.

After a few moments of much needed recovery, he runs a gentle hand down my back. "You're something else, Trix Delaney," he says.

He pulls out, and I take a moment to catch my breath, pull my panties back up and get my breasts back in my bra.

"Can I give you a ride home?" he asks, like what we've just done is so transactional.

Of course, it's a transaction. Those were the rules, Trix.

I turn around just in time to watch him pulling his shorts up, and I take a second to appreciate his amazing ass before responding.

I guess he didn't want to bite me after all.

"Yeah, sure."

He turns around to face me, and his expression changes. He looks at me just standing there in my mismatched underwear, probably all blotchy and red-faced, hair a mussed-up mess, yesterday's make-up melted and smudged.

But he doesn't look at me like I'm a mess. His eyes flit over my body and then land on my face like I'm the most beautiful thing he's ever seen.

He takes a step towards me and pushes some hair off my face. "Or—"

My heart pounds as I wait for him to finish his sentence. He's taking me home, or—? Or what?

"Or—?" *I prompt.*

"Well, it's just a one-night stand, right?"

"Right," *I nod.*

"But it's not even night yet. So, by my calculations, we have at least another—" *he looks at the silver watch on his wrist, which I'm assuming isn't genuine silver at all, maybe platinum or white gold?* "Eight hours before midnight."

I look up at him and blink. "You want me to stay?"

"Well, I feel like that was just a taster, and I wouldn't mind a full meal, maybe even a dessert." *His eyes twinkle like he has ideas for me.*

"So, you do want to bite me."

"Yeah, I do, but I also really want to fuck you again, Trix. If you're up for it? It seemed like you enjoyed that little taster as much as I did."

He enjoyed it. Maverick Stone enjoyed sex with me! He enjoyed it so much he wants to do it again!

I shrug. "Yeah, it was okay, I guess."

He grins at me, blue-green eyes full of mischief. "Liar. You fucking loved every second of my cock in you."

I'm blotchy already, but the heat moving through my entire body now is going to absolutely make me red all over.

He rests a palm on my cheek. "And if that's how much you loved my cock, imagine how you'll feel about my bite."

MAVERICK STEPS into my trailer and I squeeze out of the way to let his jacked-up form into the small space. He brushes me with his shoulder and even though his body is cooler than mine, the heat that his closeness sends through me makes me hot enough for the both of us.

After last night's dream, which once again felt more like *re-experiencing* than just *dreaming* about it, my desire for him is at an all-time high today.

But I have to be strong! Nothing good will come of fucking this man again!

"What scene are we filming today?" I ask, grabbing my script and taking a seat on the couch.

He just looms over me like some kind of mountain.

"Don't you ever check the app?"

"I told you, I can't get it to work!"

"Give me your damn phone."

"No!"

"Why not?"

"We said no swapping numbers."

"I won't take your number. I'll just look at the fucking app!"

"Fine!" I pass him my phone, and as he runs his thumb and index finger over the screen, I have to try really hard to block out where those fingers have been.

He throws the phone back at me, and I only just catch it.

"Sorry, forgot humans were so bad at catching."

"Fuck you."

God, I wish! I wish I could fuck him and not spend the next two years dreaming about him!

But what's the point? I'm already ruined. He's already destroyed me for all other men. Nothing will ever compare to sex with Maverick Stone. Why even try to fight it?

Thank god he never went down on me, thank god I never sucked his cock, thank all the gods that we never kissed. I'm already a mess. If we'd done all that too, I don't know how I'd cope with life.

"We're filming the kiss today."

My heart leaps into my chest at the idea of his mouth on mine, fucking *finally*.

But no! No no no no no! I can't kiss him! I especially can't kiss him in front of the entire cast and crew, with lights blazing on us, a boom about to knock us on our heads, cameras getting it from every angle. That's just not how I imagined it. And I've imagined it *a lot*.

"Oh."

"I just wanted to give you a heads up. I know this may be — uncomfortable for you." He runs a hand through his hair. "Honestly, it's uncomfortable for me too."

"Right."

I look down at my script, flipping pages to find the scene he's talking about.

"This scene isn't until nearly the end of the movie, so why are we filming it now?"

"Haven't you noticed literally nothing gets filmed in order?"

"We did the meet-cute at the start."

"Apart from that."

We sit in silence for a few moments while I pretend to

read the script, but I'm just staring at the words in big capital letters on the page — THEY KISS.

"If you had just kissed me that night, maybe this wouldn't be so—"

Fucking terrifying.

He glares at me. "May I remind you *once more* that *you* are the one who came up with the no kissing rule?"

Something I regretted ever since, but can't admit to now. But it was a good rule. It's all been hard enough *without* the kissing. Add kissing into the mix of what we've shared, and I will *never* get over this man.

He sits down next to me, filling the space with his muscles and his huge presence.

"Do you want to practice?" he asks gently.

"What?"

"Before we get out there, before the cameras and the lights and—"

"What, like you're just going to kiss me right now?" My heart rate goes off the charts, and my palms become swimming pools. And I know he can tell.

"For practice. So we know how we're going to do it on screen. It's very normal for actors to practice kissing."

I shake my head. There is nothing normal about any of this!

"Is that a no?" he asks. "Because I really think it will be better if we do it for the first time now, not in front of everybody."

I stand up and walk over to the sink. This is all so clinical, so practical. This is *not* how I want to kiss Maverick Stone for the first time. But neither is doing it on set in front of everyone.

I want to kiss him for the first time in his bedroom or on the beach or somewhere where we're alone and in a situation where *he wants to kiss me,* not when he's being told by a director to do it!

"I'm just trying to help you," he says.

"I'm good," I tell him. "I don't need to practice."

"It will be better if we do."

"Let's just run the lines."

"Fine," he says, flipping to his page of the script.

BUT NOW THAT it's actually happening, I wish more than anything that we'd practiced and that this wasn't going to be our first kiss. We had sex three times. His cock has been inside me. He's given me what — six orgasms? Not including the ones I've had on my own thinking about him afterwards, which has been literally hundreds.

So, in theory, *kissing* him should be no big deal.

But now I'm panicking. The lights are too bright and it's too hot. There are too many people standing around watching. The sound boom is *way* too close to my head.

He catches my eye, and I can tell he knows I'm freaking out.

"Give us a minute?" he says, gesturing to Ziva.

She just nods and goes back to talking to Brandon.

Maverick puts a hand on my lower back, sending tingles into my entire body, not helping me *at fucking all.* He guides me through the set of the hotel room to a back window. It all looks so real, and if it wasn't for the entire fourth wall full of lights, cameras and random strangers, I could almost imagine that we were really here. Just us two, in a fancy hotel suite.

The story is that we run in here looking for the disk, but the bad guys are too fast for us. Maverick is about to swing through and out of a twenty-story window to get to them. But first, just in case he dies, he has to kiss me first.

This is seriously the worst plot that exists.

"You okay?" he asks.

"Yes," I lie.

"Can we get some water?" he calls out, and instantly a bottle appears in his hand. He opens it and passes it to me.

I take a gulp, but it doesn't really help.

"I'll be gentle," he says. "No fangs." He lets out a laugh like he's trying to make a joke and put me at ease, but it doesn't work.

"Just follow my lead," he says. "I've got you, Trix. Trust me?"

I nod, and he guides me back to our starting positions.

"Makeup! She's too shiny!" Ziva calls out.

Someone arrives and pats my face with a cloth. Someone else touches up my lipstick and then blots it, I guess so it doesn't end up all over Maverick's face.

Oh god, this is happening!

"Can we get rid of anyone who's not essential?" Maverick asks.

About twenty people disappear, but there are still around fifty other people here, holding cameras, sound gear, lights, clipboards.

Ziva calls out "Action" and then we run our lines.

"We've survived so much," Maverick says. "Chances are fifty-fifty I'll survive the fall, but I need to take the risk to save us all. That information in the wrong hands—"

I place a finger on his lip, like the script tells me to. "I know," I say.

He moves my hand away. "If I don't make it, I want you to know—"

I look up at him, batting my eyelashes how we practiced with Ziva earlier. "Know what?"

"There's no one else I would rather have done all this with."

"And then you kiss!" calls out Ziva.

Maverick steps towards me and takes my face in both his hands, cupping my cheeks and angling my face up towards his. His hands are firm and strong, and just like they always do whenever they are on me, they make me feel both completely *safe and totally out of control*. His eyes tell me the same thing: *you're safe with me, Trix.*

His gaze falls to my lips and then suddenly, his lips are on mine for the first time.

My eyes flutter closed as he moves one hand to the back of my head, bringing my face even closer to his and taking total control of the kiss.

And I forget.

I forget everything.

I forget that fifty people are watching us. Right now, it feels like we're the only two people in the world. His lips on mine, his tongue finding its way over my bottom lip and pushing into my mouth, exploring me deeper, kissing me harder. He kisses like he fucks — hard and dirty — and I can feel my whole body relaxing into him, turning me into floppy, messy goo that one of the janitors will have to clean up later.

Holy fuck, if this is what kissing him is like, why weren't we doing this the whole time?!

I'm vaguely aware of a voice in the background, but I ignore it as Maverick moves a hand down to my waist, pulling my body closer into his. A small groan escapes into his mouth as my breasts press against his black suit jacket and into his hard chest.

His other hand moves to the back of my neck, and he has complete control of my body like this. Then he starts stepping back towards the bed.

Wait, was this in the script?

He throws me down onto the bed, landing on top of me,

his strong hard body crushing me in the most delicious and perfect way. My traitorous legs wrap around his waist all by themselves, and I push myself into him.

I would fuck him right here. I don't even care if fifty people are watching. Maybe it's not just a fantasy! Maybe I'd actually really like it!

I let out a moan, and he grunts a little as he pushes his erection into me. Damn his black pants, damn my fucking jeans!

"Cut!" This time I hear her, but Maverick doesn't immediately stop. He keeps kissing me, holding me down on the bed, and I don't have the will to stop kissing him back.

"I said cut!" Ziva shouts.

Maverick finally releases his mouth from mine, and then he grins down at me.

Laughter and applause erupt all around us, and reality hits. We're not two star-crossed lovers, one of us about to throw themselves out of a window to save humanity or whatever, we're just two actors playing a scene.

None of this is real, I try to remind myself. *This is just acting.*

"Perfect," Ziva says, staring into the monitor. "We'll need to edit out the dry humping, that went a bit far for a thirteen, but the chemistry of that kiss was off the charts!"

"You want to get another just to make sure?" Maverick asks.

Oh god, please can we do it again?!

Ziva shakes her head. "The first kiss is always the best. The chemistry wears off after a few takes."

But it's been nineteen months, and our chemistry is still hot as fuck.

It's only then that I realize I'm still lying on the bed with Maverick grinning down at me. He gets up off the bed and then offers me a hand.

I ignore it, and with quite a bit of difficultly, eventually get myself up to standing.

I look over at him, hoping to catch his eye, to see if he's just as unsettled by this as I am. To see if his previous offer still stands. To shoot him a look that says, "Meet you in your trailer in five?"

But he's not even looking my way. He's just smiling at a very attractive woman from wardrobe who's fixing up his shirt sleeves.

CHAPTER TWENTY-EIGHT

$\mathcal{M}$averick

"THE ORDER of Concordia was originally founded in 1589 in England as a council of elders from the supernatural clans of vampire, werewolf, witch and fae. The following two hundred years were a dark time in history for supernatural beings who were being discovered, hunted and killed in great numbers. The Order of Concordia enabled supernatural clans both to work together to escape persecution and to bring down retribution on those who were responsible for the killing of our kind. Once the great threats to supernatural beings had been eradicated from the earth, the Order of Concordia no longer needed to exist in the way it once had. By the early 1980s, the Order of Concordia had devolved into an organization that was only concerned with the rights of were-wolves. After attempted werewolf attacks on vampire-kind in the 2020s, the Order of Concordia was newly reinstated as the New Order of Concordia to bring harmony to the clans once more. As there are still many supernaturals who do not believe in equal *rights for all supernatural beings, the New Order of Concordia works in secret to protect the rights, life and legacy of all supernatural beings."*

The New Order of Concordia Codex page 2

THE ORDER MEETS SOMEWHERE different each month. We each take turns choosing the location, swapping our home advantage. The Order re-formed just eighteen months ago. The morning before my first time with Trix.

My first time, like there's going to be more times. God, I hope there are more times!

The werewolves had briefly taken over the Order, an ancient council of supernaturals originally created for mutual protection and collaboration centuries ago. The weres had twisted it into their own anti-vampire hate club, but the tables have turned once more and now we're attempting this collaboration thing again.

As I walk into the dive bar Claudia, our werewolf councilor has chosen for this evening I feel ill at ease. I can smell *wolf* all over this place and I don't like it. If something happened, if it turned out Claudia was still working against us, I'd have a hell of a time getting out of here.

She smiles at me as I walk into the back room, her deep tan skin glowing, curtains of silky straight black hair sleek around her face. She waves me over to a table shoved in the back under shelves of Jim Beam and ketchup. Henrietta gives me a wave and James gives me that stern, fae look that they are all known for. His grey eyes have never crinkled with a smile in my presence. I'm not sure the guy is even capable of it.

James previously worked as a butler for Max, but he's working for some tech company now, making a mint by the look of his new Rolex and well-fitting suit. The fae have always been good with money, gold, precious gemstones, any aspect of the material realm. Vampires get rich too of course, mostly through influence, glamouring and long-term investments, but the fae have this kind of golden touch which makes them excellent entrepreneurs or business execs. Their deals go through like magic.

Witches tend to be more middle-class. They have magical ethics, oaths, balances and harmonies of energy they work with that keeps most of them well-off but rarely insanely rich like us vampires and faes. Henrietta has more money than most witches due to her job working as Max's assistant. I have no idea what she spends her income on but judging by the cut of her sleek black dress and the simple but expensive looking silver jewelry she wears, it might go on some of that. It definitely doesn't go on hair products. The woman's red hair curls out in all directions at total odds with the sleek style of her outfit and expressionless look on her face.

The weres, on the other hand find jobs, money and success more difficult than the rest of us. From a distance Claudia looks well dressed, but as soon as you get close you can see the wear on her striped sweater.

I grab a bottle of Jim Beam from the shelf and a water-stained glass from a nearby tray and pour myself a drink.

"Anyone else?"

Henrietta gives a nod, but the others two shake their heads.

I find another glass for Henrietta and pour.

"You're going to have to pay for that," says Claudia, not realizing that thirty bucks out of the millions I make every year doesn't mean much to me.

"Fine," I say, grabbing a hundred from my wallet and throwing it on the table.

James looks at me like I've just committed treason against

the fae king or something. "Could you be any more obtuse?" he frowns.

Claudia's face heats but she grabs the hundred and shoves it into her purse. "It's fine."

That money is so definitely not going to be used to replace this bottle of whiskey.

"Shall we begin?" James asks, showing off his Rolex as he looks at the time. That's another thing about the fae, not only are they good with money, they want *everyone* to know it.

I glance at my own watch, a white gold Patek Philippe that I suspect cost a lot more than his Rolex.

His eyes flash to my wrist and I can tell by the horror in his eyes that I am correct. My watch is worth more than his!

Henrietta glares at us both. "Can we quit with the pissing match?" she says, not missing a beat.

Claudia's lips press together and I realize, I *am* fucking obtuse. Flashing my hundred thousand dollar watch in her face while she's worried about the cost of a bottle of whiskey.

Trix is right about me. I am an ass. Jesus, what does she even see in me?

That kiss has been on my mind all fucking day. The way she melted in my arms, the way she wrapped her legs around me on the bed.

"Maverick?" James asks. "You said in the chat you had something important to discuss, would you like to start?"

"A couple vampires have gone missing," I say, taking a swig of whiskey with my non-watch hand.

I have no plans to give them details, but this should get some pulses raised if they know anything.

"Who?" James asks with a frown.

"Can't share that information," I say.

James looks truly disturbed by this news, and he should be. If vampires are going missing and the fae *isn't* involved, there's no reason to think they're not in danger also.

I stare at him, trying to suss him out as I rub a hand over my chin.

"You think we have something to do with it?" he asks, his grey eyes going cold as steel.

I shrug. "You tell me. Is this fae retribution for what happened—"

"We have no interest in retribution. We all just want to move on."

"That's what you always say, but if it was the other way around, I doubt vampires would be so forgiving."

"I suppose our kind is just better than your kind," he says with a sarcastic smile.

My eyes move to Claudia. Her pulse is raised, but no more than it was when I entered the room. She's nervous around me.

I narrow my eyes at her. "Know anything about it?"

She shakes her head. "Why would I?"

"Because you have, in the very recent past, tried to kill my kind?"

"Maverick," James warns.

"Take a breath, Maverick," Henrietta says. "We're working together here now."

"Are we?" My eyes flash back to Claudia. Her pulse is faster now, but it may just be because I'm staring at her like I might rip her throat out at any second.

"Perhaps if you give us some more information," James says.

I let out a sigh. None of them are giving anything away. This seems to be the first any of them are hearing about this.

"I'm not at liberty to say more," I say. "Just that three vampires are missing."

"Missing as in—" Claudia starts.

"Disappeared, taken, kidnapped, lost, in rehab, ignoring our calls, we're not entirely sure."

"It would be very difficult to kidnap a vampire," James says. "Almost impossible, unless—"

"Unless what?" I demand.

"Silver bullets," he suggests. "Enough of them have been known to slow a vampire down enough to—"

"I know what they can do," I tell him. "But at each of the locations they went missing from there were no signs of any kind of struggle."

"You've been very quiet," Claudia says, her eyes landing on Henrietta. "Aren't your special senses picking anything up?"

"I'm just getting a blank at the moment I'm afraid. I can try to pull some cards later. I don't want to do it here in the bar. I can text the group chat with anything I discover."

James rolls his eyes. "Great. Tarot readings in the group chat now, can you do my horoscopes for me too?"

"Knock it off, James," I tell him. "You know Henrietta is good at what she does. If she hadn't saved our asses from the werewolves that time, you'd still be doing dishes at Max's mansion."

That shuts him up.

"If everyone could just keep an ear to the ground and text me if you hear anything that could even be slightly related to this situation, it would be appreciated."

"Of course," says Claudia.

James nods.

And of course, Henrietta is already on the case.

"I hope I don't need to remind you all that if it turns out any of your people are involved in this, it could be *very* bad for you."

"We get it, Maverick," says James. "Trust me, we know the consequences."

"I for one would not be willing to risk the deaths of my people over a couple of vampires," Claudia says, her voice oozing with judgement. I believe her though. What reason would she or the wolves have to kidnap vampires? Max is already pumping his own money into their community.

I wouldn't give them a cent, personally. I've only seen one vampire ripped apart by wolves, but one was enough.

"Right, any other business?" I ask.

These meetings are usually pointless. None of us really trust each other enough to share what's happening in their communities, but these meetings are an important reminder that we'll all be stronger and safer if we work together instead of against each other.

"I have a job opportunity," James begins. "We could use some wolves for a couple of weeks."

The other thing about the fae is that they also run the mafia and a bunch of other criminal organizations.

"What's the pay?" asks Claudia.

I finish my drink and reach for the bottle. Alcohol has such little effect on me, but it's better than pretending to pay attention to the rest of this boring meeting about mafia jobs and why werewolves don't get paid as much as humans.

"I'm worried," Claudia says. "Last time we did a job for you one of my boys didn't come back."

"It's dangerous, that's why the pay is so high," James tells her.

"That's exactly why we should get paid *more*," she says.

"Can't you just ask Max for more money?" Henrietta asks.

Claudia looks down at the table and her expression says it all.

Getting Max to help them the first time was in exchange for his life. To ask him for anything more would just be pure humiliation.

"Claudia," Henrietta says. "If you like, I can do a protection spell later tonight for the wolves doing the job."

She nods. "Thank you, Etta."

Etta? When did these two become so tight?

"Want me to do a spell for the fae involved, too?" Henrietta offers.

James shakes his head. "We have our own magic." He doesn't need to add that fae magic is better than witch magic, the tone of his voice says it all.

When the meeting is finally over, I make my way back through the den of wolves and onto my motorcycle, speeding through the city back to my Malibu home.

When I'm on the back of my motorcycle, my thoughts clear. And when they do, the only thing that remains is the feeling of Trix's arms around me as she straddles my back and my motorcycle, and the ghost of her warm, sweet lips on mine.

CHAPTER TWENTY-NINE

WE GET two days off for Thanksgiving, but instead of enjoying my first day off in what feels like forever and finally catching up on some much needed sleep, I spend the day cooking for my extended family, enjoying a meal with them and then video calling Fern, my biological cousin in London who doesn't even celebrate Thanksgiving but wanted to use the opportunity to tell me how grateful she is that we found each other.

I only found out about Fern a few months ago. I've always wanted to know more about who I am and when I saw an offer for a DNA test come up on my social media, I immediately hit the purchase button.

I was kind of hoping my DNA would be a bit more exotic, but it turned out to be mostly British. But finding Fern was such a blessing. We haven't met in person yet and we're both so busy. She runs a pub in London's West End, and I have Trix and Treats *and* my new acting job.

"We'll get it sorted," she tells me in her chic London accent. She pushes her short purple hair behind her ear. "I've got to go love, a gang of football hooligans just walked into the pub!"

"Any of them cute?" I ask with a grin. Fern is single and very much looking.

She turns to them, makes a face and then looks back at me. "There's one I might shag later if he's up for it."

"Good luck!" I tell her with a laugh.

"You too, hun! Enjoy the party!"

I get off the call and throw my phone on the bed that I wish I could just curl up in for the rest of the night. But I can't miss Brandon's Thanksgiving party.

I've been informed by my new assistant Louise, a twenty-something intern who constantly runs after me like I'm a toddler about to fall over and hit my head, that this is an exclusive party that only the biggest names and most important people in the industry are attending. I've also been told I should dress for the occasion.

It's my first Hollywood party and I should feel excited, but as I go through my wardrobe to find something to wear, I suddenly start to feel dizzy, like I can't keep myself upright. I grab onto the side of the closet and take a moment to steady myself. After a few deep breaths I think I'm okay, just tired.

It's no surprise. I don't even remember the last time I had more than a few hours of sleep. But tomorrow I'm going to sleep all day, bake all evening and then get another full night's sleep.

Once the wooziness or whatever it is passes, I go back to rummaging in my wardrobe again and I wonder how late this thing will go. Perhaps I can just make an appearance and then disappear.

I look at my dress options. A teal 1950s style dress that I only realize now is exactly what Maverick described when he told me about his housewife fantasy.

For a moment I consider wearing it.

Maverick has been distant this last week. Ever since the kiss scene he's kept me at arm's length. No flirting, no innuendo, no acting like a hero to save me from Cassius or runaway trains.

I keep trying to remind myself that we were *acting*. But I wasn't acting.

And the way he kissed me, god. It didn't feel like acting. Not a single second of it.

I came up with the kissing rule for a reason. I knew if I kissed him, I'd fall for him, but the truth is that I fell for him the second he caught my eye in the diner and asked me to come back to his place.

I put the dress back. I'm not Maverick Stone's fantasy. I'm just a co-worker he'd happily fuck for something to do to kill time.

And god, what if he's there with some other woman? The last thing I need is to humiliate myself by showing up in *that* like a neon sign above my head saying *I still want him*!

In the end I decide on a glittery gold knee-length dress. It's still shiny and fun but has a more refined feeling than some of my other clothes.

I tousle out my loose, freshly dyed green curls, finish my make-up by adding a little gold eyeshadow to my lids and add some gold unicorn earrings to my look.

I take a selfie and upload it to socials with the caption: "Happy Thanksgiving! I'm giving thanks for this incredible opportunity to work on this movie with so many amazing artists and creatives! What are you grateful for?"

The negative comments immediately start coming in. Someone says that my dress *so* doesn't go with my green hair and I almost consider getting changed because of it, but fuck those people! And then I get a notification that my ride is here, and I don't have time to change, anyway.

I worked at Max Montrose's mansion for nearly a year, and I never got used to the opulence of it, but Brandon Curtis' mansion is twice the size. I feel like an ant walking into an Ancient Greek temple as I wander up the front door, twinkle lights along the path guiding my way.

A burly guy in a suit stands at the door with a tablet. "Name?" he asks me.

"Trix Delaney."

He checks his list, nods and lets me through. A woman at the door takes my leopard print wrap and I immediately regret giving it away. It's not exactly warm in here. I guess vampires don't feel the cold, so why would they need to turn up the heat?

The place is ridiculous. In the entryway a crystal and gold chandelier looms above me, and then I step into some kind of parlor where the party is in full swing.

The whole place is a feast for the senses, lavish and ostentatious in every way. It's light and bright — everything is white, gold and marble, from the paint on the walls to the carpets, and even the furniture looks like it's been embossed with gold leaf. It probably has. I'm struck by the huge oil painting of Brandon that sits over the mantel and looks at least a hundred years old. I don't even know how old Brandon is, but I get the feeling he's been around for a while.

My nerves kick in now as I look around and see some very recognizable faces from movies I've loved. Some who definitely look like they haven't aged a day since their movies were made.

I look around for Poppy but can't see her anywhere. I

send her a quick text telling her I'm here and I need her as my emotional support person since I can't find anyone I know.

I gravitate towards the bar, and my stomach lurches when I see who's serving.

Ben.

The guy I dated for those six weeks in an attempt to get my mind off Maverick. We met when I catered my first Hollywood event as Trix and Treats. He was one of the servers the agency I hired sent over. He had been trying to make it in Hollywood for nearly a decade, and I was drawn to his drive and determination. He would audition all day and work jobs like this at night. We hardly saw each other in those six weeks because we were both so busy, but we texted a lot and for about five seconds I almost considered something serious with him. But I still couldn't stop thinking about Maverick and so as soon as I had that thought, I knew I needed to end it.

Usually, I'd avoid an ex like the plague, but he's the one with the alcohol.

"Trix?" he asks, giving me an uncomfortable grin. He's still cute with his messy red hair and pale blue eyes. He also looks kind of good in his tux.

"Hey," I say.

"Turkey tail or pumpkin pie?" he asks me.

I'm grateful that he's just gone straight in with the options. "What's in the pumpkin pie?"

"Cinnamon schnapps, coconut cream and a dash of nutmeg."

"Sounds great, I'll take one."

He busies himself with ingredients, and as he does, I see a stack of business cards on the bar for Cate's Catering.

Fucking Cate's Catering!

Rejection washes over me as I realize Brandon hired

Cate's Catering for this party instead of me. I could have come up with an incredible menu for this!

I'm still fuming when Ben hands me my drink. I give him a grimace and take a sip. It's nice, but I refuse to enjoy it now that I know Cate's Catering is behind the recipe.

I wander over to the ornate marble mantle and try to look casual, like I'm not here on my own, like I'm important and know people, but the truth is — I'm not and I don't. The only person I know is the guy working the bar. Oh well, at least everyone is so into their own conversations they won't notice the shiny wallflower in the corner.

I drain my drink, and the alcohol hits me fast. I take my glass back to the bar and order another. Ben raises an eyebrow.

"I don't need your judgement," I tell him.

"You know," he says, grabbing a fresh glass, "I saw that article Hollywood Daily did on you."

"You did?"

"You're a walking Hollywood dream."

"Yeah. I guess."

"And you kind of owe me, right?"

"What?"

"Well, you did break up with me in a pretty shitty way."

"If I waited to do it in person it could have been weeks with our schedules."

"Yeah, but you could have called instead of texted."

I grab the drink he's just poured me. "But we always texted."

"It's fine. I'm over it." He gives me a bright smile. Too bright. "Could you help a guy out? Get me an audition with Brandon Curtis?"

I wonder if this is what it's always going to be like now.

People who knew me briefly just wanting to use me for their own agendas.

"Sorry, I don't have that kind of power with him."

I probably could ask Brandon for a favor, but there's nothing about Ben that makes me want to do him a favor. This whole exchange feels so off.

"I'll give you my card, so you can pass it on."

He passes me a card that I don't even look at but politely put in my purse.

"What happened to Juliette, anyway?" he asks. "Rehab or something, wasn't it?"

I shrug. I've been so busy trying to bake and act and not throw myself on Maverick Stone that I haven't thought much about Juliette. No one has mentioned her on the set for weeks. Everyone just kind of got on with making the movie, and it's almost like she really did just disappear. I guess that's what happens in this industry. You get one shot, and if you blow it, that's it.

I take a sip of my second drink, and this one is even stronger.

"Trix!" Poppy grins at me as she glides towards me in a red satin dress. Her reddish-brown hair is up in a French twist, and she looks stunning!

"Thank god you're here!" I wrap my arms around her and squeeze her in a tight hug.

Between the sweet burn of the alcohol and Poppy's presence, I suddenly feel okay again.

"It's so good to see you!" she says into my hair.

"You look beautiful!" I tell her.

I pull back and take in the gorgeous, very expensive dress she's wearing. Max is looking at her in a way that suggests he is already thinking about getting her home and ripping it off her.

"You look—" she frowns at me. "A little tired."

I roll my eyes. "Great, thanks."

"Trix, lovely to see you." Max holds out his hand, finally tearing his eyes off his girlfriend, and I give it a quick shake before pulling him in for a hug too.

"Hey Max."

"I must do the rounds. Are you two alright here for a few moments?"

"Fine," Poppy says, waving him away. "Enjoy the party."

She turns back to me once he's gone. "I didn't mean anything by it. You just don't seem quite like your usual perky self."

"I've just been busy."

"You're doing a lot, Trix."

"Everyone is doing a lot," I shrug.

"Not as much as you," she says. "If you need help, money, investment, anything, just let us know."

I smile at her, all teeth. "It's all good."

A tray of hors d'oeuvres moves past us, and it looks terrible. Nothing edible on that entire plate.

Poppy smiles at the waiter and is about to take something when she sees my face. "Oh, no thanks," she tells them.

"I could have catered this better. Why didn't Brandon ask me?"

"Because you're the star of his *movie*? And movie stars don't cater parties. They attend them."

She orders a turkey tail from Ben, and I order another pumpkin pie.

I suddenly feel dizzy again and grab onto the bar to steady myself.

"How many of those have you had?" Poppy asks. "You know I'm usually all for getting drunk and disorderly, but you might want to stick to just a couple of drinks tonight."

"I don't need a lecture," I tell her.

"Sorry, I just—" Poppy's mouth drops open and I follow her gaze to see what she's staring at.

And there he is. Maverick Stone, looking like the sexiest man of the decade (which Hollywood Daily voted him as last year) dressed in a dark blue suit that fits his broad shoulders in that perfect way—

Jesus, fuck!

Every eye is on him, including the eyes of the beautiful dark-haired woman who's on his arm.

We've been over all this. We're not together, we never were and never will be. He's been with other women since he's been with me. I saw him with that Donna, and so this shouldn't be a total shock to me. This shouldn't feel like some kind of ultimate betrayal.

But it is, and it does.

I try to remind myself I have no claim over Maverick. I had sex with him three times nineteen months ago. We agreed it was a one time thing. Now we're co-workers. He offered sex up a couple of times, and I shut him down each time.

The woman he's with is dressed in a black satin dress that hangs from her skinny yet filled out in all the right places body like a glove, showing off her every perfect curve. Her long, dark, curly hair bounces around her shoulders like she just had a blowout. She probably has. Why didn't I think of going for a blowout? Oh yeah, because when the fuck would I have time to get a blowout?!

"Trix? You okay?" asks Poppy.

Maverick catches my eye and then looks away, gently guiding the woman towards Max, where he introduces her to him.

"Who the fuck is *she*?" I ask, but I do not want an answer. I don't want to know. I just want to get out of here.

"Trix?" Poppy asks. "What's going on?"

"I can't be here."

"Okay, let's go out the back for some air or something."

"I don't want air. I just want to go home." I scramble in my purse to find my phone to book a ride.

"Are you sure? There are so many people here you should meet."

"I honestly don't give a fuck," I tell her.

"Trix, please tell me what's going on with you. I'm supposed to be your best friend. Let me help."

"My best friend? I've hardly seen you since you hooked up with Max and started school."

"That's not fair. You've been busy too!"

I know it's not fair. Poppy has been busy with her new life, but I've also been busy with mine.

"Whatever," I say.

I order the ride, still holding onto the bar with one hand because why the fuck do I feel so damn drunk after just two and a half drinks?

I let go of the bar and walk through the crowd, past movie stars I've idolized and people who could make or break my Hollywood career in an instant, but I don't care about any of them. I just need to not be here. I just need to get on the other side of these doors, outside into the cool night air and as far away from Maverick Stone as I can possibly get.

But I don't even make it to the door.

Suddenly, the drink I don't even remember I'm still holding smashes on the floor, and shards of glass and sticky alcohol hit my bare legs, which give way as I fall.

CHAPTER THIRTY

*M*averick

I'M THERE QUICKER than any mortal man could be, and I hope that the few guests here who are human will be drunk enough not to notice. I can always glamour them later. Right now, I just need to get to Trix.

"Trix!" I slide down onto the floor next to her. "Fuck!"

"Call an ambulance," Brandon's voice booms.

A sudden frenzy of people rush around, gasping and screaming and making calls.

If it wasn't for my audience, I could bite my own wrist, force some of my blood down her throat to heal her from whatever has caused her to collapse like this. But I can't. Not here in front of all these people. And it's killing me.

Not only would it be insane to do that in front of humans, but it's against vampire law for vampires to let humans drink from us under any circumstances.

Of course, that doesn't mean it doesn't happen. It absolutely happens. But it's not *supposed* to happen, and as head vampire councilor of the Order, I definitely shouldn't be breaking any vampire codes of ethics, but something is wrong with Trix, and I'd break any law to save her. Her heart rate is low, way too low, and I would absolutely give up my role, even my standing with the Fraternity to make sure she's okay.

"Trix!" Poppy runs to her side and then glares at me. "What did you do?"

"Nothing! She just fell!"

"How did she fall? What did you do to her?"

"How could I do anything to her from over there?" I point to where my date Marianna is standing, looking bored by all this.

"Trix!" Poppy shouts again, giving her arm a shake.

"Everyone move away, give her space," Brandon says. "Maverick and Poppy, you stay with her. Everyone else, I invite you to please enjoy some appetizers and champagne in the ballroom."

He must put some influence into his words because everyone starts mumbling about snacks and drinks and begins to walk away from us.

I don't even realize I'm holding Trix's limp hand until I find myself starting to squeeze it.

No handholding.

Well, fuck that rule right now! It doesn't count!

"What's wrong with her?" Tears fall down Poppy's cheeks and onto Trix's gold dress.

Max appears at Poppy's side. "She'll be okay," he says. "One of us will heal her if we need to. There's nothing to worry about."

She looks up at him and blinks. "Promise?"

"Of course, my love," he says, and I can't help but feel jealous as hell at what they have.

I bring Trix's hand to my lips and I whisper to her, "Baby, you're okay."

A siren screams in the distance, and I know the ambulance is coming, but I don't want to wait.

I start to lift her, but Poppy screams at me to stop.

"Don't move her," Poppy pleads. "You're not meant to move her!"

"I could heal her in a second if you'd all just fucking let me!"

"Maverick, calm down," Brandon says. "There are eighty humans in the next room and the same number again of vampires who are more than willing to uphold vampire law."

"Fuck vampire law!" I growl.

"It looks like a simple case of exhaustion," Brandon says. "You know how common it is in this industry. She'll be fine."

"You!" Poppy stands up and gets in Brandon's face. "This is all your fault! She's been working so hard, sleeping two hours every night so she can feed your crew *and* star in your movie!"

"I told her I'd find another caterer," Brandon says. "But she's stubborn."

"What the fuck, Poppy!" I shout. "She's been sleeping two hours? Why didn't you tell us?"

Poppy starts crying, fucking hell.

"You already *knew*! You knew she was trying to do it all, and you did nothing!"

"We'll find a solution," Brandon says.

"Yeah, well, you better!"

Poppy keeps busting Brandon's balls while Max tries to calm her down, and I just sit there holding onto Trix's hand because I can't fucking *do* anything!

I rub my thumb over her cheek, which I've never seen so pale.

"Trix, sweetheart, come on," I murmur to her. "Open your eyes for me, baby. Don't you dare fucking leave me."

Her eyes flicker open for a second.

Thank fucking Christ!

"Don't call me baby," she croaks, before they close again.

I'm still calling her name like a madman when the paramedics arrive and push us all out of the way.

"How much has she had to drink? Has she taken any drugs this evening?" one of them asks.

"She only had two drinks, and Trix doesn't do drugs," says Poppy, stepping in and taking over. "We think it may be exhaustion. She's been working two jobs, not sleeping much."

"How long has this been going on?" asks another as they get her onto a stretcher.

"A month," Poppy says. "Maybe longer."

"We'll need to take her in, give her an IV, run some tests."

"Is she going to be okay?" Poppy asks, lip trembling.

The paramedic nods. "Most likely."

They can't give a guarantee. But I can give her one.

"Who's going with her?" one of the paramedics asks.

"I am," I say.

"No, I am!" Poppy says. "She's my best friend!"

"Yeah? Well, she's my—"

Poppy glares at me like I better say something that trumps *best friend*.

"I'm going," I say. "It's final."

She looks at me like she suddenly gets it. She gets that whatever is between me and Trix *does* trump best friend.

"Fine, you go, but me and Max will be right behind you."

I SIT in the back of the ambulance watching Trix's eyes flutter open and then close again. I keep telling her that everything is going to be okay. And it will be, if I can just get two seconds alone with her to give her some of my blood.

"Where am I?" she asks groggily, weakly tugging at the oxygen mask they've put on her.

"Just keep this on for now," the paramedic tells her, placing the mask back on. "You're in an ambulance, Trix. You collapsed at a party, but you're going to be okay."

Her head flops back down, her eyes close again, and I cling onto her with dear life.

When we arrive at the hospital, I try to go with her, but I'm stopped by a nurse. "Sorry, sir. Immediate family only." Recognition crosses her face as she realizes who I am. "You know this girl?"

"Woman," I tell her. "And yes. She's the co-star on the movie I'm filming. She's also my—"

I could just glamour her. I don't need to lie. But tonight, I desperately want to play this part.

"—girlfriend."

"If she was your fiancée, we might let you but—"

"I was going to ask her tonight," I say with a sad smile.

She looks at me skeptically.

"Another few hours and she would have been my fiancée." I run a hand over the eternal shadow on my jaw.

She's still looking at me like I'm some kind of creep who gets off by sitting at the bedsides of beautiful women in hospital rooms.

Fuck this.

I look into her eyes, and she quickly falls into my gaze and under my control.

"I'm her fiancée and I'm going in with her."

Glamouring is kind of old school. Most modern vampires who have some morals prefer not to use it unless absolutely necessary. I generally use it a little more than I should, but I definitely consider this necessary!

"Of course, sir!" she says, getting out of my way and letting me through.

I stand in the corner and watch as they put Trix into a bed and hook her up with IVs and whatever the hell they're doing. I never worked on a medical drama, I have no idea what's going on here.

A nurse comes in to take some blood, but even though I see the thick red liquid moving up the tube and haven't fed in a while, I have no desire to drink it, I only want to *give* my blood to her so she can be completely healed again.

Her eyes flick open, and she looks around at the room.

"You're in the hospital. Can you tell me your name?" asks a doctor.

"Trix," she mumbles.

"Is that short for something?"

"Beatrix. Delaney."

"Okay, Trix. It looks like you've been under a lot of pressure lately. We think you collapsed from exhaustion. We're going to do some tests just to make sure it's nothing else. We'll give you a few things that will make you feel better for now, but mostly you just need some good rest."

"I can't rest," she says, trying to lift her head off the pillow. "I have too much to—"

"It's not a choice, I'm afraid," the doctor says. "You'll need at least two weeks off work. Maybe longer."

"Two weeks? I can't! No!" A tear falls from her eye, and I rush to her side, gripping her hand again.

"It's okay, Trix. You just need to get better."

"Oh, fuck!" She wipes a tear away and sighs.

"We'll give you some time with your fiancée and then we'll keep you here overnight for observation. You should be able to go in the morning as long as we're happy with your test results."

As soon as they leave, she glares at me. It has a little less energy in it than usual, and it makes me ache. How I yearn for that fire she sends me with just a look, those daggers she throws at me with her warm eyes, those harsh words that I know she never really means.

"Fiancée! What the—?"

"Trix, don't work yourself up. I just said that so I could come in with you."

"And now it will be all over the internet!"

"So, what? Who cares?"

"I care! My followers already fucking hate me!"

I swipe away her tear with my fingers, and then even though I'm desperate to kiss that mouth, I place a kiss on her forehead.

"Don't worry about the haters on the internet. What are they doing with their lives? Fucking nothing. You're better than all of them."

Another tear falls, and I catch it with my thumb, wiping it away.

"Two fucking weeks? Fuck!" She bangs her head against the pillow.

"You won't need two weeks."

"What? Why not?"

"I'm going to give you some of my blood. It will heal you. You'll be fitter and stronger than you've ever been in your life in just a few minutes."

She looks up at me, confused, tired, a shell of the girl... *woman* I've grown to care so much for.

"But I might have to sneak you out of here first."

CHAPTER THIRTY-ONE

rix

I TRY to make sense of what's just happened, but I'm still confused as hell. I feel the ghost of Maverick's hand wrapping around mine, and the word *fiancée* repeats over and over in my mind. Then I remember the party, falling, the glass smashing. I remove the thin blanket covering me and look down at my leg. Someone has cleaned the wounds, and it looks like a couple of stitches are holding a slightly bigger gash together.

And then the doctor's booming voice fills me with dread, telling me I have to rest for *two weeks.*

Hell no!

I swing my legs off the bed and try to stand, but I quickly realize that if I let go of the side table that I may end up on the floor again.

Fuck!

Maverick walks into my room dressed as a doctor and

holy fuck, the guy needs a role in a medical drama STAT because he wears the shit out of those scrubs!

and I realize what's happening now.

I'm in a coma.

And of course, in my coma dream state, Maverick would be my doctor. Who else would my subconscious cast in this role?

"What the hell are you doing?" He runs to my side and holds me steady, his firm hands on my waist, his diamond blue-green eyes shining with worry.

"Getting out of here."

"No, you're not. Not without my help." He hands me a pair of scrubs. "I got you these, but I don't think you're going to be able to walk out of here."

"Yes, I am. I can! I'm fine!"

"Jesus, Trix! What's it going to take for you to realize you have a problem?"

"I just need to catch up on some sleep, that's all."

"Get back in bed. Now." When Maverick Stone tells you to get in bed, you listen, and so I sit back down on the bed.

"Do not fucking move."

I nod, and I sit and wait.

He returns a few minutes later with a wheelchair and a heavy black coat.

"Whose coat is that?"

"I don't know, I found it in the waiting room."

"Maverick!"

"Just put it on over your hospital robe and get the fuck in."

"Won't they be worried if I don't stay for observation?"

"Baby, I'll observe you all night long."

Somehow, even after everything, his words still bring a little warmth to my cheeks.

Maverick gently pulls out my IV, but it still hurts, and I yelp.

"Shhhh," he says, pressing a finger to my lips.

Oh god, why does that feel so good?

He helps me into the coat, covering my ugly robe, and then lifts me up, gently placing me into the wheelchair. He grabs my purse and dress and shoves them in my lap, and then we're off.

He pushes me straight to the elevator like he owns the place, like he's Dr. Stone, a sexy doctor with a passion for saving the lives of hot women.

We get in the lift and we're thankfully alone, at least we are until the elevator stops on the next floor down. A couple of nurses get in, take one look at Maverick and squeal.

"What are *you* doing here?!" one of them asks.

"Filming a movie," he lies.

"Can I get a selfie? Pleaaaase?" the other one asks.

Maverick looks at one of them, and I watch as her demeanor changes, her facial expression going slack.

"The only place you've ever seen Maverick Stone is in a movie," he tells her.

He does the same thing to the other nurse. "I was never here. You won't remember any of this."

Then the doors open and he wheels me out, leaving them dazed and confused behind us.

"Is that what it's always like?" I ask him as he's wheeling me through the main doors.

"Mostly."

"Do you always glamour people like that?"

"Not always."

He wheels me straight into a taxi.

"Malibu," he tells the driver before helping me in and then sliding in next to me, ditching the wheelchair on the curb. "And please hurry."

. . .

Maverick carries me into his house, placing me gently down on his couch, and all I can think of is the first time I was here, the first time we had sex.

"You ready for this?" he asks, towering over me in his scrubs.

"Ready for what?" I stammer.

"To drink my blood."

Oh fuck!

"What will it do to me?"

"It'll make you feel a bit crazy, kind of high. You'll feel strong, like you have vampiric powers. It will wear off over the next few hours, but for a while you'll feel pretty damn good. And you'll be healed. Completely."

"Do people know about this? That your blood heals? That would be—"

"Yeah, there's a reason we don't tell people about this."

"You could cure everyone."

"We'd be put in silver cages and bled dry."

I bite my lip and shake my head. "I won't tell anyone. I promise."

"I know. You've more than proven you can keep a secret."

His fangs thrust out of his mouth, and he's about to bite into his own wrist, but he pauses to look up at me. God, why are his fangs so fucking *sexy*?

"You don't have to," he tells me. "You can just rest the old-fashioned way. I could take care of you."

My heart leaps at the idea, and suddenly resting for two weeks if it means getting to stay here with him doesn't seem so bad at all.

"Will there be a… another blood bond?" I ask.

He looks at me so tenderly. "The bond between us has been strong, I know. It's been affecting me too."

I let out a breath. Shit. He felt it too?

"Is that why—?"

"Why you still want me?"

I'm too tired to pretend I don't want him, so I just nod.

He shakes his head. "It should have worn off a few months after I bit you."

"Will this be like that was? Because I don't think I could—"

He shakes his head. "It'll be different."

I don't know if different means better or worse, but I want it. I want him. I want his mouth on me. I want his healing blood. I want to *feel better*, and when I'm with Maverick, I always feel better. Even when he's being an ass and pissing me off, I always feel *better* when he's near me.

"Okay."

He bites into his wrist, and blood drips down his arm. He brings his wrist up to my mouth, and it brings back memories of when he first bit me, but this time, it is different. This time *I'm* the one getting fed.

I close my eyes and drink, and I instantly feel the power of him moving into me, through my veins. It's like I'm drinking Maverick's strength, courage, confidence, his talent, his energy, his *everything*.

"You like that, gorgeous?" he laughs as I keep sucking his very life-force out of his wrist.

And holy shit, it feels good! I have never felt so alive or energized! My fatigue disappears, my aches from being on my feet all day are gone, everything suddenly comes into focus, and I feel like I could stay awake forever!

He pulls his wrist back, but I grab him.

"Now, now, Trix, you've had all you need," he chuckles.

"I'll never have all I need," I growl at him.

He just laughs again. "Feeling a little wired?"

I throw myself onto him, pushing him down onto the

couch, straddling him. He's still stronger than me, and I'm sure he could push me off if he wanted to, but he doesn't. He just laughs and runs his fingers through my messed-up hair.

"I want to fuck," I tell him. "Right now."

"I thought that was off the table?" He gives me a dirty smirk like he knew it was never off the fucking table.

"It's back on the table. Bent over the table."

He laughs again, and it feels so damn good to know that I'm the reason for his smile! I can feel him getting hard against me, and I cannot fucking wait to have sex with him while I feel so invincible!

"What if *I've* taken it off the table?" he says.

"You wouldn't."

"I think I have to."

"What?! Why?"

"Trix, baby." He runs a gentle hand over the side of my face. "You just collapsed at a party. I just broke you out of the hospital."

"Yeah, but I'm all fixed now," I say, rubbing myself over his hardness.

"Not like this," he tells me.

"What? Why?"

"I'd love to have sex with you again, Trix. I've never pretended otherwise, but not when you're all pepped up on vampire blood."

"Why not? We had sex when you were drinking from me."

"That was different. And not the first time we did it."

"You only bit me the second time. Why?"

"Because I wanted you to know what it was like with me without The Bite."

"How come?"

He shrugs. "Sex with The Bite is different. It can be more about The Bite than the sex, and I wanted it raw with you."

I feel the pulse between my legs heat and quicken, and I feel him hardening in response. He wants it as much as I do!

"Fuck me," I tell him.

He shakes his head with another chuckle. "If you still feel this way in a couple of hours once the high has worn off, I'll consider it. Until then, I know another great way to burn off some energy."

"What's that?"

"How about a midnight swim?"

CHAPTER THIRTY-TWO

$\mathcal{M}$averick

I'VE ONLY GIVEN blood one other time. It was after a bombing in London during World War II. The government had found out about vampires, and they had recruited as many vampires as possible for the war effort. Those of us who were still human but had excelled in the armed forces were recruited for a secret mission and turned by a vampire officer who wanted to create a vampire army.

I had various roles during the war, from working as a spy (I am fluent in German, Russian, French, languages aren't hard to learn for vampires) to protecting important government and military officials.

One evening, after a long day of following officials around the city, I headed to my local pub to find a woman who was up for The Bite and maybe a good fuck as well. Donnas and Dons aren't a new thing. During the war, there were more of them than now. In times of suffering and hardship, humans have always sought us out. The Bite is better than any other drug on the market. It's free, and there are no side-effects except for the human becoming slightly obsessed with the vampire who bit them.

As soon as I walked in, I noticed Lizzie sitting at the bar. I'd been with her a few times before. She was very beautiful — dark hair in pin curls, red lipstick. She was the first woman I'd been with who I gravitated towards more than once. I was under no illusion that it would ever become more. During the war, you didn't make plans. It wasn't exactly monogamy, but if she was there, I'd choose her over anyone else in the pub.

She caught my eye across the crowded room and gave me a smile and a wave. Excitement rushed through my body, not just because I knew I was going to drink and fuck tonight, but also because it was *her*.

The air-raid sirens started up and everyone scattered in all directions, heading for air-raid shelters or the underground tunnels. But the sirens were late, and there wasn't enough time. The pub was hit.

The wood that went through my body wasn't one of the three types that can kill vampires. Only elm, ash or yew will kill a vampire, and this was oak. I pulled out the wood, instantly healing and then pushed off the bricks and quickly started removing debris at lightning speed, not giving a damn who might see me. I needed to find Lizzie, and it was just a bonus that I saved so many other lives in the process.

I'd seen a lot during the war, but my heart still nearly broke when I pulled a pile of bricks off a young child. The innkeeper's daughter. She couldn't have been more than six years old. She was still alive, but only just.

Without thinking, I bit into my wrist.

The blood bond is not like a crush for children, it's more like a parental attachment.

After she'd had my blood and was completely healed, she wrapped her little arms around me and said, "Thank you, dada!"

I had to blink away the tears. I carried her in my arms and went about finding the little tike's mother. When I found her, she was also on the verge of death. I let her drink from me, and when I found her husband, I gave him my blood as well.

Seeing the three of them in a tight embrace, knowing I saved their entire family, I knew I had done some good for once in my eternal life. I know it didn't make up for all the killing I'd become so numb to, but it returned a little of the humanity that I had thought I lost back to me.

I never found Lizzie in the rubble, and I had to believe it was because she was safe in an air-raid shelter somewhere.

Many people were saved because of what I did that night, but giving blood is a dangerous game. If anyone knew what we could do, it wouldn't be long before our blood would be sold to pharmaceutical companies for billions of dollars while we all rotted in cages somewhere. After the war, vampires made sure all military records of us were burned and anyone who remembered us was glamoured or killed.

To give blood to a human is considered an act of treason against the Fraternity. Not because we don't want to heal and help humans, but to protect our kind. I know Brandon will look the other way when it comes to Trix. He needs her on set as much as I do. But if anyone else knew what I'd just done—

I watch her now, standing on the sand, stripping off the borrowed coat and hospital gown until she's wearing nothing but a pair of lacy champagne-colored panties. She laughs manically as she runs into the water, diving right in, and I know without a doubt that needing her on set is not the only reason I gave her my blood tonight.

I had feelings for Lizzie, but what I feel for Trix — it's more than anything I've felt for any woman, ever.

A grin spreads across my face, and I run after her, throwing off my borrowed scrubs and leaping into the water after her.

AFTER A FEW HOURS of chasing each other around in the water and running races up and down the beach, (I didn't run at vampire speed but still beat her) she flops down on the sand in nothing but those panties and the top of my borrowed scrubs.

"Okay, I think it's wearing off now," she says with a laugh, gasping for breath.

I lift her up and throw her over my shoulder, giving her gorgeous ass a gentle slap.

She screams. "Put me down!"

"You don't need to use any more energy," I tell her.

"I still have energy to have sex," she assures me.

"You need to go to bed."

"With you?"

I slap her ass again a little more firmly this time. "Behave."

"Never!"

I haul her into the house, into my bedroom and then throw her onto the bed.

She gives me a wicked look, and for a moment I think about accepting her offer. It may not come around again. But my blood is still running in her veins, she's still a little high, and the rest will do her more good than I would do keeping her awake all night.

"Go to sleep, Trix," I tell her.

She pouts and flops herself down on the bed. "But I really

wanted to—" Her eyes close, and she drops off to sleep before she can even finish her sentence.

I pull the comforter and blanket over her, switch off the light and then make my way into the living room to get some rest on the couch.

CHAPTER THIRTY-THREE

"I WANT you in the shower next," he tells me.

The way he says next makes me wonder how many times he's going to want me.

I'm still standing in the kitchen, dressed in nothing but my mismatched underwear.

All I can do is nod.

He grabs my hand, and I pull it back. "No handholding, remember?"

"Fucking rules," he mumbles. "Fine. Follow me, then."

And so I do. I follow him through the house and into his bedroom. It's a bright open space, the bed is covered with white sheets and a comforter. A light grey blanket and blue and white cushions make it feel like I'm at an expensive holiday resort. I look at the bed for too long and wonder if we should have added no bed sex to the list.

He walks through the room to a door at the other end, and I follow him into the biggest ensuite I've ever seen. The sleek white and grey bathroom has an enormous tub with spa jets, a large vanity with two sinks and a double shower.

I shouldn't feel jealous, but it occurs to me that there's a reason Maverick has a shower with two large rain shower heads, and it's not because he's using both of them.

He slides the glass door open and turns the taps on both showers.

"How warm do you want it?" he asks.

"Hot."

"Get in," he says. "I want to watch you."

I let out a nervous giggle. "You want to watch me shower?"

He raises an eyebrow like I'm going to be in so much trouble if I don't do it.

I flick the clasp of my bra, and it falls to the floor.

His eyes languish over my body, and I'm getting wet all over again just from him looking at me like that.

I slide my panties down and turn to get in the shower.

I stand under the water, and it feels heavenly after the last twenty-four hours of chaos and craziness.

Maverick steps into the shower, standing under his own showerhead while he watches me intensely. It's the first time I've gotten a good look at his cock, and the thing is magnificent...

I WAKE UP, my pussy still pulsing from the shower dream. I move my hand down towards my clit so I can release the pressure, but when my fingers brush over the very high thread count of the sheets, my whole body stills, and I realize where I am.

I'm in Maverick Stone's bed.

It's dark, and I have no idea what time it is. I tap my watch, and it lights up, telling me it's nine a.m.

"Why is it dark?" I mumble as I try to find a light switch. I flick it on, illuminating the room, the white sheets, comforter and grey throw that's been put over me.

I make my way over to the window looking for a way to open the blackout blinds. I press a button on the side and the blinds slowly open to reveal sunlight and an incredible view of Malibu beach.

"Wow," I whisper to myself.

I take a shower on my own. Visions of what happened in here last time race through my mind while I wash off the salt water and sand from my midnight swim and races on the beach with Maverick last night. I keep glancing at the door, hoping he'll walk in here for a replay of what happened last time. But he doesn't come.

Everything changed last night. When he squeezed my hand in the back of the ambulance, I knew I couldn't pretend any longer. When he gave me his blood to heal me, I knew that no matter how much it would end up destroying me, I couldn't stay away from him any longer.

Pushing him away has been exhausting. Denying my feelings for him has only made it all harder.

Now I can only hope that I haven't made such a mess of things that his offer to fuck and bite me anytime still stands.

When I'm done, I step out, dry myself, tousle my hair with the towel and then look in the mirror. I look… *great*. Refreshed, awake, my skin looks excellent, no blemishes, and even some of my wrinkles seem to have disappeared…

And also — I'm *grinning*.

It must be from the vampire blood. And damn that vampire blood was incredible!

I tie the towel around me and go in search of clothes.

I find Maverick's walk-in robe and even though I've been in his house this whole time, there's something about being around all his clothes that feels like I'm stepping into his secret world. The room is full of t-shirts in neat piles, jeans on hangers, and a whole heap of suits he'd look so fucking good in. I run my hand over the rows of clothing, inhaling the scent of his clean laundry.

I grab a grey t-shirt with a brand logo on it and throw it on. It's practically a dress on me, and because I'm still feeling extra confident from his blood, I don't bother to borrow a pair of boxers.

I make my way out to the kitchen and see Maverick staring down at a tablet, bags of groceries surrounding him.

He looks up at me, and his expression changes from thoughtful into something heated as he takes in my bare legs.

"I borrowed a shirt. I hope that's okay."

"Sure," he says, looking back at the tablet.

Okay, so not exactly the response I was hoping for.

"What are you doing?"

"Catering," he replies without looking up.

"What?"

"I'm helping you."

"How?"

"I'm going to do the catering."

I let out a laugh. "*You?*"

He glares up at me.

"You think I've never made a meal before?"

"No, I don't."

"The thing about me, Trix, is that I'm very willing to learn."

A black and white cat appears in the kitchen and starts rubbing around his legs.

"You got a cat!" I bend down to pat the cutie, and it purrs at my touch.

"It's Juliette's," he says. "His name is Percy."

"She called her cat Percy?"

"No. I didn't know his name, but I thought if he was

coming to stay with me at the beach, he should have an ocean name."

"Percy?"

"It's short for Poseidon," he says like it should be obvious.

"Hey, Percy," I coo at the gorgeous thing. "When's Juliette coming back for him?"

"We don't know."

"You know you can't cater with a cat in here."

"I already got the permits."

"What? How? Those took me months to get!"

"I have connections."

"You glamoured someone into giving you a permit."

He looks up at me with a frown. "And?"

I hold my hands up in surrender. "That's cool. Totally unfair, but, whatever!"

"If you want me to get you a permit for anything, I'll fucking get you one. Just ask." He broods back down at the tablet.

Damn, he's sexy as fuck when he's pissed.

"What's your story anyway?" Still feeling bold from the blood, I lean over the tablet, accidentally on purpose nudging my breast into his arm.

"My story?" He stands up and puts some distance between us.

"Yeah, like where did you come from?"

"It's boring." He picks up the tablet and stares down at it as he takes another step back from me.

"I bet it's not."

"I grew up on a farm in South Dakota," he says, still looking down. "I enlisted in the army when I was thirteen."

"Thirteen? That's so young. I'm so sorry."

He looks at me and sighs. "Don't be sorry. It was a long time ago."

"When were you, you know—"

"Made?"

"Yeah."

He doesn't look up at me, but a dark expression crosses his face. "I worked my way up through the ranks of the army. Survived the First World War through sheer dumb luck and a bunch of good men who wanted to protect me because I was the youngest. World War II comes along, and I'm older and wiser. Good at my job. Higher up in the ranks. Because I was such an excellent soldier, a superior officer who wanted to make a vampire army of immortal killing machines turned me."

I let out a little gasp. "I'm sorry, I didn't mean to—"

He finally looks up from the tablet, and I can see the pain in his eyes.

All this time I had Maverick Stone pegged as a cocky, self-absorbed, egotistical movie star. I mean, I knew he was a vampire, but I'm only just now realizing that he comes with a very dark past. And a vampire army? That's *dark*.

"Okay, so what's the plan here?" I ask, waving my hand over the groceries and trying to lighten the mood.

"Show me what to do. Teach me, then I'll do it at vampire speed. You can still be in control, but it will be done in no time."

"I'm sorry, what?"

"This is how we fix your situation."

"*You're* going to work for Trix and Treats?"

"I'm going to *help* you, so we don't have a repeat of last night. Giving you my blood was a one time thing, so you're going to need to actually *sleep* if you want to make this movie work."

I just blink at him.

"I looked into hiring a kitchen and some staff for you, but I thought you'd freak. Decided it was better to warm you up a little by making you let me help you here for a few nights first."

My stomach flips at the innuendo in his words.

"I can't make anything cook faster, but I can get it prepped in no time."

My phone rings, and it takes me a second to realize where it is — in the pocket of the coat Maverick borrowed from the hospital, which is still lying on the couch in the living room.

I run over and answer. "Mom?"

"Honey, where are you? Are you okay? We just heard Stacey and Bob on the radio saying that you'd been in *hospital*? And that you're engaged to Maverick Stone! Honey, what on earth is going on?"

"Hang on," I tell her before sliding open the door to the porch and stepping out into the beautiful morning.

"Beatrix!"

"Mom, everything is fine," I tell her. "I'm fine, but I'm not engaged to Maverick Stone."

Unfortunately.

Maverick gives me a look through the glass. Of course, he can still hear me. He grabs his own phone and frowns down at the screen.

"Why not? That man is gorgeous! Beatrix, you bag that one!"

"Mom," I start. "It was just a misunderstanding."

CHAPTER THIRTY-FOUR

averick

"CONGRATULATIONS ARE IN ORDER! Maverix, what the internet is now calling Trix Delaney and Maverick Stone, were spotted exiting Hollywood Memorial Hospital together last night. According to sources on the medical staff, wedding bells are about to ring! Although it looks like filming for Double Agency *will officially be on hold for at least the next few weeks until Trix recovers from a very serious case of exhaustion."*

Hollywood Daily Blog

TRIX WALKS BACK into the kitchen, throwing her phone onto the counter. "Well, everyone knows."

"I saw."

"And they think we're *engaged!*"

"Uh huh."

"What are we going to do about it?"

"Nothing."

"We just let them believe it?"

I look up at her, and I want to take my thumb and rub out her frown line, but I'm trying to learn how to cook here. "Yeah. That's what you do. You just ignore this shit. Eventually, it blows over."

"But it's not true!"

"Make a statement on your social media or something if you're worried about it." I frown down at her phone on the counter. "I already sanitized that surface," I complain at her.

She takes the phone with a huff, wanders into the living area and starts typing like she's stabbing the keyboard on her phone. I try to focus on my task at hand, but Trix is so damn distracting.

"I put up a post telling them we're not engaged."

"Fine."

She bends over a little to put her phone on the coffee table, and I get a glimpse of the bottom of her ass. Damn if she doesn't look like a wet dream wearing nothing but my shirt. I run a hand over the scruff of my jaw and grimace. Now is not the time for me to be having my way with this woman in my kitchen. Not only have I already sanitized the surfaces, but the realization I had last night that I might be developing feelings for her has been deeply disturbing to me.

Sure, I want to help her with the whole cooking thing, but this was also just an attempt to keep busy, to get my mind on something else.

"Can you please put some clothes on?"

I stare down at the tablet, still having no idea what I'm reading. I don't even need to look at it. I've already memorized all the recipes Ali so gracefully sent to me after I had my new assistant Kai get in touch with her. I'm not sure why it took me so long to realize that a straight male assistant would be the perfect match for me. He won't crush on me and I won't be tempted to have sex with him. It's ideal.

No, I do know why I never thought of it before, because before the idea of a woman following me around who was up for a bite or a quickie whenever I was, felt like a dream.

Now, the idea of meaningless sex with randoms makes me feel ill.

I am so fucked.

"I don't have anything to wear but the dress I wore last night or the scrubs you stole," she tells me.

"Jesus, woman, at least put some pants on." I look up and glare at her.

She gives me a flirty smile. "Remember when you said if I still wanted it after the blood wore off—"

My jaw tightens. "I'm busy right now," I tell her. "I just want to get this done. If you still want to, we can fool around later."

The idea of fooling around with her later hits me right in the cock *and* in the heart, and I know I am completely, royally, fucking screwed.

"Maybe we could fool around *first?*" she suggests, lifting the edge of the t-shirt just high enough to reveal that she's not wearing any panties.

I'm thrown headfirst into an ethical dilemma. Help her with the food so she doesn't collapse again or fuck her all night long and have her exhausted again, leaving me more obsessed with her than I already fucking am!

My cock twitches at the idea that I could just give her some more of my blood.

Bad idea, Maverick!

"Dammit Trix, please! Just put some fucking clothes on!"

She holds up her hands and disappears into my bedroom, but the idea of her in there with no panties on makes me so turned on that the last thing I can think about right now is *baking*!

"Fuck!" I slam a zucchini onto the counter and follow her into the bedroom.

Her grinning face appears out of the walk-in robe. "You came!"

I close the door behind me and lean against it. "If we're going to do this, we need rules."

"We already have rules," she says, stepping out of the walk-in and leaning against the doorjamb with her shoulder.

"We need some amendments."

"Okay."

"This isn't a relationship. It's friends with benefits."

"Maverick," she says, my name sounding like sweet, sexy fire on her lips. "We're not even friends."

Fine. Whatever. If that's what she needs to tell herself, I'll try to tell myself that too.

"That's all this can be," I tell her, reminding myself at the same time. "I don't do relationships. Never have, never will."

"Maverick."

God, my name sounds so fucking good in her mouth. I want to take her right now, demand she say my name a hundred times while I fuck her!

"Do you really think any sane woman would *want* a relationship with you?" She turns and slowly makes her way over to the bed, and knowing she's completely naked under my shirt is *killing* me. I'm already so fucking hard for her.

"What the hell is that supposed to mean?" I say, stepping towards her, unable to stay away.

Yeah, sure, I've never been a relationship guy, I'm never going to be, it's not in my nature, but still, it stings.

"I know what you are," she says, her back still to me.

"Oh yeah, what am I?" I ask, closing the space between us and pressing myself into her back.

She lets out a gasp as I press my hardness against her.

"Say it. Out loud," I growl into her ear.

"Womanizer," she whispers.

I let out a laugh and take a step back, leaving her there, heart pounding, quivering gently, wanting me as much as I want her.

"Right now, the only woman I fucking want is you, Trix. You're the only one I've wanted since last time we did it."

She lowers one knee to the bed and then turns to look at me. "Same."

God damn!

She gets on all fours, and my shirt rides up, showing her perfect bare ass, and I'm fucking *done*.

I pull off my shirt and follow her lead, kneeling behind her. I run my hands over her back, up over her stomach and cup her perfect breasts. I lean over her, kissing the back of her neck and she moans. I squeeze her nipples gently and then my hands travel down to her hips and I hold her there, thinking of how good it's going to feel to be inside this perfect, beautiful woman again.

"Holy. Fuck. Trix," I say.

She gasps as my hand moves between her legs. She's already so wet and I've barely touched her. I slide my fingers over her wetness. I want so desperately to taste her, to use my tongue to bring her to orgasm, but that's not part of the rules, so I have to settle with using my fingers.

CHAPTER THIRTY-FIVE

rix

HIS FINGERS SLIDE UP and down in long strokes, and I can't wait any longer. "I'm ready," I tell him. "Do it. Now."

"But it's so fun to tease you," he laughs, giving my clit a little flick, lighting the spark of what I know is going to be another fucking amazing orgasm with him.

"You fucking bastard," I say through my teeth.

He just laughs, removing his hand and leaving me feeling desperately *wanting*.

"Maverick!" I practically beg.

He slides his hands over my back and down to my hips, gripping me firmly.

Oh, thank god, he's about to fuck me again!

Of course, I wanted this. I wanted this from the moment I slid into an Uber outside his house after the first time we had sex. I wanted to come back here, to be with him again and again and again. I wanted him every fucking day for all those months.

And now that I'm here, in this incredibly compromising position, my bare ass in the air, his hands on me, I'm so mad at myself for not accepting his offer to fuck me in his trailer the instant he made it.

Because somehow, me and Maverick— we just *belong* together.

Fuck my feelings, fuck the dreams, fuck my heart, all I want is *this.*

"Trix, you are fucking perfect," he says, pressing his strong fingers into my waist.

I let out something between a giggle and a sigh as his words warm me, all of me, my pussy, my belly, my heart.

He moves one hand down to my inner thigh and makes a slow path back up to the wetness pooling between my legs.

"Still no oral? Because I'd really like to suck your clit until you scream my name."

"No!" I tell him, even though that sounds *delicious* as fuck.

If I'm going to do this again, I at least need to stick to the rules!!

"No kissing on the mouth?" he asks.

"No," I say, trying to be strong. But god, if he kissed me right now, I would not stop him.

"But kissing you feels so fucking good."

"You'll have to settle for just fucking me."

He slides his hand over my wetness again, and I whimper.

"Tell me you want it," he says, with a tenderness that could make me come undone right here and now.

"You know I want it."

"Tell me. I want to hear you say it."

"You already know how much I want you," I practically pant.

"Say it."

"I want it. I want you. Fuck!"

He chuckles, his fingers running down my back again. He moves my hair off my neck, places a kiss on the back of my neck, and I shiver.

"Is this kind of kissing okay?" he asks, placing another kiss a little further down that sends shivers all the way down to my pulsing clit.

"It would be more okay if your cock was in me while you did it," I say.

He laughs and slaps my ass lightly. "Beg for it."

"Are you fucking serious?" I ask, turning to face him, and holy shit if he doesn't look like sex personified kneeling over me with his ripped chest, those old tattoos and dirty grin.

Fine.

"I'm begging you," I tell him.

"Beg me like you mean it," he says, one hand on my hip, the other finding its way back to my pulsing hot center again. "Use those Juilliard acting skills."

"Fuck you," I tell him.

"No, you're supposed to say, *Fuck me.*"

"I've been begging this whole time!"

He slides a finger into me, and I moan at the feeling of him inside me.

Fuck yes, more!!

"Beg for more," he says.

"You fucking beg for more," I tell him, pushing back into his hand.

"Trix, I'm begging you." He pumps a large finger in and out of me, a glorious promise of what's to come, and I don't even know if I can wait that long because I'm already on the edge. "Please, *please* let me fuck you," he says. "Not just today, but every fucking day of our lives."

His finger pauses for a moment, and I wonder if he meant to say that.

"Beg harder," I tell him.

He chuckles and pulls his finger out of me. I'm about to complain when I feel the tip of his cock at my opening.

"Please, Trix," he says. "*Please*. Please take it from me, Trix. I'm begging you, baby. I'm begging you to take my cock in your perfect, soft, wet—"

I slam back, filling myself with his huge hard manhood, and he lets out a loud groan.

"Fuck! Trix!" he yells. He grabs my waist and slowly slides in and out a few times before finding his rhythm.

The feeling of him inside me after all this time, and after all the play begging, is glorious, and it doesn't take long at all for the first orgasm to hit me. I shudder and shake and scream his name, and when I'm done, he pulls out and throws me onto my back.

"I want to watch you come the second time," he tells me. "After I drink from you."

His fangs extend, and I gasp at the sight of them. Not in fear, but in excitement of what I know is coming next.

He opens my legs wide and enters me again. I moan from the pleasure of being filled by him, and he grunts as he finds a new rhythm from this new angle. His lips find my neck, and even though it's not in the rules for him to bite me here, I don't stop him when I feel his teeth enter me. The pleasure of it hits so hard and so good. It's like every cell in my body is orgasming.

He fucks me harder and faster while he drinks from me and I look up at him, this sex god, this ripped fucking *god*, this rich, famous, movie star *vampire* who has his cock inside me and looking at me like I'm all he's ever fucking wanted.

Holy fuck!

And then the second orgasm finds me, and it blows my fucking mind. Every cell is coming, every hair on my body is standing on end. It's like the universe finally fucking aligns, and me and Maverick are right in the center of it.

He grips my hips tighter and thrusts even harder into me, and within seconds he's groaning and releasing himself into me and *another* orgasm hits me, or is it the same one that's still going? I don't know! I don't care! I've lost the ability to understand time and space as we're peaking together, gripping each other like we're never going to let go as we both ride the waves of pleasure, fucking *finally*.

When the waves have died down into little ripples, he relaxes onto me for a moment and grins.

I grin back.

"Fuck," he says, as he pulls out, leaving his "unviable" seed inside me.

He rolls onto his side and sighs deeply. "You're the best I've ever had," he says.

I just laugh. "You don't have to say that shit to me."

He turns his head on the pillow to face me. "I'm serious. I may be a lot of things, but I'm not a liar. I'll always be honest with you."

"Okay."

"And you really are the best I've ever had." He runs a hand over my cheek and into my hair. "You make me feel like—"

"Like what?"

He turns onto his back again and looks thoughtfully up at the ceiling.

"Like I'm human."

CHAPTER THIRTY-SIX

rix

TRIX & Maverick's Rules of Engagement updated version:
No kissing on the lips
No oral
The Bite okay anywhere
No glamouring
No cuddling
No holding hands
No sleeping over
No calling or texting unless it's to arrange a meet-up
Meet-ups are only for baking and sex
No dates, no movies, no spending time together
Never tell anyone, ever
Act like it never happened

. . .

"Is that the secret to the key lime bars?" Maverick asks as he watches me press crushed up cookies into the tray. "Cookies?"

"Yeah, pretty much. And the coconut cream gives it that extra freshness."

"Okay, I think I've got the gist of this," he says. "Get out of the way and I'll get everything in the oven and on the stove."

"Are you sure about this?"

"Yes. Now go sit over there." He ushers me towards the living area, and I reluctantly sit on the couch.

Then suddenly he's a blur of color whizzing around the kitchen like some kind of giant sexy hummingbird on speed.

In less than five minutes, he comes blurring over to me and sits, reappearing at normal speed.

"What the—?!"

"I told you I was fast." He sets a timer on his phone. "Now we just wait for everything to cook, then you can tell me if it's passable and if you think you can deal with this solution to your problem."

"I'm sure it'll be—"

"Oh, I forgot something." He walks back into the kitchen and returns with a steaming cup of coffee, handing it to me with a smile.

I look at the coffee a little stunned. "You bought coffee?"

"I got a taste for it."

I take a sip. "It's good!"

"I had my new assistant pick me up the best coffee in the city."

"What's your new assistant like?"

"Kai? He's great. How's yours?"

"It's so weird having an assistant. I don't even know what to get her to do."

"Ask her to do anything you want."

"That seems so—"

"It's her job."

He puts his feet up on the coffee table and casually puts an arm around me.

"Nope," I say, lifting his arm, which weighs a ton, and putting it back in his personal space.

"I can't even put my arm around you?"

"No, it's too relationship-y."

"Okay, so what can we do when we're together but not naked?"

"According to the rules we just made, we're not supposed to even spend time together."

"Sure, but we didn't allow for times when the muffins would be baking, or when I'd need to recover between rounds."

I quirk my lip at him. "You've never needed to recover between rounds."

Another benefit of enjoying benefits with a vampire.

"If we go for another round right now, who's going to watch the soup?"

"Okay, well, maybe we're allowed to just talk, at least while food is cooking," I say.

"Are you going to be okay with this?" he asks.

"Talking?"

"No. Soup, sandwiches, muffins. Me helping you."

I shrug. "Sure."

He gives me a look.

"What?"

"You seem so resistant to anyone ever helping you, but you're totally fine with this?"

"I'm not totally fine with it. But after passing out at the party, I realized, maybe I can't do it all. And besides, the benefits part of the arrangement appeals to me too much to say no." I give him a shrug and a dirty smile.

Percy meows and jumps onto the couch between us.

"Where do you think she is? Juliette?" I ask him.

"We don't know. Brandon's had a P.I. looking for her, but we haven't been able to find anything."

"She's not in rehab."

"She's a vampire. She was never going to be in rehab."

"You're worried about her."

He lets out a sigh. "I'm not supposed to talk to you about any of this."

"Okay."

He runs a hand over his jaw. "But vampires are missing."

My brow tightens. "Vampires? Plural?"

"Three now. They've all left these resignation letters, resigning from the Fraternity, but there's something that just feels off about the whole thing."

I don't know much about the Fraternity of the Everlasting Rose, the secret society of elite vampires who secretly run the world, or at least Hollywood, but it doesn't seem like the kind of thing you just *resign* from.

"We've had Henrietta read the tarot for us, and she assures us no one is going to suffer the Certain Death but—"

"Certain Death?"

"It's what we call it when a vampire gets staked."

"Oh."

"It's very hard to kill a vampire," he assures me.

"Are you in danger?"

He laughs. Loud.

"Baby, I can take care of myself."

Of course he can. He's a vampire. And not just any vampire, he's Maverick Stone.

I must look worried because he gives me a confident smile. "I can take care of you too, sweetheart."

I grin up at him.

"Patience," he tells me, giving my thigh a squeeze. "We've got a couple of batches of cookies to get in the oven."

"And then?"

"And then, I'm all yours."

All yours.

"Okay, tell me your story," he says, changing the subject.

"What story?"

"Your origin story, now that you know mine."

"I barely know yours," I say, but I don't want to force anything else out of him after the effect talking about his history seemed to have on him.

I take a deep breath. "Okay, well, my birth mom gave me up, I lived with my grandmother for a while, and I ended up in foster care for a few years before my real parents adopted me."

"Oh, Trix, I'm sorry."

"Yeah, it's okay. I've been through a lot of therapy. Done a lot of work on myself… I mean, I'm not totally fixed or whatever, but I'm okay. At one point I was kind of just functioning, but I'm better now."

"I get that. Never feeling like you'll be fixed."

"What I went through is nothing compared to what you—"

"Keep going with the story." He gets a little more comfortable, elbow on the back of the couch, turning towards me. "If you want to. No pressure."

"That's kind of it. After years of being a closed-down kid, I eventually found a way to let my mom and dad in. It was food that helped me. Cooking with Mom, Dad enjoying the treats we baked. That was even better than therapy."

"Now I get why you're so into this, and why it's hard for you to hand it over. Baking saved you."

"Yeah, it did. I always loved acting too, though. It was my big dream for a long time. When that dream didn't work out, I went back to my safe place, my healing place — the kitchen."

"What made you quit acting?"

I take another deep breath. "I spent a year in New York auditioning for shows, plays, TV, anything and everything."

"What work did you get?"

"Nothing."

"Nothing?"

"An entire year of auditioning and I didn't get a single role. Not even an ad for tampons."

He shakes his head. "How is that possible? You're fantastic."

I shrug. "I don't know. I knew it was going to be tough, so I gave myself a year to make it. When that date arrived and absolutely nothing had happened for me, I left. I went home for a few months, and then after moping for way too long about it, I decided to go to culinary school."

"You know, a year isn't that long in the industry. It can take a lot longer than a year to make it."

"How long did it take you? How did you get into movies after being in the army?"

He rubs the back of his neck awkwardly. "After the war, I went into hiding for a few years. I lived in a small cabin in the woods of Colorado. A couple of nights a week I'd drive into town and see a movie. I loved the movies. They are what saved me. The escape from reality. Those two hours in the cinema were the only times I wasn't thinking about what I'd been through. One night I heard some girls behind me talking about how they planned to head out to California to try to make it in movies. I asked them if I could tag along, and a week later the three of us drove out to Hollywood. While they struggled to get parts and eventually went home, I glamoured my way into my first film."

I try to ignore the pang of jealousy at the idea of Maverick hooking up with *two* hot girls.

"Does glamouring people into doing what you want ever feel like cheating?"

He shrugs. "Yeah, sometimes. I don't do it so much these days, and I honestly prefer the challenge now." He gives me a sexy smirk like he's been enjoying the challenge of us. "I'm older and wiser. But I've done plenty I'm not proud of."

I don't tell him that in our eighteen months apart all I did was watch his movies. His old westerns from the fifties, the cop movies he did in the eighties, the entire (terrible) *Road Rage* series.

"You just pretended to be your own relatives," I say.

"Yeah, as long as I pretended to be somewhat related to myself, I got away with it."

"Mason Jones, Jason Rose," I say, repeating some of his previous names. "What's your real name?"

"Maverick Stone."

"No way! That sounds so made up!" I laugh.

"Actually, Maverick was my father's last name. Stone was my mother's."

"What given name were you born with?"

"That has to remain a secret."

"You know I'm good with secrets."

He looks into my eyes for a second, and I know that we share a vault.

"Charles."

A loud laugh escapes from my mouth, and when I'm done losing it, I see he's glaring at me. That sexy, brooding glare that always hits me right in my lower belly.

"It's just not very *you*," I tell him.

"I never used it. I always went by Maverick."

"Want me to call you Charlie in bed?" I joke.

He rolls his eyes at me. "Maverick is fine."

"You like it when I say your name while we're in bed."

He raises an eyebrow, and the timer goes off for the first batch of baked goods. He disappears in a blur for exactly four seconds and is back on the couch again. The cozy smell of cookies finally reaches the living room, and it should feel at odds with this Malibu mansion, but it just makes it feel like home.

"Did you have any siblings?" I ask him, trying to get back on topic.

"Yeah, I had eight of them."

"Wow."

"You?"

I shake my head. "Not as far as I know, but I took a DNA test recently and found out I have a cousin in England. We talk online all the time. Fern is great. I'm so glad I found her."

"You have family in England?"

"Yeah. My grandmother immigrated from there. She used to own the pub that my cousin runs now. It's been in the family for generations, apparently, since before the war. I really want to go over and see it one day."

"What's the name of the pub?" he asks suddenly.

"The Silver Dagger," I say. "It's in the West End."

His eyes glaze over, and it's like he's suddenly not here with me. He's somewhere else. *Where?*

"Maverick?"

He shakes his head and runs a hand through his hair. "Shit, sorry. It's just that — fuck. I used to go to that pub."

"What?"

"During the war. I went there."

"Fern said it got bombed in the war."

"I was there." I can almost see the reflection of bombs blasting in his eyes as they glaze over. "I was there that day, the day it got bombed. Oh, fuck." He runs a hand down over his face.

"You were there? At the pub that my family owned? What? How—?"

He gets up and starts pacing. "I saved a bunch of people that night. I think I—" he stops and stares at me for a moment, so many emotions over his handsome face. Fear, worry, confusion, hope. "I think I might have saved your family. With my blood. It's the only other time I've let humans drink from me."

I shake my head. I can't understand this. This connection between us. It's not possible. *Is it?* What are the odds of something like this? Zero. Those are the odds.

"I might be wrong. There might be another Silver Dagger in the West End."

I don't know anything about London, but we both know there is no other Silver Dagger pub in the West End.

"Are you saying that you saved their lives that day and I might only *exist* because of you?"

He just stares at me.

"Well, shit," I say, curling my legs up into a ball underneath me.

"Yeah. Shit."

I look up at him and swallow. "Do you think that's why—"

"Why, what?"

"Why this blood bond has been so intense?"

His brows knit together. "How intense has it been for you?"

"I've been—"

"You've been what?"

"Dreaming of you."

"That's normal."

"Every night for eighteen months?"

"That's a little less normal. But I've felt it too. Vampires aren't supposed to feel like this."

"And it's not just like a normal dream. It's like… it's actually *happening*."

"For me too," he tells me.

The timer goes off again, and he speeds into the kitchen and back. But this time he doesn't sit, he just paces.

"I don't know what this means," I tell him truthfully.

"Me neither," he laughs. "I know we have a connection, but I don't think it's just the blood bond, and I don't think it's whatever the hell this other thing is, either."

He looks at me intensely for a few moments. What is he saying? That he has *feelings* for me?!

"It's weird, you being so old," I say, trying to bring some lightness to the moment.

He looks at me and laughs. "Yeah. It kind of is. Does it bother you? That I'm so old?"

"Well, you act like a child most of the time, so not really."

He gives me a boyish grin. "It's not like I'm some old man. You see, we're stunted. Paused. Stopped in time. We get all this extra wisdom and experience, but it's limited. It's kind of like being in a time loop. I have no idea what it's like to be older than I am now. My body has never aged. So, it's not like I'm a hundred years old, more like 35 on repeat."

"That makes it slightly less creepy," I say.

"You think I'm creepy?" He seems insulted.

"Just a little."

"I didn't hear you complaining about me being creepy when we were in *there*," he says, nodding to the bedroom.

I feel a little blush hit my cheeks.

"So, we may have this extra connection," he says. "At some point in the past, I connected with your family. It doesn't have to mean anything."

"Sure," I say, even though it feels like it means *everything*. If Maverick Stone saved the lives of my biological family, I wouldn't be alive without him.

Now *that's* a head fuck!

"Wait, you didn't like, have sex with my great-grandmother or something, did you?"

He lets out a howl of laughter. "No. She seemed very in love with the man she was married to."

Another timer goes off, and he blurs into the kitchen and back again, this time bringing a cookie to my lips.

"Taste it," he says, nudging it to touch my bottom lip.

How is this so fucking sexy?

I open my lips, and he gently pushes the cookie into my mouth.

Oh, god.

"How is it? Did I do okay?"

It's delicious. Just like I'd made it myself. *Better.*

"It'll do," I tell him. "Thank you for helping me. But this has to be a one off—"

"No. You don't get to decide that."

I can't decide if he's being a dick or if the way he takes control is the hottest thing ever.

"You can't cook here every night."

"Why not? It's not like I'm doing it for selfless reasons."

"No?"

"This arrangement could serve us both. After filming each night, we come back here. I bake. You can help a little if you *have* to. Then we fuck for a few hours, and you still get a good night's sleep."

"Oh, you think you can go for a few hours, do you?"

"Trix, I think you *know* how long I can go for. It's just that we can't do it all night or you'll end up with exhaustion again."

"It's too much," I say. "I can't just — *move in* here."

"I have a couple of guest bedrooms if it's too relationship-y to sleep together. And it's just for the next three weeks. Until filming wraps."

And then what? I don't ask. I don't want to know. I don't want him to tell me that we can do this for three weeks, but then it has to be over.

"If you don't want to stay over, we can fuck, and I'll take you straight home. No sleeping over if it's too much. And if we film really late, you don't come back here. I do everything on my own."

"No."

"No, what?"

"No, you don't do everything on your own when we film late."

"But that's a yes to the rest of it?"

I sigh. "Okay."

He grins like he's just won a fucking Oscar. "There's no pressure, Trix. If you're on your period or whatever, you can stay home."

"Just when I think you might be a decent human, you say some shit like that."

"First of all, I'm not human. And what did I say wrong this time?"

"That you don't want to spend time with me unless sex is on the table."

"You made that rule!"

"Yeah, but you don't have to be a dick about it!"

"Trix, baby. I want to spend time with you. I would burn all those rules in a second."

"You can't say things like that," I warn him.

"Okay. So come over and just read a book or something. Ignore me. I don't care. If we're not fucking or about to fuck or just finished, I won't even talk to you or look your way. I'll pretend you're not here." I sense the playfulness in his voice, but in a way, I appreciate the boundaries we're attempting to set here. Clear lines. Defined. No room for anything but what this is. Sex and baking.

"Good plan," I tell him. "We have sex, bake and I catch up on my reading."

"You should catch up on your sleep first."

"You're right." I stand up and look for my purse. "I can come by in the morning with the van to pack everything up."

"You're leaving?"

"Well, we've had sex, and the baking is done, so yeah. I should probably leave."

"Woah, wait a second. The key lime bars aren't even done yet, and why would you think for one second that one time is enough for me?"

He grabs the hem of my t-shirt and pulls me close.

"It's kind of impossible not to want you when you're walking around in just my shirt."

I raise an eyebrow. "You like me like this?"

"What do you think?"

"I think you like it."

"How about we do it this time with the blinds open?"

"What?"

"Tinted glass, remember? But it will give you the *idea* of people watching us."

I bite my lip and his jaw clenches. I yank the t-shirt off and run into the bedroom.

"Hold up, I just need to get the other cookies out!" he calls out to me.

I hear the clanging around of trays and then he's there, fast as a bullet, staring at me like I'm the best fucking key lime bar he's ever tasted.

He pulls his t-shirt over his head and then he almost trips over his trousers trying to get them off and get to me.

"Oh, you're laughing at me?" he says with a chuckle. "You're not going to be laughing in a minute!"

And then he throws me down on the bed, and we do it again. Twice.

CHAPTER THIRTY-SEVEN

$\mathcal{M}$averick

THE NEXT FEW weeks with Trix are like a dream I never dared to dream come true. We quickly get into a rhythm that feels so damn good I want to repeat it every day for all eternity.

Our days are filled with filming. Trix in her low-cut tank top and tight jeans, her ogling me in my suit while I pull her from burning buildings and cars that are about to explode.

We spend our breaks in my trailer eating key lime bars while we practice lines, and when time permits, I take her up against the wall or on the tiny couch that threatens to fall through the trailer while we fuck and laugh. And holy shit, we *laugh* like I've never laughed in my life. We try to be quiet, but there's no way in hell anyone thinks we're just running lines, especially not the security team who follow me around constantly now. Thank god for NDAs.

After filming, she slides onto the back of my motorcycle

while Kai follows behind with her van. We bake, we fuck, we bake some more. She sticks her head in some fat romantasy novel for a while, we fuck again and then I have her asleep in the guest bedroom before midnight.

That was her choice, not mine. I'd have her sleep in my bed every night if she wanted to.

In the morning, Kai drives her van from my house to the lot. I wake her at the last possible minute, and she throws on jeans and a hoodie, no bra, *Jesus.* She's all sleepy-eyed, hair tangled, sliding onto the back of my motorcycle like a goddamn angel.

We both know what this is. We know we have an expiration date. We know this can never be more than just a fuck-fest for these few weeks while filming wraps.

But I'm having the goddamn time of my life playing this part, this role of Trix's lover.

"I have a surprise for you," I tell her.

I hand her the helmet, and her eyes narrow.

"What kind of surprise?"

I know it's risky. This could all blow up in my face. She could hate me for it. It could ruin everything between us. But it could also make everything *so* much better.

"I'll show you."

We ride towards the lot, but I stop a couple streets over outside what looks like an old warehouse from the outside.

"What is this place?" she asks, shaking out her helmet hair. God, I love how her hair looks all messed up from my helmet.

"Don't get mad, but — I hired you a space."

She just stands there and stares up at the building. "What kind of space?"

"A kitchen."

She turns and glares at me. "You did *what?*"

Ah, fuck!

I raise my hands in defense. "I just hired the space. What you choose to do with it is up to you. You can come here and cook, we both can… or you could hire a team. Totally up to you."

Her face hardens.

"Or not!" I say. "It can sit empty. I don't care. It was cheap."

"How much?"

"Not much."

She looks up at the building. Her eyes go all misty, and I wait for the fallout. For her to tell me to stop trying to run her life, to remind me that we are nothing to each other and that she can do everything on her own—

"Thank you."

My mouth drops open. "What?"

She sighs. "I've been acting like a baby. A martyr. A baby martyr. I collapsed at a party, and even then, I only let you help me because I wanted to—"

Because she wanted to fuck me.

"I've been letting *you* help me these last few weeks, and that hasn't been fair on you. I can't let you keep doing it. You've done enough."

"I've loved every single second of it."

Her lips press together, and she nods solemnly. "Me too."

"Hey, what is it?" I'm in front of her, sliding a hand over her cheek before I can stop myself.

"What happens to the arrangement now?"

"The arrangement?"

"This was transactional, right? We cook, we fuck. Without the cooking what does that mean for—?"

"For us?" I finish, the words hanging in the air between us.

Us.

I shrug. "Maybe we should just fuck and have a good

time? Maybe it doesn't have to be an arrangement. Maybe it's just two people who are into each other enjoying some time together."

She looks relieved for a moment, like she's so glad this doesn't have to be the end for us, and I realize what a fool I've been. We had the perfect situation, and in an effort to do something nice for her, I may have just fucked it all up.

Reminder to self — don't do nice things for people, especially women you're not ready to let go of.

She turns to me. Her eyes look a little damp, but she's not crying.

"This is actually good timing. The second half of the catering payment just went through yesterday." She nods. "It's time. I'm going to get Louise to hire a team for me today."

"You are?"

She nods. "Yeah. I am."

"But you still want to come over tonight, right?" I ask. "We can just… fuck and chill?"

A light laugh escapes her lips. "You know what? I think I might just head straight home tonight. Get an early night."

My heart feels like it's shattering into a thousand tiny pieces. It's the first time she hasn't wanted it, hasn't wanted to be with me.

"Do you have your period?" I ask. "Because, sweetheart, I'm a vampire. I can handle a little blood."

It's the only possible explanation, and the timing feels about right, but her rejection still feels like an axe in my chest.

She rolls her eyes at me but doesn't deny it.

"Let's get to work," she says, shoving the helmet back on her head.

CHAPTER THIRTY-EIGHT

rix

Louise: Hey Trix, everything is all up and running. The team has all your instructions and recipes, and they are in the kitchen right now. Ali will pick everything up from the kitchen in the morning.

Trix: Perfect, thanks, Lou.

Louise: Anything else you need from me?

Trix: Nope. Go home and get some rest.

"Honey?" Mom calls as I walk through the front door. "You're home!"

It's just past eight when I walk into the kitchen, where Mom is putting away leftovers.

"I thought you'd moved out and forgotten to tell us!"

I give her a smile, a hug and a kiss on the cheek.

"It's that Maverick boy, isn't it?"

I laugh at the idea of her calling him a *boy* when he's a vampire who's nearly a hundred years old.

I just shrug. "Yeah."

"I knew all those posts on your social media were bullshit!"

"Mom!" I laugh.

She drops her spoon and looks me in the eye. "What's happening with you two?"

"Nothing." She keeps staring at me. "Nothing *serious*."

Dad walks in and grins at me. "Trix! We thought you'd left home!"

"No, Dad." I give him a huge hug and realize that while I have loved every single second I've spent with Maverick, I've kind of missed being home too.

"I need to hear more about this *boy*!" Mom demands.

"Boy? What boy?" says Dad.

"There's no boy. It's nothing. Just a fling with a co-star. It happens all the time."

"Trix," Mom says. "I want details!"

"How about we do details another time? I'm dying for a shower and an early night."

"You need to eat first." She grabs one of the containers of leftovers and sticks it in the microwave, ushering me towards a barstool at the kitchen island.

"While you eat, you tell me everything."

I don't tell her about Maverick, but I do tell them both about the new kitchen and the team, and they are both thrilled that I've finally made the decision to hand some work over.

"The thing is," Mom tells me. "If you get a slow period, you can just let the team go and do things yourself again. You're not tied into anything."

"How long is your lease for?" Dad asks.

"I don't know. Maverick paid for it."

Mom gives me a look.

"I'm planning to pay him back as soon as I get my cheque for the movie."

"What are you going to do when it all ends?" Mom asks. "Are you going to do more acting? Or focus on catering?"

I finish the last mouthful on my plate. "I don't know yet. I've really enjoyed acting again, but food has my heart too."

"Maybe you can combine them," Dad suggests. "You know, like Paul Newman has that salad dressing?"

I let out a laugh. "Dad, I am *so* far away from doing anything like that."

But a little light bulb goes on inside my brain. Tomorrow I'm going to post a recipe on my social media feed and see how my audience responds. Maybe there is some way to combine my two loves.

After a hot shower, I curl up in my bed in my comfiest pajamas with a hot water bottle on my belly, because I do in fact have my period. I had no doubt that a little period blood would have zero ick factor for Maverick, but that's not the only reason I put a little distance between us today.

The last few weeks have been the best of my life, but there was something we forgot to add to the list of rules:

No falling in love.

CHAPTER THIRTY-NINE

$\mathcal{M}$averick

I GET HOME from the studio and I'm alone for the first time in weeks. Every sound echoes off the walls. Every room feels so cold and empty without Trix's laughter and smart-ass comments filling the space.

Everywhere I look, she's there. Sitting on my couch, cooking with me in the kitchen, splayed out on my bed, running her soapy hands over her gorgeous body in my shower.

Fuck.

I've never felt like this before, and I don't like it. The ache, the pain of her not being here, is like I'm missing an organ.

I throw on a pair of swimming shorts and run down the back stairs onto the sand and into the ocean for a swim under the stars. But as I swim against the crashing waves, all I can think of is our midnight swim the night she was high on my blood.

Ah, a blood high. That would fix me!

I head back into the house and down into my cellar, where I keep my bottles of blood-bank blood. I notice I'm running low, so I send my supplier a quick text to book another delivery.

I grab two bottles. It won't get me completely messed up, but it should make me high enough to stop feeling so goddamn miserable about Trix not being here for five minutes.

But all the blood bank blood just makes me want her more — her sweet blood on my lips, her warmth against me, her laughter piercing my heart, her warm lips on my shoulder…

We had a rule not to text or call, but we said nothing about messaging through social media.

@MAVERICKJSTONE CAN'T SLEEP without you here.

@trixandtreatscatering we've literally never slept together.

@maverickjstone okay, can't function without you here.

I IMMEDIATELY BERATE myself for the stupidity of that last message, and I'm about to delete it, but it's too late. I can see she's seen it.

@TRIXANDTREATSCATERING I HAVE MY PERIOD.

@maverickjstone Sweetheart. You know I like blood. Get in an Uber.

@trixandtreatscatering LOL! I'm already in bed!

@maverickjstone Get your pretty ass out of your bed and into mine.

@trixandtreatscatering Tempting, but I'm exhausted and bloated and crampy.

@maverickjstone I'm sure I read somewhere that sex is good for cramps.

@trixandtreatscatering Yeah? You know what else is good for them?

@maverickjstone What?

@trixandtreatscatering Sleep.

@maverickjstone Okay, I'll let you sleep tonight, but I'm going to need you here again soon. Come over after filming tomorrow. I'll fuck you any way you want it, and then I'll ride you home.

SHE'S BEEN quick with the replies, but this one is taking ages. I'm not ready for a straight-out rejection, but I fear that may be where this is headed.

@TRIXANDTREATSCATERING RIDE ME HOME?

@maverickjstone Yeah. On my motorcycle. Did you think I meant in another way? Because I'll ride you any way you want.

@trixandtreatscatering How about Friday?

MY COCK IS ALREADY TWITCHING, but when she puts Friday on the table, my erection threatens to rip through my shorts. It's not a rejection.

@MAVERICKJSTONE THURSDAY IS our last day of filming. Friday I've got some meetings with the other producers, but I should be done by five and home by six.

@trixandtreatscatering Works for me.

@maverickjstone And what do I do in the meantime?

@trixandtreatscatering I guess you can always call a Donna. We never said we were exclusive.

@maverickjstone I thought it went without saying. It's not like either of us has had any time to be with anyone else.

@maverickjstone Have you been with anyone else?

@trixandtreatscatering No. Have you?

@trixandtreatscatering Actually, don't answer that. I don't want to know. If you get a Donna tonight, don't tell me.

@maverickjstone Trix, I won't get a Donna. The truth is… I haven't slept with a Donna since our first night together.

I FEEL braver telling her this over DMs than in person, but I immediately regret it. What if she's been with a bunch of guys since then? I'm going to feel like an idiot.

@TRIXANDTREATSCATERING ME NEITHER. Not a Donna. Just a guy. Ah, shit, you know what I mean!

@maverickjstone I will somehow manage to survive until Friday. Unless you change your mind and want me before then, just say the word.

@trixandtreatscatering Goodnight Maverick.X

WHY DOES that X at the end of her message feel so fucking meaningful?!

@MAVERICKJSTONE GOODNIGHT TRIX.

. . .

I DON'T END it with an X but holy shit, I want to.

The house feels slightly warmer now that I know she'll be here on Friday. I'm a fucking immortal. I can survive for a couple of days without her.

I head into the kitchen to make myself a coffee. Not because I really like it, but because it tastes like *her. My heart thumps* when I notice an envelope stuck to the coffeepot.

I WONDER which one of your love interests I'll take next?

SAME PAPER, same typewriter font, but this isn't a resignation. It's a threat. And it's clearly aimed at Trix.

Sure, I was a little worried when Juliette went missing. When they took Linda, I was a bit concerned. When Vivian went missing, I was slightly on edge, but now that the threat is on Trix, I'm ready to rip the head off whoever is doing this.

I immediately call Brandon and tell him to send a team of security to Trix's house, and then I ride over there as fast as the traffic will allow.

 averick

"WHAT ARE YOU DOING HERE?" Trix asks, looking sleepy and adorable as she stands in her doorway.

Her mom answered, and I thought she was going to send me packing, but she just beamed at me and called Trix to come down.

"Whoever is taking the vampires just left another note."

I hand it to her.

"You think this is about me? But I'm not a vampire."

"I can't take the risk. Can I come in?"

She frowns down at the welcome mat. "Do you need permission?"

"No, but it's always more polite to wait for it."

"Come in."

She guides me into a lounge room with matching floral couches, fluffy cushions and photos of their family all over the walls. She gestures for me to take a seat next to her, but I stay standing.

"I have a security team on the way, and I'll stay all night. I won't leave your side until we get these fuckers."

"Everything okay?" Her dad's worried face appears from the doorway, and I give him a smile.

"Mr. Delaney, so nice to meet you. I'm Maverick Stone." I shake his hand and do my best normal, charismatic human act.

"Oh, so lovely to meet you, Maverick," he says with a gentle laugh. "I enjoy your movies."

"Yeah? What's your favorite?"

"Oh, I couldn't pick just one!"

"Dad!" Trix says from the couch. "He doesn't need you fawning over him."

I give her dad a wink. "I'm always up for a little fawning."

He laughs again. "I'll leave you two lovebirds to it!"

Lovebirds?

Trix looks mortified.

"Can I stay over?" I ask. "Will your parents be okay with it?"

"Yeah, I guess."

"I'll sit out here on the couch."

"They will definitely think that's weird."

"Then I'll sit on your floor all night. I just need to know you're safe."

She stands up and reaches for my hand before quickly dropping it because we don't do that. "Come to bed."

The words pierce a little hole in my heart, and a tiny beam of light makes its way in.

Her upstairs bedroom is like the rest of the house. Large yet cozy and it's decorated in bizarre vintage items, including a purple fringed lamp which casts a low light over the room.

Brightly colored paintings cover the walls and my own face stares back at me from a framed vintage movie poster.

"*Winning the West*? Really?" I turn to her and grin.

She covers her face with her hands. "I found it in a thrift store a few months ago. It was before any of this."

I uncover her eyes. "Never hide your beautiful face from me."

"It's so fucking embarrassing."

"Why?"

"Because it's like I'm some crazy fan or something, and I'm not, I just—"

"It's cute," I tell her.

"Oh god."

"Get into bed."

She does as I say, and seeing her here, in her own bed, all wrapped up and cozy makes me want to get in there and cuddle her, but cuddling is against the rules.

"You can sleep next to me," she offers.

I shake my head. "Even under the circumstances, I think it's best if we stick to the rules. We made them for a reason, right?"

"What will you do all night?"

"I'll keep an eye on you."

"Okay, now you're really Edward-Cullen-ing me." Her eyelids flutter a little, remnants of some glitter she must have swiped on her lids after filming shimmering under the lamplight.

"I'll read your books or something," I say, nodding towards a shelf of those romantasy books she was always reading at my place.

She gives me a soft smile and then closes her eyes. "Okay, but you should start with the series about the fae prince."

"Oh hell no. Not the fae. Do you have anything else?"

"Dragons?"

"Slightly better."

"Are dragons real too?" she asks sleepily.

"No, sweetheart. Dragons aren't real. But if they were, I'd slay them all for you."

CHAPTER FORTY-ONE

rix

MAVERICK DOESN'T LEAVE my side all week, unless it's to let me check on Ali or he has to film something without me. Even then he's like an overprotective boyfriend, making sure someone else is watching me at all times.

If it was anyone else, it would feel suffocating, but when it's Maverick, it's kind of hot. Okay, *very* hot.

On Thursday night, after our last day of filming, a big group of us end up at the bar on the lot, and those of us who are human, get incredibly drunk.

We've made a movie! We're all going to be big stars! Everything is coming up roses! We have so much to celebrate!

Apart from the fact that someone who's been kidnapping vampires may also want to kidnap and kill me.

Even more reason to get drunk!

"Trix, sweetheart, I'm going to take you home," Maverick tells me as he pulls me down from the bar where me, Ali, Ziva and Finn have been doing our best *Coyote Ugly* impressions.

And boy, Finn can *dance*!

"Finn! Someone has to cast you in the next *Magic Mike* movie!" I call out to him as I fall into Maverick's strong embrace. "Ziva! Make a *Magic Finn* movie!" I tell her. "I'll be the love interest!"

"You can play my love interest anytime," Finn says with a smirk. I'm drunk but I don't miss the look of jealousy on Ali's face.

"Ali! You can be in it too!" I tell her.

"Trix, you *so* need to go home. You're wrecked!" Ali laughs down at me.

"But I'm having so much fun!" I complain, wiggling out of Maverick's arms. He could stop me, hold me tighter, keep me in his embrace, but he doesn't.

He's always like this. He's protective, strong, but he always lets me go when I ask, he always gives me the power.

I look up at him, his blue-green eyes full of care. He's not embarrassed that I was dancing on the bar or that I'm drunk off my face.

Suddenly the room starts spinning and I reach out to him to steady myself.

"Okay, we're going home," he tells me, not pretending at all that we're not together.

"OooOoOoOoooh!" coos Ali.

Maverick just gives her a stern look. I wish he'd give me that stern look. Of course, all I have to do is ask. Because Maverick is mine!

Wait, what?

Since when did I start thinking of him as *mine*?

"Let her stay!" Finn shouts to me. "You're not the boss of her and she doesn't want to go!"

"Yes, she does!" he growls.

"Trix, what do you want?" Finn stares down at me from the bar. "Choose your own destiny!"

I look up at Maverick and there's two of him.

Oh goody!

"Maverick," I purr. "I choose *Maverick.*"

Maverick rolls his eyes playfully then gives Finn a look as if to say *fuck you, she chose me!* And then he throws me over his shoulder and carries me out of the bar.

We get into the back of a black car and the instant it starts moving I feel like I'm going to hurl.

"We're not going on the motorcycle?"

"Sweetheart, if I put you on the back of my motorcycle right now, you'd vomit into your helmet, and it would not be pretty."

"Also, I'd probably fall off," I say, struggling to even keep my head upright.

"Yeah. This is safer."

"You want me to be safe."

"Yeah, baby, I do."

I fall asleep in the car and only wake up again when I realize I'm once again being carried by Maverick, this time up the steps to the door of his mansion.

He hits the lights and then carries me into the bedroom.

"We're going to sleep together?" I ask with a smile.

"I'm on the couch," he says, pulling off my sneakers and mom jeans.

"Fuck me," I tell him, reaching out my arms in a pathetic attempt to grab him.

He chuckles but shakes his head. "Get your ass to sleep. Don't forget, tomorrow is Friday."

"Friday?"

"Remember, you said you'd fuck me on Friday," he reminds me.

"I did?"

"Yeah. And so you're going to need your rest. I'm going to want it at least three times."

"Four," I tell him with what I think is a seductive grin, but probably isn't.

I WAKE UP AT MIDDAY, surprised that I don't have the hangover from hell. I lounge around in his luxurious bed for a little while longer, posting a quick update to my socials that filming is done and sharing a few pictures of me and Maverick. And then I share a recipe for ancient grains bars. While there's not as much engagement on my food posts as there are when I post Maverick's face, there are definitely people interested, especially hard-core movie buffs who are excited to eat what the stars are eating on set. Everyone wants to eat what Maverick Stone eats! If only they knew what he really ate...

I check my messages, hoping to see something from Maverick, but all I see is messages from people I don't know. Most of them I just let Louise open and respond to in her professional manner now, but my finger pauses as I see one from Hangry Book Publishers.

@HANGRYBOOKPUBLISHERS: Hi Trix, we hope it's okay to reach out this way. We've been watching your socials with interest and would like to speak to you about a potential book deal. We're thinking the book could launch around the same time as the movie and we could take advantage of some cross promotion. We're confident we could get you on a book tour including TV opportunities. We have connections with the Food Channel, and we can set up a meeting with them to discuss a potential TV series. In the meantime, we can offer you a three book deal and advance in the high six figures for the first, but this is negotiable. Let us know if this is something you're interested in…

HOLY SHIT!

My heart races, and then my mind tells me to take a beat. I've never heard of this publisher. This may be a scam. But then I go to their page and see that they have 150k followers and have published some of my favorite chefs and cooks!

IN THE HIGH SIX FIGURES.

I let out a squeal and immediately have the urge to message Maverick and tell him.

I'm grinning, looking at our last exchange, but then I remember the rules.

Immediately messaging him my good news is too relationship-y. I'll tell him tonight when he gets home.

TRIX: Louise, could you do me a favor?

Louise: Yeah of course! I've been hired until the end of December, I'm still your assistant until then. Ask me anything!

Trix: I need you to pick up a dress from my house. My mom should be home. I'll let her know you're coming.

Louise: Sure, anything else?

Trix: I also need some groceries.

Louise: Just let me know what you need, and I'll bring it to you. Where are you?

Trix: I'll send you the address.

Maverick doesn't usually eat anything but key lime bars, but I think he's going to enjoy this.

I bite my lip as I plan the dinner of his dreams.

CHAPTER FORTY-TWO

$\mathcal{M}$averick

@MAVERICKJSTONE: sorry baby, I'm running late, just got out of meetings. Be another 45. X

I TYPE the X without thinking, and as I put my phone back in my pocket, I feel a rush of — *something*. It's the strangest feeling… comfort, ease, *normalcy*, all alongside a nice dash of fear and agony.

All the way back to my Malibu mansion, I obsess about the message I sent her. The way I messaged her was so intimate, so relationship-y, and we had rules for a reason.

I don't want to stop doing what we're doing, and even though I'm fucking terrified, I want more with her. I *want* to be the guy who messages her to tell her I'll be home late. I want to be the guy who drives through the LA traffic a little faster than the speed limit just to get to her two minutes earlier. I want to be the guy who looks after her when she's drunk off her face and dancing on a bar.

I want to be that guy for her.

I want to be *her guy.*

I want to be *hers.*

And I want her to be *mine.*

But it's not possible. I am not made for this. I have no relationship bones in my body. I am a vampire. I am immortal. I am going to live forever, or at least until I piss someone off enough for them to give me the Certain Death, but even then, chances are high I'd take them on and win.

But Trix is human. She's weak. She's going to get old and die.

My stomach plummets at the thought.

And it's not that I care about her getting old. If she would let me, I'd spend every single day of her human life by her side. *But eventually, she will die, and I will be without her.*

I have never had these feelings before, and I am scared out of my goddamn mind. Of everything I have faced in my life — poverty and hardship, joining the army at thirteen, two world wars, getting turned and dealing with the insatiable thirst and eternal despair of being a vampire, movie critics who couldn't find one nice thing to say about me, *losing* Trix is what terrifies me the most.

There's only one thing for it. I have to end it. Now. Before *it* all breaks my fucking cold dead heart.

Traffic is heavy, and forty-five minutes turns into double that. By the time I park my motorcycle and make it inside, I'm praying Trix hasn't given up on me. That she hasn't left. I need to tell her right now that it's over, I may not have the guts to do it later.

"Trix?" I call out as I flick on a light.

And there she is, asleep on the couch, Percy in a ball by her feet.

"What?" she asks, squinting through the light. Her makeup is all smudged, and her hair is sticking up on one side, but she's still the most beautiful woman I've ever seen.

How the fuck am I going to end this?

Why the fuck am I going to end this?

Because you're a vampire and she's a mortal. Trix is not your happily ever after. You don't get one of those. But without you, she can still have one.

"What are you still doing here?" I ask. I don't mean it to come out like an accusation, but that's how she takes it.

You're doing this for her.

Percy jumps off the couch and meows at me like I'm an evil bastard for not feeding him as soon as I walked in.

"Oh my god. I'm such an idiot." She buries her face in her hands.

"Trix?"

"I thought maybe—" She lets out a strangled laugh and looks at the ceiling. Her deep, warm eyes return to mine as she sits up on the couch. "I don't know why I—" She looks around frantically for a moment before grabbing her phone. "I'll get an Uber. I'll just go. *Fuck.*"

As she starts typing something into her phone, I take in what she's wearing. A teal fifties-style dress, tight bodice, long puffed out skirt.

Oh shit, this is my fantasy.

But it's gone wrong. So very, very, fucking wrong.

"Trix, I'm sorry I'm late. There was traffic and—"

"No," she says, without looking up from her phone. "This is all on me. None of *this* was in the rules." She picks up the edge of her dress and then lets it fall. "I'm such a moron," she mumbles.

"Hey, you're not a moron," I say moving towards her. "I messaged you, but it was already late, and then there was traffic."

She looks up at me, and it's then that I realize her makeup is not just smudged, but she has black tear tracks down her cheeks.

Fuck. I've made her cry. This is the fucking worst!

"I didn't see your message," she blinks.

Knowing she was sitting here crying over me just kills me.

And in that *dress*?

This is exactly why I need to end this. She shouldn't be waiting on anyone. Especially not me. She should be with some normal human guy who shows up on time after work.

"There's meatloaf on the table," she says, getting up and grabbing her purse. "Well, it's made with lentils, so it's plant loaf, I guess."

She should be with someone who actually *needs* to eat her plant loaf.

"Trix." I take a step towards her.

"This was all just a big mistake," she says, blinking at me numbly. "All of it."

I've been desperately trying to convince myself I need to end it with her, but now that she's talking about ending it with me, I just want to die. Again.

"No, it wasn't. It isn't." I put my hands on her shoulders. She's so warm and beautiful and perfect.

"I have to go."

I drop my hands. I don't want to hold her here against her will.

She looks up at me like it's going to be the last time she's ever going to look at me like this and my chest aches. There's a physical pain like I'm being stabbed in the heart with an ash stake.

"Trix, please don't go," I plead.

"I wanted to do your fantasy," she says with a sad smile. "I wanted to *be* your fantasy."

"Trix," I move closer to her again and cup her face in my hands. Her bright red cherry earrings wedge themselves between my fingers. "I want this fantasy more than you know, but—"

"But?"

"But it's going too far. I want — but I don't know how to—"

She takes a breath and looks up at the ceiling. "You're right. I went too far. I'm sorry."

"No, it's not you. It's me."

She lets out a strangled laugh. "Of course you're going to fucking end it with a line."

"I don't want to end it. That's the problem."

She blinks, and I wipe a little of the mascara off her cheeks.

"I think I'm—"

Oh, fuck, am I really going to say this?

"What?" she asks.

"I think I'm — I'm falling… for you."

Be brave you asshole.

"I'm falling in love with you."

Her beautiful warm eyes widen.

"But I can't do the love thing. I can't do the relationship thing. I'm not capable of it. And I don't want to hurt you, and so that's why we need to end this."

She just keeps staring up at me, not saying anything, but I can see a million thoughts in her eyes.

"Trix, please say something."

She pauses for a moment and I'm waiting for her to say she loves me too, that the two of us — me, a fucked up immortal with a past full of darkness and her — a gorgeous mortal full of life and light can somehow make it work.

"No, I get it. We had the rules for a reason. And you're right."

"I am?"

"This was only ever supposed to be about sex."

"The sex with you, Trix, it was otherworldly."

"Past tense," she whispers.

I run my hands down her arms, careful not to hold her hands.

No handholding.

"If we continue like this, it's going to kill me," I say.

"Could we have… one more time?"

I should say no. But I don't.

"Let me be your fantasy, just for tonight. I still really want to do this, if you still want it."

I should absolutely say no.

"It seems only fair after you've fulfilled so many of mine," she smiles sadly.

My jaw tightens as I consider what she's saying. I'm already in too deep. What's one more time?

She shakes her head. "Sorry. I'm being unfair. You've said what you want. I should—"

I throw my arms around her, grabbing her ass and lifting her up. She wraps her legs around me like she's holding on for dear life, just like that first time. I carry her over to the dinner table that she's set for two. A cold plant loaf and two almost burnt-out candles in the center.

This is my ultimate fucking fantasy, and I want to play it out with her. I want to play pretend one more time.

"Just for tonight," I tell her.

She nods. "One more time."

I swipe my thumb over her cheek again, removing some more of the mascara tracks.

"Are you sure?" I ask.

"So sure."

"Turn around and bend over," I tell her.

She does as I ask, and I have a hell of a time tackling the layers of her dress to lift them up.

"Okay, this was easier when this was just a fantasy," I say.

She lets out a laugh, and I eventually get the last layer flipped over, revealing the fact that she's completely naked under this dress.

I'm immediately hard for her.

"Jesus, Trix, how am I going to let you go?" I say, as I check with my fingers to see if she's ready for me. She is. She always is.

Her pulse runs faster with each circle I make of her clit. She lets out a whimper and I know that she wants this as much as I do.

"Are you ready for me, gorgeous?"

"Always," she says.

I line myself up, feeling her silky smooth folds opening up for me. I grab her waist and oh so slowly, slide myself inside of her.

One more time.

She stretches out to fit me and I push inside deeper. Deeper into her.

And then I'm as deep inside her as I can get, wondering why the fuck I would ever let her go.

rix

IT'S NOT EXACTLY how I thought this night would play out. Me crying on the couch because I had no idea where he was or what he was doing, followed by a confession of *love*. But now that he's inside me, none of it fucking matters.

If it's our last time, I want to just enjoy it, but his words *I'm falling in love with you* keep resounding in my head as he thrusts his cock into me.

"Fuck, baby," he growls. "You're so fucking good."

He just goes for it. Fucking me so hard my thighs are slamming into the table. But I'm loving every second of it.

"Harder," I beg. "More."

"You're insatiable," he chuckles.

"Only for you," I tell him.

My words have him gripping my hips and thrusting even deeper into me and I come harder and faster than ever before with him, screaming my ecstasy over the plant loaf and blowing out the candle stubs.

He comes a moment later, faster than he ever has, calling out my name as he shudders behind me.

It's quicker than I expected. But it's done. Our last time. And it was good, *so* very good, just like it always is with him. In a moment I'll leave, knowing I had an amazing time with this man. It was wonderful. Every single second of it. Filming, fucking, biting, fighting, playing out our fantasies.

As he pulls out of me, I feel the emptiness like a hole in my heart.

It's over. But I'll be okay. I'll get over it one day. I'll—

He grabs my shoulders and lifts me up from the table, turning me around to face him. His eyes blaze down at me.

"I'm not done with you yet," he tells me. "Give me until midnight."

There's something deeper in his gaze. Something more. It's like he wants me on a deeper level than he's been able to give or receive before, and I'm all fucking for it.

Just for tonight.

I just nod. Of course, I'll be his until midnight. I'll be his forever, whether he knows it or not.

He slides his hand down my arm. "I want to hold your hand," he tells me. "Is that okay?"

"Okay."

His fingers slip into mine, and my heart leaps at the warmth and comfort of it. He stares down at our hands, fingers entwined, and then, still holding my hand, leads me into the bedroom. He closes the door behind us and switches on the light.

"You want the blinds open?" he asks.

"Closed." I know that no one can see us through the tinted glass anyway, but I don't even want the idea of it. I just want *him.* Just *us.*

He closes the blinds and then turns me around, unzipping my dress and letting it fall to the floor. I feel myself physically shaking.

He turns me around again, taking in my naked body, but his gaze returns to my eyes. That deeper look, that look of... oh my god, is this *love?*

Are we *in love?!*

Oh, holy shit.

He runs his fingers over my collarbone. It makes me shiver, and he grins up at me. That something extra in his eyes makes me melt, and his touch makes me completely disintegrate.

He pulls off his shirt and then presses his naked chest into mine. Our bodies are a perfect fit.

"What if there were no rules tonight?" he asks.

"What do you mean?"

"I want to kiss you. Not for the cameras. But for real."

"Are you sure?"

"It was your stupid rule," he smirks. Then he adds, "I've never been surer."

He moves his face towards me, and I gasp as his lips press into mine. His tongue presses my lips apart, and I open up my mouth for him, tasting his sweet, salty kiss for the first time without a crowd of people watching. I thought he put on a good show before, but this is another level. I feel his kiss so deep within me — my belly, my heart, my fucking soul. He definitely kept something back, something just for me.

He pulls away from the kiss, and I gently bite his lower lip to try to get him to stay.

"Trix," he says, almost in a whimper.

"Maverick."

He steps back and lets his pants fall to the floor, revealing his perfect, huge manhood, vampire-hood? Whatever it is, it is *glorious.*

He closes the gap, our naked bodies pressing together. He lingers, kissing my cheek, my forehead, my neck and finally my lips again.

"You taste so sweet," he says.

He walks me to the bed, and I fall back, my legs opening for him. He moves on top of me and kisses me again, hot, heavy, like he's been starved of kisses his whole life, and I kiss him back with just as much need, hunger. All this time of not kissing Maverick Stone feels like a waste of my life!

"You're so wet," he says as he rubs his rock-hard cock against my opening.

"It's you," I tell him. "It's your cum from the first time."

He groans in approval. "How many times can I fill you before midnight?"

Oh my fucking god.

"There's not much time," I say, opening my legs wider and pushing myself into him. "Fuck me now," I groan.

"I don't want to fuck you, sweetheart."

I pause and frown at him. "What?"

"I want to make love to you, Trix."

Oh shit!

"Can you handle it?" he asks me. "I know you can take my massive cock, but can you also take my heart? Just for tonight?"

Oh god, this is bad, so, so bad. If I do this, if we do it like this, I don't know how I will ever get over him. I will never get over him. My life will be ruined. I will never be able to be with another man.

"Yes," I tell him. "You already have mine."

That look in his eyes shifts again, and I know my words have changed him. He knows I feel the same.

He presses himself into me slowly, gently, and it feels like I'm being fucked by an angel.

"Trix," he says, into my neck.

"Bite me," I say, turning my head to give him better access to my pulse point.

"No, baby. Not tonight. I just want to pretend."

"Pretend to be in love?"

"No, that's not pretend. Is it pretend for you?"

I shake my head. "No."

"I just want you to pretend — that I'm human."

His words hit my heart, so deep and pure. I feel a tear escape and roll down my cheek, but I don't wipe it away or pretend not to be feeling everything I'm feeling right now. I just wrap my legs around him and pull him deeper into me. He finds my hands and links his fingers into mine. He thrusts into me while we stare at each other like we're each other's only reason for existing.

"Maverick," I say.

"Yes, baby?"

"I know we're making love and all, but can you do it a little harder now?"

He laughs and plants a gentle kiss on my mouth.

"I'll give you whatever you want," he says. He lets go of one of my hands and hooks my leg over his shoulder and then thrusts into me *hard.* I let out a yelp, and he pulls back a little.

"Too much?"

"More."

"Your wish, my command," he gives me a dirty smirk and continues to thrust deeper, holding my leg with one hand, squeezing my hand with his other.

He places my leg down and moves his now free hand to my breast, playfully pinching my nipple as I gasp. He does the same to my other breast, and when my nipples are screaming with warmth and pleasure, he moves his fingers down to my clit and rubs up and down in time with his thrusts, all the while still holding my other hand.

I squeeze my fingers into his as I feel myself reaching my climax.

"Come for me, baby," he says. "Tell me it's all for me."

"It's all for you, Maverick," I tell him as the orgasm hits. My whole body clenches, and I squeeze his hand like I'm going to break it, but of course, I won't. I let out a howl of pleasure as I reach the top, and then I'm floating along waves of such immense pleasure I never want to go back to the shore.

"Call me something else," he says, still thrusting into me hard as I lie here in absolute ecstasy. No bite required.

"Like what?" I whimper.

"Something fucking romantic," he says, still thrusting into me.

A laugh escapes my lips. "It's all for you, my lover. My love. It's all for you, baby."

"Tell me I'm the only one," he growls into my neck.

"You're the only one."

"Are you just saying that?" he asks, glaring down at me, his eyebrows knit together. I think it's the first time I've ever seen him vulnerable. Thrusting into me, holding my hand. *Making love.* "Please. only say it if you mean it."

I run my hand up to the back of his neck, running my fingers through his sexy, messed up, dirty blonde hair.

"You're the only one," I say. "You're the only man I'll ever want."

He thrusts into me hard and heavy on my words, and it's not long before he hits his own peak, riding me and the waves of his own pleasure as another climax hits me too.

"I fucking love you," he says, as he thrusts into me one last time, his unviable seed spilling out inside of me.

"I love you too," I whisper. I grip his hand even tighter as tears fall down my cheeks.

CHAPTER FORTY-FOUR

rix

THE WORDS TUMBLE out like rocks down a mountain, an avalanche that's going to bury us both.

I love you too.

Those words have never been uttered from my lips until this moment, and their sound seems to echo through the room as we both just lie there, staring up at the ceiling, still clutching each other's hands, neither of us knowing what to say or do now, because none of that was anything like what I expected.

Sex with Maverick has always been unbelievable. But it was just *sex*. This wasn't just sex. This was me falling in fucking love with him.

And then I realize that's not true. I've been falling in love with him this whole time. From the first moment in the diner when his eyes locked with mine, I knew there was more to Maverick Stone than just the hot movie star whose face was on every billboard in town. The first time we had sex in his kitchen, I knew it was more than just sex.

There's always been something between us that's just undeniable.

Maybe it's just because he saved my ancestors. Maybe there's some fucked up ancestral trauma bonding us.

Or maybe we're just somehow *meant to be together*.

I've thought that a million times with guys I've crushed on or dated for five minutes. I've always gotten myself into that delusional headspace, thinking I've found my soulmate just because some guy is semi-cute and nice to me.

But this isn't like that. This is—

This is fucking *real*. *Too* real.

And this is it. The last time.

He doesn't do relationships. He's not capable. And what do I know about love? Fucking nothing.

He squeezes my hand and I hold my breath, waiting for him to speak, to say the "rules" are stupid and we should just be together like this forever, or at the very least to tell me he wants me to stay all night.

"I'm going to take a shower," he says, sliding his hand out of mine and disappearing into the ensuite.

He doesn't invite me to come with him.

He doesn't tell me to stay.

He just *leaves*.

As soon as I hear the water run, I grab my dress from the floor and put it back on. I leave the bedroom, not daring to look back at the bed we just made love in. I grab my shoes and my purse and head out the door.

The Uber is only two minutes away, thank god, but those two minutes are the longest of my life. Standing outside his Malibu mansion, I think of the first moment I arrived here, sliding off his motorcycle, staring up at his mansion, wondering if I was making the worst mistake of my life.

It wasn't a mistake. How can love ever be a mistake?

But that doesn't mean this doesn't hurt like hell.

The car arrives, and I jump in the back. I look back up at the house and I hold my breath, waiting for him to come to the door, to call out my name, to stop me from leaving, to tell me I'm the one, to chase the car down the street just like he would if it was one of his movies.

But this is not a movie, and he doesn't come.

CHAPTER FORTY-FIVE

$\mathcal{M}$averick

I HEAR her leave while I'm still in the shower. She tries to be quiet, but I hear everything. I hear the rustling of her dress as she puts it back on. I hear her putting on her shoes. I hear her leave. I hear her car driving away.

I don't remember the last time I cried. Maybe it was the night of the bombing in London. Maybe it was never.

But tonight, I fucking cry.

CHAPTER FORTY-SIX

WEEKS PASS, and I avoid everyone and everything. I skip the official wrap party and instead me and Ali have our own celebration, getting drunk at her apartment. I get so messed up at Ali's, the next morning she looks at me like I'm losing it. I am.

"Are you going to be okay?" she asks the next morning.

"I will be," I tell her, even though I have no idea how long it will take for me to be okay. But I have to believe that one day I will.

One day I will get over this. One day maybe I'll find someone who makes me feel a little bit like Maverick does.

A pain hits my chest whenever I think about him, which is all the fucking time. They say time heals, but those first eighteen months didn't heal shit.

I'm still having dreams, but now instead of dreaming

about him fucking me in his kitchen, I dream about him holding my hand. I dream about him telling me he loves me.

I dream of us making love.

It's so much worse. But in some ways, it's also better.

Because now, even though my heart is broken into a million pieces, I know what it's like to be in love.

I've been loved. I have loved.

I can't control any of this. I can't stop the dreams. I can't stop my feelings for him. I can't change the fact that I'm so in love with him it feels like I can't breathe most of the time.

But I can go back to therapy.

I can sign the three book deal with Hangry House Publishers and talk to the Food Channel about a TV show.

I can move my team out of the kitchen Maverick hired for me and into my own place. A place I pay for all myself.

I can trust my team to make food that's *almost* as delicious as if I'd made it myself and I can start donating more of my time and food to local soup kitchens.

December gets busy, and Trix and Treats is catering events almost every night. But I have my team to help me.

Keeping busy helps, but somewhere deep in my soul I know that no matter what happens next, eventually, I will be okay.

At least, I think I will until a notification pops up on my phone reminding me of tomorrow's event.

Max Montrose's Christmas Eve party.

CHAPTER FORTY-SEVEN

$\mathcal{M}$averick

I LOOK at myself in the mirror and practice my fake smile. In a designer navy blue suit with a festive red tie, I look the part of a movie star going to an exclusive Christmas party in the Hollywood Hills.

I don't look like a man who hasn't rested for two weeks. I don't look like I'm in absolute agony every time I get into bed and *she's* not there. I don't look like I'm living off a diet of stale blood bank blood and Hallmark Christmas movies.

I don't look like I've broken my own fucking heart by breaking the rules and falling in love.

It's been two weeks since she left my bed and walked out of my life.

I never knew two weeks could feel like two years, two decades, two hundred years.

I don't know what I'll say when I see her at Max's party. I don't know if I'll be able to speak. I don't know if I'll just break down and cry, beg her to come back. I don't know if I'll be able to put on a show and act like nothing happened.

That was part of the rules, after all.

Act like it never happened.

I ditch the tie and walk to the garage where I get on my motorcycle. I immediately feel the familiar aching pain at the emptiness of not having her arms around me, and I head out towards the Montrose mansion.

"MAVERICK, LOVELY TO SEE YOU." Max claps me on the back and welcomes me into his parlor where the party is in full swing. Everyone is dressed festively in red, green, gold and silver. The house is decorated with Christmas trees plural, he has two just in the parlor, tinsel and string lights. It's like a Christmas wonderland in here. Max has never cared for Christmas before, and I can only assume this is all Poppy's doing.

I spot the director Jessica Palmieri and Stacey Graves, Max's co-star from the indie movie he wrapped earlier this year, but most of the other guests are vampires. The remaining members of the Fraternity are all here, mostly looking somber. And why wouldn't they? It's been months and we still have no fucking clue where Juliette, Linda and Vivian are.

I haven't told anyone apart from Brandon about the letter threatening Trix, but the pieces of conversation I pick up are enough to make me realize that every vampire here is already concerned enough. There's a strong sentiment in the air that Brandon is to blame for this, and I don't think it would take much for them to demand *his* resignation as president, maybe even from the Fraternity.

There is change in the air for the vampire community, and not for the better.

I've been such a miserable shit these last few weeks, deep in my own self-pity. I sent all the security Brandon had arranged for me over to Trix's house, asking them to shadow her and keep her safe, and to let me know if they see anything suspicious. I suspect that she's a million times safer away from me, anyway. Another reason not to reach out, to tell her I can't live without her, tell her I'd do anything for one more night.

My eyes search everywhere for Trix. I knew she was catering this party, but she told me weeks ago that she'd bring a dress and join the guests once everything was ready. But I don't see her anywhere. I shouldn't be watching doorways and wondering when she'll walk in. She should be here, by my fucking side.

Fuck.

I spot Poppy dressed in a red and green floral dress standing by a buffet of food in the dining room. This is where the food is. This is where I'll find Trix.

And then what? I don't know.

What do you say to someone after confessing your love, fucking them like the world is ending and then ghosting them for two weeks?

It was too hard? I didn't know how to handle it? I have never loved anybody before, and I suck at this? You're human and you will die and leave me all alone for the rest of eternity, and I won't be able to live without you? I'm sorry I broke your heart, and mine, but it's better this way?

Or maybe I'll suggest we fly to Vegas and get married immediately.

I don't know what I'll say to her when I see her. I just have this desperate need to see her, to breathe the same air as her. I just want to *be* near her, even if it kills me.

"You okay, Maverick?" Poppy asks.

"Yeah, fine."

She gives me a look like she knows I'm not fine.

"Where's Trix?" I ask.

"She's not here."

My mind can't comprehend this. "She's not here?"

"No."

"But she's catering the party."

"Trix and Treats is catering, but Trix isn't here. Ali is running things tonight."

My heart feels like it's just fallen out of my body and onto the ground.

She's not here.

I mentally calculate how long it will take me to get to her house. She might not want me there, she might tell me to go, but just like the teenage boy at the end of the movie, I'm willing to take the risk to look like an absolute fucking fool if there's even a one percent chance she'd be happy to see me, throw her arms around me, kiss me on the goddamn mouth and tell me, "fuck the rules!"

Poppy frowns up at me and then realization dawns in her big hazel eyes. "Wait, you and *Trix*?"

"She didn't tell you?"

Her eyes get even wider, and she shakes her head. "I thought maybe—when you were so determined to go in the ambulance with her at the Thanksgiving party but no, she never said anything to me."

Trix never told her. She kept her promise. She stuck to the rules. Even now.

"It's over now," I assure her. "And it's for the best."

"Well, that explains why she's been so miserable lately."

"She has?" My heart shouldn't light up at the knowledge that she's been in pain, but it makes me better to know that everything I'm going through, she's going through, too.

"Why?" Poppy asks.

"Why, what?"

"Why is that what's best?"

I sigh. "You know me, Poppy. You know my life, you know who I am. Surely you wouldn't want someone like me dating your best friend?"

"I want whatever would make Trix happy," she says. "She's been in such a bad mood since the movie wrapped. I thought she was just coming down after the high of filming. Max gets like that when something wraps."

"She'd be more miserable trying to have any kind of future with me. You know what I am. You know how hard it is to be with — someone like me. And I'm not even half the man Max is."

"Do you love her?" she asks, point blank.

"Yes," I answer with absolutely zero hesitation.

"I don't care what Max is, only *who* he is. But if you're not man enough to go after Trix, to tell her how you really feel, to at least *try* to make something work with her, then she is better off without you."

She's right.

"If you want to keep living this life, different Donnas every night, parties, fame, whatever, then go for it. But if you want something *more,* you know what to do."

Poppy leaves, I fill a plate with food made from Trix's recipes and I head outside, sitting alone at a table on the patio in the cool evening air.

Max has a view to die for and that's exactly what he did for this view. But as I look down at the lights of the city below, all I can think is that Trix is down there somewhere.

I eat every bite as if it's part of her soul, her heart, part of her light, and it's all so delicious I want to cry.

This is insane. A vampire sitting on a patio having a private pity party by gorging himself with human food.

I need to make a decision.

But the decision is already made.

It was made two weeks ago when I told her I loved her. I've tried to convince myself I can't, that I'm not that guy, not monogamous, not boyfriend material, but maybe with Trix I *can* be that guy.

I need to go after her.

"Thanks for the party, Max," I tell him on my way out.

"This was the worst party I've ever hosted," he sighs. "It's so somber. All the vampires are looking over their shoulders worried they could be next."

"I don't think any of us will fully relax until we find out who's behind this and all the missing are returned. Any of us could be next."

"Even you?" he asks.

I let out a laugh. "Any of us but me. I'm the last vampire they're going to mess with."

"Good to see you," Max says. "Take care."

EVERY TIME I COME HOME, I find myself holding a spark of hope that Trix will be here. That she'll have dinner on the table, that she'll be wearing that sexy as fuck dress, ready for me to take it off her and have my way with her.

I hope that she'll be on the couch dressed in nothing but my t-shirt, watching one of my old movies, about to order a pizza for us both.

I hope that she's in my bed, still there, the last two weeks never having happened.

I hope she'll just fucking *be here.* Even if she's mad, even if she hates me, even if all she wants to do is yell at me for how stupid I've been.

But she isn't. The only thing that's here is a delivery of blood sitting at my front door.

Fucking finally.

They don't usually leave the delivery if I'm not home, but

whatever. I could really use a drink right now. I open the door and bring the box inside, ripping it open and grabbing one of the familiar wine bottles that the blood is delivered in. I pull the cork out and pour the blood into a tumbler that's sitting on the coffee table, filling it right to the top.

I drink it fast, filling a second glass and drinking nearly the whole bottle. It's a large dose, more than I need. But a blood high wouldn't be the worst thing right now.

But I don't get a blood high, I don't even get the usual satiated feeling. It's almost like I'm drinking that synthetic blood Max was on when he was going through his "not harming humans" phase.

"What the fuck is this?" I look at the small amount of blood remaining in the bottle and start to feel a little groggy.

My peripheral vision goes, and I feel a wave of panic rush through me.

Oh fuck, this is how they are doing it!

I reach for my phone and dial Max's number.

"Maverick?"

But I'm too late. "It's—" I say. "The blood—"

And then I'm out.

CHAPTER FORTY-EIGHT

rix

"I KNOW HE LOVES ME," I say, plating up some more carrot lox on a not actually silver platter.

"What?!" Poppy exclaims. "What the hell is going on with you two? Why did you tell me to tell him you weren't here? You need to talk to him! He's miserable!"

"Nothing," I shrug. "Not anymore. I just didn't want to face him. I'll get over it."

I won't.

"He looked so broken when I told him you weren't here."

I look up, heart pounding. "He did?"

"Yeah, he did. It looks to me like all this is killing him as much as it's killing you."

"Well," I say, passing the platter to one of my team. "He's the one who said he didn't want a relationship. And I'm not going to chase him. I'm not going to try to *force* him into a relationship with me when he specifically stated on a number of occasions that he doesn't do relationships. I'm not going to be that girl."

"What girl? The girl that fights for love?"

"No! The pathetic girl who doesn't read the signs, who doesn't listen. The delusional girl who thinks she can *change him*. We all know who Maverick Stone is. He's never going to be boyfriend material. I just need to accept it and move on with my life."

Yeah, good luck, Trix.

"What if he was? What if he wanted to be with you? What if he could change?"

I sigh. "He isn't, and he doesn't, and he won't. He's made it clear."

"What about what you want?" Poppy asks.

I want him to turn me into a vampire so we can literally be together forever.

"I just want to move on."

"We're nearly out of dessert again," says Ali. "They're hardly touching the savory stuff, but the sweets are going fast!"

"On it," I tell her, opening the fridge to pull out a platter of mixed desserts. I place the platter on the counter and see an envelope sitting on top of the tray.

"That's weird, what's this?"

"Maybe it's from Maverick! Open it!" Poppy demands.

I'm about to open it when a wave of nausea hits me. I feel like I'm going to vomit and then everything suddenly goes dark around the edges of my vision.

"He's in trouble," I whisper.

"Who?"

"Maverick."

"How do you know?"

"I just... I feel it."

"The blood bond," Poppy says. "Sometimes when Max's

emotions are really strong, I feel them—" Poppy grabs the envelope and pulls out the letter.

"I, Maverick Stone, hereby resign from the Fraternity of the Everlasting Rose. I no longer believe that the organization operates in the best interests of vampire-kind, and so I submit my resignation. It would do all other vampires in the Fraternity well to consider their own involvement in this outdated secret order and to look to the future instead of the past when it comes to vampire legacy, influence and affluence."

"WHAT THE—?" Poppy begins.

I don't even realize I'm moving until I'm yanking the kitchen door open and running over the gravel path towards the van.

"Trix!" Poppy calls after me. "Wait!"

But I don't wait. I don't think. I just know I need to get to him. *Now.*

Maverick is in trouble and so fuck the rules, fuck pretending I'm not in love, fuck acting like I'm going to be fine without him.

If something happens to Maverick, I'll never be fine again.

I'm about to hit the gas when Poppy appears in the seat next to me.

"Max, Brandon and Henrietta will be right behind us," she says, catching her breath.

I speed down the driveway, giving my old friend Malik a wave of thanks as he opens the gate for us, and then I drive as fast as I legally and safely can in this truck.

"God, this was stupid," I say after about ten minutes of winding in and out of traffic. "Max's car would have been faster."

"What matters is that we're on the way," Poppy says.

"Who would do this?" I ask. "Who would kidnap vampires?"

"We don't know he's been kidnapped," Poppy says.

"Oh, don't pretend Max hasn't told you what's going on," I say.

"Maverick told you?"

"He just told me they've been going missing. That's all I know."

"Max doesn't know any more than that," she assures me. "Brandon has had some private investigators looking into it, but they still haven't come up with anything."

"Someone was in his house," I say. "In Max's house. Someone planted that letter. Who?"

"I don't know. Max's security is the best money can buy. If it was on your platter of desserts, maybe it was someone from your team?"

I shake my head. "No way. I vetted them all—"

"Maybe someone put the letter in there while you were packing?"

I try to remember who was there when we were packing the van outside the kitchen. There were definitely moments when no one was watching the van.

"What about Henrietta? Can't she see visions or read the tarot or something?" I ask, my voice getting higher with every question I ask.

"All she gets is blackness."

"What does that mean? What blackness?"

"She said it's like something is blocking her vision. She can't see anything."

I drum my fingers anxiously on the wheel like it's going to help us get there faster.

"Werewolves?" I ask.

"They wouldn't dare, not since Max started paying for all

their college tuition and other extras. If they went against us now, after everything he's done for them, the Fraternity would be ready to kill them all."

I don't miss the way she says *us* like she's one of them.

"Are you going to let Max change you?"

She lets out a nervous laugh. "Oh, god, that's a big question! Not right now, but in the future. Maybe when I'm the same age as him."

"Isn't it the sort of thing you need to be sure about?"

"I've got eight years to think about it," she shrugs. "But I honestly can't imagine life without him."

"Eternity is a long time. You want to make sure it's the right guy."

"Not even eternity would be long enough for me and Max."

We sit in thick silence for a while as the traffic slows to a crawl.

If I was on the back of Maverick's motorcycle we'd be there by now.

"Would you?" she asks.

"Huh?"

"Would you change? For Maverick?"

"Yes."

More silence.

"I know it's probably really hard for you to even consider this, but do you think there's any chance that Aiden has something to do with this?"

I look over at her, and her mouth forms a hard line.

"The idea that my own brother—the one person I had on my side growing up, my own flesh and blood—could be part of this plot to kidnap vampires *is* really hard to consider. He was always there for me. He was my rock. The only family I really had. But he also chained me up in a fucking crypt. He was going to let his girlfriend, and let's not forget—*Max's wife*—kill me. The two of them would have killed us all if they'd had the chance. So yeah, it's hard to consider, but it's also... plausible. But without Lottie? He wouldn't be strong enough. Lottie is dead and how would a two-year-old vampire take on a vampire like Maverick?"

She's right. Lottie Luelle is dead. The Certain Death is called Certain for a reason and Maverick is fast and strong and immortal. How on earth would a younger, weaker vampire kidnap him?

We sit in silence the rest of the way, both lost in our thoughts, trying to put the pieces of what feel like completely different jigsaw puzzles together.

By the time we arrive outside Maverick's house Max, Brandon and Henrietta are just seconds behind us.

I run straight up the steps and bang on the door. I know he's not here, but I still call his name as I try the door.

It's open.

I run into the space that almost feels like my own home after all the time I've spent here but it's so quiet, empty and hollow without Maverick.

"Where's the security team you hired for him?" I practically yell at Brandon as he and the others enter the room.

"The security guard said he didn't see anything. Just a delivery a few hours ago," Brandon says.

"They must have taken him out the back way," Max says. "Down the beach."

"Why the fuck was there only one security guard out there?" I demand.

"He sent the rest of his team to look after you, Trix," Brandon says.

My heart sinks.

"What? Why?"

But of course, I know why. I'd kind of gotten used to the black cars following me around, I didn't think anything of it when I noticed there were twice as many of them as before. When he knew we weren't going to be together anymore, that he wouldn't be there to protect me, he sent his team to look after me.

I look around the room, over at the posters of his handsome face, the near empty bottle of blood on the table.

"The blood," Max says. "That's what Maverick said to me on the phone. *The blood.*"

"The blood?" Brandon takes the bottle in his hand, swishing it around and giving it a sniff.

Max looks down at the box filled with eleven more bottles. "This box, this isn't quite…"

"What? What is it?" I ask as both Max and Brandon stare down at the box.

"It's not the usual box that the blood comes in," says Max.

Brandon looks at the label. "This didn't come from our usual supplier."

"It's the blood," Max says, standing up, his gaze fierce. "We need to alert the Fraternity."

"I'll contact them," Brandon says. "Can you take a bottle to your lab and get it tested?"

Max nods, lifting a bottle out, another envelope attached to it.

We all exchange glances, and then he opens it.

"This one is for you," he says, passing it to Brandon.

He reads it out loud: "Brandon Curtis. Step aside or everyone you care about will die. Return the Fraternity to its rightful heir or you and all those you care about will receive the Certain Death."

Max's jaw clenches. "Fucking Lottie… but *how?*"

CHAPTER FORTY-NINE

rix

"WE NEED TO DO SOMETHING!" I pace the living room as my stomach twists into knots and tangles at the idea that Maverick — strong, powerful, movie star, vampire army hero, *Maverick* has been taken. Taken from *me*.

"Just try to relax," Brandon says. "We will find him."

"Oh yeah? Like you found the others? Juliette has been missing for *months*!"

"It should be easier to find him with the blood bond you share," Henrietta says, grabbing a deck of tarot cards out of her purse.

"Wait, you knew about them?" Poppy asks.

"I can sense it," Henrietta says.

"I'm sorry," Max says. "Trix and *Maverick*?"

"It was immediately clear from their chemistry on set," Brandon says.

"How long has this been going on?" Max demands.

"None of your business," I tell him.

Max turns to Poppy. "You knew about this?"

"I only just found out!"

"Trix, why on earth would you get involved with—?"

Poppy elbows him in the ribs. "You think you can judge? Our relationship is not exactly normal."

Max huffs and Henrietta starts shuffling the cards, laying them out on the coffee table as we all gather around her.

"Eight of Swords," she murmurs. "He's trapped, taken against his will—"

"Can you get anything on the others now?" Max asks. "I know you've been blocked with this, but we need *something* to go on."

Henrietta closes her eyes and her face squishes up in deep concentration. "Everything is still just… blackness." She pulls some more cards, frowns, puts them back in the deck and shuffles again.

"Anything at all would help," Max says.

Henrietta turns to me. "You're not getting anything? Through the blood bond?"

"I felt sick, and I felt panic. Then there was darkness," I say.

"Okay, good," says Henrietta. "Your bond is strong."

No shit.

"Try to tune into it," Henrietta says, shoving a huge clear quartz crystal in my hand.

"Tune into it?"

"Just think of him," she says.

I close my eyes and think about Maverick, his blue-green eyes, his strong jaw, his messed up dirty blonde sex hair, his naked body on top of mine, the way he made love to me that last time—

"What are you getting?" Poppy asks, bringing me out of the fantasy.

"Nothing!" I shake my head in frustration. "I don't know what I'm doing!"

"Trix, you may be our only chance to find him," Max says softly. "To find any of them."

"What about all the Donnas he knew? All the other women he shared a blood bond with? Maverick had a whole list of names in his phone," I say, reaching for his phone still sitting on the table. "He claimed so many Donnas." The idea of it still pains me, but if any of these women could help us find him—

Max frowns. "Maverick never kept a Donna's number."

"He did," I say. "He told me, that day in the diner—"

Max shakes his head. "If Maverick wanted a Donna, he'd call the club. Vincent's. They have a service."

Poppy gives him a look.

"I've never used it," he tells her.

"What about all the girls he claimed?" I ask. "Didn't he see them all the time?"

Max lets out a laugh. "Maverick only claimed them so that they wouldn't be bitten by other vampires. It was his way of keeping them safe."

"What?"

"He was always worried about the Donnas after—"

"After what?"

"In the eighties there were a lot of deaths. A lot of girls who enjoyed The Bite were drained," Brandon explains.

"Maverick began claiming as many girls as he could in an attempt to keep them safe from the killer," Max says.

I shake my head. "He was trying to *save* them?" I think of the woman he was kissing that night. He definitely didn't seem like he was trying to save her.

"Of course, Maverick benefited from it too," Brandon says with a chuckle.

I just glare at him.

Henrietta grabs my hand. "Take a breath. Let's try again. Focus. Think of Maverick."

I close my eyes and he's instantly there, just like he always is. His fingers slipping into mine, pressing my hand down firmly onto the pillow while he slides inside me.

"Okay, the connection is there… now focus on where he is *now*," Henrietta tells me.

A vision suddenly comes to me. "Joshua trees," I tell her.

"Good, good! What else?"

"He's in a car."

"Tell me everything you see, and anything you feel."

"He's angry. I can feel it, like he wants to kill someone, rip someone's head off—"

I can feel the anger like it's my own, my whole body pulsating with fire, ready to run, ready to kill, ready to do whatever it takes to get him back.

"I see a sign for the I-40 interstate!"

"Can you see which direction they're going?"

I shake my head. "I'm just getting flashes."

"Okay, what other flashes are you seeing? Even if you think they don't make sense, tell us what you see."

"I see—"

Oh shit.

"What is it?" she asks.

My eyes open, but I can still feel the rage through our bond.

"Cassius."

CHAPTER FIFTY

 averick

I COME to in the back of an SUV. My hands and feet are bound by silver, and it hurts like hell. I try to cry out, but I'm fucking gagged. I kick the seat in front of me. I don't have my usual strength, but I kick hard enough to get their attention.

Cassius turns around in the passenger seat and glares at me.

Oh, fuck, not this asshole!

"Hello again, Maverick," he grins back at me.

"Fuck you, asshole!" I attempt to say, but it comes out garbled.

His eyes narrow, clearly getting the gist of the intentions behind my words.

"Take his gag off," Vincent says, keeping his eyes on the road and not even glancing back at me.

Cassius clearly doesn't want to, but he does as he's told.

The power dynamic between them is so clear. Now I know why the bar is called Vincent's.

"What the fuck," I spit as soon as he pulls my gag off.

Cassius just laughs.

"We're not going to hurt you," Vincent says, glancing at me in the rear-view mirror.

Cassius's evil gaze upon me doesn't resonate with Vincent's words.

"We have an opportunity for you," says Vincent.

"Yeah? You could have just called or emailed." I struggle in my chains, but it just burns, so I give up, staying still to reserve my strength. I get the feeling I'm going to need it later. Whatever was in that blood knocked me out for a while. I have no idea how long I was out, but I'm not completely depleted. *Yet.*

"We had to do it this way. It's what she wanted," Cassius says.

"What who wanted?"

"You'll find out when we get there," Vincent says.

I look out the window. It's still dark outside, but the moon is half full, casting shadows on the Joshua trees.

The desert.

I glimpse a sign telling me we're on the I-40.

I try to get a feeling for *which* desert this is, but we could be anywhere. Joshua Tree, Nevada, New Mexico.

Fuck.

My eyes start to close, and I can't stop the fatigue that comes over me. I'm out of it again until I'm jolted awake by a sharp turn and the bumps of a dirt track beneath the wheels.

Oh, shit, are they taking me into the desert to kill me? The Certain Death? Shit!

"You'll be found eventually," I tell them. "Everyone will be out looking for me."

"Yeah? Like you were out looking for Juliette?" Cassius

asks. "You were too busy making that movie and sucking on that human for the last two months to give a shit about Juliette. What makes you think Max and Brandon and the rest of those losers will do anything differently to find you?"

"Fuck you."

But it's true. What were we even doing to find them? Hiring a couple of investigators? Getting Henrietta to pull us some tarot cards every once in a while?

We all cared more about our movie than we did about the missing vampires, and now I'm the one who's going to pay for it.

The lights of a ranch up ahead come into view.

"What is this place?" I demand.

"You'll see," says Vincent.

They stop the car out the front of the house, get out and then hold the door open for me. I try my best to get out of the car, but my legs are still bound, and so I end up on my fucking ass.

Cassius laughs.

"Get him out of those chains," Vincent tells Cassius.

"No way, he'll run."

"He won't run," Vincent says, eyes narrowing at me. "And if he does, he won't get very far."

Cassius grabs a pair of bolt cutters from out of the trunk of the car.

"Just the feet," Vincent tells him.

Cassius once again does as he's told, and my legs are free.

And instinct takes over. I fucking run.

CHAPTER FIFTY-ONE

$\mathcal{M}$averick

I RUN for about two minutes. Adrenaline coursing through me, overpowering whatever it was that was in that bad blood, until I'm taken down by silver bullets in my back. I'm weaker than I realize and hit the desert earth with a thud. My hands are still bound, and I can't reach the bullets in my back. I just have to let them burn while they lift me up, Vincent on one side, Cassius on the other. They drag me like a sack of bricks towards the house.

"You fucking dicks," I say, spitting a little blood from the effects of the bullets still in my back.

Cassius laughs.

"Just shut up and listen," Vincent says. "We're here to *help* you, asshole."

It's my turn to laugh now. "How is binding me with silver and shooting me in the back fucking *helping*?"

"You'll see," says Vincent.

"Jesus, fuck, if you say *you'll see* one more fucking time!"

They drag me up the steps of the big old ranch house. Christmas lights wind around the railing, and a holly wreath on the door threatens to fall off when Vincent jerks it open and shoves me inside.

"We've got him!" Cassius calls out.

"Get him cleaned up." Aiden appears in front of me, frowning at the state I'm in.

Fucking *Aiden*!

"Then bring him round the back," Aiden says with the confidence of a guy in charge, but without Lottie by his side, his strength and power is incredibly limited. Even in my weakened form, I could take him. Well, maybe if it weren't for the chains still around my wrists and the Blake brothers on either side of me.

"*You*," I say. "You fucking—"

Aiden gives me a sly grin and disappears out the back of the house.

Vincent puts on a pair of leather gloves, shoves his fingers into my back and I let out a howl.

"Get rid of the bullets," Vincent tells Cassius, and then he kicks my feet to push me through the house.

I feel the wounds in my back already healing, but the chains around my wrists are still burning.

"Take these off," I say, shoving my hands in Vincent's face.

He steps back, not wanting to be touched by the silver. "Not until you've heard what she has to say."

"What who has to say?"

Cassius appears and rolls his eyes at me. "If you could just shut your fucking mouth and listen, this will all be so much easier. In an hour from now, you'll be fucking thanking us."

"I'll never thank you for anything, you piece of shit," I tell him.

He just laughs. "You haven't forgiven me for that little

Trix thing." He gives me a shrewd smile that I want to punch right off his face.

"It's not a *little thing* to go against vampire law."

"Yeah? Well, maybe the law is about to change." His eyes go wide, and I know that whatever is *out the back* is not going to be good.

He shoves me out of the door, onto a back porch covered in rocking chairs and more Christmas lights and decorations, and down into a huge yard that opens up into miles and miles of nothing but desert. Adirondack chairs surround a fire pit, and Juliette, Linda and Vivian sit, all smiling and laughing at something hysterical the other woman I can't quite see yet has said.

"What the fuck is this?"

The fourth woman turns around, a sick grin splitting her beautiful face.

"Maverick, darling! How nice of you to join us!"

CHAPTER FIFTY-TWO

$\mathcal{M}$averick

"ONLY THE OLDEST, strongest and wisest vampire in the clan should hold the role of President of the Fraternity of the Everlasting Rose. Any vampire strong and cunning enough to bring the Certain Death to a president has proven their worth and will automatically be appointed as the new president."

The Fraternity of the Everlasting Rose handbook page 559

"HOW THE FUCK ARE YOU ALIVE?" I ask, taking in the scene before me.

Lottie Luelle's platinum blonde hair shines in the half-moon light. She's dressed in a black satin slip dress, cowboy boots, and a dark red embroidered Afghan coat, giving her the look of a sinister seventies groupie. Lottie was a silent film star. She starred alongside Max in so many movies of that era, and it's clear by the bandana twisted around her forehead just how much she's still struggling to give up the roaring twenties aesthetic.

It's a chilly night, but vampires don't feel the cold. As I look around the group, they're all dressed in sweaters and wraps, holding wine glasses full of blood and toasting smores. Vivian doesn't have her wig, but she wears a slouchy red beanie. They look like they're at some wellness retreat for rich people, not a group of vampires who've been — what? Kidnapped? But no one here looks like they are here against their will.

"Oh, darling, it's going to take more than a little stake to the heart to kill *me*." She fingers the strands of pearls and jewelry around her neck, paying extra attention to a metal pendant at her chest. I notice in the fire's glint of light that it's dented. "Please, Maverick, darling. Take a seat."

With few other options available, I sit.

"Max saw your blood turn black."

"I *was* dead," she says. "But you see, darling, I came back. I rose *from* the dead."

Lottie always had a flair for the dramatic. All the letters of resignation, the creepy ransom letter about Trix — it all suddenly makes sense. Of course it was Lottie Luelle mind-fucking us all.

"Risen from the dead?" I let out a laugh. "I think the more likely explanation is that Max made a mistake."

"Oh, he *did* make a mistake," Lottie says. "Trying to force the Certain Death onto me was the biggest mistake of his life."

"So what the fuck do you want with me? With us?" I gesture to the others sitting around the fire.

"We're starting over," she tells me. "The old Fraternity has been corrupted."

"What?"

"Brandon Curtis has no claim over the Fraternity, and the direction things are going in is quite appalling. The *New Order of Concordia* indeed! Paranormals working together?" She clutches her pearls. "I just won't have it!"

"Max killed you, but he didn't want the job, so he passed it on to Brandon. That's how it works."

"He had no right to do that," she says. "Even if I *was* dead, which clearly, I am *not*, you can't just go passing around the presidency of an ancient institution to any old Tom, Dick or Harry!"

"Brandon is an excellent leader," I say. "Everyone thinks so."

She throws her head back and laughs. "If he's such a good leader, how have *four* of his vampires gone missing on his watch?"

"Is that what this is all about? Making Brandon look bad?"

"Oh, darling, he doesn't need *my* help to do that."

"You want to take the Fraternity back? You should have taken Brandon, not me."

"I don't want it back," she says with a huff. "I want to start something new. A *Sorority*. It's always upset me that the Fraternity was so *masculine*. That's why I started by recruiting the most powerful women in the Fraternity. We're going to do things differently this time, aren't we, ladies?"

The women around me all nod and raise their glasses. "To our queen," they all say in unison, like a bunch of Stepford wives.

Oh, holy shit, this is not happening.

"Why the hell am *I* here?"

"Oh Maverick, you're a friend to women everywhere." She gives me a look like she wants a piece of me, and I just glare back at her. In no version of reality will I ever get into bed with this piece of evil.

"I want to turn you to my cause," she says. "I want you to

understand that being on *my* side is the *right* side, and then I want you to help me turn the others. You have influence with the rest of them, you see. And your role with the Order will be useful too. I'm hearing rumors that the fae are gaining power again. I'd like to stop that from happening—"

"Brandon is my friend," I tell her. "And so are Max and James. I don't want anything to do with — whatever the fuck this is."

"*Sorority*," she says. "You'll change your mind. Once we have Trix."

My heart catches on fire and burns against my rib cage.

"If you stay, if you join us, if you go against Brandon and Max, she will be safe. We won't harm her. If you do anything that goes against my will, I will crush her like the pitiful, pretty little butterfly that she is."

"If you fucking touch her—" I'm out of my seat in an instant, but before I can reach her, I'm grabbed by Vincent and Cassius and thrown back into my seat.

"What is it with these human girls?" Lottie asks. "Wouldn't you rather be with someone of your own kind? It's much more interesting. Much more fun." Aiden appears at her side as if on cue.

"Juliette is a much better choice for you," Lottie says.

My eyes flash to where Juliette is smiling at me, but something in her eyes feels wrong, *dead.* Even for a vampire.

"You will share Juliette's room, and her bed, up on the second floor," Lottie tells me.

What the fuck?

"I'll be going to my room now," she says, linking her hand in Aiden's and pulling him along after her. I have no doubt that she has some kind of feelings for Aiden, but it's very clear who's got the upper hand in that relationship. God, I hope Trix never feels like that with me. Like I'm the vampire holding all the cards in our relationship.

Our relationship.

Now that I'm here, facing whatever the fuck this is, all I can think is that I shouldn't have let Trix go. I shouldn't have just gone and taken a shower like a coward. I should have told her I wanted her. That I was scared shitless but I still wanted to be with her. That I wanted to spend the rest of my fucking life with her.

Now I may never get that chance.

No, I decide. I can't let my mind go there. I will get out of here, just like I got out of a million life-threatening situations in the wars, and just like in my movies, I will get a happy ending.

Vincent and Cassius follow Lottie and Aiden inside, but I get the feeling they will never be far away.

"What the hell is going on?" I ask the others. We're never going to be alone here. Lottie and the Blakes will hear everything we say, but I have to at least try to get answers.

"Lottie Luelle rose from the dead," says Juliette wistfully.

"She is our queen," says Linda.

"All hail the queen," Vivian says, raising a glass.

"You're all acting insane!"

Juliette reaches out to me, placing a hand on my thigh. I swiftly remove it, and anger crosses her face. "But Lottie said I could have you," she pouts.

"What the fuck? You can't *have* me. I'm not hers to give!"

And besides, my heart very much belongs to someone else.

And if I ever get out of here, I'm going to tell her exactly that.

CHAPTER FIFTY-THREE

*M*averick

"There is a type of mint that only grows in the desert of Nevada called Mentha Imperium, which can be used to control the minds of those who ingest the substance for a brief period of time. This is very dark magic, and those who are called to work with this medicine must proceed with extreme caution."

Herbalism for Witches and Warlocks, page 372

JULIETTE SITS down on the bed — an old wooden ranch-style thing covered in crochet blankets. She tosses her dark hair and pats the spot next to her.

I don't sit.

"What is this place?" I ask, looking around at the kitschy decor. It is *so* not Lottie Luelle.

I do notice however, that there are blackout blinds over the window, sitting behind curtains that are covered in little yellow corns.

Many vampires, including Lottie, have never been too

keen on the idea of sun serum. She's always said she believes that vampires are creatures of the night for a reason. It will be dawn soon, which means everyone will be getting some rest inside. I took a dose of sun serum yesterday, which should give me maybe another 24 hours of sunlight, one more day. But that's all I'll have before I'll have to live as a creature of the night again too.

I had really hoped that the days of darkness were behind me.

"Airbnb," Juliette says.

"What the hell? Lottie rented an Airbnb for her new cult?"

"It's not a cult," Juliette sulks, running her hands through her long dark strands of hair. "And she didn't exactly rent it."

Of course. Lottie probably drained the throats of whoever owned this property. I don't want to know.

"Juliette." I sit next to her and lean in close, whispering as quietly as I can. "What is going on here?"

She looks up at me like *I'm* the one who's lost my mind. "We told you already! Lottie is back from the dead. She's our new leader. She's our *Savior.*"

It only gets worse.

"You can't really believe that." But even if she doesn't, she can't tell me. Lottie will hear everything through these walls.

I search the room and eventually find a small pad of paper and a pencil in a drawer and write her a note.

Tell me what's happening here. We can find a way out!

I pass her the pencil, and for a second it looks like she's going to write something, but then the blank stare moves over her face again.

"Why would I want a way out? I love it here. I'm happy." She smiles at me. It's all fake and twisted. Even Juliette could act better than this.

I throw the pencil and paper across the room.

"Perhaps you just need a drink, darling," she says. Oh god. Lottie even has them *talking* like her.

"Are there any humans around?" I ask her.

She shakes her head. "We don't drink from humans anymore."

"What?"

"Humans can't be trusted. We only drink from a special supply of blood we have here."

I grab Juliette's shoulders. I'm about to tell her not to drink the blood, but I don't want Lottie to hear and know I'm onto her.

The blood I drank knocked me out. That's how she got the other vampires here. Whatever blood they're drinking now must be affecting them in some way too. There's no way that if Juliette was in her right mind that she would go along with this, that she would choose to be here over starring in her first movie and being her own goddamn queen!

I don't know how I'm getting out of here. But using my acting skills feels like the first step.

"I'd love a drink."

She grins, takes my hand and leads me back downstairs to the kitchen.

Vincent and Cassius are sprawled out on the couches in the living area, and I can tell they're not on the blood. They're here of their own free will.

They must be in on it. They're the ones delivering the bad blood. Fucking assholes.

Juliette grabs a wine bottle full of dark red liquid and finds two glasses.

She pours them and sits down at a rickety old kitchen table. She taps my glass with hers in a cheers and takes a gulp.

I take a sniff. It's real blood, but there's something extra in here. Something… herbal. Minty.

Juliette downs the drink in a flash, wiping blood from her lips and giving me a grin.

"Drink up, Maverick," she says, eyeing my still-full glass.

"I prefer to sip," I tell her.

"The sun will be up soon, so we should get to bed." She gives me a look like she thinks I'm *actually* going to share her bed with her, and not just to rest in.

"I think I'll sit with my drink a little longer, and then take a shower," I say. "I'll meet you up there."

"I'll go get ready for you," she smiles.

I watch as she walks away, Vincent eyeing up her ample backside as it sways past him.

Throwing the blood down the sink, I wonder how long I can survive here without blood. A couple of days, maybe a week if I wasn't already weak from what they gave me last night. And I know if I drink whatever blood is here, I'll end up like the rest of them, a puppet for Lottie's new power play.

I rinse my glass, fill it with water and go join the Blakes in the living room. I sit down opposite Vincent, smacking my water glass on the coffee table.

"Can we help you with something?" Cassius asks.

I twist my lips. I can't say everything I want to say. Not here. Not with Lottie and the others being able to hear every word. So I just glare at them both and hope that they understand what I'm saying with my eyes. That I'll fucking kill them both once I'm out of here.

Vincent stands and nods towards the door. He knows a place where we can talk. Cassius starts to follow us, but Vincent shakes his head. Cassius flips him the bird and throws himself back on the couch.

We walk out onto the front porch, down the steps and then towards the black SUV that brought me here.

Vincent gestures for me to get into the car. Once our doors

are closed, he turns on the radio. Loud. Some eighties pop song that I remember dancing to in a club around the same time all the Donnas started getting drained, blares from the speakers.

"What?" he asks quietly, barely audible even to me over the music.

"Is it safe to talk?" I ask in the same quiet tone.

"More than any other form of communication."

Not a yes.

"What the fuck is this?" I ask.

"Lottie is starting a new vampire order."

"Yeah, I got that, but why is everyone acting nuts?"

"Just do what you're told. Drink the blood. Accept your fate."

"Fuck that," I say. "Get me some real blood."

He lets out a loud laugh, and I hope that Lottie doesn't hear it.

I narrow my eyes at him. He's taken a risk even sitting in the car with me. If Lottie found out that we were even having this conversation, deliberately out of her earshot, Vincent would be fucked.

"If you get me out of here, I'll get you into the Fraternity."

He runs a hand over his dark stubble. "Why would I want to be in the Fraternity now that Lottie is building a new vampire order that will crush the Fraternity as soon as it's strong enough?"

"Because hers is built on lies and manipulation?"

"And the Fraternity isn't?"

"Brandon isn't like the other leaders we've had. You know him. He's an upright guy."

"You think vampires want an upright guy leading them? Nah, fuck that."

"You think Lottie is better?"

"Brandon's too loose with the rules."

"You'd prefer him to stake Cassius? He has the right after what Cassius did to Trix."

"Oh please. Cassius could have drained her. But he didn't. He let her go. What more did you want?"

I grit my teeth. "You know this isn't going to work. As soon as the others find out that they are drinking bad blood, laced with whatever the fuck it is, that they're under her control—"

"The blood is fine," Vincent says. "The girls just really believe in the Sorority."

"You drink it then."

He raises an eyebrow. "I already ate."

"Lottie didn't let you in when she was president, so why are you working for her now?"

"I believe in her vision."

It's bullshit. He has his own agenda here.

"You want to be in the fraternity? Help me out of here, and I'll make that happen," I tell him.

He seems to be considering it for a moment. The Blakes aren't stupid. Vincent is old and he's smart. He's under no illusion that this is going to work out. But after centuries of his applications for the Fraternity being denied, he may still be convinced.

"What about Cassius?" he eventually asks.

"Fuck Cassius."

He laughs at that.

I hate both of these assholes, but Vincent didn't leave bite wounds in Trix's arm. The memory of it is enough to make me want to snap both their heads off their necks.

"I'd need assurances."

"You have my word."

"But you're not the president. Your word doesn't mean shit."

"No, but I am the vampire councilor of the New Order of Concordia."

A dark eyebrow quirks. "So, it is true, the Order is back up and running?"

I nod. It's supposed to be a secret, but fuck it. It's the only leverage I can think of.

"Yes," I say. "And so I do have sway. But more important than that, if you don't let me go, you won't only have the Fraternity coming to find me, you'll also have the wolves, fae and witches after you."

"Who are the others?"

"Huh?"

"The other councilors?"

"I can't tell you."

"Bullshit."

I roll my eyes. "Believe what you want. But trust me, if you're on Lottie's side, you're going to be on the wrong side."

CHAPTER FIFTY-FOUR

rix

A WINE GLASS overflows with blood and stains the earth.

Crows caw in the distance.

A door swings open on a dilapidated ranch house that looks like something out of a horror movie.

Juliette runs her hand over Maverick's thick thigh...

I STARTLE AWAKE, and it takes me a second to realize I'm on Maverick's couch. It's light. Already morning. I'm wearing one of Maverick's sweatshirts, and the scent of him is strong. It makes my heart both leap and ache because all I have is the sweatshirt. He's not here.

We stayed up talking for hours, trying to formulate a plan to go rescue four kidnapped vampires from *somewhere* on the I-40. Maybe. We have no idea how far they drove or what exit they took.

Me and Max wanted to just *go*. To just get in the car and *drive*. But Henrietta advised against it. She said it was better to stay here, keep working with me on amplifying the blood bond so we can find exactly where he is before we just went off "half-cocked" (her phrase) driving around the country in hopes we'll stumble onto them.

I sit up and look towards the kitchen that held so many happy memories for me, but now it's filled with worry as Max, Poppy, Brandon, Henrietta and some guy I don't know sit at the kitchen table talking in hushed tones about blood bonds, Joshua trees and interstates.

I glance at the front door, half expecting him to just walk through it with some pathetic excuse as to where he was all night. I'd forgive him anything right now.

But all I see is the moment I walked out of it. Before I bolted.

But I had to. I couldn't stay. He didn't want me here. He didn't want my *love*. He didn't even want a relationship.

My heart aches as I realize that none of this is about me and what I want. it's about *him*. This isn't some love story that ends with us living happily ever after. It's not what he wants.

But if — *when* we get Maverick back — I will tell him exactly how I feel about him. I will tell him I love him. That I want to be with him. That I want a relationship with him, even if I have no fucking idea how to do that. I'll tell him I want fucking forever with him.

If he says that's not what he wants, well, at least I won't spend the rest of my life wondering what if?

"Why did you let me sleep?" I ask as I walk into the kitchen, rubbing my eyes.

"Sometimes the blood bond is stronger when you're asleep. You're able to pick up on each other more," Henrietta explains. "Did you dream?"

"Blood," I tell her, taking a seat at the kitchen table. "And there was this old ranch house."

She hands me her phone. "Search ranch houses on and around that interstate and see what you can find. It's a long shot, but you never know."

I take the phone from her and start searching, but it's only showing results from Airbnb.

"This is Lucas, by the way."

A very tall and very attractive guy with dark skin and eyes and short clipped hair smiles at me from the other side of the table.

"Lovely to meet you, Trix."

"He's a very powerful warlock," Henrietta says. "And my fiancée."

Henrietta bagged herself a hottie. "Congratulations." I force a grin. It's hard to be happy for anyone else's love story right now.

She forces a grin back, and I get the feeling she's not as happy about it as she should be.

"We got the results back from testing the blood," Max tells me. Poppy leans on his shoulder, looking half asleep.

"What was wrong with it?" I ask, not looking up from my search.

"Laced with colloidal silver," Max says.

"Oh, fuck!"

"Just trace amounts," Max continues. "Not enough to do a huge amount of damage, but definitely enough to knock a vampire out for a few hours at least."

"For immortals, you're pretty easy to fuck with," I say.

Max scowls and Brandon chuckles.

"It's almost undetectable," Brandon says. "But I suspect that if Maverick had been less distracted, he might have noticed it didn't smell or taste quite right."

This is all my fault. I'm the reason he was so distracted when he left the party.

And there it is. The house from my dream.

It doesn't look as creepy in this picture. It looks like a regular ranch house, but it's definitely the same place.

"I found it."

"Is this what it looks like?" Henrietta asks over my shoulder.

"No. This is the exact house." I bring up the details. "Arizona."

"Are you sure?" Max asks.

"Certain. Now let's go."

"Go where?" Lucas asks.

"To get Maverick!"

Lucas shakes his head. "You're not going anywhere. If they could kidnap four vampires, imagine what they could do to you."

I glare at him.

"He's right. Max and I will go." Brandon scrapes back his chair and stands.

"If you think there's magic involved, I may be able to help," Lucas says.

"I'll come too," says Henrietta.

"It's not safe, Etta." Lucas tells her. "I can handle this."

She frowns at him. "These are my friends, and I will be going."

"We'll take my car," Max offers.

"Okay, so what are we waiting for?" I ask.

Max shakes his head. "You can't come with us."

"Fuck that," I say. "Maverick is my—"

There's a silence I don't know how to fill.

"I'm coming with you," I finally say.

"Me too," says Poppy.

"Oh no, no, no, no!" Max takes her by the shoulders. "It's not safe, my love."

"Trix and Henrietta are going!"

"Poppy, I won't risk your life."

My stomach sinks.

Am I risking my life?

Poppy's mouth moves into a hard line. "Stay with me, then."

"I can't. Maverick is my friend, and he needs me."

"I need you."

"I promise you I'll return." He pulls her into an embrace, and I burn with jealousy.

I want that. So fucking bad.

"What am I supposed to do while you're gone?" she asks.

"I'll call Claudia."

"What? Why?"

"If you're with the werewolves, you'll be safe."

"Are you serious? What if it's them doing this?"

"I trust them." Max looks down at his phone, frantically texting at vampire speed. "She'll be here in fifteen."

Fifteen minutes later Poppy has her werewolf babysitter, and I'm in the back of Max's Aston Martin, Henrietta in the middle seat and Lucas next to her, Brandon in the passenger seat and Max at the wheel.

And all thoughts and worries of risking my life disappear in the rear-view mirror.

$\mathcal{M}$averick

Lying here next to Juliette, who's sleeping like the dead, when it should be Trix I'm next to, is making it impossible for me to rest.

And besides, I don't need rest. I need *blood,* and I need to get the fuck out of here.

I can feel myself weakening from the bad blood, the lack of real blood, and so my hearing isn't as good as usual, but I can't hear anyone moving around. It sounds as if everyone else is asleep or at least resting deeply.

My first thought is to creep up on Lottie and stake her in the heart. But as far as I'm aware, there is no elm, ash or yew wood anywhere around here, and even if there was, last time someone staked her to death it didn't even work.

I make my way through the dark house and run my fingers over all the wood I can find. Oak, walnut, nothing useful. Nothing that will bring the Certain Death to Lottie.

But how the fuck did she survive it last time?

Max isn't stupid. He told me that he and James staked her through the heart. He said he saw the blood turn black. There is no way she could have survived that. Is there?

I'm weak, but I could still run, and if the others are off the sun serum, the sunlight could slow them down, and besides, it could be my only chance.

But when I reach towards the handle to open the back door, my hand hits a shield of… nothing? I try again, and the same thing happens. It's like there's an invisible force-field around the door. I try the front door, then a window, same thing.

Magic.

Lottie working with witches? She hates witches almost as much as she hates the fae.

But then, she's always done whatever it takes to stay on top.

Okay, so if I can't get out of here during daylight hours, I'm going to need to find some decent blood so I can regain my strength and make a run for it when this door is open again.

I look in the kitchen pantry. It's stacked with boxes of blood just like the one that arrived at my house before the Blakes kidnapped me.

No thanks.

I can only assume that Lottie and Aiden are still drinking human blood. But if they are, they wouldn't leave it in plain sight. They wouldn't want the others to drink it and come to their senses.

It's such a bizarre plan. What's she going to do? Just drug the entire vampire community until they're all under her control?

I look at the boxes. Oh, holy shit, that's exactly what she's going to do. If she's taken over blood distribution for vampire kind, pretty soon every vampire who uses the blood bank supply will be under her control.

Well, nearly everyone. There are still some vampires who only feed directly from humans. I'd still do that myself if I wasn't so addicted to Trix and found it impossible to drink from anyone else.

A scuffling noise startles me. I still, stop breathing and listen.

There's someone in the basement.

CHAPTER FIFTY-SIX

averick

THE BASEMENT DOOR is hidden at the back of the pantry behind a tower of boxes of blood.

The door opens. There's no magic on this one.

I take the stairs as quietly as possible, praying with each step that Lottie doesn't hear me.

"Holy shit," I mouth. Three dead bodies, two others barely alive, chained to a supporting beam.

I squeeze my eyes shut and then open them again like that will somehow erase the scene in front of me.

And then I realize who the humans are. One of them is Beth, a Donna who I claimed. She is mine, and according to vampire law, I am now entitled to kill whoever the fuck has done this to her.

And I will.

My eyes move to the other human who's barely breathing.

Finn fucking Huxley. Jesus.

I go straight to Beth's side. She looks up at me but has no idea who I am or what's going on. She's had the shit glamoured out of her.

I need to feed, but if I take her blood, I could kill her. Finn's eyes are rolled into the back of his head, and he looks even worse than she does.

If I could, I'd let Beth drink from me first to heal her, but once my blood is running through her veins, it will take hours before I'll be able to receive any benefits from feeding from her. Her blood will taste like vampire blood, and it has no effect, good or bad, for vampires to drink from each other.

"Beth," I barely whisper. She looks up, and it makes me think she can at least *maybe* remember her name. "I'm going to get you out of here, but I can only do that if I drink from you."

She nods and moves her head over, like she's so fucking desperate for The Bite that she'd die for it.

Fuck.

I bite into her neck and start drinking. It's not intoxicating like it's been with Trix these last few weeks. It's nothing but survival. A means to an end. When I feel her heart rate start to drop, I immediately stop, pull out and heal her wounds over.

I go over to Finn and do the same but take even less blood from him. He's so out of it he has no idea I'm even doing it. I'll ask for his forgiveness later. Maybe. If he lives.

I bite into my own wrist and give them each a few drops of my blood. I can't give them more than that. They can't be full of life when Lottie next comes down here. But hopefully I give them enough to keep them alive, to survive for as long as it takes for me to get out of here and get help for us all.

Finn looks up at me for a second and tries to talk. I shake my head and put a finger to my lip, point to the ceiling and then my ear, in the hopes he'll understand that Lottie is listening.

"Get me out of here!" he begs in a low growl. "I know this place, I can—" His eyes droop closed again, but his heartbeat is a little stronger than it was.

Beth's is too. As long as no one feeds from them again too soon, they may live.

I silently scale the steps, and I'm already feeling better. Not as strong as I need to be to get out of here, but I should at least be able to pass a message to Trix down the blood bond.

As I make my way back up into the kitchen and start quietly re-stacking the boxes of blood in the pantry, I feel a warm nudge from Trix through our bond.

There she is!

Thank fuck!

I send a wave of warmth back to her. *I'm alive, I'm okay, I miss you like hell.*

I feel it immediately returned — her warmth, her light. It feels like sunshine in this darkness.

I've had blood bonds before, but I never knew it could be like this, that we could communicate like this through it. And then I wonder if all those sex dreams, all those times I couldn't stop thinking about fucking her, if all of that was just us sending each other messages.

I close my eyes and lean against the pantry door, sending my thoughts and love in her direction, and when I feel like she's there, I start sending images.

I bring to mind the I-40 sign on the interstate, the dirt road we turned down and the house. My blood boils as I send her Cassius and then Vincent, Juliette, Linda and

Vivian. I send her images of the boxes of blood and the feeling of the spell or whatever is stopping me from getting out of the house. I send her Lottie and Aiden.

And then I send one more thing down the blood bond.

I fucking love you, Trix.

CHAPTER FIFTY-SEVEN

rix

Mom: *Merry Christmas honey! Now, where are you? Did you fix everything with Maverick? He's such a nice boy. I hope you can work it out, but you know I worry when I don't know where you are, especially on Christmas! Why don't you bring him over for lunch?*

Trix: Merry Christmas Mom! It's kind of a long story, but I won't be able to make it home for lunch. I'm so sorry!

Mom: Is everything okay, honey?

Trix: Yeah. I think so. I hope so. I'll fill you in when I'm home, hopefully tomorrow.

I HATE LYING to my mom, but it's not like I can tell her the truth. That I'm spending Christmas sitting in the back of Max Montrose's Aston Martin, staring out the window, watching Joshua trees fly past on my way to rescue the vampire I'm in love with.

I clutch my heart suddenly. It feels like it's bursting open, and I can *feel* Maverick as if he's here with me, one hand on my heart, the other on my cheek, holding me close.

"Maverick!" I gasp.

"The blood bond!" Henrietta grabs my hand. "What are you seeing? Tell us everything."

"The I-40, the house," I say. "It's the same house from my dream and the listing. We're going to the right place."

"Thank goddess," Henrietta says.

"Cassius, Vincent." I take a pause and try to make sense of all the images suddenly flying through my mind. "The missing vampires."

"All of them?" Brandon asks from the front passenger seat.

"Yes. And boxes of blood. Like the one we saw at Maverick's house. I don't know what that means!"

"It's okay," Henrietta says. "Just keep telling us what you see."

"He can't get out. There's some kind of spell over the doors and windows—"

"A spell?" Lucas asks. "But vampires can't use spells."

Henrietta rubs my hand. "Anything else?"

"Lottie," I say. "And Aiden."

"That's not possible," Max says. "I staked her myself!"

"I'm just telling you what I'm seeing."

"Is there anything else?" Henrietta asks.

I fucking love you, Trix.

"No."

My heart lurches, and I don't know if I'm doing this right, but I send a message straight back.

I fucking love you too. I'm coming for you.

Henrietta grabs the tarot cards from her bag.

"Henrietta," Lucas says. "You've been trying to read on this for weeks and keep getting nothing, why do you think it will work now?"

"I have more information now," she says as she shuffles. "And now that I know that it is some kind of magic that's been blocking me, maybe I can try to weave my way around it."

She fans out the cards and holds them out to me. "You pick the cards. Your open connection with Maverick should help."

"How many?"

"As many as you like. At least three."

I pull three cards out of the deck and hand them back to her.

She turns the first one around. "The Tower," she says. "Unexpected events, a sudden change. This is the past, Maverick being taken." Henrietta turns over the next card. "This is the present, the Queen of Swords reversed."

"That's Lottie's card," Max exclaims. "It always comes up when you read her."

"That's right." She turns the last card over. "Death reversed. It's true. She's alive."

"How on earth can anyone survive Certain Death?" Max asks.

"Shuffle again," Lucas says. "You must have pulled incorrectly."

"I don't need to shuffle again," Henrietta says shortly.

"There are myths and legends," Brandon says. "Stories of ancient magic, sometimes witch or warlock, sometimes fae, that could protect a vampire from death in all realms. But never have I encountered an actual occurrence of it."

"Renaud. Lottie's father," says Max.

"Yes. He used to collect those strange occult artefacts." Brandon rubs at his golden stubble.

Max changes lanes to take the next exit. "Those artefacts were nothing but junk."

"Perhaps there was more to them than that," Brandon muses.

"There was a pendant that she wore," Henrietta says. "It caught my eye the last time she came to the mansion. It had an ancient witch mark on it."

"Dear god," says Max. "That ugly old thing she always used to wear?"

"It's just an idea," Henrietta says. "I'm not even sure what it was, or what it meant. Just that it was maybe connected to my people."

"You're clutching at straws," Lucas tells her.

Max thumps the steering wheel. "But I *saw* the blood run black. I know what I saw!"

"It's just a vision," I tell them. "Maybe it's muddled. Maybe it doesn't mean what we think it means. Maybe it doesn't fucking matter *who* has Maverick, we just need to get to him!"

"Can you pull an outcome card for us, Henrietta?" Max asks. "What are our chances here?"

She turns the card over. "The Devil," she says.

"What does that mean?" I ask her, but from the creepy as fuck imagery of a naked man and woman in chains at the feet of the Devil, it's pretty clear what it means.

Henrietta stares at the card for a moment before turning it over and placing it back in the deck. "We should proceed with caution."

CHAPTER FIFTY-EIGHT

$\mathcal{M}$averick

"Maverick, darling, drink your blood." Lottie looks at me over the fire. Tonight she's dressed in tight jeans, cowboy boots, a silk blouse, a floral scarf wrapped around her head and that Afghan coat again. She's really dressing for the part of a desert cult leader.

After I'd seen what was in the basement, there was no way I could go back to my room and pretend to sleep, so I sat on the couch and read through a bunch of fat romantasy novels some previous guest had left behind. It was the same series Trix had in her bedroom, and Jesus, I was not expecting so much *sex* in books about the fae! Don't people know that vampires are much better at sex than the fae?

As soon as the sun dropped behind the mountains, casting a dark blue twilight over the desert, I could open the door and leave the house. But by then everyone else was awake.

The whole gang is here by the fire tonight. Aiden at Lottie's side, Cassius and Vincent on either side of them like bodyguards. Vivian adjusts her red beanie and attempts to cuddle up to Vincent while Juliette and Linda sit on either side of me.

"Maverick," Lottie warns, nodding to my drink.

"I'm not thirsty," I tell her.

She throws her head back and laughs. Two seconds later, everyone else laughs too.

"I expect you'll be feeling a little rough from last night," she says. "If you don't drink, you'll become too weak and be of no use to our cause."

"And what exactly *is* your cause, Lottie?"

"Oh darling, all I've ever wanted is just to make things right. After everything that happened with my father."

The group falls silent. Even when we weren't all on drugged blood, no one would dare to speak against Lottie's father in front of her. But she's right. He wasn't a good leader. Before Lottie took over as president in the 1950s, her father was involved in embezzling funds. Among other things, Renaud Luelle was known for his ability to locate rare artworks and artefacts. Picassos, Monets, ancient Egyptian statues — he could get you whatever your heart desired for a price. He ran a very profitable little side business until it came to light that he was selling fakes and using other vampire's money to fund his own personal collection.

"I tried to make things right," Lottie says. "But the system was always against me. I had no power to change the rules, to change vampire law. But now I can start over. I can create laws that benefit all vampire kind."

"Yeah? Laws like what?" I ask.

She lets out a huffy sigh. "Well, for starters, we must eradicate the world of the other supernatural beings."

My jaw clenches. "And why exactly would we want to do that?"

"Vampires are the superior supernatural race," she says. "The wolves are a blight on our world. Half of them would be in prison if it weren't for my husband Max subsidizing them financially."

Aiden, who's sitting beside her, clenches his jaw now at the mention of her husband.

"As for the fae, well. You know what happened there," Lottie says.

"What did happen with the fae, my queen?" asks Juliette.

"The fae came to us with information that my father was... involved in certain questionable activities," she says. "This angered the Fraternity, and one of our members staked my father." She takes a sip of blood. "But it was a rouse. The fae were controlling my father. They thought if they got rid of Daddy that we'd all fall. Little did they know that I would take over and bring some peace and calm to everything."

Sure, peace and calm after Lottie staked the vampire who killed her father and all the fae who had been involved, were suspected of being involved, or even *knew* someone who'd been involved were murdered or imprisoned.

"James Truscott was the brains behind the operation," she says. "The one controlling my father. And so, we made him watch while we killed all his friends and family. And then we put him to work as our butler." She lets out a sick laugh.

The memory of it all brings a dull ache to my chest. I never killed a fae. It is said that to kill a fae is to lose your soul, and I had lost enough pieces of my soul in the vampire army. But there were enough vampires in the Fraternity who would happily do Lottie's bidding for me to sit that one out.

That I just stood aside and let it happen still haunts me. But what was I supposed to do? Tell the other vampires to stop? Try to protect the fae? Lottie would have killed me too.

Eventually, we put it all behind us. Or at least tried to. I have no doubt that James becoming Max's butler was less about James' punishment and more to do with a constant daily reminder to Max that Lottie was in charge. That she was powerful. That she could do anything she wanted. That she'd kill everyone Max ever loved if she felt like it.

"Fuck," Juliette whispers, taking a sip of blood. "And so, our great queen made everything right in the end."

"I tried to, young Juliette, but as I said, I was bound by tradition and rules that were set out for us so many centuries ago. I made some mistakes too. But my own near Certain Death experience has changed me. I know I am here to do good. To create great change for our kind." Lottie takes a gulp from her own glass of blood, which I'm pretty sure is *not* the same blood that's in my glass.

"Maverick, darling," Lottie says, grinning at me like some evil clown show. "Drink your blood, or I shall have to end you."

I look down into the drink, and I desperately try to send a message through the blood bond that the blood is *bad*. And then I take a sip.

CHAPTER FIFTY-NINE

averick

THE FIRST FEW sips of the blood are fine. I still feel like myself. Relatively normal. And then suddenly I begin to notice just how lovely Lottie is. Her skin is like oat milk, her laughter like an angel singing.

It's no wonder Max was besotted by her and married her! If only I had met her first!

I shake off the strange thoughts, things that would never usually cross my mind and put my glass down on the ground next to my seat.

"Darling," she says, her eyes piercing into me through the flames. "You must drink more. Regain your strength. Be ready for when they come."

"When who come?" I ask as a fog begins to form in my mind.

"Are we getting some new sisters?" Linda asks with a dumb smile on her face.

"No, darling. Not yet. First, we must do away with the scourge of vampires who are against us."

"Vampires are against us?" gasps Juliette. "But who could ever be against *us*?"

"Exactly!" Lottie says. "The only ones against us are the bad ones. The ones who want to take our power, our liberty, our freedom!"

"All hail the queen!" says Vivian, raising her glass.

"All hail the queen!" follow the others.

"Aiden, darling. Please get Maverick another drink. Some of the extra special blood I think."

"I'm good," I say, rubbing my sweaty hands on my thighs.
Sweat? I never sweat!

Aiden disappears, and I try to get my thoughts together.
I'm being drugged.

I try to send this thought down the blood bond, but I can't find it. I can't find Trix. The thought terrifies me.

Aiden returns a few moments later with a wine glass of blood almost full to overflowing.

He passes it to me with a very slight grimace. He doesn't want this either. He doesn't want to be here. He doesn't want to be doing this.

I look around the circle, and I see it in everyone's eyes. No one wants this. No one is here under their own free will. Even Cassius and Vincent aren't helping Lottie because they truly *want* to. Whatever their agenda is, it has nothing to do with loyalty to Lottie and her bizarre vampire cult.

It's all fake. All pretend. All of it.

"Drink, my darling," Lottie says.

"No," I tell her.

And then she pulls a gun from her coat and points it at me. "If you don't drink, I'll shoot you with a round of silver bullets. You're too weak to get far, especially after you gave some of your blood away to my friends."

Fuck, how does she know?

Of course she fucking knows!

"Which is an offence punishable by Certain Death, I may remind you. At least, under the old laws it is. Perhaps if you stay and join me, we can rethink some of those laws." She smiles that devil smile at me. "It would be such a shame if the world never got to see another Maverick Stone movie, wouldn't it? Oh, but perhaps I'll star in the next one with you." She stands up and walks towards me. "I'll be your leading lady and together we'll own the silver screen. I'll be a star once more." The cold metal of the gun hits my forehead. "Now drink, before I fill you with silver bullets and then stake you in the heart for being a traitor to the queen."

And so I drink.

CHAPTER SIXTY

rix

Poppy: Where are you? Are you okay? Why isn't Max replying to my texts?!!!

Trix: He's driving. We're not even there yet.

Poppy: I'm so worried about you all!

Trix: Max can handle himself.

Poppy: That's what we thought about Maverick and look what happened!

Trix: Okay now you're freaking me out.

Poppy: Look after each other. Get my Max back to me safely. And get yourself back safely! I can't lose everyone I love in one go! This is the worst Christmas ever!

Trix: Oh yeah, Merry Christmas!

"THIS MUST BE IT," Max says, slowing down and taking a left turn onto a dirt road.

We've driven all day, and it's already getting dark. The sky turns purple, casting shadows over the desert landscape as the first evening stars begin to twinkle.

Lights are on in a house up ahead in the distance, and I just *know* this is the place. I can *feel* it.

But then something strange happens. About halfway down the road, the car stops dead.

"Car trouble?" Brandon asks.

"I never have car trouble," Max grumbles as he frowns at the dashboard. "The car still looks fine. It's just — stopped."

He puts the car into reverse and drives backwards for a few seconds before driving forward again, but the same thing happens. The car just *stops.* He swears, turns the car around, and drives back down the road.

"Magic?" Brandon says.

"I'd say so," Henrietta says. "Let me out so I can take a closer look."

"Be quick. We don't want to draw attention to ourselves," Max says.

Henrietta gets out and starts running her hands over the invisible shield or whatever it is.

Lucas follows her out and shakes his head. "It's clearly a very complicated warding spell. There's no way we can get past this."

Henrietta gets back into the car. "A ward," she says, "I can take it down, but I need a few things."

Lucas frowns at her. "How are you going to take down a *ward?*"

"What do you need?" Brandon asks.

She grabs her phone and starts tapping. "There's a market just a few miles from here. I can get everything there."

. . .

We drop Henrietta and Lucas at the market, and the rest of us take a seat in Lucky's diner just down the road.

"Welcome to Lucky, Arizona," a waitress greets us with a forced smile. She's in her late twenties with long brown hair and dressed in a peach and mint green dress that matches the aging decor of the place. "Happy holidays folks. I'm April, and I'll be your server this evening." She's peppy in a way that makes me think she's been on her feet all day and would rather be anywhere but here. "We have a moist maker Christmas special and a pecan pie with—"

"Just a coffee," Brandon says. "Thank you."

"I'll have the same, please," says Max.

April fills their cups with coffee neither of them is going to drink.

"Trix, you must be famished," Brandon says, passing me a menu.

"I can't eat," I say, shoving the menu back at him.

"A veggie burger and fries," Max tells the waitress. "And a Coke."

"Sure, won't be long."

"Maverick has survived worse," Max says. "Much worse. You know he was in the army—"

"I know. Two world wars."

"He can handle himself," Brandon tries to assure me.

"If he can handle himself, why did he get kidnapped?"

Henrietta and Lucas appear, both sliding into my side of the booth.

"Get what you need?" Brandon asks.

She nods.

"You should both eat," Brandon tells them.

"Maybe some pie," Lucas says, eyeing up the counter.

"Henrietta has what she needs, let's just go," I say.

"What about my pie?" Lucas complains. "We've hardly eaten all day."

"We don't have time to sit around chatting over coffee and pie," I say, frowning at him.

"The moon will rise in a couple of hours," Henrietta says. "Waxing gibbous. If we wait until then, it will be quicker and easier for me to take the wards down."

April reappears with the Coke Max ordered for me. He slides it over to me, and because we're clearly not leaving just yet, I take a sip. I had no idea how thirsty or tired I was. I down the whole thing in one go.

"Another?" April asks me curiously.

"Thanks," I say, sliding the empty glass towards her.

"Anything for you folks?" April asks Henrietta and Lucas.

"Can I get the pancake stack?" Henrietta asks. "And a side of cottage fries."

"Just a slice of pie," Lucas says, giving Henrietta a look.

When April has disappeared again, Lucas turns to Henrietta. "You know your magic will be stronger if you don't fill yourself with fat and carbs."

My mouth drops open, and I'm about to defend her, but I don't have to.

"My magic will be just fine, thank you," she says. "And besides, you ordered *pie*!"

"My metabolism is better than yours."

Okay, I might be starting to see why Henrietta doesn't seem ecstatic about marrying this guy.

After a few moments of uncomfortable silence, Lucas fills it. "It's curious, isn't it?" he asks. "Vampires rarely work with witches. They so often think we are beneath them. But if we worked together, we could be unstoppable."

Brandon raises an eyebrow. "This is exactly why we have the New Order of Concordia. So we can work together." He straightens up the menus. "And besides, I've always been truly in awe of Henrietta's abilities."

A slight flush hits Henrietta's cheek.

"Henrietta is a powerful witch, but a ward that can stop a car from entering is very strong magic," Lucas says.

"Just because you can't do it doesn't mean I can't," she shoots back at him.

I can't help the audible whoosh of air that escapes from my lips.

"Oh, I could take that ward down," he says. "But I want to see you try first. It's good practice for you."

"If you think you can do it faster, do it," Henrietta says. "Getting our friends to safety is more important than my ego."

Lucas raises an eyebrow. "I'd be happy to." He clears his throat. "After my pie."

CHAPTER SIXTY-ONE

rix

"Wards can be created out of intention and will and can be as simple or complicated as the witch can manage. A simple ward for a beginner can be created by visualizing four pillars of light in each corner of the space you want to protect and then strands of light connecting each pillar. A more detailed description of the process can be found on page 107. See Protection Spells for Advancing Witches and Warlocks *for information on creating more complicated wards."*

Protection Spells for Beginning Witches, page 22

Max parks on the side of the road just before the turn off. Henrietta takes a few moments to chant incantations and draw symbols in the air over the car to keep it hidden. I can still see the car, but I trust her magic. I think. Lucas watches with disinterest.

"Fascinating," Brandon says when she's done. "The way you speak that language. Is it something similar to old Norse?"

"It's nothing like Old Norse," says Lucas, waving a hand at the car before stomping away towards the dirt track that leads to the ranch house.

"Wait," she tells us before we follow him. "I'll place an invisibility sigil over each of you." She draws a little symbol over my head, and I feel a buzzing sensation that makes me feel warm and safe. "It will last a couple of hours at most." She draws the same sigil over Max and Brandon. "We will still be able to see each other, but no one else should be able to see us."

When she's done, we walk in silence down the dirt track that leads to the ranch house. When we reach the spot where the car stopped, we all stop dead in our tracks. It's as if there is an invisible wall in front of us. But it doesn't feel like a wall, it feels like — nothing?

"It's a complicated spell," Lucas says, running a hand over the space between us and where we want to be. After a few minutes, he shakes his head. "This isn't something we can do ourselves. We would need to call the coven in, and there's no way they would be willing to work with vampires."

"What are you saying?" asks Brandon.

"It's impossible to pass," Lucas says.

"So, what do we do now?" I can feel tears stinging in the back of my eyes at the idea that we've come this far only to be stuck on this side of the ward.

"It doesn't feel that complicated to me," Henrietta says, mostly to herself while she runs a hand around the invisible shield.

"It has many layers," Lucas says, shaking his head.

"If I can undo the base ward, then I can assess the next layer."

"You can't just *undo* a ward," he says.

She runs her fingers along the invisible wall and begins to walk. Everyone follows behind her, Lucas at the very rear of our group, huffing about the absurdity of it all.

"I found a pillar." Her fingers grasp an invisible pole. "There are many ways to set a ward. A basic way to do it is to begin with placing up beams of light and energy. If you can *remove* a pillar, the whole thing can come down. If it's made with a crystal grid or physical objects, you would need to find those first, but I don't sense anything physical here..."

"And how does one remove a pillar?" Brandon asks.

"With a great deal of concentration and effort," she says. "And a little candle magic." She pulls some white candles from her purse, along with some herbs, oils and a picture of Jesus she must have picked up from the market.

Okaaaay.

"If you ask politely, any deity will help you," she says with a smirk.

She fusses around with the candles, placing them where she found the pillar.

"This is such a waste of time," Lucas says. "You won't get very far that way."

Her eyes flash open. "And what do *you* suggest we do? Rip it down with some chaos magic? Blow a hole in the side with a fire spell?" She steps back from the ward and glares at him. "May I remind you, Lucas, that there is a reason you and I have been made a match, and it's because I'm just as powerful as you. If not more so!"

He glares right back at her. "The only way through is with the help of the coven. You can't do this alone."

"You said it yourself. They won't come. And the coven will put us both on trial if they know we're out here helping vampires."

Lucas clears his throat. "You're right. We shouldn't be out here. We should all just go home."

We all glare at him.

"We didn't come this fucking far just to *go home*." I growl at him.

Henrietta ignores us all as she lights candles and begins to chant, waving her hands around over the ward.

We watch as she pulls at the invisible pillar, and after what does indeed look like a great deal of effort and energy, she falls back on her ass and lies down on the scrub. "It's done."

"Henrietta," Brandon goes to her. "Are you alright? Can I get you something? How can you recharge your energy?"

She shakes her head. "I just need to rest a moment, and then I'll tackle the next layer."

"Another layer?" I ask.

"Webbing," she says. "And beneath that, I suspect something else as well. It could take all night."

"We don't have all night," I say, looking over at the house in the distance.

Maverick is so close, but still so out of my reach.

CHAPTER SIXTY-TWO

"Someone's coming," says Brandon, as tiny headlights appear back at the start of the dirt road.

Henrietta blows out the candles. "The sigils will keep us hidden, but let's still get out of sight. Just in case."

Brandon, Max and Lucas go one way, and me and Henrietta go the other. The two of us crouch down behind some desert scrub and wait.

A large black SUV stops at the border of the wards, and Cassius and Vincent get out.

Fuck.

"We know you're out here!" calls Vincent, waving a gun that I have no doubt contains silver bullets through the air.

My eyes flash at Henrietta, and she shakes her head like something is wrong.

"We saw your car," Cassius says. "Nice ride, but you won't get far without it."

The two of them start wandering in the direction of Brandon and Lucas and Henrietta's breath hitches.

"The sigils will still work, right?" I whisper.

"They should, I don't know why the one on the car didn't work…" She squints at the top of my head where she put the sigil. "Yours is still good."

"Come out, come out, wherever you are!" Vincent calls, pointing his gun right where the others are hiding.

"How long will it take you to get this ward done?" I ask her. "Really?"

"An hour or two at least," she says. "Honestly, I'm not sure I can even do it."

"I'm going in."

"What? How?"

"Keep working on it."

"Trix, what are you—?"

Vincent and Cassius still have their backs turned, and so I take my chance. I run as quietly as possible towards their SUV. I get in the passenger side, and then slide into the back of the car, nearly landing on three humans who are gagged and tied in what looks like silver chains.

Oh fuck.

They look around, almost at me, but it's clear they don't see me. I'm invisible. Shit, this magic thing works! I grab a blanket and throw it over me just in case, and I get into fetal position. I have no idea if this will work, but I'll do anything it takes to get Maverick back.

Anything.

"Where the fuck are they?" Cassius asks, getting back in the car.

"Who cares? It's not like they can get past Lucas' wards."

Wait, what the fuck? Lucas?!

Suddenly, it all makes sense.

"They'll be wandering around out there all night. We'll come out in the morning when it's light and get rid of them."

The car starts, and a few moments later we're still driving.

I'm through the wards.

But now what?

CHAPTER SIXTY-THREE

THE SUV STOPS, and a few seconds later the back door opens. Vincent, wearing gloves, starts pulling the humans out of the back. He takes the chains off them, throwing them in piles on the ground.

Cassius appears and helps him.

"Ah, fuck, watch out!" Cassius yells as one of the chains brushes his arm.

Silver.

The humans look drugged up, weak. They've lost too much blood. I feel like shit just standing here not doing anything to help them, but I quickly remind myself the best way to help is by finding Maverick and getting us *all* out of here.

While Vincent and Cassius are focused on their task, I take my chance to quietly slide out of the car.

And there, in front of me, is the house. The house from

my dream, the vision Maverick sent me through the blood bond, the house from the Airbnb listing I found.

Christmas lights are strung around the porch, the lights are on inside, and it's clear by the sound of laughter and music that Maverick is not the only one here.

I silently follow them up to the house, slipping through the door before Cassius closes it behind me. He pauses for a second, looks in my direction and then shakes his head, walking forward with his brother and the weak humans.

The house is as kitschy as ranch houses can get. Old pine furniture, corn print curtains, pictures of chickens and horses on the walls. What the hell are a bunch of vampires doing hanging out *here*?

Vincent and Cassius throw the humans down on the kitchen floor and start moving boxes around in the pantry before opening up a hidden door leading to what I guess is a basement.

Is that where Maverick is? Down there? I have the feeling that if I go down there to find him, I'm never coming out.

And then I hear it. Maverick's laugh.

What the fuck?

I follow the sound, tiptoeing through the open door at the back of the house and out into the yard. And there sitting around the fire, his arm wrapped around Juliette, with a huge ass smile on his face, is Maverick.

CHAPTER SIXTY-FOUR

$\mathcal{M}$averick

ROAD RAGE III, *one and a half stars*
I love Maverick Stone... as a concept. *He's very fucking cool in these movies. 100% iconic AF. No one can deny that watching these movies is an excellent way to waste a Sunday afternoon, but while his biceps can fill out an XXL t-shirt in a way that makes even the best of us fall over ourselves, the truth is, the guy can't act for shit.*
@Filmmmbufff3456

I'VE HAD TOO much of the blood. My senses are fucked. I'm saying stupid shit. I'm finding Juliette and Lottie incredibly attractive.

But there's still a part of me that's aware. A part that *knows* I'm drugged. That knows the best way to get out of here is to play along, just enough to convince everyone I'm a little more drugged and under their influence than I am.

Some people think I can't act for shit, but what those people don't know is that even the "acting like shit" for the big movie franchise *is* acting.

Even movie star Maverick Stone is just another fucking character. The real Maverick, that's the only character I don't know how to play.

The only time I've ever felt like I wasn't playing a character was when I was with Trix.

Trix. I feel myself sobering up just thinking about her.

Goddamn, just the thought of her is enough to send me into a spiral that I'll never come up from. But I can't entertain the idea that I'll never see her again. She's the reason I will get out of here.

I look down into my half-full glass. This is the trick. Always keep your glass half full. Too full and it's suspicious that you're not drinking; too empty and someone will get you another.

And then I see it. A flash, a vision down the blood bond. I see this fire from the porch above us. I see myself with my arm around Juliette, and I feel deep, intense *rage*.

Trix is fucking furious at me.

Fuck, Trix is here!

"Gimme a minute, babe," I tell Juliette.

"Where are you going?" she complains.

I grab her almost empty glass. "To get you a top-up."

She grins and lets me take her glass. She does *not* need any more. The only thing worse than a vampire who's high is a vampire high on bad blood.

I walk hesitantly through the kitchen, trying to figure out what the fuck is happening. A hallucination, probably. I'm off my fucking face.

Vincent and Cassius are stacking boxes of blood in the pantry. Cassius turns to scowl at me, and then I hear it. The scuffling of more humans in the basement.

And all I can think is that one of them might be Trix.

I glare at Cassius. "Who's down there?"

"What are you talking about?" he huffs.

"Who did you bring?" I growl. "Is it her?"

Vincent laughs. "You could both drink from any woman in the city, what's so special about *her*?" He thumbs toward the door.

"You fucking bastards, I will—"

I lunge towards them, but fuck! This blood makes me so weak!

"You will what?" Cassius laughs, kicking me to the floor. "Lie there and take it?"

He kicks me in the stomach, and I curl up into a ball. *Fuck!*

"At least, that's what she did." Cassius grins down at me. "When I fucked your girl."

"You fucking bastard—" He kicks me again, this time in the shin, and holy fuck, I forgot how much getting beat up hurt!

"Forget the girl, and forget him," Vincent says, giving me a shove with his foot. "He's just going through the process."

What process?

"He's a liability," says Cassius.

"He's weak. He's not fully under her control yet, but he will be. Give it another day, he'll be as nuts as the rest of them." He hands me a bottle of blood from the boxes in the pantry. "Have another drink. You'll feel better."

So, the bad blood not only has some kind of mind-altering drug in it, it also weakens us. Why would Lottie want her vampires weak?

So she can be the strongest one.

So she can rule us.

Cassius and Vincent walk off, leaving me lying here, weak, kicked and beaten.

I squeeze my eyes shut to block out the pain… and then I feel a tender hand on my shoulder. It's *her* hand. I'd know it anywhere.

My eyes flash open, but she's not there.

I must be fucking delusional. I'm so fucked up on this bad blood.

And I don't know how I'm going to do it, weak and half mind-fucked by Lottie, but I've been in worse situations. I will get out of here, but I need to do it fast.

CHAPTER SIXTY-FIVE

THE BLAKES LEAVE, and a few minutes later Maverick
manages to sit up. I've never seen him like this before —
beaten and bruised. He looks almost human. He runs a hand
through his messed-up hair and makes his way to stand. His
brow furrows as he looks around the room.

"I'm out of my goddamn mind," he groans.

I follow him as he gradually makes his way up the stairs
and into a bedroom.

But when I see sexy black lingerie on the pillow, I can't
help the rage burning behind my eyes! Why is there lingerie?
Why the fuck did Juliette have her arm around him?!

His eyes widen, and I realize he's looking at me. The sigil
must be wearing off already.

"Am I insane or are you here?" he whispers.

I open my mouth to rip through him, to yell at him for
being such an asshole, for putting us in danger, for making

me sick with worry — but I don't say any of it, because suddenly his lips are on mine, and holy shit, it feels so fucking good and right for us to be together, even here, like this. Even after he had his arm around Juliette. He pulls me close, pressing every inch of his body into mine as he kisses me with desperation. I kiss him right back, wrapping my arms around him.

He's safe. He's here. Everything is okay.

When he releases me, there's so much pain in his eyes. I open my mouth to speak, but this time he puts a finger to my lips and shakes his head. He points to the outside of the house and then to his ear. *They will hear us.*

He scrambles around the room until he finds a pad and a pencil, scribbling fast.

Lottie drugging us. Missed you.

A smile spreads over my face as I read the last part. I grab the pencil and write.

I missed you too!! Now how the fuck do we get out of here?

He shakes his head.

Magic keeps us here, he writes.

Henrietta is working on it, I write back.

I have to pretend. They will suspect. Kill me.

He looks over at the lingerie on the pillow.

Nothing with J. Only want you. Weak. Need blood.

I look up at him and nod.

He pushes back a strand of hair and cups my cheek. He kisses me again, hard and fast, and then his lips make their way to my neck, and I'm suddenly in ecstasy at the short, sharp pain followed by the immense pleasure of his bite.

CHAPTER SIXTY-SIX

$\mathcal{M}$averick

Fuck, I don't want to stop. I don't want my lips and my mouth to ever *not* be somewhere on Trix's warm, gorgeous body. She writhes in pleasure on the bed while I grind my hips into hers and drink. All I want is to rip her jeans off, take my fill of her in every way. She grips my back and begs for more.

Somehow, I find the will to pull back, satiated by her blood but not satiated in all the ways I want so desperately to be satiated by her!

I lick my finger and run it over the bite marks. Her eyelids flutter a little at the sensation of it, and a smirk lights up the corners of my mouth.

"Thank you," I mouth before I kiss her on the lips one more time. But not for the last time. Never the last time.

I don't need to write it down this time. Our blood bond is back, and it's back with fury. I can feel her heat, her desire for me, I can feel her *love* for me, and her love makes me feel even stronger than her blood.

I look into her eyes and tell her without a word what I'm going to do now. I'm going to give her my blood and make her strong so that we can take these fuckers down together.

She grins and nods at me.

I'm just about to pierce my wrist when—

"Babe!" Juliette's voice calls from the hallway.

I point to the wardrobe and push Trix inside. I open the door and call back to Juliette. "Yeah, babe?"

"You're always disappearing!" She bursts into the room and frowns at me.

"Just freshening up for you." I give her a smile, and she instantly buys it.

"Come back down. Lottie's been asking about you."

Shit.

"Gimme one minute?" I toy with a strand of her hair, and she bats her eyelashes at me.

"She wants you now, and so do I," Juliette says, sticking a pointy dark red nail into my chest. She smiles and then flicks her hair and walks out, swaying her hips in an attempt to make me want her. But I could never want her.

I could never want any other woman again.

I only want Trix. *Forever.*

I look back to the wardrobe door, silently pleading through the blood bond for Trix to stay in there and stay safe, and then I follow Juliette back down to the fire pit.

But when I get there, there's no sign of Lottie or Aiden. Of course, they're probably feeding off the new humans while everyone else drinks the bad blood.

"She's so wonderful, isn't she?" murmurs Juliette. "Our queen. She gives us everything we could ever want and need." She squeezes my thigh and looks at me with those creepy goo-goo eyes they all seem to have.

"She is a true icon," says Linda, looking just as gooey as she stares up at the half-moon in the sky above us.

They both look to Vivian, and for a split second I think I see hesitation, but she smiles at them both. "To Queen Lottie!" she says, raising her glass.

Not this shit again.

"Maverick?" Juliette nudges me. "Silly, you forgot to toast our queen!"

I plaster a dumb smile on my face and raise my glass. "All hail Queen Lottie!" I say.

CHAPTER SIXTY-SEVEN

rix

FUCK HIDING in a cupboard while Maverick is out there in danger. I rip up our notes and then shove them in my pocket.

I'm probably going to die here, but fuck dying in a cupboard! If I'm going to die tonight, I'll at least die trying to save the man I love.

I walk out of the room and down the stairs as stealthily as possible. I notice a matching set of candlesticks on the mantel in the living room. I grab them, one in each hand. I have no idea whether they're silver or not, but here's hoping. I make my way into the kitchen and stop at the doorway, trying to psych myself up for whatever comes next, when suddenly a pair of muscular arms wrap around my neck and force me to drop the candlesticks.

"How the fuck did you get in here?" Cassius's voice growls into my ear.

Cassius!

"Magic," I tell him.

He lets go, but when I try to run, he's too fast. He grabs my wrist and pulls me close to him.

"You're a witch?" he asks, with curiosity more than anything.

"I'm just here for Maverick."

"What is it about that fucker?" The question feels sincere, like he really wants to know why I chose Maverick over *him*. He loosens his grip a little, and I can see it in his light blue eyes. He does have a thing for me.

"You had your chance with me," I tell him, trying to pull out of his grip.

"You ran."

"Before that. When I worked for you. You knew how I felt about you."

"You rejected me. You said you didn't want it."

"I liked you, but I was just scared. That's why. But now, now I'd never be with you."

His grip tightens on me again. "You're not scared of Maverick."

I shake my head. "Maverick isn't a monster."

He throws back his head and laughs. "Oh, sweet, stupid Trix, he's more of a monster than any of us."

"What? No!"

"In the army, Maverick killed more people than the rest of us put together. He was a killing machine. And not just soldiers, civilians too."

I shake my head. "No. He wouldn't—"

"He did. He was a baby vampire then. Completely out of control. Ruled by his thirst."

"Well — I don't care about his past." I thrash around, trying to get out of his grip. "He's not like that anymore. People can change."

"Sure, people can. But vampires never do."

"Trix, darling, I thought that was you!" Lottie appears in the doorway, Aiden standing just behind her. "How did you get past my wards?" she asks with a curious smile, like she's asking me where I got my dress from.

"She's a witch," Cassius says.

"Nonsense," Lottie says. "She's not a witch, she's just a little girl with an attitude."

"Just because I'm not two hundred years old doesn't make me a *little girl!*" I keep struggling in his grip.

"What do you want me to do with her?" Cassius asks.

Lottie ignores him. "Come out and sit with us, Trix." Lottie takes my hand. It's *cold,* so cold. Cassius quickly lets me go.

As we walk out to the fire pit, I lock eyes with Maverick. He may be a good actor, but he's not hiding the fact that he'll unleash hell on Cassius, Lottie and anyone else who tries to hurt me.

This is a terrifying situation, but, holy fuck, it feels good to know he still wants me.

"Juliette, why don't you move around and let this little human sit next to Maverick?"

"What? Why?" Juliette complains.

"Because I said so, darling." Her tone is sugar, but the intention behind it is ice cold. "Actually, you can all take your leave. I'd like a little double-date with Aiden, Maverick and Trix."

"Double date?" Juliette whines.

Lottie gives her a look.

"Of course, yes, my queen," Juliette says with a bow.

"My queen," says Linda, standing up and bowing.

"My queen," Vivian says, bowing as well.

"And you, Cassius," Lottie says. "Your services are no longer required this evening."

I hold my breath while I wait for him to tell her about the others out by the edge of the wards.

His eyes flicker to me and then back to her. "I could be useful—"

"Useful?" Lottie laughs. "You think it's *useful* for me to have humans just walking through our wards? You think you're doing a good job by bringing her to me, even after she's somehow managed to walk in on *your* watch?"

Cassius's mouth forms a hard line. "No." He takes a beat. "My queen."

"Do as I say," she says. "Or I will do away with you."

"Yes. My queen." He does that same sick bow towards her, flashes his eyes at me for just a moment and then takes a few steps backwards before turning and walking away, following the others inside.

"Sit," she commands me.

I drop into the seat beside Maverick while she slides into the seat on his other side.

"Now," Lottie says. "How ever did you find your way through those wards? I was assured that the warlock who put them in place was very high up in his coven."

"It's not my fault if your magic is shit," I spit at her.

She just laughs. "Oh, this one is feisty!" She grabs my hand across Maverick's lap. "I think in other circumstances you and I might have been friends." She squeezes my hand, and shivers of ice curl up my spine.

"My queen—" Maverick begins, but she cuts him off.

"I know you're pretending, Maverick, darling. You haven't filled your glass all evening."

She lets go of my hand and grins at both of us.

"I can see the appeal with this one." She runs a hand through Maverick's hair. "I suppose he never mentioned to you we were once an item, weren't we, darling?"

My stomach churns at the idea of Maverick being with *her*.

"*You* kissed *me*, and it was one time," he growls.

"But wasn't it wonderful? It just occurs to me now that Max may not know that story, perhaps I should tell him."

"Like he'd believe anything that comes out of your mouth."

"Now, now, Maverick. I just wanted to enjoy a few drinks with you both, maybe help you see my side of things." She looks to Aiden, who's been sitting silently by her side. "Some more blood for Maverick, please, darling. Bring him the good stuff, and perhaps a glass of the special red for Trix? And another for me, too." She shoves her glass into his face.

Aiden stands, following her orders, and I glare up at him.

"Poppy would be disgusted by what you've become," I tell him. "She wouldn't care that you'd become a vampire. She'd still love you and want you in her life, but hurting her friends? She'd be so ashamed."

He shows no remorse, just turns and walks into the house.

"Do you both take me for some kind of idiot?" Lottie asks, leaning towards Maverick and dusting a piece of invisible soot off his shirt. "Do you think I did not know the girl was here? I can hear *everything*. Every footstep, every breath. Every pencil scratch on paper. I can especially hear people getting into wardrobes." She moves a little of Maverick's hair from his forehead, and I want to rip her arm off. "You should know me better than that, Maverick."

"What do you want with us?" he asks.

"I just want my power back, that's all. And you know, I'm not all bad, so I'll give you a choice. You can either bow down to me now and join my Sorority or you can receive the Certain Death."

"That's it?" I ask. "We just have to bow down to you?"

Maverick turns and glares at me, a hard *no* in his eyes.

But who cares if it will get us out of here? It's not like we have to *mean* it—

"Of course, I'll know if you don't mean it," she says, reaching over and taking my hand again, squeezing it way too hard with her icicle fingers.

Maverick grabs her hand and pulls it off me. "Touch her again and I will end you," he tells her. There's something ancient, dark and deep in his voice that makes me shudder in all the best ways.

God, help us get out of here so that I can make love to this man again!

Lottie just laughs. "Oh, Maverick, don't you remember what happened last time someone tried to end me? I rose from the dead!" She grins at him. "Now, which will you choose? Bow down to me, your rightful Vampire queen, or face Certain Death?"

"Lottie, you're forgetting one thing," he tells her. "There's always a third choice." And then he lunges at her.

CHAPTER SIXTY-EIGHT

$\mathcal{M}$averick

SHE DOESN'T EXPECT IT, and so I have the upper hand — for a split second at least. I push Lottie toward the fire. Fire won't kill us, but it does burn. The skin on her face turns red and blisters in the flames, but she quickly shoves me back. As she pushes me down onto the desert earth, straddling me with her strong thighs, her face is already healing.

Lottie looks weak when you don't know what she is. She was turned when she was twenty, just a waif of a girl, but she is old, and she is strong and now I have no idea what I was even thinking trying to take her on. I've had some blood, so I'm stronger than I was, but I'm nowhere near my best.

But even on my best day, could I win a fight with Lottie?

I quickly shut down all negative thoughts. I have to believe I can win. I have to believe that I will get out of here, that I will get Trix out of here. I have to believe that even though I have been a monster, that I have caused pain and suffering to so many people, that even though I haven't always been a good man, that I somehow still deserve a little happiness.

"Why couldn't you just play *nice*?" Lottie snaps. "Don't you understand my vision? I only want what is best for all vampire kind!"

"How is drugging us all into submission what's best for us?"

"Because sometimes people don't know what's best for them. And besides, who wouldn't want to be drugged all the time? It takes away the *pain*, my darling. You have so much pain, don't you, Maverick? All those memories from the war? The trenches, the death, the killing… don't you want the pain to go away?"

Flashes of death, bombs, bullets, all the senseless fucking pointless killing appear in my mind's eye. I squeeze my eyes shut. The pain is still there, but it's not like it was. Because now, among all those horrific memories, I also have good ones.

Acting has been my therapy, and memories of good times on set, camaraderie with my co-stars, friendships made, and success on a level I never dreamed possible come to me now. Knowing that millions of people around the world enjoy what I do has brought me joy, making the darkness a little easier to bear.

But what has lifted me out of the shadows even more than that are the memories I now have of my time with Trix. Sitting with Trix on my balcony, watching her eat an entire pizza while she laughs at stupid shit I say. The sound of her sweet laughter filling my home, my heart. The two of us tangled up in my bedsheets, *making love.* I'm falling in love, and while that's not an antidote to every bad thing that's ever happened, it has lightened my heart enough to stop me from living in absolute misery.

I glance over at Trix now, where she stands behind Lottie, watching in horror.

I cannot let her lose me.

I summon a burst of strength and push Lottie off and away from me, scrambling on the ground to get to Trix.

Lottie laughs as she gets to her feet. A second later she's standing over me, the sole of her cowboy boot on my neck.

Ah, fuck.

"I don't *want* to kill you, but I will if I have to. I would much prefer for us to get along. To work together. Think of it, darling. You and me on the silver screen. I could finally give Max that divorce, and *we* could be together, on screen and off. Wouldn't you like to know what it's like with me, darling? It's all very nice to engage in the odd roll in the hay with a human, but vampire and vampire together, that is the natural way. And you and I together, we could have it all."

"The drinks, Lottie. My queen."

She lifts her boot and turns towards Aiden. "Darling!"

Of course he's heard the whole thing, but he just stands there, holding the drinks like nothing more than her servant.

"Give me that," she says, reaching for the tray.

I sit up and look for Trix, but she's gone. Good. I'm glad she's gone. I hope she finds her way back to the others. I hope she gets the hell out of here. I don't even care what happens to me. If she's safe, my Certain Death will be worth it.

"Give me Maverick's drink," she demands. Aiden passes her a glass of blood. "Now drink or die."

What a fucking choice.

But one I don't have to make. Lottie's hand grips my nose, and she pours the blood down my throat.

I struggle in her grip, and I try to close my mouth. It's not like I really *need* to breathe, but my body doesn't always know that, especially in stressful situations. I gasp and feel the warm, thick drink move down my throat.

I can only assume that the "good stuff" is the blood I drank at my house, before I got taken. And so I wait to go under… but nothing happens.

Okay, maybe the "good stuff" is something else. Maybe it's just the mind-altering blood. I wait to start feeling goo-goo about Lottie again, but I don't.

"Why isn't it working? Why isn't he out?" Lottie's face contorts. "Aiden, get me some more!"

I don't know why the blood's not working, but clearly I'm meant to be knocked out, so I let my head fall to the ground, close my eyes and act the part.

"Never mind, he's out now," she says.

"Do you want me to get the Blakes to do something with him?" Aiden asks.

"That won't be necessary. I quite enjoy playing these games with him." She gives my foot a little kick, and I let it go limp. "I'd like to be here when he comes to so I can torture him a little more. But get me some silver rope and some gloves."

"Yes, my queen," says Aiden.

"But first, my drink, darling?" I hear glasses moving around on a tray. "And did you bring a special glass of wine for the girl?"

A pause.

"Where is the girl?"

"I don't know, my queen," he says.

"Find her!"

"Yes, my queen."

A few minutes later, I hear familiar footsteps and the sound of silver chains rattling.

I open one eye just a slit, and there stands Trix. Glaring at Lottie like she's going to kill her.

Fuck, Trix! Why couldn't you just run?

"Oh, you are a spirited little thing!" laughs Lottie. "Now drop those chains, or I'll stake Maverick right here, right now. Won't that be something to see? His blood turning black, his soul, or what's left of it at least, leaving his body."

A look of terror crosses her face, and she drops the chains. "Take me, do what you want with me, drain me, I don't care, just don't hurt him."

Trix, no!

"Drink your wine, Trix, darling," says Lottie. "You'll be forced to if you don't."

"Is this drugged?" Trix asks.

"It's just a little something to soothe your troubled mind," Lottie says. "When you drink it, you feel all nice and lovely. All warm and fuzzy. Your worries will just melt away. Doesn't that sound nice? I'm sure you have some worries you'd like to melt away. You'll forget all about your struggles with your business. You'll forget all about your business!" she laughs. "And you'll surely forget all this palaver with Maverick and Cassius. Although what a lucky girl to have two of the most eligible vampire bachelors in the city wanting you." I hear Lottie take a gulp of her drink. "What is it about her, Aiden? Do you see it? Why do the boys go so crazy for this green-haired little Pixie?"

She's jealous as hell. Neither me nor Max wanted her. In fact, apart from Aiden, I don't think any man has ever wanted to be with Lottie without being under some kind of duress.

"I don't know, my queen. Perhaps it's because she's so unusual."

"What do you mean by that?" Lottie's voice is harsh, hard.

"She's just a little weirdo," Aiden says. "I certainly wouldn't be interested in a freak like her."

I will kill him. Give him the kind of Certain Death other vampires will talk about for centuries.

"You think she's just a little freak?" Lottie muses.

"Yes, my queen. Just a freak."

"And then, what am I?" she asks, taking another gulp of her drink.

"You are a queen," Aiden says. "You are *my* queen." He steps towards her, takes her face in his hands and kisses her.

With Lottie and Aiden caught up in their embrace, I stand silently. If I can surprise her from behind—

"Aiden," she says, stumbling back. "I feel I've taken a turn. I suddenly feel quite ill."

"My queen?" he asks, worry in his voice. "What is it?"

"What did you do?" She clutches her pearls as her wine glass slips from her grasp and smashes onto the ground, blood splattering her coat.

"My queen!"

And then Lottie drops to the ground.

CHAPTER SIXTY-NINE

rix

AIDEN STARES with horror at Lottie's unconscious body. He glares at me and then looks at Maverick who's now sitting up, eyes wide at the scene before him.

"Maverick!" I throw myself into his arms, hot tears of relief washing down my cheeks.

Maverick's huge arms squeeze me tight, and he kisses me on the top of my head, sending heat through my entire body. I look up at him, and he wipes a tear from my cheek before pulling me in for a breathless kiss.

He's okay. I'm okay. We're safe now.

"We can do this as much as we want later," he mumbles into my lips. "Right now, we have to get out of here."

Aiden falls to the ground beside Lottie. He seems very upset for someone who just made this happen.

"Aiden, you saved us," I say.

He looks up at me with a hateful look in his eyes. "What did you do?"

"You did it! You swapped the blood!"

He ignores me, running a hand over Lottie's limp face, then down to her pearls and the necklaces around her neck. He yanks off one of her necklaces and then turns to me.

"Why would I save *you*?" he spits. And then he runs off into the first light of dawn. He fucking *runs*!

"We should go after him!" I try to get out of Maverick's embrace so I can chase him down.

Maverick shakes his head. "No. He's no threat without Lottie. We need to get her bound and—" he gives me a look. "And as soon as I can find the right wood, I'm going to have to stake her."

I just nod.

"Bind her with the chains," he says. "I would help, but I can't touch them."

"I've got it." I lift the heavy chains I'd brought back from where Vincent left them by the SUV. I thought maybe I could take Lottie by surprise, strangle her with silver, but Aiden made it so I didn't have to.

I wrap the chains around her limp body, and they burn her skin. It's disgusting, the smell of burning vampire flesh makes me want to vomit, but I keep going until she's wrapped like a mummy.

"I'm not strong enough to move her," I say.

"I'll find some gloves." Maverick walks towards the house and Juliette, Linda and Vivian appear on the back porch.

"Our queen?" Juliette asks, confusion all over her face as she looks down at Lottie. "Why is she—? What's—?" She blinks and rubs her forehead.

Maverick puts his hands on Juliette's shoulders, and I try to quiet the jealousy. He doesn't want her. He wants *me*.

"Everything is okay now," he tells her.

She looks around like she's never even seen this place before.

"Where are we?" Linda asks.

"What's Lottie doing here?" asks Vivian. "I thought she was *dead*?"

"You've all been drugged," Maverick tells them. "Lottie was forcing you to drink bad blood. It made you her servants. She was controlling your minds."

I stand up and look down at my feet where Lottie is out of it, wrapped in silver chains. "But she can't hurt anyone anymore," I say.

Maverick's eyes reach mine, and just as I'm about to run into his arms to celebrate the end of this dramatic tale, the Blake brothers appear, and in an instant Vincent has a stake to Maverick's neck and Cassius has a gun to my head.

$\mathcal{M}$averick

I MAKE quick work of ducking out of Vincent's grip and the stake at my throat, but he's fast, and he's on me again in a second.

"Stay still, Maverick, or Trix dies," Cassius says, nudging the gun into Trix's temple.

I stop dead. I'll do anything he says to keep her alive, and he knows it. I raise my hands in surrender.

Vincent grabs my hands and binds them with silver rope behind my back, and it burns like hell.

I look to Juliette, Linda and Vivian but they're all still out of it, looking around like they have no clue why they're here or what the hell is going on.

"I'm bound. Now put your gun down, Cassius," I plead.

He does as I ask and then proceeds to gently move loose tendrils of Trix's hair away from her neck.

Even my rage isn't strong enough to break the silver rope,

and knowing he's about to give Trix The Bite is fucking *killing* me.

Cassius' fangs in her neck, him getting his fill from my woman, her ecstasy at *his* bite.

Rage rips through me and I lunge forward, but Vincent holds me back with a chuckle.

I will get free, and I won't rest until both these assholes die the Certain Death!

"I hardly got a taste last time," Cassius says, running a finger down Trix's neck and way too fucking close to her breasts. "Maybe this time I'll bite her here." He places a kiss at the top of her breast and Trix kicks him in the shin.

He just laughs and leans in closer to her.

I struggle against the rope but all it does is burn!

"What on Gaia?" Henrietta steps out onto the porch and observes the scene in front of her. Lottie passed out and bound in silver chains, three vampires looking around like idiots, Me bound in silver rope with Vincent lording over me, and Trix about to be bitten by Cassius Blake.

Brandon appears behind her, and I let out a sigh of relief.

Some guy I've never seen before steps forward and Trix struggles against Cassius' grip on her. "Lucas! You fucking traitor!" She yells at him. "You put the wards up! You've been working for *them*!"

Lucas puts a hand to his heart and feigns shock. "Who? Me?"

Henrietta turns and glares at him. "I knew it, goddess-damnit! Why didn't I trust myself?"

He shrugs. "It was just a job for me sweetie, and you didn't trust yourself because you never do. You should really work on trusting your intuition a bit more. That's what makes you so weak."

"I spent hours getting those wards down! People could have died because of you!"

Brandon yanks him by the arm. "You piece of shit!"

I haven't seen Brandon angry for decades. He's going to absolutely destroy this guy.

"You just wait until the coven hears about this!" Henrietta warns.

"But they won't, will they? You go to the coven about this, and I'll tell them that you work for a vampire. What will they say about that?"

Wait, what? This guy is a warlock who's been working for Lottie?!

I guess that explains the wards on the doors and windows.

"Fuck you," Henrietta says.

"You and I will get married, and live happily ever after and we'll never talk about any of this again," Lucas tells her.

Brandon grips him harder.

Henrietta glares at him. "Like hell!"

"If you don't marry me, you will lose your standing with the coven. You'll be out. *Solitary.*" He says it like it's the worst of witch slurs. Maybe it is.

Henrietta's face pales.

"Witches are another breed, aren't they?" Cassius says, his mouth still too close to Trix's neck as he watches this witch's lovers tiff.

"If you're going to bite me, just fucking do it already!" Trix yells at him.

"No!" I yell out, struggling against my rope to get to her.

Cassius' pale blue eyes flick to me. "I won't hurt her. I just want to taste her—"

"You fucking asshole!" I yell. "If you touch her, I *will* fucking annihilate you!"

His fangs protrude and he grins at me before looking down at her neck and—

I launch myself in Cassius' direction, finally getting free

from Vincent's grip. I shove my shoulder into Cassius and Trix is free.

"Run!" I command her.

She runs, and relief washes over me as I sink to my knees.

Run, Trix, Run! I push the words down the blood bond, desperately hoping I'm still strong enough for her to hear them loud and clear.

Vincent stands in front of me, stake in hand.

Max appears, speeding onto the scene, a gun at Vincent's head now.

"Stake Maverick, and I will end you," Max says.

But Cassius is fast, and in a heartbeat, he has Max pinned to the ground.

"Fuck!" Max growls as he struggles to get out of Cassius' grip.

Vincent lifts the stake, and I have a sudden realization that it's my time. This is how I go. I say a quick prayer that the others will be fine. That Max will get out of here, that Trix will live a long happy life without me. All I want is her happiness.

And then I see my life flash before my eyes. My childhood on the farm, my youth in the army. I don't see the bad, I only see the good. Running through cornfields, joy echoing in my own laughter. The friends I made in the army, the good times we had as lads, joking around, playing cards. I don't see the moment I was turned; I see the people I helped, the family in the pub, the others who lived that night because of me. I don't see the bad reviews, I just see the smiles on the faces of the fans, the light that I've brought to this world even in all the darkness. And then I see Trix. Her smile, her kind eyes, that expression she makes when she's in the throes of passion.

I love you too.

And it's all okay. It's okay if I die right now, because

despite everything, my life has been good. It has been worth something. There has been suffering, there has been pain, but holy shit there has been *love.*

And so I take a breath. I am ready.

With eyes closed, I wait for the blow. Wait for the end.

But it doesn't come.

Instead, I hear a loud *thwack* and a gurgle. I open my eyes to see Vincent on the ground, a silver chain wrapped around his neck. I look up in awe, and there's Trix, glaring at Vincent who's now writhing around on the ground in pain, unable to free himself of the chain at his neck.

Trix grabs the silver rope at my wrists and yanks it off, grabs another silver chain from the ground, turns to Cassius and lunges at him.

He holds his hands up in surrender and drops his gun. "I never wanted to hurt you, Trix," he says softly.

"Too fucking late!" I roar, getting to my feet. I grab Vincent's stake, run towards Cassius and hold it at his throat. "I told you I'd fucking end you."

"No," says Trix. "Please! Don't hurt him."

My eyes flash fire towards Trix. "He tried to kill you! He was part of all of this!"

She shakes her head. "He saved me. He switched the drinks."

Cassius blinks and then laughs. "What?"

Trix steps towards us. "It wasn't Aiden, so it must have been you. After Aiden poured the drinks, you swapped the glasses around, so that Lottie would drink the bad blood."

"Is this true?" I ask, pressing the wooden point into Cassius' skin.

He looks into Trix's eyes. "Yes."

I probably shouldn't believe him, but I do. He cares about Trix, in his own fucked up way. He didn't want her to die. He saved her from Lottie.

Fuck.

I push the stake in deeper, inching into his skin. "If you ever fucking touch her again, I will come for you."

He nods in my grip.

I push him away. "Get the fuck out of here."

Vincent, still lying on the ground with the chain around his neck, calls out — "Cass! Help me!"

Cassius takes a step back and shakes his head. "I want nothing to do with any of this," he says. "This was always about you, Vince. I just wanted to run a club and have a good time. I never wanted any of... *this.*"

Cassius looks at Lottie bound in chains, at me still holding the stake and then his gaze lands on Trix. "I'm sorry," he says. "Truly."

"You're dead to me, Cassius!" Vincent calls out to him as Cassius starts walking away. "Dead to me!"

CHAPTER SEVENTY-ONE

rix

"THE ONLY WAY a vampire can die the Certain Death is from a stake made of ash, elm or yew straight to the heart. Nothing else will kill them."
Vampire Hunter's Guide page 32

HENRIETTA LOOKS at the pearls and pendants around Lottie's neck. "Where is it? The pendant?"

"He took it," I tell her. "Aiden."

"What was it?" Maverick asks, slipping his fingers into mine like it's the most natural thing on earth. My heart gives a hard and fast thump and then rests into an easy beat, knowing that it's all over now. And while I don't know what's going to happen next, right now, my hand is in his and despite the carnage around us, it somehow feels like a perfect moment.

"A pendant, magic," Henrietta says. "We think it's why Lottie didn't die the first time she was staked."

"Fascinating," says Brandon. "That witch magic can save a vampire from Certain Death."

He gives Henrietta a look like he's got some big ideas for her.

"What did it look like?" Lucas asks, stepping towards Henrietta.

"You get the fuck away from her," Max seethes, pulling him back. "Don't talk, don't move. You're lucky you're not dead."

"What shall we do with him?" Brandon looks Lucas up and down like he's trying to figure out the most painful way to kill him.

"If you don't let me go, the coven will come after you," Lucas says.

"He's right, and they'll come after me too," Henrietta sighs. "But if Lucas tells them about my involvement, they will know he was working for vampires and kill him too."

"So, you can't tell," Brandon says. "Or you'll be killed."

"Just let him go," Henrietta says. "There are worse things than being solitary. Like marrying him for one."

"The last thing we need is warlock blood on our hands," Max says.

Brandon gives him a shove. "Go. Never speak of this again, or we will come for you."

Lucas turns and runs up the stairs, tripping and falling over himself twice on the way. He disappears through the house and hopefully out of our lives forever.

"What about Lottie?" Maverick asks, kicking at the chains wrapped around her. "We can't let *her* go."

Juliette, Linda and Vivian, who now seem to be totally out of Lottie's control, and the rest of us, apart from Vincent, who's still wrapped in chains by the fire pit, step towards Lottie, making a circle around her chained-up body.

"No," says Brandon. "We can't let her go."

For a moment we all just stand there, staring at her. At the vampire who lived through one staking already.

Lottie's eyelids flutter open as if she's aware of us all standing over her. She looks down at the chains wrapped around her and laughs. "You think chains can stop me? I've risen from the dead once, I will do it again!"

"Not without your pendant," Henrietta says.

Lottie looks down at her neck and sees that she's no longer wearing it. "Give it back!" she growls, sounding possessed. "Where is it?!"

"Gone," Henrietta says. "Aiden took it."

"Aiden! That little weasel! I will end him! I will kill him!"

Lottie looks towards the three vampires she'd been keeping captive. "Help me! I am your queen! Get me out of these chains and kill these traitors!"

They look at her as if they have no idea what she's talking about.

"You drugged us?" Juliette asked.

"For your own good," Lottie says. "You were happy when you were drugged. You didn't have to worry about anything. You were at peace!"

Juliette glares at her. "You wanted power so badly that you took it away from *us*."

"I wanted power for us all!"

"By taking away our autonomy? Our free will?" Juliette picks Vincent's stake up from the ground, and a fire flames in her eyes. "How fucking *dare* you take away my power!"

And in a blur of movement, she's in front of Lottie, stabbing the stake through the chains and into her heart. And this time, it goes all the way in.

CHAPTER SEVENTY-TWO

averick

LOTTIE'S BLOOD turns black as the sky begins to brighten in a kaleidoscope of cotton candy pinks.

"No one takes my power!" Juliette seethes, standing up and wiping Lottie's black blood on her jeans.

"I must stay and watch this time. Make sure there isn't another spell or charm protecting her." Max wipes his forehead with the back of his arm. This is the second time he's had to watch his ex-wife die. Devil that she was, Lottie had more of a connection with Max than anyone.

"I'm out of sun serum," I say, blinking up at the sky.

Max hands me one of the familiar small bottles, and I gulp it down, immediately feeling more like myself again.

I may have been made for darkness, but every day I *choose* sunlight.

"I'll watch her too," Juliette says. "If you've got any more sun serum?"

Max hands her a bottle. "That's my last one. Linda, Vivian, you may want to get inside." They do as he suggests.

Vincent tugs against the silver chains that now tie him to one of the Adirondack chairs. "I haven't taken any sun serum! I need to go inside too!"

I shake my head. "I think a day of sunlight could do you some good."

"What will happen to him?" Trix asks.

"He'll go a little crispy, be in some pain for a while. He'll live."

"A little crispy? It will burn the fuck out of me!" he squeals.

"Well, maybe you should have thought about that before you fucked with my woman!" I kick him in the shins, and he grimaces. He's already weakening in the early light.

I turn to Juliette. "Thank you." It's a weird thing to say, but I'm glad I didn't have to be the one to kill Max's wife.

"She never fucking liked me," Juliette says, glaring down at Lottie with zero remorse.

"There are humans in the basement," I say. "We need to get them out."

Brandon nods. "I expected Lottie would have a supply somewhere."

Trix does *not* need to see what's in the basement. "Trix, Henrietta, would you stay here and keep an eye on Vincent?"

They both nod, and I'm glad Trix doesn't fight me on this. I don't even know that I'm prepared for what I'll find down there.

Me and Brandon walk through the kitchen and into the pantry, quickly moving the boxes of bad blood out of the way.

I open the door and walk down the stairs, trying my best to ignore the overwhelming scent of death.

When we get to the bottom, we see three new humans have arrived. They all look off their faces, but their heart rates are high enough.

"We'll glamour them and let them go," Brandon says.

I kneel down next to a dark-haired woman and look deep into her eyes. When I know I have her complete attention, I tell her, "Everything is okay. You just had a big night out with some friends. You'll feel a little hungover and the memories of last night will be hazy, but you'll know you had a good time."

She nods dumbly.

"You won't remember anything of this place or what you saw here. You won't remember getting home. But you'll know everything is fine."

She nods again. I break apart the cable ties that bind her feet and hands, and she stumbles up the stairs. I do the same again with the other human while Brandon does the same, sending his human up the stairs after them.

And then we look at Beth and Finn.

"We should have helped them first," I say. "They're barely alive."

Brandon gives me a look, and I don't like what he's saying with his eyes.

"It's the only way," he says. "They're too close to death. They have too much venom already in their veins."

"No."

"If we don't, they *will* die."

I shake my head. "We could still try healing, giving them our blood."

He takes Beth's limp hand. "There's no time."

Brandon has already claimed Beth as his progeny, which means Finn is mine.

Ah, fuck.

I sit down next to him, and Brandon's right. I can barely even hear Finn's pulse. He's going to die any second.

Finn fucking Huxley.

I take a breath, forcing my fangs through, and I bite him. But I don't drink; I only give him even more venom. He cries out in pain, and I begin the sickening process of turning him.

CHAPTER SEVENTY-THREE

I DON'T ASK what happened in the basement. I don't need to. I can tell by the look on Maverick's face when he comes up hours later that nothing good happened down there.

He wraps his arms around me. "Let's get out of here."

We drive back to LA in Max's car. Brandon and Max in front, me in the back between Maverick and Henrietta. I doze on and off, my head resting on Maverick's shoulder.

It's only when traffic picks up and I realize we're nearly back in LA that my heart sinks. What happens now? How does reality work now that Maverick knows exactly how I feel about him?

Max takes the exit to Malibu, and soon we're all standing in Maverick's living room, Max with his arms around Poppy like he's never going to let her go, her crying into his neck, so grateful that he's safe.

When they're finally done with their embrace, Poppy rushes over to me and hugs me tight.

"I'm so glad you're okay, Trix."

"Me too," I tell her.

"You saved Maverick's life."

"We all did."

Maverick steps forward and runs his fingers down my arm and into my palm. He pushes his fingers into mine, and it strikes a match inside me.

"Without you, without our blood bond, I'd still be there under Lottie's toxic spell."

"Lottie?" Poppy gasps. "But I thought—"

"I'll fill you in at home, my love." Max puts an arm around her, and she nuzzles into him. "Everyone ready to go?" Max throws me a look like he's not sure if he's driving me home or leaving me here.

I look up at Maverick. "Do you want me to stay?"

"I'm never going to let you go again," he says, before kissing me on the top of my head. My eyes close at the gesture, the warmth, love and safety behind it.

I'm safe with him.

Maverick walks everyone to the door, and I stand next to him and say my goodbyes.

They all act as if this is the most normal thing ever — me and Maverick. *Together.*

He closes the door and leans against it with a sigh. "Thank god, I thought they'd never leave."

"They were ready to give their lives to save you," I remind him with a smile.

"And I'll be grateful to them forever for it. But—" He takes a step towards me. "It's you I'm most grateful for." He reaches out and takes a piece of my tangled hair in his thumb and forefinger, rubbing it in a way that makes my lower belly heat.

"I acted like such an asshole. The way I just *left*. Took a fucking shower." He runs a hand over his jaw. "I'm sorry. So sorry."

"I'm sorry I ran. I should have stayed. I was just…"

"Scared," we both say at the same time.

"It's scarier without you," he says. "I'd rather spend every day of forever fucking terrified and know I'm yours, then spend one more second without you."

My breath hitches as he pushes my hair behind my ear.

"So, what now?" I ask.

"I think you know what now," he smirks. "But this time it's going to be different."

"Yeah?"

"Yeah. There are no more fucking rules. I'm going to hold your hand and I'm going to make love to you and I'm going to eat your fucking plant loaf and your pussy and—" he grips my ass and lifts me like I weigh nothing, my legs opening and wrapping around him.

"And?" I prompt, as he carries me to the bedroom.

"And I'm going to love you forever."

My heart blooms open, like a bud of a flower that has been hidden away in my chest cavity my whole life and the sunlight has finally reached it.

Maverick throws me on the bed, rips off my jeans and my shirt and stands over me, looking at my mismatched underwear with a dark, sexy, ravenous look in his eye.

"Fuck, you're beautiful."

I grin up at him. "So are you."

He pulls his shirt off, revealing his ripped chest and ancient tattoos, and drops it to the ground. "I'm disgusting," he says. "I haven't showered in days."

"I don't care," I tell him, sitting up and grabbing at the waistband of his jeans.

"You want to fuck me like this? Covered in grime and blood and—"

"No," I tell him. "I don't want to fuck you."

A surprised look crosses his face. Of course he'd be surprised. Who wouldn't want this Adonis to fuck them?!

"I want to make love to you," I say.

His eyes light up, and I unbuckle his belt.

"Say it again," he says.

"I want to make love to you, Maverick."

He lets out a growl and in an instant he's out of his jeans, climbing onto the bed in nothing but his boxer briefs stretched over his huge cock that's already hard for me.

I bite my lip as I take him in. He's huge, ripped, gorgeous, so fucking beautiful.

"The things I'm going to do to you," he says, pulling down one bra strap and planting a kiss on my shoulder.

"Yeah? What things?" I ask with a grin.

He reaches around to my back and unclasps my bra before peeling it off and throwing it across the room.

"First, I'm going to kiss you. A lot. *Everywhere.*" He runs his fingers over my naked breasts, and my nipples instantly harden at his touch. I arch into him, and he takes it as a hint to bite. And holy shit, when he bites my nipple, even without fangs, it feels like ecstasy.

He looks up at me and smiles. "When you're ready for it, one day I'll get my fang into your nipple. You'll fucking love it."

"I'm ready now," I tell him.

He raises an eyebrow, and his lips collide with mine, his tongue possessing my mouth, exploring and swirling in a way that has me pushing my hips up so I can rub on his erection still hiding in his briefs.

He surfaces from our kiss and smiles at me. "There's something I want even more than to bite your nipple."

"What's that?"

He runs his hands over my breasts, firmly squeezing each nipple, making me shudder. His hands move down my belly and to my hips where he gives me a little squeeze before grabbing the band of my oh so damp panties and pulling them down.

"Something I've wanted to do since I first saw you in that fucking club."

He gets my panties off and then opens my legs. For a moment I think about telling him to stop, to wait until I've had a shower, I'm not exactly clean either, but the deep inhale he takes as he looks down at my naked pussy tells me it doesn't matter to him at all.

He slides down between my legs and grins up at me, and then his cool breath is on me and I'm desperate for more. "Oh!" I call out as his tongue touches my clit. I can feel him smile, and then he starts to make slow, delicate movements at first, warming me up and easing me into it.

"You taste incredible," he mumbles into me. "So beautiful."

His movements speed up, and he quickly finds the rhythm I like. He sucks my clit into his mouth, and I buck into him, begging for more.

He understands what I'm telling him and slides a finger into me, sending pleasure into so many fucking nerve endings inside me.

"Fuck!" I call out, feeling my orgasm begin to build.

He curls his finger, and I'm done. I cry out in ecstasy while he continues to pump and curl his finger and suck my clit and holy fuck, did anything ever feel so good?

Suddenly, I feel his fangs protrude.

Oh fuck.

"I want to bite your thigh," he tells me, while I'm still riding the waves of pleasure.

I grab his hair in my fist. "You better fucking bite me!"

He chuckles and swaps his tongue for his finger, circling my clit as I feel the sudden sharp pain in my thigh, just inches from my opening. Then the high, the incredible fucking high that feels like a million mini orgasms, spreads up into my clit and through my whole body until I'm on the edge of something so beautiful, so magical I can't even comprehend it.

I cry out, and I hear him moaning, drinking, experiencing his own ecstasy at the taste of my blood.

I'm still floating on clouds of bliss when he sits up and looks at me, my wetness, my blood and a huge grin on his lips.

"More," I beg him.

He grips my thighs, opens my legs wider and settles himself in between them. His briefs now off, his huge cock hard, glistening and ready to take me.

"Please, Maverick," I beg.

"Oh, so *now* you're going to do the begging thing?"

I let out a light laugh. "Anything you want. It's all for you. I'm yours."

"Tell me again," he says, nudging his cock at my soaking wet entrance.

"I need you inside me first," I plead.

"As you wish." He pushes his cock into me, and I thrill at the feeling of it. The stretch, that moment of feeling like there's no fucking way I can take this huge cock. I take a breath and relax, knowing that he does fit. He fits me perfectly, in every way.

"Tell me," he begs, sliding in and out of me in a delicious way that makes me want to just lie here forever with him.

"I'm yours," I tell him as he thrusts into me a little deeper now that I'm stretched enough to take it.

"I'm yours, too," he tells me. His fingers find mine, and his lips press against mine, and we're joined. Now. Always. Forever.

"Forever," I tell him as his thrusts start to speed up.

"Forever," he repeats. "You and me, for fucking ever."

I grin into his neck, gripping his hair while he rides me.

"I'm forever, undeniably, yours," he whispers into my cheek.

And then his mouth finds my nipple, his fangs grazing against it, sending sparks through me. He bites down, and I feel his fang pierce my nipple, and I hit a new fucking high.

My body arches so high I think I'm going to hit the roof. I call out his name as he licks a trail of blood from my breast.

I'm in complete bliss. There is nothing better than this. Then his body stiffens, and I grip his shoulders as he moans into my neck and comes inside me, calling my name, telling me he's mine for all eternity.

We bask in the light of whatever magic we've just made for a moment, catching our breaths, and I try to find my way back to this place in time and space.

After a few moments, he pulls out and rolls over.

For a moment I worry that he'll pull away again. That he won't be able to do this. That he'll run or that I will.

But this time, instead of telling me he's going for a shower, he pushes a strand of hair out of my eyes and says, "Marry me."

CHAPTER SEVENTY-FOUR

$\mathcal{M}$averick

"Vampires must never engage in romantic relationships with humans. This is an abomination. If a vampire wishes for companionship, he should find it with another of his kind. Vampires who engage in this sort of thing will—"

Remaining piece of a burned Fraternity of the Everlasting Rose periodical from 1923

Trix throws her bouquet, and Poppy catches the multicolored roses, grinning as she looks over at Max, my best man. Trix's mom is still dabbing her eyes with a heavily used tissue while her dad rummages through his pockets to find more. Ali steps in with a tissue box she must have found in a corner of the chapel somewhere.

Max grins back at Poppy, and I have no doubt they are going to be next.

We invited Brandon too, but he stayed at the ranch house to look after the new baby vampires and help the vampires who'd been drugged to recover and get back to full strength. I didn't want to be too far away from Finn. The first few weeks as a new vampire are the worst, but Brandon assured me he had everything under control, and he usually does.

The day after my pathetic attempt at a post-sex proposal we had a belated Christmas dinner with Trix's parents. When Trix was busy in the kitchen doing something with the potatoes I asked them formally for her hand in marriage. That evening, I did it right. I took her to the beach and got on one knee, presenting her with a diamond antique ring I'd bought during a blood high after I'd seen *An Affair to Remember*. When I came down from the high, I barely had any memory of the movie or buying the ring. I'd been carrying it around for nearly a century with no intention to ever give it to anyone. It was just a trinket I'd collected. Until now.

She said yes, and a week later, here we are.

Fucking married.

Grinning brighter than life, Trix looks over at me, wiggling the huge diamond and gold band on her left hand. I immediately close the space between us, planting another kiss on her sweet, warm, gorgeous lips. Lips that are now officially, in accordance with the law, *all fucking mine.*

"Give me just one second. Then I'm yours forever," Trix says with that smile that lights up the darkest corners of my soul. "I just need to see Poppy real quick about some bridesmaid business."

"What if I don't let you?" I tease, pulling her even closer, my hand drifting down to her perfect ass that looks so damn good in her short white sequin dress.

"Then you won't get to see me in sexy wedding night lingerie later," she whispers into my ear.

I immediately let her go. "Don't be long, *wife.*"

Holy shit, who knew that would feel so fucking good to say?
"I'll be right back, *husband.*"
And even better to hear.

She gives me a wink, and I immediately remember what we did last night. Her mouth around my cock, my tongue on her wet hot center. As a flush hits her cheeks, I can only assume she's thinking about the same thing — a life of damn hot sex, and no fucking rules. Shit, I'm going red too. We both giggle, and she bounces off towards Poppy, who's still smiling over catching the bouquet.

"It's a shame the others couldn't make it," Max says, stepping beside me. "But it's better that Henrietta stays with her cousins in England for a while. She can't go back to her coven, and so many vampires now know she's a witch."

"We'll visit her," I say. "Me and Trix are going to honeymoon at the castle in Scotland and then make a trip to London. We'll see Henrietta on the way."

"London?" Max raises an eyebrow at the mention of his home city.

"Trix has a cousin there, and I think it will be good for me to go back. Healing. Therapy. Whatever."

"How is Finn doing?" he asks.

"It's never easy," I say, trying not to remember the fresh hell of being turned. "But Brandon, Juliette, Linda and Vivian are looking after both him and Beth. Supplying them with enough blood to stop them from going on baby vampire rampages. In theory."

The truth is, there's very little you can do to stop a new vampire from killing at least a few times. It's part of how they learn to know how much blood they can or can't take from a human.

"They'll find some real scum of the earth types to feed to them," I say. "But I'm sure they'll both be fine in the end."

"Well, we turned out alright, I suppose." Max looks over

at the guy in sunglasses and a white sequin jumpsuit who just married us. "Does she know it's really him?"

I give him a wave and a smile. "Not yet. I'll tell her later."

Max laughs. "Perhaps we can all grab a drink together later. It's been a while."

"Definitely."

I'm staring at Trix again. This ray of sunshine that has changed my whole life. Me, Maverick Stone, *married*! Wait until the press get hold of this! I chuckle to myself at the thought of it.

"Are you sure about this?" Max asks.

"Bit fucking late now if I'm not."

"Forever," he says. "It means something different to us than it does for them."

"You don't want forever with Poppy?"

"Of course I do." He lets out a sigh. "We've been talking about her being turned. Honestly, I wish she wouldn't even consider it."

"Shouldn't it be her choice?"

"Yes. But she needs to make an informed one. I don't feel that she truly understands what she'd be giving up. Has Trix asked you?"

I shake my head. "No."

"You haven't even talked about it?"

I turn to my best friend and plant a hand on his shoulder. "I took a vow to love her for as long as I live. And I will. Whether I get five hundred years, fifty years or just the next five minutes. I will always love her. For every second of my immortal life, I will love her."

I turn and watch her. She is truly the most beautiful thing I've ever seen, and she's all mine. *Forever*. However long that is.

She turns and grins at me, and I swear I can feel my heart start beating in my chest again.

EPILOGUE

IT'S BEEN years since I was back home, and for good reason.
The place sucks. Lucky, Arizona, is one gas station and a
diner away from being officially scheduled as a ghost town.

I pull my baseball cap low and walk into the diner,
disappearing into a booth in the corner. Lucky's Diner is
one of those places that looks anything but lucky. The
cracked peach vinyl seats have been here since the seventies, and the peeling mint wallpaper and chipped linoleum
flooring are obvious signs that this place makes zero
money. But it's the decades worth of fryer fat and burger
grease impregnating its walls that has me throwing the
cuffs of my hoodie over my nose as I lean back in the
booth.

Since I was turned, all my senses have heightened. Some
of this I'm okay with. For example, sex was always good, but
now it is *sub-fucking-blime*. But the smell of meat, which I'm

pretty sure is at least a couple days past its best, frying in old grease makes me want to puke.

I don't even know if I can puke now, but maybe I'm about to find out.

"Your pie, sir."

Her voice.

Now *that* is something I'm happy to experience with my new vampire senses. That sweet voice, that gentle lilt. It hits me right in the chest cavity where my heart used to beat.

April Abernathy. The girl who always had her face in a book, head in a cloud, dreams too big for this shitty town. It just kills me that all these years later, she's still here working at the diner when she had so much potential to do something amazing with her life.

She was also my high school girlfriend until I well and truly fucked that up.

"Watch it, girl! You just damn near knocked my coffee over!"

My blood heats at his words, and I raise my head slightly, taking her in.

April. Sweet, gorgeous April, long brown hair in a ponytail, cheeks burning, stands there staring down at him. "My apologies, sir. It's been a long shift. I'll get you some more coffee."

She turns to walk away, but the guy, a middle-aged truck driver type, grabs her by the wrist.

"I don't want no more damn coffee, I want some good old-fashioned customer service like we had in the old days!"

"Sir," she says, gritting her teeth. "While our decor may be outdated, I can assure you that you haven't time traveled, and women in *this* century are no longer expected to treat men with respect that they absolutely do not deserve."

I hide a chuckle in my hoodie sleeves. Damn, April hasn't changed a bit. Beneath her pretty as a prom queen looks and bookworm nature was always an absolute fucking fire-cracker. She's still got it.

"I 'aint paying for this pie!" the guy yells. "I demand to see your manager!"

Clive Dixon suddenly appears, towering behind her. The football star of Lucky High still looks in good shape, but judging by his apron covered in food grease, I guess all those football scholarships never led to anything.

"Is there a problem here?" he asks.

"Too damn right there's a problem! I 'aint paying to be treated like this!"

"If you'll just calm down sir, I'll be happy to listen to your complaints," Clive says.

April gives him a look like she can't believe he's not kicking this guy out, and neither can I.

"How about I box up a full pie for you? You can take it with you, on the house."

April's mouth drops open.

"April, honey, can you box up some pie for the gentleman?"

She looks like she's going to murder them both. "Sure, *honey.*"

Why the fuck are they calling each other honey?

Oh, no. Fuck no. Not April and fucking Clive!

She moves behind the counter, throws some pie into a box and shoves it over the counter towards Clive, her face burning.

Fuck this shit!

Clive hands the guy his box. "I'm not paying my bill!"

"No problem sir, enjoy your evening."

The guy gets up, still pissed, even after a free meal and pie that he does not fucking deserve, and I follow him out to where his truck is parked on an empty lot next to the diner.

"You piece of shit," I tell him when he turns and notices me. "Is that how you talk to women? Or all diner servers?"

"Fuck off," he tells me. "She had it coming."

"Nah, man. You're the one who has it coming."

My fangs rip from my mouth, and the guy screams. High-pitched, whiny, like the pathetic excuse for a man that he is.

I'm fast, and it only takes me a second to grab him, pull him behind his truck, rip into his neck and drink.

The thirst for blood is insatiable. No matter how much I drink, no matter how many humans I drink from, I'm always fucking thirsty.

Even now, when his heart rate starts to drop, I want to keep going, to satiate myself, to eradicate this dick from the planet.

Finn, stop.

I ignore the voice and keep drinking.

Stop, or he'll die.

I don't stop.

Finn!

"Fuck!" I release my fangs from his neck and look at him. He's covered in his own blood, close to death on the dusty ground.

They told me I'd kill someone eventually, that it was just something that *happened.* But I'm not ready for it. I'm not ready to become a fucking murderer.

He deserved it. He deserved to be scared shitless and almost drained to death, but does he deserve to *die*?

"Oh, fucking fuck!"

I grab my phone from my pocket and call my maker.

"Yeah?" Maverick answers.

"I fucking did it again!"

"Jesus, Finn!" he sighs. "Where are you?"

"Lucky, Arizona."

"What the fuck are you doing there?"

"I just wanted to see this girl—" I begin, and fuck me, tears start leaking from my eyes. It takes me a second to realize I'm crying over April and Clive, not over the man who's about to die, and that makes me feel even more like a monster than before. "I'm a fucking monster," I wail, sinking behind the truck and staring at the man's lifeless body.

"Does he still have a pulse?"

"Yeah. Just."

"Make sure the puncture wounds are healed. Call an ambulance and then get the hell out of there."

I look back at the diner and even from this far, I can hear April laying into Clive while he apologizes profusely. I'd give anything to be working in that diner with April, arguing with her over pies and shitty customers.

But I'm not human. Not any more.

"Finn?"

"Yeah, yeah. I'm on it."

"And one more thing."

"Yeah?"

"For fuck's sake, stay away from the girl."

The Immortal Hollywood series concludes in:

My Unholy Everything

She's the preacher's daughter.
He's an unholy abomination.

Rising star Finn Huxley is living the Hollywood dream—fame, money, *girls*… but beneath the surface lies a nightmare.

Memories from the night he was turned into a vampire haunt him, and his insatiable thirst for blood controls his every waking thought.

But while Finn has been giving The Bite to every woman in the city, there's only one girl who will ever have his heart. A girl who's so good and radiant that she would never want him now that he's eternally damned.

April Abernathy has always done what everyone else expected of her, but beneath her good-girl exterior lies a hunger for more. A hunger that was only ever satiated by secretly kissing Finn Huxley in cornfields.

When Finn returns to town all these years later, more tortured and broken than before, April is drawn back to him like a moth to a very hot and deadly flame. So when Finn's publicist offers her payment in exchange for fake dating Finn to help with his bad boy image, she jumps at the chance.

But Hollywood is not a cornfield in Arizona, and Finn Huxley is no longer the boy next door. Now he's a dangerous immortal with a target on his back.

Violent crime is on the rise, blood supplies are drying up, vampires are at each other's throats and Finn will do anything it takes to keep April safe from the darkness lurking in Hollywood's shadows…

Even if that darkness is him.

Finn and April's story coming December 2025
Pre-order here: https://mybook.to/unholy-everything

. . .

Sign up at:
www.stormyohara.com for updates, sneak peeks and deleted
scenes!

ABOUT THE AUTHOR

Stormy O'Hara is the alter ego and pen name of a well-known spiritual author who divides her time between writing stories, reading tarot and exploring ancient monuments in the Peak District of Derbyshire where she currently lives.

Stormy believes in the magic, power, creativity and connection of the human heart, soul and spirit and no generative AI is ever used in the creation of her books.

www.stormyohara.com
www.instagram.com/stormy.ohara
www.tiktok.com/@stormy.ohara

ACKNOWLEDGMENTS

Thank *you* dear reader for joining me on another adventure through the movie star mansions, movie sets, LA beaches and vampire bars of the world of Immortal Hollywood!

As an indie author every single purchase and read through of this book truly matters to me and honestly makes a huge difference to my life and in my heart!

I wrote these books because I wanted to read them. I wanted vampires that were desperately trying to cling onto their humanity, bad boys trying to be good men, men/monsters who were tortured but absolutely redeemable by the power of love! Just like we all are! I wanted to write something hopeful in a world that doesn't always feel that way at times.

I hope this book made you feel a little lighter and more hopeful.

As an indie author doing most of this on my own, I don't have a huge list of people to thank, but a giant thank you goes out to my amazing beta readers—Gaby, Erica, Sonya and Caz. Your thoughts and suggestions have been so incredibly helpful, but mostly your positive feedback and words of support have really kept me going when I was deep in the pit of author self-doubt and despair!

Thank you to my friends who've held the vision for my fiction writing success even when you've had a whole heap of your own life stuff going on. Hannah, Nicole, Emma, Maria and Chezza, thank you for always believing in and rooting for me!

And as always, to my biggest fan, first reader and the guy who inspires all my grumpy heroes, all the rest of my love and gratitude go to you, Ian. I am so forever, undeniably, yours.

xx

www.ingramcontent.com/pod-product-compliance
Lightning Source LLC
Chambersburg PA
CBHW050604170726
48283CB00001B/100